CW01463868

AMONG THORNS AND STARDUST

HAYLEY ANDERTON   MERI BENSON   DESTINY EVE

AMY JOHNSON   DAWN CHRISTINE JONCKOWSKI

MARIE SINADJAN   MEGHAN TOMLINSON

Copyright © 2024 by Amy Johnson

Individual copyright belongs to the authors

All rights reserved.

No part of this book may be reproduced in any form or by any electronic or mechanical means, including information storage and retrieval systems, without written permission from the author, except for the use of brief quotations in a book review. This book is a work of fiction. All names, characters, places, and events are fictitious. Any resemblance to actual events or people, living or dead, is coincidental.

∼

Cover Art by Luisa Galstyan

www.behance.net/luisaartist1

Formatting by Amy Johnson

www.fiverr.com/johnsonamy895

DEDICATION

To the ones who have inspired us to dream and everyone who still believes in fairy tales.

TABLE OF CONTENTS

ABOUT THE
Stories

Into the Arms of Morpheus

Amy Johnson

A lifetime of captivity in her own home has made Princess Liana curious. Maybe a little *too* curious. When a dare from one of her so-called friends leads to her pushing one wrong button, Liana realizes that her parents' efforts to protect her were not unwarranted. A monster descends upon her planet, and there's nothing anyone can do to stop him. In their haste to protect their only child, Liana's parent's force her into cryostasis. But what will be left when she wakes up—*if* she wakes up?

∼

Everything Made Beautiful

Dawn Christine Jonckowski

In the kingdom of NexusNova, beauty is bought at a price, and there is no place for the ugly. Disfigured from a childhood accident and crippled by her mother's selfish debts, Briallen will never be able to afford better looks, but finds contentment alone in the shadows. Until a case of mistaken identity at the Prince's ball introduces her to the one person who might actually see what lies behind the scars.

∼

Skyscraper

Hayley Anderton

Rapunzel has never left her high rise building. But when a mysterious stranger appears on her balcony, she begins to question more about the world outside and why she has been locked away from it for so long.

∽

Aliandra

Destiny Eve

After meeting the alluring thief Aliandra, adventurous Princess Jazmyn embarks on a quest for the Spirit of Arsalan: a mystic orb that is the reason their world is at war. But are either of them—or anyone—worthy enough to possess it?

∽

Stardust and Steel

Meri Benson

When Andromina's father goes missing, she'll travel into unregulated space to find him. Though she'll never expect what she finds on a hidden planet in this Beauty and the Beast retelling.

~

Just A Byte
Marie Sinadjan

In the not-so-distant future, The Corporation is the fairest of them all.

But nothing is as it seems. After an attempt on her life, Blanche finds herself caught up in a rebel plot against her stepmother Adriana, CEO of The Corporation, and the queen of Modding.

~

Wild Swan Chase
Meghan Tomlinson

On an interstellar search for her missing brothers, Lark Svanur may have met her prince via subspace code. But when she discovers him stealing top-secret parts from one of her brothers' ships, can she trust him to help her save her eleven brothers from the lab of her bird-obsessed stepmother, or will their happily ever after be over before it begins?

Days pass.
Then weeks.
Then months.
Then, years and galaxies.
She doesn't know she's
finally getting to explore the
galaxy, just like she wanted.

Liana simply sleeps.

INTO THE ARMS OF *Morpheus*

Amy Johnson

Nebulae

When stars are born in the distant cold of space, planets stop spinning to watch. Comets pause their endless cyclical journeys to listen for the crackling of creation. Even the moons cease their circling to investigate.

It always begins small—a whisper of a prayer carried on water droplets or pinged between satellite signals. That hope is a center of gravity, pulling everyone and everything inward, holding up the dreams of a civilization, building and building until—

A gasp.

An explosion of light and fire.

And a scream, unlike any heard in this galaxy or the next. The cry of a child—no, a star—hot enough to burn the world with one touch but too innocent to ever consider it.

The planets breathe sighs of relief and resume their rotations. Comets coast by once again, waving at the newborn celestial body. Even the moons gleam down at her before retreating behind their guards.

And the littlest star rests, not knowing how important she is or how astronomic her light will become.

Gatherings

O n the ground floor of the *Palais* Talia, the entire planet is celebrating. Music drifts around an immense ballroom, wrapping each individual in the warmth of kinship and the spark of optimism. Bodies merge in dance until unique species are indistinguishable. Together, they are nothing more than an astral amalgamation, liquid light.

Among them, they pass a tiny, sleeping *princesse*. A hand-woven silk shawl the color of stars both swaddles her and protects her from the curious, tender touches of hands and fins and tentacles and various other appendages. The beings gaze down at her and whisper well wishes in their native tongues, and yet she never rouses.

"At last," they coo, touching her porcelain cheek. "Talia's saving grace."

"*Rei* Lucian must be so proud," another whispers. "An heir at last."

One presses purple lips to her head. "Spitting image of her mother, isn't she? *Reina* Emille's clone. Lucky *princesse*."

She travels around the room, and not a single being wishes her harm. No one would dare. This is a meeting of allies, after all. Who would dare endanger the long-

5

awaited offspring of the mighty rulers of Talia after all they've done for the galaxy?

No one in this room, at least.

No one on this *planet.*

While the tiny *princesse* makes another round, the music starts again and drinks are refilled. At the edge of the ballroom, a *garde* leaves his post. His eyes trail his charges—the infant heir and her hovering nurse—for another moment before he steps away toward a stairwell. The space is dark, but not quiet. All the way down, the noise of the celebration follows him. It keeps him company in the narrow passage where there are nothing but a few candles to show him the way.

The hallway ends at a steel door, one that looks rather out of place in the *Palais* Talia. The *palais* itself is white marble, carved straight out of the mountain and protruding from the glistening waters that cover the planet. This door is sleek silver, causing it to stand out from the otherwise natural aesthetic of Talia.

On the right side of the door is a small keypad. Green illuminates the digits, casting eerie shadows on the stone walls. The *garde* types a string of six numbers, and then he tucks his hands behind his back and waits.

Soon enough, the silver slides away, and the *garde* enters a different type of gathering—one without music or laughter. Six beings sit around a long table, each one more unique than the last. There are three females, each wearing their own version of a crown that matches the planet they rule, and three males. They all have tablets propped on the table in front of them, and in the center is a holographic image of the planet Talia—a shimmering, pink, perfect replica, down to the sprawling capital city, where the *Palais* Talia sits at the base of the largest mountain. The *palais* is surrounded by an odd sea that covers ninety percent of the planet. The only gaps in the wall of fresh sunrise-colored water are small white islands scattered throughout. In the sky around the translucent orb, silver crafts travel their usual surveillance paths.

The entire hologram is surrounded by a semi-translucent white netting. If one were to stand in space, they wouldn't be able to actually *see* the perimeter surrounding Talia. Here, though, in the safety of Talia's council room, one can see and touch the newly-installed security measure.

The *garde* takes his place along the room's edge after nodding once to his *Rei*, a tall, light-haired Talian sitting at the head of the table. A crown of white pearl sits atop his head, encrusted with a variety of glittering gemstones. All eyes are glued to the Talian sovereign, even as his flit to the *garde*.

A promise passes between them: *She is safe.*

Rei Lucian nods back, relaxes his shoulders, and returns to his meeting.

"*Csar*, you have a report for us, I believe." His voice is pure authority, deep and controlled. Power undercuts each word, and with just one sentence, every being in the *palais* knows who's in charge.

The *Csar*, the sovereign of an aquatic planet hosting entirely blue beings with webbed appendages and frilled gills around their necks, clears his throat. "Yes, Your Majesty. So far, our security upgrades have all been successful. All allied planets have working perimeters."

"And the defense scans?"

"The radars are constantly running and can pinpoint any incoming projectile. Missile, slug, craft—doesn't matter. The AI we programmed into each one knows the difference and has the ability to assign defense protocols on its own."

A little ripple of murmurings crosses the room as the allied sovereigns note their gratitude and agreement.

Then, from a little ways down the table, a small being raises her three-fingered hand. On her head is a sand-colored braided cord—the crown of Nihara. "Permission for speak?"

Even through her poorly-spoken Universal Tongue, her voice is rough. It's also deeper than one might expect from an individual no taller than a meter. On her planet, though, where she is the sovereign, everyone is this small. It's best not to mention that, though, especially if you like your kneecaps intact.

"Granted, *Tanno* Meiji," Lucian says, directing his eyes to the female.

"Thank you." Meiji climbs up to stand in her chair and

looks around the table. "The Nihara installed each perimeter. We make no mistakes, no miscalculations. No accidents. Is faultless."

The room emits a collective sigh. They know the worth of Niharan tools. If Meiji says it's faultless, then it is.

Rei Lucian nods to Meiji, and she flops back down into her seat. "Very good. And we've fully stocked all of our weapon storages? With extras?"

Another member of the council, a man whose skin glints with the silver and black of innumerable mechanical implants, rises from his seat. There is no hair or crown on his head, but tattoos coat his bare skin. Some of them glitter like stars; others move on their own, dancing from one screen implant to the next.

"My people have transported weapons for several days now. You should be more than prepared," he says. His voice even sounds mechanical. Its rough edge is just grating enough that several beings at the table shift in discomfort.

Even in space, where "other" is the norm, the intense cybernetic nature of the Gollems still aren't wholly welcome.

Rei Lucian, who didn't even flinch when the sovereign Gollem spoke, nods. "We appreciate your assistance, *Rebb* Cyrno."

The sovereign Gollem points a cybernetic finger at the other man. A few of the *gardes* shift, but a hand from

Lucian keeps them in place. "You will do well to do more than *appreciate* us. When the time comes, when this inevitable battle knocks on your door, you will show no mercy, correct?"

No one speaks. A blanket of tension collapses over the room. Beside Lucian, *Reina* Emille—wearing a pearl-encrusted crown that matches her husband's—sits up a little straighter. She slips her hand across the dark stone of the table and grips Lucian's arm.

"*Rebb* Cyrno," she says, in a voice that can only be compared to liquid mercury—cold and poisonous. It doesn't match her soft appearance. "*If* Malfios shows his face, no one at this table will hesitate. Not after what he's done to all of us." She pauses, and her husband meets her intense gaze. "Especially not now."

Now that we have an heir.

The unspoken words circle the table until everyone understands the weight of this promise and the importance of the little star-swaddled infant currently being coddled on the dance floor.

Another voice rises from the heavy quiet. "Speaking of our reason to gather, I am happy for you both."

All eyes fall on the last female sitting among the war council. If it wasn't for the gentleness and femininity in her voice, one might not be able to tell her gender. Her face is shrouded from the nose up by a solid gold mask, one that glints in the candlelight and is rumored to hide her omniscient third eye. The rest of her is covered by an impenetrable black cloak. A single command from her is enough to have the war council on their knees, even if they are some of the most powerful beings in the galaxy.

"Thank you, *Sybil* Ionia," Emille says, breaking the silence.

The other female's mouth turns upward in a smile. It lasts only a breath before it falls away.

"A child is a blessing, yes. But thieves love their treasure, don't they?" Ionia clasps her hands in front of herself. "We've seen darkness on the horizon. Hold your light close."

The other beings at the table shift uncomfortably, unsure what to make of the Sybillian's prophecy. They may be a highly respected and ancient race known for foreseeing disasters, wars, and blessings alike, but sometimes it's easier to ignore their tangled prophecies than to take the time to pick out the knots.

"We will be sure to do that," Lucian says, twining his fingers between his wife's. "Now, if everything is set, I would like to bring this council to a close. We have a celebration to—"

Before he can finish his sentence, a harsh crackling fills the room. One by one, the *gardes* tear out their small ear pieces as they push away from the perimeter, overwhelmed by the sharp interference. Some rush to their sovereign's side; others leave the room to protect their infant ward.

Lucian rises from his seat, still holding Emille's hand,

and begins shouting at his *gardes*. "What is happening? Where is that coming from?"

"No idea, sir," one says. "A passing craft is interfering with our comm network. Investigative crafts are departing as we speak."

"Did we seriously not see this coming?" Lucian snaps, rushing out of the room with his wife on his heels. The rest of the war council follow fast behind him.

The *garde* closest to him presses buttons wildly on his tablet. "We were monitoring the ship, but it seemed to be a passenger flight. It's not weaponized for an attack."

"So why mess with our communications?"

The group enters the ballroom, where the music has died. Most of the guests have retreated to the walls and are clutching their comms. Whispers float toward the sovereigns—of static in the feeds, of an impending attack, of *Malfios*. The spark of optimism has dimmed into flickering fear. From the crowd, the *princesse*'s nurse appears, clutching the child. Emille's entire body relaxes. Of course she trusts the woman, but nothing feels better than having her only child in her arms.

"We aren't really sure, sir," the *garde* says, voice thick with confusion.

Lucian clenches his teeth so hard that a muscle in his jaw twitches. "Figure it out," he barks. The *garde* swallows and purses his lips. With a nod, he jogs away, still pressing buttons. Lucian turns to his queen. "Take her somewhere safe, Emille. I'll find out what's going on."

Emille nods, her dark hair falling away from its elaborate twist. It lies on her shoulders, within the baby's reach. A single pudgy, pink hand reaches up to touch the strands. Then, from the inner depths of space, two blue eyes find the sovereign. His entire demeanor softens, like a spell has fallen over him. Her eyes are gravity, eternally drawing him in. The mighty Lucian, creator of intergalactic alliances and leader of his planet, melts under his daughter's gaze. He runs a finger across her cheek and feels her heart thrumming through her shallow, salmon skin.

"Could it be him, love?" Emille whispers.

Lucian's fingers freeze on his daughter's forehead.

Could it be? Yes, there is a chance that their enemy has caught up to them. That's not what his wife needs to hear, though. She wants comfort, to know she's safe with him. And yet, they do not lie to one another. So Lucian just looks up into her eyes and says nothing.

The silence tells all.

"After everything," Emille says, pulling the baby into her chest, "we cannot lose her."

Lucian shakes his head, dizzied by the sudden loss of contact. "We won't. I promise. Liana is safe."

At the sound of her name, the *princesse* coos happily and begins chewing on her mother's cloak.

"I'll send a *garde* with you, just—"

For the second time tonight, the sovereign's words are cut off. This time, it isn't by obnoxious interference or screeching comms. Instead, it's one of the tele-screens' activation sounds, nothing more than a soft chime. All eyes turn to where the thin screen hangs above the western wall of the ballroom.

At first, there's nothing but the Talian logo dancing across the screen. The three royals huddle together, Emille and Liana tucked behind their king. The room holds a unified breath as dread and tension mix into a sickening smog around them. Panic grips their stomachs in its clawed hand.

After a moment that feels like an eternity, the Talian logo fades. A figure takes its place. He is shrouded in black —hair, lips, clothes. Two horns curl away from his head, disappearing into the darkness behind him. On the starless screen, his shape is nothing but an outline and two piercing red eyes.

The whispers crawling along the marble floor fall still and silent, crushed like their speakers by the weight of fear enveloping the room.

Rei Lucian says nothing. He won't bend to this creature, to this being who has ravaged planets for reasons unspoken, who has slaughtered entire species and decimated ancient bloodlines, and who wants the planet Talia for himself. The beings around the room—both Talian and guests alike—wait, holding their breaths.

Unsurprisingly, it's Malfios who speaks first.

"My dear Lucian," he purrs. Like the shadows themselves, the male's voice is deep. Whether that's by design or a gift from Nature, no one knows. But both sovereigns and slaves have been lured in by the comfort of that voice, of the sweet rest its night promises, only to be forever lost in it. "I believe something is wrong with my communication systems."

Lucian's brow furrows in confusion, but he keeps his mouth firmly sealed until he can formulate a response. He knows from experience that Malfios can smell weakness, and confusion might as well be a gap in the sovereign's armor.

"I have excellent repair technicians, if you need their assistance," Lucian finally says. Sometimes it's best to fight fire with kindness and blankets. Other times, you must smother the enemy. "What makes you think there's an issue?"

Malfios chuckles, the sound resembling a peal of distant thunder. "My invitation to this party, of course. It must've gotten lost in transmission."

The temperature in the room drops ten degrees. Behind Lucian, Emille shivers and clutches Liana closer into her. The baby just coos softly.

Lucian opens his mouth to continue down this deceptive play, but Malfios cuts him off with a harsh growl. "Don't even consider lying to me, Lucian. That's enough."

Across the room, a *garde* breaks free from the statuesque line of visitors and rushes towards his charge. He says nothing as he sidles up beside Lucian, but he holds his tablet face up.

Two words flash in gentle Talian blue across the screen.

PERIMETER SECURE.

She is safe.

"If you say so," Lucian finally says, looking up at his planet's sole enemy. "It is no secret why you weren't invited, Malfios. Why are you here now, interrupting my celebration?"

The outline on the screen shifts. "Do not worry, I don't plan to attack you. Not today, anyway." He laughs, but this time it isn't warm or inviting. There's something off about the sound, and Emille shudders. "I would just like to know why you've invited half the galaxy to Talia. Did you finally get bored with that prudish Emille and find another wife? Or are you skipping polygamy and going straight for a harem?"

Lucian swells with pride and anger. "You'll do well to stop speaking of a sovereign that way. *Reina* Emille holds just as much power as I do. It won't end well."

"Yes, yes, I see all your weapons pointed at me. Lower your hackles, and answer my question: Why are you celebrating?"

While the two males stare at each other, waiting for the other to crack, a Niharan—small, with hair whiter than a newborn star—emerges from the crowd and hands Emille a shawl. The female motions for the *reina* to kneel, and when she does, the Niharan drapes the fabric over her shoulders. Emille blinks at her in stunned silence. Why does she need this? She isn't cold, really, just worried. That emotion alone courses through her veins like ice.

But then the female mimes pulling the shawl over and around her small chest, and it clicks. It's to hide Liana.

Emille cannot stay here in this room with her days-old infant. If Malfios finds out that they have an heir, after decades of praying and hoping for one and grieving all the losses along the way, he will stop at nothing to kill the *princesse*.

And Emille cannot let that happen.

This demon will not take her motherhood from her.

Not again.

So, she follows the Niharan's directions and pulls the shawl tight around her chest, covering Liana entirely. The baby giggles a little, but at Emille's soft pat, she quiets.

"Why should I tell you?" Lucian asks as his wife begins to slink away from him. "After everything you've done to our galaxy?"

The shadow on the screen bristles. "Lucian, you have about five seconds before I lose my—"

His words die in his mouth as Emille turns and speed-walks towards the exit. The crowd collapses in, success-fully covering her from sight. She ducks into a stairwell and slumps against the cold marble wall.

Lucian, still staring up at his sole enemy, grasps the empty air behind him. His anchor is gone, and he's left to float in this sea alone. It's a good thing he's dealt with

Malfios before. Patience is the only retaliation that works against the short-tempered being.

Beside Lucian, the guard flashes his screen toward his *rei*. A timer has replaced the message from before. "Comms secure again in five seconds," the *garde* mumbles.

"Listen, Malfios," the sovereign says, looking back up at the tele-screen. "It's over. We have built our walls, strengthened our alliances. You are no longer welcome. Crawl back into your shadows, or find another galaxy to terrorize."

At first, there's no response. A second passes, and then, before the line is disconnected, Malfios laughs.

"So naïve," he says, the wicked smile laced in every word like a scattering of radiation. "This is only the beginning. I will tear this galaxy apart one family at a time, Lucian. Starting with yours. You cannot keep me out for—"

The ballroom falls silent as the timer flashes a series of zeros.

It's the *rei* who exhales first. Lucian's shoulders drop, a barely noticeable shift, and for a moment, he's just a being—not *the* being. Then, all eyes are on him once again. He takes a slow breath, straightens his spine, and turns away from the tele-screen. His eyes scan the crowd of terrified guests. They're holding one another and trembling in their garish outfits. In the far corner of the room, shadowed by the doorway, is his wife, staring at him.

"You are safe," he finally says, voice drifting across the frozen expanse. It's soft and warm, a ray of sunlight waiting to wrap them all in its comfort. "He cannot get in —now or ever. The perimeter will always do its job." With a smile, Lucian adds, "I promise."

It's the last two words that sweeps their doubts away. A promise from a Talian means everything, but from the Talian sovereign? Those words may as well have been etched into the solid marble walls.

But walls crumble.

And nothing is forever—not even promises.

For tonight, though, these beings choose to trust their *rei*, choose to forget the imminent enemy and enjoy ignorance. Who can blame them when there's no telling how dark the future will be? One by one, they take their partners' hands again and begin to merge together in hesitant swaying.

Lucian doesn't dance with his kinsmen, though. Instead, he eases through the gliding crowd, touching shoulders as he goes. Talians and guests alike whisper their thanks to him as they return his feathery touch. His mind doesn't linger on them, though. It paces the distance between him and Emille, and as soon as he is in front of her, the voices of worry abate.

He takes her into his arms, and their bodies meld together. Baby Liana reaches up between them, her chubby fingers poking at their chins, but they don't break apart. Not for a long moment.

She is safe.

They are safe.

His promises to the residents of Talia might be etched in temporary marble walls, but his duty to these two women is timeless and indestructible, like the galaxy and its thousand-year-old glittering stars.

It isn't the little *princesse* who breaks her life-givers apart. It's *Sybil* Ionia. She clears her throat and waits, hands clasped behind her back.

Lucian gives his Emille one more light kiss and then turns to his ally.

"I'll have the guards double the safeguards tomorrow," he says, anticipating her chastisement. "It was a fluke, Ionia."

The Sybillian nods. "Mistakes can reveal cracks, Lucian."

The Gollem leader slides up behind Ionia. His frown has deepened even further. Right behind him is the aquatic *csar*. They all wear the same expectant expression, waiting to see what Lucian will do.

"We continue the same way," he finally says. "Open and constant communication between ourselves, though. Any sign of Malfios or any chinks in the perimeter's armor, and I want to be notified immediately."

The three of them nod.

Ionia's eyes fall on the *princesse*. "We've seen an approaching darkness," she says. Everyone recognizes her repeated warning. "Malfios will have your light, Lucian. Best cover it with a basket."

The *rei* looks at his daughter—the one who has his white-blonde hair and her mother's perfect blue eyes. His blessing and his undeniable weakness.

"I know," he whispers, touching Liana's head.

"If I were you," the Gollem sovereign says, "I'd keep her as far away from the outside world as I could for as long as I could."

Lucian's response sticks in his throat. There's no lie in Ionia's warning. Talia is the only thing standing in the way of Malfios's total domination. If the heir is killed, the planet ends up without a leader, open to be scooped up by the monster waiting in the dark.

Liana must be protected. In order to do that, she must be a secret.

In that moment, Lucian makes up his mind.

His daughter will grow up isolated from the world beyond this atmosphere, safe from knowledge of the waiting threat. She'll know nothing of Malfios, and he will know nothing of her.

Secrecy is the only way to save her.

Explorations

Liana isn't supposed to be here.

Her *rei* has made it very clear that the space-craft hangars are *absolutely* off-limits. He'd even stood his ground when she batted her giant eyelashes at him and feigned forgetfulness. No amount of begging and pleading would sway him, but that didn't mean she hadn't tried. Her father was notoriously weak when it came to Liana, and she had most definitely *never* taken advantage of that.

Except maybe once. Or twice.

Truth be told, there are a lot of things (and places) forbidden to Liana. The *palais* rules have been tattooed on her brain since the moment she learned how to walk. If she followed every one of her parents' restrictions, the *princesse* would never leave her room. But life is too short to live in a gilded cage.

The desire to escape has always been an itch in her chest, one she can never quite reach. She can't sit still, can't resist exploring the dark hallways. There's something about the forbidden—about all the secret rooms in the *palais*, about the sealed books in the library. She needs to see it all, touch it all, experience it all.

So she stopped asking permission sixteen years ago. Forgiveness is much simpler to beg for.

Liana does have some sense of self-preservation, though. She isn't an idiot. Just curious. If the *rei* and *reina* catch her, her bedroom door will be locked before she can even say sorry.

So, on tonight's covert exploration, the *princesse* wears all black—pants instead of her typical dress, long sleeves, and her blonde hair tied up and tucked into a hood. Anyone who sees her will probably laugh and ask whose closet she raided, but the outfit is a culmination of every spy book she has ever read. *Spy* isn't a word that exists on Talia. It's ancient Terran, and a word most Talians do not understand.

If it wasn't for her many hours spent in "punishment lockdown," as she calls it, Liana probably wouldn't know it, either. But there isn't much to do *except* read when she is trapped. What better to read than her ancestors' records and publications?

That obsession with the archaic has brought her here —again—wearing all black and attempting to blend in with the shadows. Honestly, it's an effective disguise, minus the bright blue eyes that illuminate any space they inhabit, like lighthouses in a midnight sea.

Luckily, the hangar is mostly empty. There's a *garde* across the room, leaning against the wall, a tablet in his hands. But otherwise, the pilots have all retired for the evening. That means the crafts themselves are abandoned.

Liana takes a careful step forward and cranes her head

out into the open. In one corner of the room, there's a security camera that feeds right back to her father's surveillance center. A *garde* sits in front of those screens at all times. The *princesse* glances down at the mini-tablet in her hand. The time blinks back at her.

Any second now, the *garde* at the desk will have an unbearable desire to relieve himself.

And it most definitely will have nothing to do with the giant pitcher of *nimês* juice that Liana brought him as "thanks for his hard work."

Liana's eyes dart back up to the camera and train on the tiny corner of the black lens. There's no way to see the mechanism shifting inside, not from this far away, but that's not what she's looking for. No, all she needs is a—

Suddenly, a miniscule red light starts flashing in the blackness. Liana almost cries out in excitement. The *garde* has started recording the feed, meaning he's stepped away from the screen.

That means she has exactly two minutes to cross the camera's path to the crafts.

Tucking her mini-tab back into her sleeve, Liana sprints across the hangar, every step muffled by her soft-soled shoes. The *garde* never looks up from his tablet; the camera never stops flashing. Completely undetected, the silent *princesse* shoots up the ramp of the closest space-craft and disappears into the surveillance-free interior.

Liana makes it about two steps in before the motion-sensor lights click on. Soft blue hues fill the belly of the ship, spreading down into the hangar below. It's irrelevant now, though, because the *garde* won't investigate a random craft's lights turning on. Could be anything—a little forest *souris* (or *mouse*, as the Terrans used to call it) or dust motes. It won't be worth walking over for.

So, Liana pushes her hood back and relaxes.

Before her, the belly of the starship stretches out. The open expanse is no bigger than her bedroom, but it couldn't be more different. Here, the walls are sleek steel. They reflect the floor lights, breathing as hydraulics work and whispering as computers awaken. Silver storage crates line one wall, and there are benches stationed in front of the other.

Loading deck, she reminds herself. This part of the ship is called the loading deck.

For a moment, Liana pretends she isn't the sheltered daughter of a sovereign. She straightens her spine, walks over to the benches, and studies the small handles built into the wall. Gripping the nearest handhold, she slides open a long drawer and pulls out an extra flight suit. It's too long for her, of course—she was never tall enough to learn to fly—but she can drape it across her shoulders and *pretend*.

The lilac material of the flight suit is slick to the touch, like it was made for repelling water instead of projectiles. She's seen these things at work, though. They're almost impenetrable—a piece of Niharan tech mixed with the Gollem's artificial minds.

After running her hand along the suit one more time, Liana drapes it across the open drawer and steps away. Her feet carry her down the hall.

Past the common room where three chairs sit around a table that's been anchored in the center of the room. The *princesse* stares for a minute, imagining herself sitting and laughing with other pilots, forming unbreakable bonds of trust and love.

Past a medbay with two pristine, cushioned beds. For a second, she pictures herself lying there while a medic patches up a wound on her shoulder.

Past three staterooms with their doors propped open to reveal an assortment of personal items.

Liana doesn't stop to pry here. She, of all people, knows the value of privacy. Instead, she pulls the doors closed and moves on.

With a wall of computer screens on her left and right —support systems and weapons, respectively—this is her favorite part of the spaceship. Two chairs sit in front of a massive glass window.

For a moment, she can picture it.

"Captain on the bridge!" someone yells, and all three chairs spin toward her.

Liana laughs and shakes her head at her three best friends. "At ease," she says with a smile. "Reports?"

"All systems functional," her engineer chimes, beaming at her from his station. The gunner rattles off the same thing, followed by her navigator, and Liana breathes a sigh of relief.

With a nod, she sits down in the biggest chair, turns to face the window, and takes in the infinite expanse in front of her.

Neverending stars glittering in all corners of her vision.

Planets that cast shadows over them.

Comets sailing beside *her* craft.

The entire galaxy to explore.

No locked doors.

No restrictions.

No gilded cage.

Forgetting where she is for a moment, Liana sits in the captain's chair and gapes at the window. There aren't any stars out there, of course—just another craft's ramp and the roof of the spacecraft hangar. But that sight alone fills her with such an intense longing that tears well up in her eyes.

Anger blooms under it.

She knows why her parents keep her here. They've always been open about their desire to protect her. It's from *what* that Liana doesn't know. Maybe if they'd just tell her, then she could rest. Maybe she could stop *wanting*.

Deep down, though, Liana knows it won't be enough. She's already tasted endless knowledge in the form of whatever books she wants. If they give her a cup of knowledge, she will search the furthest corners of the universe to find more.

It will never be enough.

Sighing, the *princesse* turns the chair toward the control deck. Her fingers dance across the buttons, itching to press one or two, just to find out what they do. She traces the edge of a rather enticing green one with an "A" printed on it, wondering, weighing the consequences.

What could it hurt?

Just one little—

"What you doing, *princesse*?" a gritty voice asks.

Liana's hand jerks away from the button, and she screams. The chair spins wildly as she flings herself out of it, grappling for any weapon within reach. There's nothing, of course, so she simply balls up her tiny fists and prepares to fight to the death.

Unfortunately, it isn't her worst nightmare incarnate standing in front of her.

It's *Tanno* Meiji.

Her worst nightmare—*Rei* Lucian with a disappointed scowl on his face—might be a better sight.

The elder Niharan glares up at Liana, looking for all the galaxy like a nîme berry that's been left in the sun for too long. Her tunic, which the *princesse* knows for a fact used to fit her perfectly, envelops her now-shrunken form. Her back curves in a harsh "U," so much so that Liana is convinced the only thing holding her upright is the gnarled gray branch she uses as a walking stick.

But it isn't her weathered, ancient appearance that frightens the young girl. It's her ability to sneak up on someone when they least expect it and use her giant brown eyes to gaze deeply into their souls. *Tanno* Meiji doesn't visit Talia often anymore, but when she does, she pins a target on Liana's back.

"I was just . . . taking a walk," Liana lies, her voice trembling slightly. *Get it together. You're a crown* princesse, *for stars' sake.*

Meiji's eyes narrow. "Inside starship?"

Knowing very well that there's absolutely no way to lie her way through Meiji's soul-devouring glare, Liana risks a grin instead. "Would you believe me if I told you I got lost?"

The *tanno* huffs in disbelief. "Full of lies, you," she growls, pointing her stick at Liana. "Too young to be breaking rules. And rules that protect you at that! You should be ashamed."

The *princesse* hangs her head and the rest of her blonde hair falls around her shoulders, which sink in defeat. Why did she think she could get away with this? She isn't a spy. She's a guarded *princesse*, a sealed artifact that's only meant to be seen behind thick glass.

"Please don't tell my father," she whispers, looking up at the elder Niharan.

Meiji is still glaring at her. Truthfully, she's spent most of her life glaring at someone. "Ought to." Then, without any warning whatsoever, her walking stick swings out wide and whacks the back of Liana's knees. The girl nearly buckles as the sharp crack echoes around the ship's bridge.

"*Tanno!*" The elder's title comes out a breathy hiss of pain as Liana grabs for the searing skin, but it doesn't slow Meiji down. She cocks her hand back and readies another strike. Liana's self-preservation kicks in, and she squeaks, leaping around Meiji and bolting toward the ramp.

The Niharan chases her all the way, clacking her stick against the metal walls.

The once quiet spacecraft hangar doesn't exist anymore. Instead, it's a cacophony of barked commands, shouted warnings, and sharp stick slaps. When Liana comes dancing down the ramp, fighting back tears, she nearly runs straight into a line of *gardes*.

As if tonight couldn't get worse, the *rei* is standing behind them.

If she wasn't dead before, she is now.

The stick-clacking stops and *Tanno* Meiji slides up beside her to face the sovereign before them. He doesn't pay her any mind, though. His eyes are glued on his trembling daughter.

Half an hour ago, she'd been filled with adrenaline—felt it coursing through her veins like electricity, driven with molten want. Liana can still taste that on the back of her tongue, but it's slipping away. In its place is shame, cold and bitter. She knows the rules, knows that their purpose is to protect her, not punish her.

From what, she doesn't know, but does that matter?

Here she is, risking everything they built for her, and for what?

Liana looks once at her father, at the wrinkles in the corners of his eyes and the permanent creases between his brows. His hair, once sandy blond like hers, is now gray-streaked. The crown on his head seems too heavy to bear.

One thing hasn't changed, though.

When his eyes meet hers, he still melts. Every trace of anger slides off his face, and only adoration is left. His little star. She might be the reason he's gone gray, but he would do it all again with no hesitation. *Rei* Lucian would give her the galaxy if he could.

But he can't.

It isn't safe.

Liana forces herself to look away before she cries. "I'm sorry, Papa," she whispers.

And all he can do is sigh. "I know, *étoile*. I know." Parting the *gardes* like they are nothing more than water, he takes his daughter into his arms and leads her away from the spacecraft and all the temptations it holds.

Back to her gilded prison.

Guests

Her father may not be able to punish her, but her mother can. The next morning, Liana wakes to *Reina* Emille standing at the edge of her bed wearing the galaxy's deepest scowl. Her arms are crossed over her chest, and she's still dressed in night clothes.

Not a good sign, Liana thinks as she scoots to the edge of the bed. If someone other than her husband is going to see her, Emille always takes the time to look perfect—hair, makeup, and clothes.

"Appearances are everything," she says often as she sips strongly brewed *nimês* juice, Liana sitting across the table from her. "Your enemies and allies alike will take one look at you and form an assumption. Dress the way you want to be perceived, and control the narrative."

But how does Liana want to be perceived? Cold and serious like her mother? Soft but commanding like her father? A mixture of both? She has no idea. Does anyone at seventeen?

No, *eighteen*. It is daybreak. Today, the little Talian *princesse* is eighteen.

Too old to be scolded by her mother, she thinks.

"Morning, Ma—"

Emille cuts her off with a sharp, "Not a word, Liana Fleur Thorne."

The "too old to be scolded by her mother" *princesse* flinches. With a sigh, she swings her feet off the bed and stands. Soft orange light dances across the white tile, filtered through the sheer curtains that cover the singular window of Liana's bedroom. Not looking at her mother, the *princesse* crosses the room, plops down on the plush bench that runs under the window, and slides her tablet out of its protective sleeve.

Her most recent read is open before *Reina* Emille can pick her jaw up off the floor.

"Liana Thorne," Emille hisses. She takes a step toward her daughter, but the girl holds up a slender finger—the universal *wait* sign. Metaphorical smoke curls out of the *reina*'s ears.

After a lightyear-length minute, Emille repeats Liana's name.

This time, the girl looks up. "Can I speak now?" she asks, voice level. Little does her mother know that the hand gripping her tablet is trembling in sheer terror. This woman could eat her for breakfast, and the galaxy wouldn't even *blink*. Who does Liana think she is?

The sovereign huffs and uncrosses her arms. "You know what, Liana? I'm not going to react. I just don't have time for your teenage sass this morning. Get dressed." She pins Liana to the windowsill with a glare. "Now."

"What for?" Liana dares to ask as she clicks her tablet into sleep mode and turns.

"I would have told you if I'd been able to find you last

night." *Reina* Emille shakes her head and moves to Liana's massive closet. Even from the outside, one can see the piles of discarded dresses and mismatched shoes. A scarf hangs from one of the door handles, and there's a brassiere draped across the other.

"I came to find you after dinner to tell you all about the surprise your father and I have planned, but when I knocked, you didn't answer." Emille's voice is thick with mock surprise. "So I came on in, of course, because you're my *daughter*. And what did I find?" She thrusts a pale pink dress in Liana's direction. "An empty bed and my only child missing!"

The *princesse* takes the dress but refuses to cower. *Too old to be scolded,* she reminds herself. "So it wasn't *Tanno* Meiji who found me?"

"Oh, it was definitely Meiji, but she wasn't the only one looking." Emille pulls a pair of black flats out of the shoe pile and sets them aside. "Half the castle was hunting you."

That causes Liana to wince. All for a little exploration.

Before the full weight of that can sink in, though, another question rises to the top of her mind. "Mama, why is *Tanno* Meiji here anyway? She only visits for Papa's council meetings, and the next one isn't for at least thirty days."

"Another thing you would have known if you'd been in your room." Her mother plucks a brush off her vanity and uses it to point at the chair. Liana finishes pulling on the dress the *reina* selected before sitting. "They're here for your birthday. Your father and I planned a party. It was *supposed* to be a surprise."

But then you ruined it.

Liana can hear the undertones bringing down the otherwise exciting news.

Too scared to ask anything else, she just says, "They?"

"Meiji is here with her two granddaughters," Emille says, pulling the brush through Liana's tangled hair. Pulling is a bit of a stretch, though, because there's nothing *graceful* about the action. It's more like a yank or a jerk. "*Rebb* Cyrno brought his son, too. I forget his name."

Of course you do, Liana thinks bitterly, watching her mother twist strands of hair away from her face. *How could you remember any of them when they're only allowed to visit once a year?*

When she was much younger, the other heirs made an effort to include her. They often vid-commed her or DMed her links to relevant galactic social news. As time passed, though, they all grew lives of their own, blooming like flowers in an open clearing while she shriveled in the shadows. It was awkward to talk about movies Liana hadn't seen, musicians she'd never heard. Maybe they just got tired of watching her face fall when they talked about their quick hops over to the next planet for a holiday.

Whatever caused it to end was irrelevant. Their friendships just *weren't* anymore. Full stop.

But they were coming today. Just the members of Papa's council and their children. Never anyone new. Never anyone *exciting*. As her mother fights a particularly nasty knot out of Liana's hair, the *princesse* stares at the hands folded in her lap.

The words "surprise party" had set her heart racing, but could a gathering of no more than five really be called a party?

She should be grateful. Should say her thanks and smile.

Instead, Liana's chest aches. Why had she thought things would be different just because she was one year older?

With a final sign, *Reina* Emille sets Liana's crown upon her head—a tiny twisted string of gold with embedded pearls and crystallized white flowers. She looks down at her daughter, at the child she's sacrificed everything for.

"Happy birthday, *étoile*," she whispers, pressing a kiss to the side of her head. "I hope you understand why your papa and I do the things we do."

The sad truth is that she *does* understand, but that doesn't make her hate it any less.

∾

Luckily, the day gets much better after her scolding.

Liana spends several hours in the front courtyard of the *palais*, socializing with Talians and drinking fermented *nimês* juice. Her mother doesn't even take it away when she catches her sipping it. The beach is filled with laughter and friendly conversation, with birthday wishes and thanksgivings. When the sun peaks in the sky, everyone moves into the shade of the *palais*, where the music being played through tele-screens echoes between marble columns.

But the air is fresh with the tang of saltwater and the sun is warm on her bare shoulders.

It doesn't matter if the music is slightly outdated or if her head is spinning from too much *nimês*—she's enjoying herself. For the first time in months.

The party breaks for lunch, and Liana finds herself drifting to an isolated circle of guests, two of whom are smaller than the usual crew and one who glints silver in the blinding sunlight. The two girls are dressed in simple, tan wraparound dresses and sandals, but elaborate embroidered designs trim the bottom. Their skin is tanned from many hours under their six suns, their clothes sandy from the unavoidable desert landscape.

The boy, on the other hand, is dressed in an immaculate black outfit. The jacket clings to his frame and stretches to the back of his knees. Like his father, the Gollem heir is semi-mechanical. Half of his head has been replaced by cybernetics. Through a thin glass plate, one can see the gears and wires as well as hear his thoughts shifting.

"Well, hello, Liana," one of the girls says, raising a glass to the *princesse* as she approaches. "Happy birthday!"

"Thank you," Liana says, smiling at each of them. "It's been way too long. How have you all been?"

The Niharan twins shift awkwardly.

The Gollem heir breaks the silence. "Same as always." His voice is stiff, awkward. Why had she even come over here? "Meetings and classes, training and parties. It's all a bit boring, really."

Liana tries (and fails) to hide the scowl she feels building up. What does he know about boredom? Has he ever spent days locked in his room with nothing but a book to keep him company? Ever called his "friend" seven times and been ignored over and over again? Ever been forbidden to leave his own planet? She doubts it.

"That sounds . . ." She spins her hand through the air as she searches for the gentlest word. Finally, she settles for a lie. "Just awful."

"It really is," he says, oblivious to her sarcasm. "Just last week, Father made me travel *alone* to Sybil to meet with Lady Ionia and listen as she went on and on about some 'intergalactic web of deception' and 'darkness upon us.'" He uses his free hand to air quote the Sybillian dignitary's words. "Honestly, it was a waste of time."

All Liana can do is bite her tongue and think about how she would *die* to travel to Sybil.

"No frakking kidding," one of the twins says. Liana has no idea which one it is. She stopped being able to tell them apart when she was seven. "Amma makes us sit through three hours of etiquette training every day. If I have to listen to her explain which frakking fork to use one more time, I might stab her with it."

The two of them dissolve into their own conversation while Liana is left to figure out what the frak "frakking" means—even though she has a pretty good idea. It's all a little too ridiculous for her, but walking away would be rude. These people will be her war council one day; she should learn to get along with them.

"Speaking of boredom, Liana looks like she's suffering from it," the other twin says. *So that's how I told them apart,* Liana thinks as she jerks back to attention. One has a deeper voice, like her mother.

The *princesse* hurries to set her drink down on a side table. Maybe she's had a bit too much if she's lost control of her face. "No, no, it's not that! I'm tired; that's all."

They study her for a long minute before the deeper-vocalled twin suggests, "How about we play a game? This is a party, after all."

"A great idea," her sister agrees. "Any suggestions?"

While they throw out ideas—pétanque (not enough for two *good* teams) or werewolves (they agree the wolf would be too easy to guess with only four players) or Who

Am I? (but Liana doesn't know modern celebrities) or maybe a simple round of Go Fish (no one is carrying a deck of cards, though)—Liana's gaze drifts up to her window.

Her tablet should still be sitting on the windowsill, right where she left it. For once, she'd much rather be up there, reading about the Terrans and their adventures on that blue and green Earth with its countries and snow.

Just then, an idea comes to her.

"What about Truth or Dare?" she asks, unknowingly cutting off the Gollem heir.

All three of them cut their eyes to her, digesting her words. Then, one of the twins smiles. It's a sly, wicked gesture, one-sided and twisted, and Liana lacks the socialization to accurately translate it. The *princesse* takes it as excitement and lets it bleed over to her.

"What a great idea," the twin says, setting down her drink. "I know it's your birthday, but can I go first?"

That all-too-familiar itch flares up in Liana's chest. "Of course."

The other two heirs look at each other, wary expressions crossing their faces. Liana doesn't notice though; she's too busy clinging to the edge of her seat and fighting the urge to *scratch*.

"Truth or dare, *Princesse* Liana?"

The word rushes out like undammed water, like a spacecraft thrown into hyperspeed. "Dare."

Dares

The *palais* is quiet.

Candles extinguished.

Curtains drawn.

Tele-screens powered off.

For once, there are no *gardes* standing in every corner, no maids spot-cleaning the windowsills.

Instead, it's just four sovereign heirs standing in the center of the ballroom, soaking in the stillness of desertion.

"You don't have to do this, Liana," the boy whispers, knowing his voice will carry to her all the same.

A sharp hiss slides out of one of the twins. "Yes she does. A dare is a dare."

He shoots her a glare. "It's just a game. I don't want her to get in trouble."

"They'll never even know!" A hand falls on Liana's bare shoulder. "Go on, then, *princesse*. We'll wait here."

Liana nods, fighting back an excited grin.

Her task is simple: break into a locked room. The castle has an abundance of those. When she mentioned that to the others, though, they added a little more.

Break into the locked council *room.*

For a moment, Liana feels like she's standing on a precipice, staring at the glittering pink ocean that is the rest of her life. *This* is the moment she's been preparing for. All of the spy books, all of the sneaking around, all of the quiet—it's all been building up to this. It's her parachute as she prepares to leap into adulthood.

Excitement courses through her, and with a small nod, she gathers her tulle skirt and glides toward the stone archway that leads to her father's council room. The flats *Reina* Emille chose for her make no sound against the marble, adding to the secretive aesthetic.

Like the ballroom, the hallway is empty. Habit forces her to check the cameras in each of the corners, but the red recording lights blink in each one of them. They're all at the party, just like she expected them to be—just like they were commanded to be. Why didn't she think of sneaking around on her birthday *years* ago?

It's all too easy, she thinks, approaching the silver door. Chuckling to herself, Liana reaches for the handle, and—

Meets a solid wall.

The *princesse*'s stomach drops. How could she have been so naïve? Of course there's no handle; it's her father's frakking council room. (Maybe she *does* know the meaning of that word.) Picking the lock would have been like taking candy from a baby, especially since she learned that simple skill when she was eight. But a solid steel door?

Desperate, Liana digs her fingers into the small gap between the two silver plates and attempts to pry them apart. It's useless, she knows that, but as quick as the excitement dies, horror is born.

This *cannot* be her dead end. This room. It must hold so many secrets, so many . . . possibilities. She's had it all planned out in her head: Once her friends accept her and know she is both smart and one of them, her parents will see that it is safe for her to socialize outside of Talia. They'll loosen her cuffs, maybe even let her visit one of them. This is supposed to be the first day in the rest of her life.

And Liana will *not* let a stupid door stop her.

Huffing, she digs her heels in and pulls even harder, her face turning red from the effort. Beads of sweat make their way down her neck and forehead.

"Stupid—door—"

As soon as the words leave her mouth, the door fights back. Liana loses her grip and flails sideways, her shoulder slamming into the wall. She winces and starts to grab for the door again when she spots something on the wall.

A small black box with the digits zero through nine printed on them.

A keypad?

A breathless smile spreads across her face. She doesn't need superstrength to pry the door open, she just needs super intelligence to guess the code! That's much more manageable.

Smoothing her dress, Liana leans down to stare at the

tiny keypad. Most likely, it's a date. It's always a date in her spy novels. Maybe it's her mother's birthday? Or the *rei*'s? Or would it be the date of Talia's creation? That last one's silly—it would just be 00-00-00 because time didn't exist here yet. Maybe the date of Earth's demise, when their ancestors left their planet once and for all?

It'll be something really important to *Rei* Lucian.

And she has to get it right on her first try, or it'll probably set off an alarm of some kind.

Taking slow, deep breaths to help her concentrate, the *princesse* asks herself: *What was the most important day in Papa's life? What means the most to him?*

And just like that, she knows the code.

With a sugar-sweet smile on her face, Liana types in her own birthday—today's date, eighteen years ago—and then steps back.

Two seconds pass, but then, all at once and with a *whoosh*, the doors slide away. Liana takes a deep breath and steps off the precipice.

Into the rest of her life.

Or, at least, into a small room that's surprisingly cold. The decór is simple: a singular black oval table with six chairs stationed around it. In the center is a hologram disk. Liana reaches across and taps the edge, and Talia itself appears in the air before her. She studies a globe projection like this almost daily during her lessons and can recognize different islands and landmarks.

This globe is much more detailed than hers, though. It

has the perimeter, glittering white and shifting slightly as the holo spins. Liana runs a finger through the image and pretends that she can pierce that impenetrable border. Sure, it protects them all from stars-know-what, but it also keeps them all in.

Without the proper clearance, no one gets in or out.

Especially not her.

Sighing, Liana powers down the holo disk and continues her exploration.

She pauses at her father's chair, the biggest of the six. The cushions are worn where his shoulders have rested; the once black arms have faded with age and wear. What gives it away for Liana, though, is the small dip in the right armrest where the paint is missing. *Rei* Lucian's dining chair is the same way, the result of his anxious picking.

Liana slides the chair out and sits down in it. The grooves from his body engulf her, but in the most comfortable way—like when she was a little *princesse* walking around in his shoes, wearing one of his uniform jackets. A smile spreads over her face at the memory.

This will be her seat one day.

Her mind instead of his. Her word over all.

Liana doesn't know how she'll manage. She can never compare to her father. Not in a thousand years.

With a soft sigh, the *princesse* slides the chair back and starts to stand back up. Then, she notices a tablet lying face-down on the table. Without a second's hesitation, she picks it up, toggles it out of sleep mode, and starts swiping through the interface.

A second too late, she notices whose it is.

The programs are different, the commands more specific. Where her reading app is, a security link sits. Where she has a shortcut to her reading goals and sketchpad, there is an icon shaped like an archaic newspaper and a small green square with a speech bubble in it.

Liana's curiosity swells in her chest until she suddenly finds it hard to breathe. The hand holding the tablet starts to shake, and the other clenches the arm of the chair. It's wrong. She knows it's wrong. This is her father's tablet. She should put it down right now, leave the council room, and carry the secret of this adventure with her to the grave.

What she *shouldn't* do is open the security app. She most definitely should not scroll through the feeds or open the travel logs. Looking at the recent threat report will probably send the *rei* to an early grave.

But the invitation is just so inviting.

And Liana can't stop herself. Even if she wanted to. Her fingers move on their own, soaking in every juicy piece of information and scratching that stars-awful itch she's been trying to reach for years. They just keep scrolling, keep clicking through to the deeper recesses of the archives, into code that even she doesn't recognize. She could easily be corrupting his tablet, and Liana wouldn't even know it.

After a few minutes of digging, the *princesse* finds an icon hidden in the collection for an app labeled "$2\pi r$"— whatever that means. Centuries later, a much older and less naïve Liana will regret not having paid attention in her mathematics study, and even the slightest mention of $2\pi r$ will cause her to sweat.

Now, though, Liana taps the icon with no thought of consequence and waits for the program to load.

Even then, she can't quite tell what it is. The screen shows a strange circle turning lazily on a black background. Occasionally, a section of the figure will blink green or yellow, but it always returns to white within a few seconds. Liana stares at it, mesmerized by the strange graphic, wondering what in the world it could be.

She's about to close the app when the top left section blinks red. The tablet vibrates violently; the screen flashes with an alert. Liana's back straightens, and she clutches the device like it's the only thing keeping her on the ground. Her eyes are glued to the screen, and for a moment, she's frozen.

In terror.

Of being found out. Of something being wrong. Of the unknown.

All she can do is wait.

The words "INCOMING CRAFT; M IDENTIFIED" appear on the screen, surrounded by a black text box. Two options sit under the dialogue: "Establish Connection," and "Initiate Security Protocols."

Once again, Liana knows what she *should* do.

But the temptation is too sweet. She's waited too long, been sheltered too strongly.

Licking her lips, Liana presses the first option and holds her breath.

No more than five seconds pass, but it feels like a lifetime. Her heartbeat thunders in her ears; her nails dig into her father's well worn armrest.

Then, the screen shifts.

Staring back at the *princesse* is a figure that will star in her nightmares long after everything changes. His smile will haunt and motivate her, driving her to both tears and vengeance.

The man, a dark-skinned and dark-haired adult with long, twisting black horns, studies her for a beat before saying in a warm voice, "You are a spitting image of Emille." He pauses and smiles. "Except for your hair. That's all Lucian. So, I'm guessing you are their daughter. I've heard so much about you, Liana."

The *princesse* blinks. "Who are you?" she manages to spit out.

He laughs, a sound like velvet and melted sugar. "I am Malfios. It is so good to finally meet you, *princesse*."

Trespassers

A tingle starts at the base of Liana's spine—the first clue that something's not exactly right. She glances up at the council room door, wondering if the *gardes* are on their way. The tablet probably set off an alarm, so they should be here soon. Surely they wouldn't abandon their tech for her party. The *rei* wouldn't let his guard down so fast.

Knowing they'll come to her rescue if something is wrong—like they always have—Liana tries to relax.

"How do you know my parents?" she asks, meeting Malfios's eyes. It's hard to do because they're the sharpest shade of red she's ever seen. She perseveres, though, because *Reina* Emille has always pressed the importance of eye contact alongside appearance.

"Old friends," Malfios says shortly, his smile never faltering. It's a sweet expression—two dimples in his cheeks, soft lips, and no teeth. Little does she know it's been curated to fool even the strongest wills. "Are you supposed to be playing on your father's tablet?"

Liana doesn't flinch, but the reminder that she's breaking half a dozen house rules is enough to make her want to. "I'm not *playing*," she says with a nervous laugh.

"Then what are you doing?"

A beat passes as the *princesse* weighs her options. She

could lie—say she was watching the security feeds for her father—or she could admit the truth. This man knows nothing about her, though. Liana can be *anyone*.

So she chooses to be someone else. Just for today.

"The *rei* asked me to watch it. Just for a moment." After a second, she adds, "He will be right back."

Malfios sits back in his chair. Somewhere off screen, Liana recognizes the soft blue of space craft lights. "No rush. I've got all the time in the universe."

Shadows move behind him, catching Liana's attention. Muffled shouts follow them.

"Tell me about yourself, Liana," Malfios says. His voice drowns out whatever is going on behind him. "Unfortunately, I don't get to catch up with your parents very often. We're just so busy, as I'm sure you know. How old are you?"

"Eighteen," Liana says, a small smile breaking out on her face. "Today's actually my birthday."

The stranger beams at her, showing a row of perfectly straight, white teeth. "Well, happy birthday, *princesse*. An adult at last, huh? Any special plans? A trip, maybe?"

"Not really," Liana says with a shrug. "I don't travel much."

"Oh? Why not?"

His voice is so soft, so genuine, that Liana can't help herself.

"I'm not allowed. Papa says it's not safe."

Malfios hums. "That is very true. The universe is a dark place these days. Horror lurks in every corner."

"But my friends travel. They're already training to be sovereigns!" She huffs in frustration. "How am I ever supposed to take Papa's place if I don't socialize with the rest of the galaxy?"

He nods, eyes glinting with understanding (or maybe hunger). "That is incredibly unfair, Liana." He looks off-screen for just a moment and then returns with his eyebrows raised. "I just had a wonderful idea. Would you like to show your father how responsible you are? It's obvious that you're a smart girl. We can show him if you'd like."

The *princesse* nods, her hair slipping out of the *reina*'s elaborate twist. "Yes, please."

Malfios leans in, and his face takes over the screen. "Do you trust me, Liana?"

The prickle at the back of her spine crawls upward. Every instinct she has screams to turn off the screen, to run across the *palais* and find her father. Something is wrong with this situation, but . . .

She's at the edge again.

Could this be her chance?

The first day of the rest of her life?

He does look a bit dishonest with his horns and red eyes, but during their conversation, he gave her his full attention. Mama would have her judge him based on his outward appearance; she'd have Liana running for the hills.

But *Reina* Emille isn't here right now.

And Liana is sick of being told what to do.

Shoving the warning tingle down, Liana nods. "I do."

"Good girl," he purrs, that fermented *nimês* juice smile crawling like sunrise across his face. "All you have to do is find the *Open* command on the app you're on right now. Can you do that for me?"

Liana nods and minimizes his vid-call window to start looking. "What does it open?" she asks as she searches.

"Just trust me, love."

She glances at his tiny picture in the corner for a brief second and goes back to scrolling. Within a minute, she's located the command—a little silver icon hidden deep in the settings. It wasn't meant to be found accidentally, that's for sure. The designer hid it well.

"Do I just press it?" she asks, finger hovering.

"Only if you want to show your father just how grown up and brave you are."

There's nothing she wants more, so Liana lets her finger fall.

Across the galaxy, a Sybillian sovereign loses her grip on her goblet as a vision takes her. The shrill sound of her keening can be heard throughout the temple, followed by a gut-wrenching, looping chant—"Talia, Talia, Talia. Darkness has found her, darkness has found her—"

54

Back in the council room, Malfios smiles at Liana one more time before sitting back. "Thank you, *princesse*. I'll see you soon." Then he ends the call, leaving Liana alone in the council room.

She doesn't move at first. The vid-call keeps replaying in her head. What did she just do? What did she open for him? More importantly, who was he? She's never heard of anyone named Malfios, but it's not like she knows everything about her parents. Considering they've successfully kept the secret of what they're protecting her from safe for eighteen years, it's also safe to assume they have more secrets.

With one last look around the council room, Liana sighs and rises from the chair. There's nothing else to explore, so she may as well report back to the heirs. It wasn't a total waste, though. Surely Malfios will come through.

The scene forms in her mind as she puts the tablet back in its place and heads for the silver door.

"Sweet étoile, *you did this for me?" her father will say, standing in her bedroom door. The morning light will halo around him, and he will look like the savior she's always seen him as.*

"Of course, Papa." Liana will close her book and sweep across the room to hug him. He'll smell of freshly-washed clothes and sugar—a result of being both notoriously clean and addicted to baked goods—and his chest will be warm, like always.

As he leans down to press a kiss to the side of her head, Rei *Lucian will whisper, "I guess it is time to let you explore your galaxy. Where do you want to go first?"*

Liana knows the answer to the imaginary question: Gollem. The tech has always fascinated her. She might even get an implant of some kind.

Since she's busy plotting how she might convince him to let her visit *Rebb* Cyrno, Liana doesn't feel the shudder of the floor under her feet. She doesn't notice the way the silver doors quiver as they slide shut behind her or that the music outside has died. She's still smiling, even as she steps into the empty ballroom.

Then, the screaming begins.

It's a singular sound at first, one terrified girl with her finger pointed at Talia's cloudless sky. As the adults around her glance up absentmindedly, the screams multiply, and the fear explodes. Many of the guests are old enough to recognize the heavy black crafts in the sky, to know exactly who the swirling red "M" insignia on the bottom of each belongs to. Others can taste the dread and panic, so it bleeds down their throats to control them.

Gardes race to their posts. Barked orders echo around the courtyard.

"Into the *palais!*"

"Remain calm! Panicking will only make things worse."

"Women and children to the front! Hurry now!"

Bodies merge into rivers. Children glance at the ships

above them. Mothers try to shield their eyes as fathers usher them into safety. The shocked screams morph into muffled cries and whimpers.

In the midst of it all, two sovereigns begin to panic, searching the crowd for their *princesse*.

Four ships hover in the sky—large enough to block the afternoon sun. The ship at the front opens its bay doors. Teardrop-shaped projectiles emerge and begin to fall toward the crowd. It's ancient tech, from the age of Terrans and World Wars.

Plus, there are no guards at their stations. So who can stop the bombs?

One by one, the ammunition hits its marks, and the ground becomes unstable. Talians trip over one another, over dead bodies, over fallen marble, over shrapnel in their race to find safety.

But there is none.

Palais Talia is falling apart in front of them.

In the ballroom, Liana braces herself in a doorway, watching the horror unfold. Some of her people have made it inside, but the situation isn't better here. Chunks of the ceiling are breaking away, and plaster is snowing down around them.

Her parents.

Where are her parents?

Did she do this? Is this her fault?

From within the crowd, a desperate scream emerges. "Liana!"

The *princesse*'s heart stops. Still holding the archway, she returns the wail with one of her own. "Mama!"

Liana starts to step down into the writhing sea of bodies, but another shockwave rocks the *palais*, knocking her backward. She clings to the wall, searching desperately for her parents.

What did she *do*?

Before she can consider running into the crowd again, a ring of *gardes* appears in the center. Liana can't hear what they're saying, but she can see their mouths moving rapidly, clearing a path to her. In the midst of the *gardes* are her parents, their dress clothes covered in debris and a red substance Liana refuses to name.

Her mother looks up, cups her mouth with her hands, and begins to shove her way to Liana. *Rei* Lucian yells after his wife, but as soon as he sees Liana crouching in the archway, he too breaks from his protectors and rushes to her.

They reach her at the same time, throwing their arms around her. Liana is crushed between them, and she dissolves into sobs.

"I'm sorry—I didn't—I—"

Emille pulls back first, brushing her hair out of her face with trembling hands. She hushes her, but Liana can see the fear in her eyes.

The *princesse* shakes her head. "I didn't mean to. I promise." Her voice quivers with the myriad of emotions coursing through her. "I didn't know what would happen."

As she talks, Lucian releases her and begins pulling them down the hallway, away from the crowd.

"What do you mean, *étoile*? You didn't mean to do what?" Emille glances up at her husband, but his face is morphed with determination. This is a scenario they've planned for, a conversation they've had a hundred times in their shared bed at night. Both of them know the emergency plan, but that doesn't make this any easier.

"I—pushed—I pushed the button," Liana chokes out, sucking in massive gulps of air. Guilt writhes in her chest, a snake constricting her lungs. "I let them in."

Lucian stops then, turning slowly to look at his daughter.

Emille is silent. Stunned. Confused. Scared.

The *palais* vibrates around them.

"You let who in, Liana?" her father asks, voice barely above a whisper. If they weren't huddled so close, she might not have heard him.

"M-Malfios." The name drags its claws up her throat as it emerges, and Liana begins to cry again.

"You've spoken to him?" Lucian hisses, sounding angry at her for the first time. Even when she snuck out of the *palais* one time to go night fishing, he didn't get angry with her.

Liana nods, chin quivering. "I broke into your council

room. It was a dare. Your tablet was sitting there, and I just —" Emotion overcomes her, and she loses her voice. Emille pulls her in for a hug, which only makes her cry harder.

The sovereign can do nothing but clench his jaw. They have taken every precaution, built up every wall. Liana was *never* supposed to know about Malfios, just as he should never have known about her. Was it simply coincidence that her rebellion overlapped with their enemy's plan, or was it some devious twist of fate? Will he live to figure it out?

Probably not.

"It was a mistake," he finally says, kissing Liana's forehead. "Everything will be okay. *You* will be okay, I promise."

A Talian promise.

Words etched in stardust, eternal and invincible.

From deep in his uniform, Lucian draws out a small keycard and slides it through a well-hidden crack in the wall. The stone shifts and strains, unsettled by the battle taking place around them, but it still manages to curl away and form a doorway. Lucian guides the two women through, and the stones close behind them.

If Liana wasn't distraught at potentially bringing her entire planet to death's door, she would have soaked in their downward walk. She might have noticed that they slipped into a different era, into silver and computers, holograms and the future. As it stands, though, she doesn't even realize they've stopped until her father shoves a lilac flight suit into her hands.

"Change, *étoile*," he says gently. When she doesn't budge, he traps her chin between his thumb and forefinger and forces her to look at him. Her galactic blue eyes are bloodshot and brimming with tears. Lucian uses his free hand to wipe them away before adding, "It's a flight suit, Liana. You've been dying to try one on for a decade."

Even longer, she wants to point out. But now is not the time.

Emille is already untying her dress. Lucian lets her go and turns his back to them.

"Papa," Liana mumbles, shrugging the dress off. "What's going on? Am I leaving?"

He shakes his head. "No. You're staying." A pause. "You've just got to go somewhere . . . safe."

As her mother helps her into the suit, Liana looks around the room. It's odd, almost like a spacecraft in style, but much smaller. There's a person-length metal table extending from an odd blue hole in one wall and a computer built into the other. The room itself has no windows. Liana tilts forward a little to peek inside the hole, and suddenly realizes just what it is.

"A cryo chamber?"

Rei Lucian looks over his shoulder, meeting her eyes. His lips are pursed; tears gather in his bottom lashes.

Liana's not leaving.

She's being frozen.

Goodbyes

Her lilac flight suit fits better than the pink tulle dress did. The sleeves are perfectly tailored to cling to her wrists; the pant legs slide easily into the black boots that her mother forces on her. After Liana zips up the front, smoothing down the flap that covers the zipper, it feels like she's wearing a second skin.

Meaning her parents had this planned.

They knew she'd need a suit.

They knew she'd mess up.

They knew Malfios would come.

"Cryo?" Liana repeats in a small voice. It comes out more like a whine than she intends, but the tone embodies her emotions perfectly.

She's read all about cryostasis, of course. In her Terran science fiction novels, it's common to freeze oneself in order to attain a longer lifespan. One particular romance novel featured women being kidnapped and forced into cryo for space travel. It isn't usually depicted as a negative experience, but that doesn't change the fact that she doesn't want to be *frozen*.

"Just for a while, *étoile*," Emille says softly, pulling her long hair back and wrapping it in a hair tie. She smooths the flyaway strands, picking out pieces of debris. "To keep you safe."

Liana's hands tremble like the floor under her. Or is her entire body shaking? How can she be sure?

"I—I can be safe with you two," she pleads, watching her father at the computer. "Please don't do this."

"Trust us, *petite étoile*. Your father had this room designed specifically for you, for keeping you safe. The stasis will protect you no matter how long we're engaged in battle with Malfios, and the walls are reinforced so strongly that the castle could collapse and you'd be fine."

As if to challenge the *reina*, the castle jolts around them again. Liana puts a hand on the wall, but her eyes stay glued to her father. Emille won't bend for her; she's an iron bar. But her papa? There's still hope there.

"Let me help you," she says, willing her voice to be still. "I can help, Papa."

He doesn't look at her.

Liana presses further. "You can't keep hiding me. I *need* to be out there. I have to learn." After a moment's pause, where her father keeps on typing, the *princesse* brings out the big guns. "Please, Papa. *Please* don't do this to me."

His hands still on the keyboard, his chin drops to his chest and his shoulders heave with deep, broken breaths.

"You are our everything," *Rei* Lucian whispers. When he speaks, the battle around them nearly drowns out his words. But nothing can cover the desperation in his voice. "You are the future of this planet, the future of *us*." Finally, he looks at her. Tears streak his dusty face. "Let us protect you, Liana. Please."

In the eighteen years she's known him, the *princesse* has never seen her father cry. She's heard him belly laugh at one of her ridiculous Terran jokes, seen him startle from fear when she jumped out at him, watched his eyebrows furrow and twist in unwilling frustration when she breaks yet another house rule. Lucian is a man of many emotions, and he has never hesitated to tell or show her all of them—pride, fear, love, excitement, or joy.

This is the man who used to balance her on his feet and spin her around the ballroom floor, scream-singing at the top of his lungs. Who watched her fall face-first in the sand when she was learning how to ride a hoverboard and laughed uncontrollably. Who scolded her up and down the *palais* when she kissed the son of a *garde* behind *Reina* Emille's giant vase after a party.

But tears?

Liana doesn't know how to handle tears. They reach inside her chest and strangle her heart, choking out every ounce of willpower the *princesse* has. As soon as one drips from his cheek onto his uniform, she knows that she has no choice.

She's being frozen.

The *princesse* nods, but she can't stop crying. "Okay, Papa," she says, her voice trembling. "I trust you."

He crosses the room in two steps and engulfs her in a hug. "I love you so much, *petite étoile*. You know that, right?" When Liana nods, body wracked with sobs, he adds, "Everything will be okay. I promise."

They stay like that, wrapped up in one another, until a horrible tearing sound comes from somewhere above them. Emille clears her throat and says softly, "Lucian, we should hurry."

He nods once, untangles himself, and gets to work.

Four sensors attach at Liana's heart, the top of her spine, her stomach, and her forehead to maintain her vitals and track health data.

One facemask, drawn tight over her mouth and nose to keep oxygen flowing and protect her sinuses from the cryo material.

One intravenous needle through a small hole in the crook of her arm, to feed her nutrients and medicine as needed.

One *princesse* laying on the slim metal table, watching her parents bustle around her, still crying.

And two parents, terrified that this is the last time they'll ever see their most precious treasure, but willing to say goodbye if it means she will live another day.

"Systems initiating," the computer says in a soft feminine voice. It is intended to be calming, but all three of them stiffen. The AI continues. "Hello, *Princesse* Liana. I am FLORA, your artificial intelligence guide. I will be ready to initiate stasis in three minutes."

Liana's eyes dart up to her parents, who stand side by side at the computer interface. Neither of them are looking at her, so she whines softly. Lucian turns first, followed by Emille, and together, they move to either side of her.

"We will not say goodbye," her father says, leaning down to kiss her forehead, "because that is not what this is. I will see you in the morning, when the world is perfect for you. Sleep well, *étoile*. Good night."

Reina Emille squeezes her hand and smiles down at her. "My sweet baby," she whispers, tearing up. "Dream of galaxies undiscovered and spacecraft galore, okay? When you open your eyes, we will be right here."

Liana nods as best as she can with the headset on and tries not to cry out as they move away from her. They retreat out of sight and cling to each other. Emille finally gives in to tears, but she cups her hands over her mouth so Liana doesn't hear her. Lucian's chin trembles as the emotion overcomes him, too.

And the AI counts down to zero.

"Beginning the cryostasis sequence," FLORA chimes. "Inducing sleep in five . . . four . . ."

Liana searches for her parents, but she can't see them. They've moved just out of sight.

All she wants is to say goodbye. Or good night. Or that she loves them.

"Three . . ."

She'll see them in the morning.

Everything will be okay.

"Two . . ."

Will it though? What will be left when she *does* wake up? Will they all hate her for what she's done?

"One..."

Does it even matter, though? Why was she scared in the first place? It's just a short ... nap ...

Liana turns her head slightly in an effort to be more comfortable, her eyes fluttering. Two shadows drift over her vision. Her parents?

Do they know how thankful she is?

How much ...

... she loves ...

... them ...?

"Zero." A pause. "Sleep state complete. Securing the *princesse*."

The two sovereigns dissolve into despair as the metal table begins to slide into the cryo chamber. From here, everything is automatic. All they have to do is watch their only child slide away.

At least she's safe.

That's all that matters either way.

They hold one another until the chamber seals and FLORA's voice fills the silver room once again. "Cryostasis complete. The *princesse* is secure. All systems are active and stable."

And then, with longing looks at the seal, the two of them leave the room, leave to discover the extent of Malfios's attack, to salvage some world for their heir when she awakens.

Victories

Malfios steps over the severed head of a Talian, careful not to slip on the blood coating the steps of the *palais*. The smell of fear is palpable in the air around him, mixed with despair and grief.

He'd been right; the Talian military was weak. That's what happens when one builds a wall and cowers behind it for eighteen years. Sure, they'd built a (nearly) impenetrable wall, but it was still just a wall. He'd been able to get through it, hadn't he?

And after that, it was simple.

Because they were weak.

As his soldiers—clad in black uniforms, their faces covered to the point that their only distinguishable feature is their bright red Mōrish eyes—search the palace courtyard for any sign of life, Malfios continues up the stairs toward the entryway.

This is his sixth victory in thirty years.

Six planets for Mōr, his homeland.

For him and all the power he craves.

With Talia in his palm, he has the rest of the galaxy at his disposal. He is unstoppable.

Well, mostly. There are still two pesky sovereigns to deal with.

The *palais* door sits crooked in its frame, torn from its silver hinges. The once-intricate design is blackened in some places and flattened in others. As he passes it, Malfios runs a dark finger through the ash, leaving a trail.

Inside, the *palais* is dark. Quiet. He stands still for a moment, remembering what the immense space looked like before the ceiling fell in, before the columns collapsed, before the walls cracked. It isn't hard to picture —candles lining the dance floor, a checkered marble floor in silver and white, a stage that holds the musicians, giant arching windows that let in just the right amount of sunlight and stardust. So many summers wasted in boyish laziness with Lucian, trying to fit into their fathers' molds.

It didn't work, apparently, because Malfios is anything but the royal prince his father wanted him to be.

That no longer matters, though. His father is dead; Malfios killed him himself.

From the ballroom, Malfios heads toward the stairwell that leads to the *palais*'s second floor. Lucian and Emille won't hide from him; they have too much pride to cower. No, he knows exactly where they are—right where he left them thirty years ago.

He ascends the grand staircase, stepping around chunks of fallen stone. An arm protrudes from one. It is bent at an unnatural angle, and blood seeps out onto the white stone. From somewhere below him, a dying moan lifts into the air. A singular gunshot follows the sound, and the dying becomes just another dead.

Immune to the carnage, Malfios takes a right at the top of the staircase. How many times did he walk this hallway, chasing Lucian or terrorizing Emille? He wonders when they decided to carpet the marble, when the paintings were reframed. Did they remove the ones of their fathers? There's no time to check.

Soon enough, Malfios stops. Through a thick wooden door, he can hear whispering. The cold smell of panic bleeds out to him, and he inhales it like a child taking its first breath. With a soft smile, he pushes the huge door open and steps into what used to be his favorite room in the *palais*.

The archives.

Hundreds of thousands of books—old-fashioned paper and digital copies—sit in sealed glass cases. Row upon row of the sleek, polished glass fills the room. Brass chandeliers hang from the ceiling, and although they may have once cast light, their candles have long been extinguished. In the center of the room are some comfortable-looking chairs and cushions, each paired with its own blanket.

And sitting on the two-person lounger are none other than Lucian and Emille, battle-worn but still regal. It absolutely infuriates him. How could they still be so calm in the face of such a loss?

"What now, Malfios?" Lucian says, his voice giving away how tired he is. Malfios can see the colors dancing around the *rei*—blue for exhaustion, purple for grief, and slips of red for rage. "You've won. What now?"

Malfios strides over to one of the glass cases and pushes it open. The room may be chaos incarnate, but the artifacts are perfectly maintained. He slides one book out of its place and gently flips through it. After scanning the first couple pages, he stops, grips the top corner of a page, and rips. The horrible sound of tearing paper nearly drowns out Emille's gasp of outrage.

But Malfios hears it. He meets her eyes and does it again.

And again.

And again.

Until the floor is littered with historical (and priceless) confetti.

"Stop," Lucian finally says, sighing. "You're being dramatic. Tell us your terms, and let's be done with this."

Malfios laughs. "My terms, huh?"

The sovereign nods.

"This isn't a negotiation, Lucian." He drops the book onto the ground and steps on it. "There are no terms. It's over."

Lucian rises from his seat, still holding one of Emille's hands. There's blood streaking her gown and she's filthier than Malfios has ever seen her, but her eyes—those are crystal clear.

Before the *rei* can counter Malfios' statement, he continues. "Where is she?"

The sovereigns look at one another, confusion crossing their faces. Then, like a mist falling over drenched land, realization sets in. Liana.

Neither of them speaks.

Malfios creeps closer. "Where. Is. She?"

Still, the *rei* and *reina* hold their tongues, their secrets, and their wills.

At last, Malfios is standing right over them. Their purples, blues, and reds overwhelm his vision, inter-mixing into a mauve haze. Such an ugly color, he thinks. Befitting to them, really.

"Last chance," he whispers, raising a clawed hand.

Both of them look up, but it's Emille who opens her mouth. Tendrils of her aura curl like worms in the air between them. The blended color shifts, suddenly more red than purple. Malfios senses her mercurial response before it spews from her mouth.

"You're pathetic," the *reina* spits out. "All you had to do was ask, Malfios. We were your friends. We loved you. Surely you know that!"

The man standing over her doesn't respond. Instead, he glares, never breaking eye contact. The hand at his side clenches into a fist.

Taking his silence as permission, Emille continues. "Whatever you wanted, we would have fought for you—

beside you, even! Why did you have to murder and lie and *take*? Your mother would be so—"

Malfios's hand moves of its own accord. It swipes across Emille's face with dangerous speed, sending the *reina* to the floor at her husband's feet and filling the room with the crack of skin against skin. Lucian steps towards their assailant, a threat half-formed on his lips, but Malfios already has a gun trained on his head.

"I will find her," he says, pushing the nagging thought of his mother back. "I will find her, and I will kill her. There will be nothing left of Talia when I'm done with it." First, he'll erase them, and then everything they represent, including the memories that haunt him.

Malfios snaps his fingers, and his men materialize behind him like shadows. "Tie them to a post in the courtyard. No food or water for the next two days. Let them *simmer*."

The men spring into motion and scoop up the two sovereigns. Emille glares at Malfios, a burning red mark staining her cheek, while Lucian attempts to fight back. It doesn't work, of course; he's outnumbered and outmatched. But it doesn't stop him from trying—pulling hair, kicking groins, biting hands.

In the end, both of them end up bound at the wrists and ankles and gagged with thick cloth. Malfios's men drag them out into the courtyard with their leader close on their heels and tie them to two metal posts that have been erected there.

Malfios gives his old friends one last forlorn look before turning toward his men and his future as ruler of a galaxy.

"Find the *princesse*. I don't care if you turn the palace upside down and kill everyone in your path. Just bring her to me." A chorus of affirmations answer him, and they scurry off to do their jobs. Malfios retreats inside the castle to do his own searching.

For two long days, the *rei* and *reina* hang there, wrists aching from their positions. They occasionally meet each other's glances and pray that their daughter is safe, that the *gardes* will survive and bring her out of cryostasis when it's time, that their planet will have some hope of a future. They do not have one, though.

At the end of the third day, Malfios has the surviving population of the planet rounded up and gathered in the courtyard—children and mothers and fathers alike, all battered and starved. Their eyes, once bright with the joy of a young *princesse*'s birthday, are dull, gray, and lifeless. They see their mighty sovereigns, already half dead, and know there is nothing left for them to wish for.

It's over.

Just like he did for his father, Malfios delivers the killing blow—two bullets straight through the backs of their heads. The audience never emits a cry of despair, but it echoes in their hearts for years after as they succumb to slavery and abuse. When their *princesse* does not appear again, they mourn her, too.

And all that's left of the mighty Lucian and Emille are their stolen bones buried in a shallow grave under a lone *nimês* tree at the edge of a slave camp and three small, unmarked gravestones where Talians sometimes pause to say their daily prayers.

Complications

While Malfios was ravaging the palace, hunting the *princesse*, and the sovereigns hung on their posts, the electricity failed.

No one noticed.

If they did, it was of no importance whatsoever. They were too tangled in their own survival, in their own hiding.

The AI in Liana's chamber noticed, though.

"Converting to an internal power source," FLORA said to absolutely no one.

That power source, though, was compromised by Malfios's presence in their once-secure server. As soon as FLORA connected, the AI lost control of her systems. Commands started initiating at random; power fluctuated spontaneously. Liana slept, but the system was losing its mechanical mind.

In an effort to break away from the corrupt server, FLORA did the only thing she was programmed to.

"Beginning Eleventh Hour sequence," she said, voice sounding as panicked as an artificial intelligence can possibly articulate—which isn't very. "Launching escape pod in ten . . . nine . . ."

Liana, sound asleep, could not tell the pod to cancel its action.

Emille and Lucian, chained and imprisoned, could not tell the pod to cancel its action.

The *gardes*, dead in droves and piled in corners of the palace, could not tell the pod to cancel its action.

And so, FLORA continued her course, and ten seconds later, Liana's pod launched itself, unnoticed, into the black of space.

Dreamless

Liana read an old Terran saying once that went like this: "If a tree falls in the forest and no one is there to hear it, does it still make a sound?"

She asked her father, who told her he didn't know, so she went to her mother, who said she didn't have time for silly questions. With no one else to ask, she'd had to resort to the scientific archives for answers.

What she discovered was this:

Sound is defined as vibrations that travel through a medium and can be heard.

Air would indeed be a medium, so that verified half the requirements. But who would hear it? An animal? So the answer was situational.

If there was any living thing nearby, then yes, it would make a sound.

As Liana's pod floats through space, there is no one to hear FLORA's monthly health reports. No one to click "read" on the computer's screen. No one to save the files. Yet she continues to do what she is programmed to.

She delivers 1,200 monthly oral reports to the purified air and the small, earless Talian dust mites who thrive in the emptiness.

Her screen shows 100 text boxes, outlining the details of these findings into annual reports.

The folders deep inside her archive fill up, not designed to self-save this many transcripts.

But she continues to do so.

Days pass.

Then weeks.

Then months.

Then, without Liana knowing, years.

She doesn't dream.

She isn't aware that she's finally getting to explore the galaxy.

Liana simply rests.

Talia mourns her parents first, then her, and then the loss of their freedom as Malfios takes control. Then, they forget. The Thorne family becomes a bedtime story whispered between enslaved Talians: a lost heir and a droplet of hope.

Landings

O n day thirty-six thousand, six hundred fifty, FLORA's alarms start ringing.

Red lights strobe in the pod's cabin.

Dust mites scuttle back into hiding.

The craft itself veers off course as something solid rams into its side.

"Warning," FLORA chimes. "Entering an asteroid field. Battery life too low to engage defense protocols."

The giant rocks continue to assault the forgotten pod, causing it to jolt harshly. The alarm turns shrill. FLORA repeats her warning until, finally, her voice gargles out one final string of nonsense and dies at last. The lights flicker out, leaving the blue haze of the cryo chamber as the pod's only illumination.

With no power, the thrusters give out and gravity takes over. The pod takes a sharp right and begins a quick descent toward a dark object. The closer it comes, the larger the shape, until flickers of light can be seen on the surface. The pod shudders as it breaks through the atmosphere of the planet, and a fire ignites on the outer shell.

Miles below, a man (if Ciel can be called that) looks up from his patrol route.

It's hard to see the sky through the haze of hundreds

of lights, between the skyscrapers and neon billboards. He knows for sure, though, that something is approaching, because an alert pops up in his HUD—the display implant set behind his eyes.

As he watches the object fall, the mechanical sector of his brain calculates its speed and time of landing. Caution causes his dozen live-screen tattoos to darken dangerously. Goosebumps rise on what little authentic flesh he has remaining on his arms.

"Manyn, do you see this?" Ciel asks aloud, even though there's no one else there.

A beep echoes in his ear, and then a feminine voice responds. "I do, boss. Rogue asteroid?"

"I don't think so. Not from this field, anyway. It's too small."

"Do you want me to go check it out?" his second-in-command asks.

Ciel studies the falling object, the way that the flames licking the outside are soft white, almost translucent. So it's aluminum. Man-made. A spacecraft? But why is it so small?

"No," he finally responds. "I'm closer. Head this way, though. Just in case."

"You got it, boss."

A chime informs him that Manyn has closed the comm channel, and with a sigh, Ciel begins trudging across the planet's cityscape toward the object's approximate landing site. Beings jostle him on each side. Not *people*, per se, because half of his planet is inhabited by wholly cybernetic beings–AIs that have broken away from their old masters. The other half is a collection of wild, unlabeled individuals.

Vide, the planet where he has been elected leader— not a *sovereign*, like the empires of old called them—is a safe haven for the outlawed and the banished, for individuals like him with nowhere else to go.

Is that what this craft is doing? Running? What have they done that is so severe they must make a crash landing on Vide? Murder? Maybe regicide? Did they insult the Sybillian queen? Intergalactic grand larceny?

He's prepared for any situation (except this one, although he is unaware of it) where he has to lay down the laws of his land and iron-fist this traveler into bending to his will.

But the sight of the smoking craft, which has been morphed into nothing more than a crumpled heap of aluminum, stops his plotting.

Emblazoned on the side is a flag that Ciel's never seen —not in person, anyway. The pale blue is chipped and worn, nearly unreadable. But who could miss the curling wave and intricate regal script? Has he not obsessed over the lore attached to this logo his entire life?

The man's heart stutters, and rare joy fills his chest.

If he's right—if this is what Ciel thinks it is—could the person inside really have survived?

With thrill coursing through his veins, he descends

into the pod's crater and begins searching for the escape hatch. When he finds it, he tugs, and a hiss fills the air. Smoke billows out around his feet. To his surprise, a soft coughing begins in the haze.

The planet's leader takes a step back and waits, one hand on the gun at his belt. A habit, mostly.

What rises from the wreckage dumbfounds Ciel, though. It isn't a hulking defense Gollem or a guns-blazing AI.

It's just a girl—wide-eyed and pale, skinny from a hundred years in cryo, stumbling on her unused limbs. She trips on the edge of the pod, and he rushes forward to catch her.

She responds in a broken, dead language. Then she mumbles something else and switches to Universal. "Thank you."

Her voice. Gravelly from disuse, but somehow silk across his ears. Her hand. Softer than any Niharan plush as it clutches his semi-mechanical arm. When she looks up at him, not even flinching, he breathes in the intense blue of her eyes—like the edges of newborn stars.

"Where am I?" she asks, glancing around them. Her hand never leaves his arm, though, and Ciel suspects it's because she knows she would fall over if she did.

"Vide." The planet's name rolls like butter off his tongue, but he loses the rest of his welcome speech in his excitement at seeing her. "What is your name?"

The girl looks up at him again, and Ciel knows that

those eyes have probably lured many a man into their depths (and they, like he, didn't mind being ensnared).

"Liana," she says softly. "*Princesse* Liana Fleur Thorn."

Ciel's face hardens, mainly because it would be embarrassing to kick his feet and squeal in excitement. He has found the lost princess of Talia, the one his mother used to tell him about, the one who he obsessed over for years, the one he used to *dream* of.

"Welcome to Vide, Liana," he says softly, helping her up and out of the crater. "There is much we need to discuss."

And Liana just nods, oblivious to how much the world has changed without her, sure in the fact that she is perfectly safe with him, and vaguely aware that this is only the beginning.

Tonight I cannot be the broken doll tied to the ends of expectation's strings and forced to dance for the amusement of others.

They don't know who I am.

But if I go . . . if they see . . .

. . . they will.

EVERYTHING MADE
Beautiful

Dawn Christine Jonckowski

They call me ugly.

And I am.

But I wasn't always.

I used to be pretty. Before. When Daddy was alive and Mother hadn't gone into debt with modifications for herself.

My older sister Celestina doesn't need mods. She was born perfect, with porcelain skin and gently curling blonde hair, crystal blue eyes, a shapely waist, long slim piano-player fingers (though she couldn't find a note if you pointed to one)—all the things one needed to build a flawless storybook heroine.

Celestina was born perfect, and she stayed perfect.

When the other hovercab crashed into ours, Daddy was killed on impact. Raging electrical fires ate holes in

Mother's face and right arm, her spray-stiff hair igniting instantly. Safety foam spurted from the vehicle's crash systems, coating my sister especially in a dense layer of protection. She cried because her dress was ruined and her curls fell out.

Me? I remember the scent of burning flesh and hair, the way synthetic fabrics melt to form a second, searing skin. I remember slowly wondering why I couldn't feel them as my fingers blackened and shriveled.

When I woke later in the burn unit, the agony on my right side brought me to howls until they pumped me full of pain blockers that were more for the mind than the body, because (they told me) I really had no right side left to speak of.

Mother appeared at my bedside on the rare moments when Celestina slept, my older sister's only damage a lightly raw throat from smoke inhalation, but accompanied by nightmares of safety foam and fog. Mother told me that Daddy was gone. Along with her own face and the flesh of her arm. My right arm and leg. But she would fix it. The kingdom of NexusNova would send her credits for Daddy's death and she'd fix herself. And then me.

I was six.

Now I am sitting in front of the flat mirror, trying to figure out how to affix a hat so it hides the scarred webs of my scalp where hair will not grow. On the other side of the room, Celestina hums along with the screen's recommendations on styling her look for the theme of the day.

The camera picks up her perfect face, superimposing hair-styles, jewelry, and clothing suggestions based on the inventory Cindrell updates every time my mother and sister return from the boutiques with more dresses and debt.

The camera cannot accurately read my face.

It wouldn't have recommendations for me anyway.

Cindrell tells me that styling by the flat mirror makes me more unique.

She's kind, my stepsister. If a bit naïve.

I sigh and try tilting the hat farther down my fore-head. The gears in my wrist give a high squeal of protest, the rotation slow and stiffening.

"You should really oil that arm, Briallen. Heaven forbid it should creak like that if the prince ever takes your hand." Celestina's eyes never leave the screen as she twists up a lock of bright blonde and directs Cindrell where to tuck the pin into the updo. I can still hear her smirk.

Never mind that I will never stand at the front of the pack of eligible girls simpering for the prince's attention, though less because of how I look and more on principle. The guards only let the pretty ones to the front anyway. Something about the Queen's orders to ensure she does not have ugly grandchildren. The royal family is certainly not above modification—the Queen famously kept everyone waiting at a ball two years ago because her face came loose and her personal modifier had been too in his cups to screw it back on straight for the better part of an hour.

Simply that starting mods too young could have dire consequences on a body.

I well know.

"Come, ladies," Mother claps thrice as she glides into the room. Her dress nips and tucks in all the right places, further proof of a body not quite born of nature. If her face didn't already make it obvious. Her natural hair is dyed to match the implants that fill half her head with rich brown tresses, all of it carefully styled at the base of her neck. Her skin is as smooth as Celestina's. No crow's feet for my mother, no fine lines writing time across her forehead, no creases of joy around her mouth.

Mother reminds us daily that smiling only causes one's face to age prematurely.

I'm fairly certain that's not scientific, but there's never been any arguing with her.

"We do not want to be late," Mother continues, appraising Celestina with a look and a tight nod and glancing at me with a barely repressed sigh. "The announcement is coming precisely at three o'clock. Celestina must be seen at the front of the crowd." She stares at me a moment before whisking the small hat from my patchy head and covering it with a wider brim that features a dense fall of barely transparent veiling that drops over my face and neck.

It's fine.

I would rather they not stare, anyway. The only reason I've not invented some excuse to stay behind—to help Cindrell feed the sheets into the laundry folder, inventory Mother's latest shoe purchases, anything—is that the news wave mandated that *all* eligible young women be scanned as attending.

Celestina at nineteen and myself at eighteen both qualify. Cindrell should qualify as well, but Mother claims that as a country transplant, she's not even in the system, so who will know.

I am not in the system, either. Oh, my name is there, so disconnected that my data shows me as something like a distant cousin. (A *very* distant cousin.) But the tech cannot scan my face. And yet Mother insists I attend in support of my sister. Who hardly needs the help of someone like me, unless it is to make her beauty shine that much brighter.

With final instructions to Cindrell on making sure dinner is on the table when we return, Mother hustles Celestina and I into the waiting hovercab. My heart clenches beneath the bodice of my dress, my sudden inability to draw breath hardly due to how the corset stays now compress my bones. Twelve years and I still cannot bear to sit in these vehicles.

I do it for Celestina. My bright and beautiful sister who must catch the eye of the prince to save Mother from the looming mountain of debt, to create for herself a better life that will afford more mods for when the lines begin to creep across her own face. But most of all, I do it for me. A crown for Celestina would afford me enough to disappear from public eye forever.

It might be nice to raise cows in the country. They certainly wouldn't be bothered by the squeaking of my mechanics.

Even the short ride to the Center Square is long enough for the springs in my hip to tighten in protest. I shift, no amount of squirming able to release the pressure.

"Briallen, stop it. You're going to wrinkle my gown," Celestina whines. She pouts and pats at the sleek skirt skimming down perfectly-shaped thighs. The tips of her golden boots peek from the long hem.

I sigh.

I love my sister.

(I hate her sometimes.)

The hovercab glides to a stop at the edge of the Square, and Mother flashes her credit cuff at the machine to pay our fare. It beeps and the doors whisk open. I exit first, not only desperate to stretch the ligatures that burrow into what's left of my hip bone, but to better highlight who comes after. They all notice me exiting the hovercab, however ungracefully, but they don't see me. They don't ever see me because they're waiting for who's next.

Mother emerges, the spray of stars that extend from

her collar catching the doorframe and springing forth in glitter and flash. I am the notification; she is the herald.

Celestina is the prize.

My sister extends one slim gloved hand. Mother catches it, supporting her trophy as she steps from the cab. Today's fashion is a berry wine sensation of fabric that slicks over every curve and dip of her perfect proportions. She is a shape so many pay dearly for, and all she had to do to achieve it was draw breath. Her golden curls pile artfully up one temple and tumble across the other shoulder, bouncing and teasing along a bare collarbone.

She is exquisite.

A chime sounds from the clock tower, and all eyes turn from my sister to the screens that dominate the middle of the Center Square, bright under the perpetual overcast of sky. Titters flutter across the crowd, young women pinching cheeks and giggling as they push to the front.

They push, but my sister glides, the crowd parting before her beauty as if to say, "Here is our golden offering. Revere her as we do, for she is flawless."

The screens flare to life, the royal fanfare warbling from the speakers, cameras blinking on as they scan the crowds to document the faces they find.

One trains on Celestina, who coos into her own shoulder, batting heavy black lashes as she peers coyly from the corner of her gaze.

Words scroll across the screens, thick and black—*Citi-*

zens of NexusNova, we beg your humble attention to the following proclamation—and the Royal Herald's face quickly brightens the screens.

"His royal highness Cael Invictus Reginald Apollo Bartholomew Francis—"

"Francis?" My nose twists at the name.

Mother swats me to silence. "Yes, Francis."

"—Rufus Amadeus is giving a ball!"

～

WELL OF COURSE THE prince is giving a ball. It's what princes do.

But this particular ball?

Is to find his future bride.

They've mandated that the young ladies of every noble household be registered as attending the ball. Which means they expect me to go, too.

So here I am, sitting on the edge of my bed clad in just my slip, a set of hex wrenches between my teeth and Celestina's gown from two years ago staring me down from the dress form in the corner. Popping another wrench into the socket in my right palm, I fit the other end into the joint on my hip and press, engaging the torque. It whirs unhelpfully, the old screws long since stripped. It was foolish anyway to hope that the wrench could provide any relief. Easing to a stand, I walk over to the mirror to take stock. The slip catches on a slipped spring on my leg, hitching the silk high on my thigh. I settle split weight, and the exhausted hydraulics emit a worrisome hiss.

Scar tissue maps peaks and valleys from just above where my ear should be down along my neck.

Mother said facial mods weren't worth investing in until I was full grown.

It was hard enough to manage the stares when I was six.

Impossible now that I'm eighteen.

She continues to find other reasons, other things on which to increase her debt.

My right arm transitions mid-shoulder from flesh and bone to metal and springs. I grew often and quickly, and practically overnight, a ligature would become painfully small. But child-size mods were custom, and therefore costly. Mother made me wear my limbs until I could no longer sleep from the pain. If she was in a good mood, the local modifier would come and weld lengthening pieces on, retrofitting the tech so the oddly-elongated limb would still bend and flex as mostly intended.

If she was in a bad mood, I'd get a mouthful of sour brandy to knock me out until morning.

The last time I got new mods was when Mother married the country baron, Cindrell's father. He had compassion on his new fourteen-year-old stepdaughter, helping me work through the kinks in the tech by teaching me a country reel and dancing with me across the rough floor of his manor. Mother ripped apart the old limbs for the copper and titanium and sold them for cash out the back door when the baron wasn't home.

He died of a heart attack—sudden and vicious and visible right in the front drive—and there was no more manor house. No more dances on uneven floors.

No more new mods.

Mother sold it all and moved us—including the step-daughter *she* had inherited in the deal—back to the pollution-clouded city.

I learned to hide the limp when that last leg became too short, clamped my lips together as my spine screamed at me every night.

Cindrell learned to become invisible, since that's what Mother told her she was.

And Celestina learned . . . nothing. Aside from how her natural beauty could be traded as currency for anything she fancied, anything from anybody.

So of course, she fancies the crown. And thus, I scrutinize my reflection as her old gown scrutinizes my frame and we figure out how we'll work together to minimize embarrassment for us both.

"I could do your hair, if you like."

Cindrell's soft, fluted voice sounds from the doorway. "Your mother sent me to help you into the dress so it doesn't tear, but I do have enough time for your hair." She enters the room fully, all gentle smiles and soft scent, despite four years of scrubbing, cooking, laundering, and generally being ordered about by her stepmother and eldest stepsister.

I sigh as she appears in the mirror next to me. "Couldn't you just go to the ball *for* me?" I ask, half jest, more desperate hope. She maneuvers me to the small vanity and begins brushing the bits of hair that still grow on half my head. Her fingers are cool, her touch gentle.

It's all I can do not to cry.

"I've always hated it when they stare," I whisper, a single tear glistening on my lower lash. Cindrell catches it on a fingertip and expertly dashes it away on her dingy apron.

"They stare because they know they are not nearly as strong as you, Briallen. To face such a shallow world with the truest face you have, with the pieces that you are held together with hope and springs." She leans down so her face is even with mine in the glass. "I know you are glorious. Someday, they'll see it, too."

It's quite the inspirational speech, perhaps one of her best.

But tonight . . . tonight I cannot be the broken doll tied to the ends of expectation's strings and forced to dance for the amusement of others.

They don't know who I am.

But if I go . . . if they see . . .

. . . they will.

"Please, Cindrell." The eyes I lift to her already burn with the film of building tears. "I'll insist you come as our attendant. Before they scan me, we'll run to the lounge. You can fit this dress, I'm sure of it. Then, you enjoy the ball—dance with everyone worth dancing with, eat sweets, enjoy what the world should be offering you— and I will stay hidden in the back corridors until it is time to switch again and return home."

She hesitates.

Which means she's thinking about it.

"Please," I beg again, turning on the stool to face her straight on. "Neither of us is in the data inventory. They don't know who I am.

"Which means they won't know who you are."

~

BUT WITHIN TWO minutes of my stepsister setting foot on the dance floor in her borrowed gown, they all certainly want to know who she is.

The prince most of all.

And after being snubbed for a dance in favor of this mysterious creature in a swirling crystal blue gown, my sister is furious with her need to know as well.

It turned out the skirt's top layer was a separate piece, removable for the ease of entering and exiting a small hovercab. Except Celestina had always wanted to arrive in all her diaphanous glory, and thus had never seen her old gown without the top layer, as Cindrell now wore it. After all, why pay attention to something so trivial while someone else is dressing you?

And also, with the number of gowns she'd had in the past two years alone, one could easily forgive her not recognizing this specific one, especially when it was on someone else. She'd certainly hardly recalled it when I emerged from my room, Cindrell in tow, ready to leave for the ball.

"I didn't know Mother had the time to buy you a new gown too, Briallen," she exclaimed, plucking gloved fingers at the short cape I'd tied around my shoulders to hide the small modifications we'd done to the bodice.

So she does not recognize the dress on Cindrell, either.

She does not recognize *Cindrell.*

I peer through some of the servants' peepholes long enough to see the prince bow to Celestina, freezing halfway to standing as his eyes catch Cindrell at the back of the room. Without a bother to finish kissing my sister's hand, he excuses himself and bee-lines for Cindrell. Waving aside the scanning drone, he bows low, taking my bewildered stepsister's hand and sweeping her immediately into the waltz the orchestra strikes.

She will be just fine.

And, dressed as a maid and ignored the same way, so will I.

So, pulling the hood of my cape up over scars and flimsy curls, I resolve to find the palace library and cozy up with a book, ideally by a hot fire that will loosen some of the fittings in my joints.

The room is easy to locate on a night like this, warm and inviting and absolutely empty of any other living thing. Recognizing the gold leaf pressed in the binding of the rare paper volume, I pluck a favorite novel from the shelf and slowly lower myself to the pile of cushions on the floor in front of the roaring flames.

A gray pouf leaps from the pile, legs shooting out akimbo from the frizzed body before the cat dashes away on a surprised yowl.

Well, *now* the library is empty of any other living thing.

I am three chapters in, heat just finally easing the springs in my shoulder, when a gently cleared throat echoes like a gong in the silent room. I snap the book shut, holding the slim tome against my pounding heart.

"Apologies, my lady. I thought on tonight of all nights, the library would be empty."

His voice sings in my ears, sure syllables of dark velvet. A voice made for night and stories. I gulp my heart back down between my lungs where it belongs, tuck fingers along the side of my hood to keep it from slipping and showing my face, and turn toward That Voice.

He leans against the end of a shelf, his pose as awkward as his voice is smooth. A long dark coat fits close around his trim torso, flaring at his waist and draping down to his ankles. The stiff high neck has rubbed a raw line on his shaved skin except at the center where the bright white of his shirt shows. Slick black trousers and high shining boots peek through the split of the coat. Dark, unruly hair sticks in all directions, flopping adorably over his ears in a clear attempt to disguise how far they protrude from his head. His nose is a tad over-large, but in an intriguing way.

In a world full of purchased perfection, his conglomerate features are striking in their exception.

He heaves ungracefully off the bookcase and ambles closer. I duck my head, pulling the hood tighter.

"Do forgive me, my lady. The queen will be sorely put out if she learns I have disturbed one of the prince's guests."

I finally find my voice. "I'm no lady," I squeeze the words through a panic-closed throat. "And the prince neither knows nor expects me. I am only a . . ." A what? A coward? A liar? A pawn in my family's plight for a crown?

". . . only a chaperone, sir."

A liar, then.

Beyond my hood, fabrics shuffle and I hear a heavy thud as he drops another cushion a respectable distance from me, a lone and unaccompanied young woman, but still facing my direction. I keep my head tipped down so only the shiny tips of his shoes show beneath the edge of my ducked hood.

Could he not leave a girl to read in peace while she avoids a party she doesn't want to attend?

"Alas, not a sir here, either." The words are shaped with a smile.

It makes me want to smile back.

But my scar tissue pulls and my lips stay in a straight line.

On a sigh, he stretches out his legs. Shin to sole show in my limited perspective. Pulling the hood close over my right eye, I dare to peek upward, just a little. His eyes are waiting for mine, full lips pulled into a crooked grin.

"Do you mind?" He gestures to his boots. When I shake my head, he drapes his left leg over his right knee and wrestles his boot from his foot. There's an all-too-familiar hiss of hydraulics as the cybernetic foot flexes at the end of his ankle.

I try not to stare.

"Thing's a damn sight better than crutches, for sure, but I can't for the life of me figure out the right formula of oil so it will not tighten at the joint inside of these boots. Or in the cold. Or when it's cold *and* I must wear boots." He rotates the metal foot, and it stutters slightly in the ball joint.

"Vodka," I reply.

He lifts a single brow, boot still in hand. "Pardon?"

"Vodka," I repeat, more confidently this time. "The cold will always make your oil seize up, but since alcohol has a lower freezing point, it offers a smoother lubrication. I've found, too, that it works better when the joints experience restricted movements that prevent traditional oil from spreading well, such as under denser fabrics and leather."

He finally breaks his stare with a blink. "I will . . . have to try that. Thank you, Miss . . . " he lets the sentence hang, fishing for my name. I pretend he's punctuated the thought with an honorific and barrel on.

"In a pinch, cruiser fuel will also work, but the stench is untenable. Better to smell as if you've had a bit of a party instead."

"You've had extensive experience," he notes, tilting his head to see under my hood. My spine curls in on itself of its own accord. When it's clear he won't catch a glimpse, he turns instead to dig through his pocket, producing a handful of very precise, very delicate, and very expensive wrenches. He rifles through with a thumb before selecting one. From the other pocket, he pulls an equally pricey power handle, fitting the wrench into the handle before angling it just so into the shiny platinum ankle joint. The *whirrrrrr* of the power handle makes a pleasant overtone to his sigh of relief as the joint loosens its pull on his bone.

It's been a long time since I knew that kind of relief. I nearly sigh along with him just on the memory.

"One picks up a thing or two in a dozen years of manipulating cybernetics."

His eyebrow lifts again. "A dozen? You or your mistress?"

And I know I've said too much. My jaw freezes as if its

own natural joint has rusted in place. He cannot know who I am, who Cindrell is. We are playing a dangerous enough game just in having the prince so instantly besotted with her, though who else he has danced with for the balance of the night I do not know. For all our sakes, I hope he has returned to Celestina and danced with her at least twice.

"I . . ." but I do not know how to finish the thought.

Fortunately, the bell tower does, clanging its first gong violently through the halls of the palace it crowns.

At midnight, the prince turns twenty-one.

At midnight, Cindrell is supposed to slip away to the powder room and we are to hurriedly switch gowns and take a hovercab back to the house, leaving a note with the doorman for my mother and Celestina, who will undoubtedly want to stay for the fireworks and continuing party.

The bell tower echoes a second clang.

"I'm sorry, I must go." My hydraulics click and hiss in a loud frenzy as I drop the book and try to scramble to my feet. He attempts to stand to assist me, but his ankle is still loosened, and he loses his own balance, precariously poised on one leg, the other tucked gull-like to his side.

"I can help you," he starts, furiously shoving the wrench into his ankle to tighten it back to usefulness.

Finally, my feet are under me. I smooth the cloak over the borrowed dress. "Thank you, I can manage just fine."

"No," he insists over the light whine of the power handle. "I can *help* you."

I still don't understand, but it doesn't matter. The sound of the third bell fills my head, makes my eyes water. I turn to hobble-run my way to the powder room. Cindrell is likely halfway out of the gown by now, panicking at where I am.

"I'm the queen's new modifier."

His words tumble out in a rush, and suddenly I can place the crooked smile and jug-like ears, can recall the announcement that scrolled across screens when he arrived at the palace mere weeks ago, his prowess already renowned at such a young age.

The story included a brief paragraph about the birth defect that bore him forth with one full leg and another that ended in a smooth, round stump where the ankle should have been. How he had modified himself only recently, and how the gorgeous work was what landed him in the palace to begin with.

"I can help you," he implores again.

The article referred to him as Shua Gorbandt.

It still doesn't matter. I pull my hood close and turn.

Too quickly.

My too-short metal leg torques as my torso continues to move, and instead I end up thrown to the floor in a heap of skirts and grinding gears.

In the briefest moments between the third bell fading away and the clapper hitting for the fourth peal, I lift and turn my head and our eyes meet in absolute stunned silence. The hood has slipped off and this man who is making his fortune fixing the unfortunate is staring me right in the face. Red heats my neck and crawls up my cheeks between the gnarled lines of scar tissue.

His fancy wrench droops forgotten between his fingers. Gathering my legs beneath me, I wobble to a stand and let him look.

So he can see.

"You cannot help me." I finally push the words between numb lips and limp as fast as I can manage toward the door.

～

THE PRINCE DANCED with no one else that night but Cindrell.

Now he is reportedly broken-hearted, as he did not think to ask this creature of perfection for whom he has irrevocably fallen for her name. And why should he have asked, when the scanning drones carry record of every attendee.

Every attendee except Cindrell.

Whose face neither exists in the databases nor was recognized by anyone she whirled past in the hours of endless dancing.

All he has of hers is a single threadbare dancing

slipper with a broken strap, dropped on the stairs as we rushed to our waiting hovercab.

(She had to wear an old too-small pair of her own, since all of mine are half misshapen in attempts to mold around the aging joints in my one metal foot.)

The palace is in an uproar to find her.

Celestina is enraged at the snub.

Mother is too furious at the same to question where I disappeared to all night.

Cindrell catches herself constantly humming the waltz from her first dance.

Three days after the ball, the prince is still refusing to leave his room, scouring the databases night and day for any trace of his mystery girl. But not a single scan matches the face in his memory.

He digs deeper.

Until.

There is only one name on the list that does not have an accompanying scan.

Mine.

∾

"I CANNOT BELIEVE he has invited *you*, and worse—that you would go without me!"

I glance over my shoulder to where Celestina's reflection in my flat mirror stamps her little foot and glowers in my general direction. Cindrell bites her lip and tucks another sparse curl behind my ear.

Under her dingy kerchief, her own shiny tresses are plaited in an intricate net that ends in a smooth chignon. I've tucked a few of Celestina's old jeweled hair pins up my sleeve. We'll add them to Cindrell's hair before we enter the palace.

The door chime alerts us to a vehicle approaching.

"And to take Cindrell as a chaperone? You're absurd, Briallen," Celestina bites. "The prince will take one look at you and think so as well."

Mother *tsks* from the hallway. "Manners, Celestina. The prince is only doing his due diligence to find this mysterious girl who doesn't exist. He does not know Briallen, only that her name did not come with an accompanying scan. Which is to our advantage." She smiles at me, a rare curve of her lips that has lines flaring out from the edges of her nose. It is not a becoming look for her, unpracticed as it is. "Briallen may be no flower, but she will certainly plant the seed that it was you he danced with all night, my dove, you who blooms this infatuating love in his heart." She looks at me pointedly. "Won't you, Briallen?"

I rise from my seat and pick up a tiny, impractical clutch just as the gong of the door chime tells us our ride is here.

"I will do my best, Mother." I bobble as quick a curtsy

as my knee joint will allow. Cindrell takes my arm, and together, we walk to the door.

Celestina refuses to see us off, and so Mother ignores us as well.

Pity.

Because it is not a hovercab that the palace has sent to collect me and my chaperone. It is a full royal Hummer, bedecked in golden scrollwork.

Celestina's jealousy would choke her.

A footman who is trained not to stare helps us into the Hummer. I fumble my way up, and Cindrell floats in after me. He closes the door. Nerves force giggles from our throats, but we flick the switch to raise the privacy screen. It emerges from behind the seat, fully embroidered with the royal crest.

By the time the footman opens the door again, it is Cindrell emerging first, the blue-green shimmer of her borrowed dress reflecting even under the perpetually overcast skies. I follow behind, slow due to rusting joints and not deference, but no one looks at the chaperone in the clean but oft-mended serving gown.

Least of all the prince.

Flouting protocol, he is running down the palace steps as fast as he can to see if this Briallen he summoned is the one who has haunted him since the midnight bells pulled her from his arms.

This Briallen—I glance down at the time-softened fabric I wear—is not.

It is a dangerous game we play to make him believe that Cindrell is.

He halts at the bottom of the stairs, chest heaving, perfect hair drooping just so from nervous sweat. But he looks at Cindrell and he . . . transforms. The pollution-laden clouds no longer hang over the kingdom of Nexus-Nova. Birds that have not migrated to our kingdom in decades seem to sing in his ears. His eyes widen and so does his smile, which he releases only enough to utter one word.

"Briallen."

I push three fingers against the small of her back, and Cindrell comes to life. She folds into a more graceful curtsy than Celestina has ever achieved, dipping her head low before lifting her eyes and her lashes slowly to meet his. Her strawberry pink lips curve into a demure smile.

"Your Highness."

And then they simply . . . stare at each other.

Until another figure makes its way down the stairs, long black coat fanning behind hurried steps so smooth, one would never know that one of those ankles is titanium and oil and not joint and sinew.

Shua.

He stops just behind the prince and gently clears his throat, breaking the spell that holds my stepsister mid-curtsy and the prince in gape mouthed awe.

"Perhaps a walk in the garden, sir, after formal introductions," he offers softly.

The prince shakes his head. "Yes, yes, of course. An excellent suggestion. Lady Briallen, please meet my chaperone, Master Shua Gorbandt, our royal modifier. My steward, who would typically accompany me, seems to find himself indisposed due to questionable diet choices, and Shua was kind enough to fill in." He leans in conspiratorially. "Do not tell, but I happen to like Master Gorbandt better anyway and shall continue to request his presence whenever possible."

Cindrell rises at the prince's address, but dips her head toward Shua, acknowledging his station. "It is an honor to have you accompany us today, Master Gorbandt. I fear we do not have a robust household, yet it is still my honor to introduce our lady's maid as my chaperone this afternoon. Please meet B—er, um, Cindrell."

I dip into an uneven curtsy, murmuring, "Your Highness. Master Gorbandt," but when I straighten and lift my eyes, it's Shua's intense gaze I find staring back. The prince offers a general "nice to meet you" somewhere in my direction, still entirely focused on my stepsister. Shua nods his head as befits his station versus what he believes mine to be and says simply, "Cindrell."

I wish I could hear how his voice says *my* name.

The prince offers his arm to Cindrell, directing her toward the privacy of the gardens. Ungainly as my gait is, I still follow close enough behind to hear his initial breathless rambles.

"Lady Briallen, you so bewitched me the night of the

ball. It took me days to discover who you are, and only because your name was the only one without an accompanying scan. Of course, you stole my breath so quickly I couldn't wait for the drones to catalog your presence, but even still. How is it that you are not in our databases?"

My steps falter even more. Shua reaches out a gentlemanly arm to steady me, but I am stubborn and anyway unaccustomed to being noticed, so I brush him away in favor of hearing Cindrell's response.

Our ruse could be over before it has hardly begun.

I don't know why this makes me feel so suddenly empty.

"Oh," my stepsister titters, barely sparing me a glance. "I am only visiting a cousin, Your Highness, from my father's side. He is a country baron; the signals have been unstable for the past few years. We have not been able to fully scan into the databases."

The prince straightens with new resolve. "Then I shall work with the council to update our infrastructure. Such a waste for a flower like you to be planted in the country beyond my knowledge and reach!"

I close my eyes and roll them behind my lids, but Cindrell only giggles more.

"And pray tell, who is your cousin that I might call on you at her house?"

Her spine stiffens, her walk slows. "My . . . cousin? Yes, my cousin. Well, my father's cousin. Once removed, you see. Through marriage, I believe. My . . . aunt. Her daughter is Lady Celestina."

The prince's face falls instantly. "Oh. *Her*." His eye twitches, and I know he knows he has said more than is proper, but my stepsister and I both secretly share the sentiment behind his words and so we say nothing about his breach of manners.

"Pardon my saying so, Your Highness, but—" here Cindrell pauses, glancing at me for help. I tip one shoulder, hoping her mind works quickly. "My cousin, Celestina, she is . . . a bit jealous. Please, if we could keep our meeting private so as to spare me her ire."

The prince's eyes sparkle with intrigue. "Of course, of course! Say no more, I shall arrange everything." And they continue on, heads bent as close as propriety allows.

I heave a silent sigh, grateful their besotted gazes finally begin to slow their steps, allowing me to keep up even as the humidity from the recent rain grinds the joints in my leg. Without thinking, I cup my hands in front of my waist, flesh and bone fingers pulling and twisting metal ones through a series of stretches and movements to keep the whole hand from locking up. Mother fusses at me every time I do it in public, as if that is the thing that will most make others stare at me.

Cindrell's kerchief rides low along my forehead, but still cannot hide the twisted flesh that crawls up my cheek.

"I have some vodka."

Shua's voice sounds over my shoulder with no preamble. By the time I turn to look at him, he's drawn even with me on the gravel path, the arm nearest me crooked again in a gentleman's offer and the other boasting a small flask.

"Is the idea of chaperoning along with me that distasteful, Master Gorbandt?"

His brows rise. "For your hand."

I stare back at him a moment too long.

"You were right, it does work. And smells a damn sight better than cruiser fluid."

Oh. Right.

I hold out my hand and he passes the flask, my metal fingers clinking musically against the container. It twists open easily, the cap modified to include a small dropper soldered to the inside for precise dosing of the creative lubricant. I let three small drops fall into the joint at the base of the thumb, then toss back a not-entirely-ladylike swig before closing the flask and handing it back.

His face splits in a grin.

We walk a respectable distance behind in silence and eventually arrive at a small table set for tea—for the Prince and Cindrell, of course. The chaperones will sit a polite distance from the couple. A plain tin of refreshments awaits us atop a rough half wall.

The prince doesn't even spare us a glance as he pulls my stepsister's chair out in a flourish and invites her to sit. She does, tucking her gown neatly behind her knees so it fits well under the wrought iron scrollwork of the table legs. He pulls his chair as close to her as manners might allow and they continue whatever exclusive conversation they began on the way through the bushes and shrubbery.

Shua offers me a hand so I can perch atop the wall, and of course, he's situated himself so it's my cold metal palm he feels in his, my twisted flesh he sees, my just-too-short leg that whines as I ease a hip onto the rock. I wonder briefly if he has settled us this way on purpose, his curiosity getting the better of his manners and hidden behind the guise of "wanting to help."

He settles his own hip onto the half wall, and even though I know that the leg nearest me ends in gears and screws, his shiny leather boot hides the hydraulics and metal from view.

It is not so easy to hide what I am.

What I am not.

He pries open the tin and offers me a biscuit. They're small shortbread drops with real cherry jelly dollops in the middle. My mouth waters. Mother only rarely purchases biscuits, and when she does, they are dry and tasteless and only for guests.

(And Celestina.)

Or perhaps for show.

(Much like Celestina.)

I've got a second biscuit in my hand before I'm hardly done chewing the first.

Mother would be appalled. At my manners? My audacity? I'm uncertain and frankly, I don't care, so I take a third while they're still offered.

Shua takes only one, studying the jelly dollop with absurd intensity, two fine lines creasing between his drawn brows.

"My grandmother brought these thumbprint biscuits to our house the single time she visited us," he offers, eyes still trained on the sticky red glob. "She wasn't a fan of my father, thought he wasn't good enough for my mother. Blamed him for how I was born. But these biscuits were the finest things I'd ever tasted, and the next year for my mother's birthday, I was determined to make a batch and surprise her."

He glances up, mirth pulling his pupils to focus. "Do you know how difficult these are to make when you're on crutches? And only nine?

"And don't know how to properly work an oven?"

A soft laugh huffs from his nose as he bites into the treat, light crumbs showering one pant leg. Biscuit-colored snow on a sharp black landscape.

"We're lucky I didn't burn the house down. Father said he could use the biscuits as charcoal to roast the last of the meat. Mother was gracious about the fact that her precious jar of cherry preserves had been scraped clean by her over-ambitious and now sobbing nine-year-old, and there wouldn't be more unless the peddlers managed to save any jars for the homes on the outskirts."

I smile as I nibble at the third biscuit, picturing a tinier Shua balanced on crutches stirring a mixing bowl of heavens knew what in a dingy old kitchen.

Technically, I know how to make biscuits. Among other things. Cindrell only has so many hands, and when the occasional guest shows up that Mother truly wants to impress, it is easier to hide me in the kitchen as an extra pair of hands and gloss over my absence, if it is even remarked upon.

"I could teach you, if you want."

Shua looks up, both of us equally surprised at the offer that has just come out of my mouth.

"You know how to make these," he finally says.

I lift a brow. "Theoretically."

His head tips back in a raucous laugh that still manages not to pull the prince's attention from my step-sister. I'm a bit affronted.

"Well perhaps I have never made *these* particular biscuits before, but I have made biscuits. And they were at least not inedible charcoal briquettes!" Just for his laughter, I reach for a fourth.

"Touché," he manages within a final chuckle. "We are all lucky that my father turned my creative tendencies to tinkering with springs and metal instead. I was not going to have any future as a baker."

I tug at my skirt, hoping to make the drab fabric dip lower over the dull and rust of my leg.

"The palace pantry has cherry preserves," Shua says,

his laugh-crinkled eyes posing a challenge to me—not my scars, not my grinding gears or squealing joints. In that moment, all he sees is a childhood memory . . . and me.

A messenger chooses that instant to emerge from the maze of hedges with an urgent summons for the prince, and we are all dutifully hustled back to the royal Hummer with a half-breathed promise to return lest the prince absolutely perish from too many moments away from Cindrell's beauty.

I wonder what they have talked about, since she can clearly share nothing that is actually truth.

But she swears to return, and I want to kick her in both of her fully-functioning ankles because how in the world can we maintain this charade? Instead, I dip my head toward Shua as he helps me into the Hummer and say, "You'll need to ensure they have sugar and shortening as well. And don't wear black."

We spend the return ride hurriedly reassembling our true identities and concocting the best version of events where the prince realizes it was indeed Celestina he must have danced with, but important royal duties have suddenly consumed him and we encourage him to come court her as soon as he is able.

Celestina is on a rampage when we walk in the door, eyes puffy from crying fits at being made to wait for the prince she so clearly deserves *right now*, dresses thrown in pouting heaps on the floor. Nothing we say matters. *Obviously* the prince should have danced with her all night in the first place and should shirk his duties to come find her because *just look at her*, she's perfect. After apparently buying our story, Mother decides that a bit of pampering at the spa will lift my older sister's spirits and leaves Cindrell and I to clear up the mess and set supper.

When they return, we also enter six more gowns and a pair of satin heels that shimmer with intricate glass beading into Celestina's wardrobe inventory. Mother informs us that we are going meatless for the remainder of the month to "keep Celestina's complexion healthy for the prince."

Which means she has spent our meal credits—and likely then some—on gowns to bribe a smile from my sister, instead of on vital nutrients for us all. I tell myself it doesn't matter and go to sleep with a familiar twinge in my hip and a new emptiness in my belly.

～

The next time we visit the palace—this time in secret under the guise of selling some of my older and valuable paper books to the library in exchange for a replacement spring and some quality oil—Shua makes sure the prince and Cindrell are positioned at a table right outside a kitchen window. Meanwhile, we laugh and bake biscuits until we have them perfected, and for once, I'm not thinking about how my scars pull when I smile or how the hot pans turn my unfeeling metal fingertips molten red.

Instead, I'm thinking about the dusting of flour over Shua's eyebrow and how he looks at me when that first sheet of perfected biscuits comes out and he pops a still warm one into his mouth whole.

Celestina asks me at dinner that night if I have cut myself. I panic, but Mother instead turns my chin toward her and with narrowed eyes asks how I came to have a crust of dried preserves just on the underside of my jaw. I tell her it must be from the small tartlet I purchased with what remained of my balance after exchanging my books. She turns my chin toward her and scrubs the jam off with her napkin, muttering about how the country baron once upon a time let my manners slip at such a crucial age and that it is a good thing the prince was mistaken and will never again invite me to the palace.

The comment has Cindrell nearly dropping the purifying jug she is carrying around the table to top each mug with clear-ish water. Mother scolds her with only a look.

That night, I dream of Shua's dark eyes and his warm hands gently brushing the twisted pits of scarred skin to collect an errant drop of cherry jam with a fingertip and taste it on his lips and tongue.

I wake with a smile and a sense of foreboding. At breakfast, Cindrell pulls me back to the kitchen to show the small bouquet of wildflowers happily soaking up water from an old canning jar. No such blooms grow anywhere public in NexusNova, not since the gray rains took over the sky and soaked the soil with liquid smog.

They could only have come from one place.

The palace gardens.

The small card tucked in them reads "Briallen." Cindrell plucks it deftly and holds it to her chest, stars dancing in her eyes. I do not ask what it contains.

"They simply appeared on the back step early this morning," Cindrell whispers happily, next burying her face in the blooms. "Oh, and this was set beneath them," she adds, reaching into her apron pocket for a small jar.

Cherry preserves, adorned with a simple red ribbon and a scrap of a note.

To new memories. —SG

A surprising urge makes me want to respond as Cindrell did and hug the little jar to my own heart. Instead, we tuck it deep in the recesses of the pantry among the spider webs and expired rice. That night, after Mother and Celestina are in bed, we sneak back to the kitchen and spend hours spooning tiny dollops of jam onto stale bread, giggling quietly, freezing at every creak of the crumbling manor in case we have woken them with our rare and unadulterated joy.

I cannot remember the last time I have smiled this much.

The sun is moments from rising behind its veil of clouds when we sneak back out to our beds.

My scars ache, but oh, my heart is full.

~

THE PUBLIC NEWS is that Prince Cael is biding his time, still searching for a bride. For *the* bride, is what the desperate mothers and daughters hear, and so every public outing is met with blonde-lined streets, young women attempting to closely resemble the girl from that night whose details now none can properly recall, aside from her bright sunshine hair and floating blue gown. A few have sought modifiers to painstakingly replace every hair with one longer and more golden. Others crowd the salons, clamoring for caustic bleaches to strip browns, blacks, reds into some level of brassy yellow.

One mother pushes her daughter to so many stylists, one after another after another, insisting that the bleach is not yet quite right. And then they disappear from social functions altogether and the rumor churns that the poor girl's hair fell out, chemical burns turning her bare head into a gnarled red map.

I pity her because, like me, she was given no choice.

Metal clicks as I open and close my right fist.

Except her hair will grow back. Eventually.

Because of all this, our trysts become chaotic and creative. Though none of us claim to be religious, Cindrell suddenly insists she must go to the cathedral outside the city to pray for her father. Mother waves her off and tells me to go, too, and to pick up her dress order on the way home. When my stepsister waves down a black line hovercab and flashes a newly acquired golden pass at the driver, I suddenly understand her newfound religiosity. My gown is plain, but respectable enough for church. We hurriedly change in the back of the cab, her pass card buying silence as well. She all but wrenches the stiff springs from my shoulder, pulling me behind her down the empty stone walk and into a dark latticed confessional. The screen slides up, and it is the prince's silhouette awaiting her secret sins.

We duck out the back doors. Down and down and down spiraled stone stairs to a dark, cool room boasting a candle-lit wine and cheese spread laid out atop a thick red fur, Shua and the stacks of old dusty skulls shadowed in the background.

One never quite imagines a catacomb to be magical, but somehow the prince makes it that way for my stepsister. They sip deep reds and crisp whites between the pop of fat grapes and thick cuts of cheeses.

Shua and I stick to the shadows of the small room, giving the prince and Cindrell what space we can. It is difficult to talk in the echoing stone space, but he gently nudges my shoulder, careful not to dislocate any overextended springs, and I look down to see a small tin full of tiny, perfect squares of golden brown shortbread sparkling with chunky sugar crystals. My scars stretch into a smile as I lift one to my lips and chew slowly, savoring the easy crumble of the shortbread, the buttery sweet on my tongue, the crunch of sugar between my molars. I don't realize my eyes have closed in bliss until I open them to see Shua leaning in, smile poised, pupils wide with the need to know how he has fared.

"You do incredible work, Master Gorbandt."

His face breaks wide open.

The prince's next plan involves rowing small boats through vine-latticed lakes stabbed through with the bare trunks of long-dead trees. Except rowing becomes nearly impossible within the foliage and my shoulder locks when I try to maneuver the oar, so we float in our two boats in the middle of the water. Shua offers me vodka, but I cannot reach the piece that has seized. He holds his hand out for the flask.

"I am a professional," he adds softly, dark eyes gone fathomless.

I turn slowly. Let him unlace the back of my dress to expose the gears and springs of my mechanical shoulder. It is not skin he sees, not flesh he touches, but the gentle pressure of his fingers against the metal driven into my bones is somehow even more intimate than if he'd undressed me whole. My heart pounds into my throat, the sting of vodka wends its way up my sinuses.

He gently tugs the laces of my dress back together, warm fingers brushing lightly against the skin between my shoulder blades.

I am on fire. Every nerve flays into a million sparking ends that arc live charges wherever his hands touch. I turn sharply to face him, heat blooming across my chest and traveling up my neck between my scars.

"Cindrell, I . . ." he trails off, and it takes me a moment to realize that he is addressing me. I wonder briefly what my name would sound like rolling out in his rich baritone. What he might think if he learns the truth about who I really am.

When he learns.

"Will you tell me what happened?" he finally asks. The question is gentle, cautious. I turn as best I can. His eyes, his fingers, his attention are all still on the disjointed curve my half-tech shoulder makes under my dress.

I don't want him to pity me.

I want him to know me. In every way possible.

The realization punches a hole straight through my lungs and I nearly cannot breathe.

He cannot know me.

Ever.

And so, to stop the ache in my heart, I tell him. I cannot offer the fullest truth. But the pieces I can admit—the accident, the years of outgrown mods because I was not valuable enough to fix—I hand over one by one.

He does not interrupt, only listens carefully, accepting every detail before thanking me for trusting him.

By then the prince has managed to call his Hummer driver to throw cables and tow us all back in. We ride in silence. But as the prince and Cindrell draw out their goodbyes with clutched hands and promises to see each other again soon, Shua cups my elbow gears in one hand and turns me toward him.

"You are strong and brave and wondrous, my lady," he offers quietly. "I have been acquainted with you only a short while, yet I know this to be true. Do not let anyone have you believing otherwise."

He looks as if he would say more, but I cannot let him. I lay my own hand briefly on his chest, feel the pound of his heart beneath layers of cloth and skin.

"I . . . " But what can I say? Words tangle on my tongue and all I finally do is nod and motion for my stepsister because we have to go and we have to go *now*.

We are climbing into a separate Hummer that will deposit us on the edge of town where we can call a hovercab when the prince boldly declares his love for Cindrell. "Marry me, Briallen," he shouts to her. "Marry me and let me make you my queen." She leans out of the open window and presses a hand to her chest, promising him her heart and her forever.

We ride back in silence, her eyes sparking between joy and fear.

I don't have the heart to tell her that this has gone too far and we must end it.

She already knows. I don't have to say it aloud.

Which is good.

Because I know that it also means I will never see Shua again.

And that causes a deep, aching twinge in my core that has nothing, nothing to do with my mods.

~

TWO DAYS LATER, a cream-colored envelope arrives at every doorstep in the city. We are all in tumult—only the most important news is printed, and this was done so at great expense. The paper is thick, the words scripted across it in raised gold ink.

The prince is throwing another ball.

For he has found his bride.

~

IT HAS BEEN the longest three days of our lives, between receiving the invitation and the night of the ball. There have been no clandestine meetings, no word from the palace. Only a single red rose left on the back step early the second morning, with the finest silver vessel resting beside it. Cindrell tucks the rose deep in the recesses of the pantry in a tumbler of water. We puzzle over the silver cylinder until I notice the finest seam and twist off the top to reveal a finely-soldered dropper that dips into the smoothest oil I have ever seen. Curious, I let one bead of oil fall into a particularly tight joint in my wrist.

The release and relief that follow are so instantaneous I nearly cry.

Without sunlight, the rose quickly withers.

"But what will we do about the ball?" Cindrell whispers furiously in my ear while behind us, Celestina is endlessly screeching about how the prince's invitation had better mean he is finally proposing to her because she will not attend only to watch him select some other trollop to marry and crown. Mother attempts to console her, pointing out how her new satin heels with the glass beading will sparkle against the midnight blue cut of her gown and certainly complement the ring she is sure to receive. Celestina shrieks again, snatching the shoes and pitching them wildly across the room. She stomps out and Mother follows, pleading with my beautiful sister to stop crying lest her eyes be puffy at the ball.

I am done.

"Grab the shoes," I hiss at Cindrell in the quiet left by Celestina's wailing retreat.

"What?"

"Grab the shoes," I repeat. "You're going to the ball."

Her eyes spark with hope. "I have just the dress, too."

An hour later, we are crowding into one of the last available hovercabs in the city. Celestina shoves me to the corner so her full skirts will not be crushed. Beneath the unwieldy skirts of my own gown, we have tied a folded bundle that contains this mystery dress Cindrell says belonged to her mother. From the bit of material that peaked out between the folds, it seems Celestina's beaded shoes will match perfectly.

I tell Cindrell to keep her head down when we arrive so we can sneak into the powder room without any of the prince's guards seeing her first.

When she exits, my stepsister is stunning.

Silver and white cascade from the edges of her smooth shoulders, skimming tight across the bodice to showcase the dip of her waist, the slight swell of her hips. Skirts flow like water down to the floor. A single slit travels up to reveal just enough of her left leg, the glitter of glass beads shining brightly on her tiny feet. When she unwinds the dingy rag from her hair, soft curls cascade down her back. She leaves them loose, the ethereal blonde trailing between her shoulder blades.

Cindrell looks, to all rights, like a queen.

I do not know what to expect of the night. I cannot think beyond giving my sweet and inexpert stepsister any sort of happy ending, past my chance to see Shua again.

It is impossible. It is all impossible.

And yet I cannot find it in me to stop her. To stop myself.

So instead I kiss her cheek and usher her into the ballroom to find her prince.

He is standing at the far end of the floor. Three steps lead from where he stands up to a small dais where his parents, the King and Queen, are seated.

The queen hardly looks old enough to have a son of marriageable age.

I know it is Shua's work, and as much as I hate how

she is using his considerable skill, I cannot help but admire even from such a distance how considerable indeed that skill is.

The prince's eyes are continuously searching the hall for Cindrell. As soon as I push her to the fore of the grand staircase leading down to the dance floor, the prince's hand shoots toward the orchestra. The music stops. The dancing stops. The world stops as a beam of light sweeps across the space to shine on Cindrell. I try to search the crowd for Shua, but the light is blinding me as well.

"Go," I whisper-shout at her in the sudden silence. Her heels click gently against the slick and shining stone stairs and slowly, she begins to descend, light pooling around her every move. The shoes throw shards of reflection with every step. The prince pushes through the stunned crowd and they are mere steps away from each other when a piercing shriek rends the moment.

"You BITCH!"

My stepsister's face goes colorless and the crowd turns as one to the offending voice, but Cindrell and I don't have to bother looking to know whose it is. Celestina is shoving her way through the shocked party-goers, face an alarming shade of red, Mother hot on her heels.

Guards instantly surround the prince, cutting him off from Cindrell as he turns to address Celestina. A dark head of hair emerges from behind the queen's throne, and I see Shua making his way toward the prince as well.

"Dear lady, contain yourself," Prince Cael orders, his full voice carrying across the space. "Briallen is a noblewoman and your cousin, and will soon be your queen. I have been courting her privately under the chaperone of your lady's maid for some time. I suggest you choose your next address with care."

Celestina pushes forward, drawn up short by the cadre of guards. "She is neither a noblewoman nor my cousin." Her words will destroy us both, and so I start to make my way carefully, slowly down the stairs, my soul begging my gears and hydraulics to stay silent and conceal my movement. "Cindrell is a servant in our household, the untitled daughter of a dead country baron. *That*," she stabs one finger into the air and the light splits, pinning Cindrell in place with one beam and swinging wildly to me with another, "is Briallen."

I quicken my descent, hoping to reach Cindrell and the prince to explain, but the blinding light has me ducking my head and throwing my whole center further off balance. I misjudge the depth and my too-short metal leg lands awkwardly on the next stair. In slow motion, I sense the foot has lost purchase and I pitch forward, a tumble of springs and skirts, until I lie crumpled at the base of the stairs. Metal twists in my bones as I count breaths and then try to assemble to standing. Springs and gears protest loudly. No one comes to help me, until . . .

"Briallen?"

It's Shua's voice. Saying *my name*.

But it is not how I imagined. There is no warmth, no resonance. Only a chilled reserve.

I cannot stop it: A tear wells in my left eye and rolls down the smooth skin on that side of my face. Scar tissue aches in the corners of my right eye. It hasn't teared properly since I was six.

Shua pulls me to my feet, but he is formal and stiff, ignoring my tears. I look in his eyes, but a wall has gone up and I fear he will not let me back in.

"You can see why *she* would not be in your database, Your Highness," Celestina sniffs, turning her head from me. I feel Shua's arm tense on mine, but before I can say a word, he drops his hands and backs away. I think it is because we have lied, but it is also because the crowd is parting and the Queen is approaching. We all bow low. The gears in my hip creak ominously. They have taken such a beating against the stone, and I worry for a moment that they will seize and lock me in this awkward bend, but there is an odd metallic ping and I straighten just heartbeats after everyone else.

The Queen stops before Cindrell, who sinks again into a low curtsy.

"Now that I see you more closely, child," the Queen murmurs, tipping Cindrell's chin up with one finger and beckoning her to rise, "I do believe I recognize you. And that gown.

"Your mother. She was . . . Nicola, if I am not mistaken."

Cindrell's eyes go wide and she nods. "Yes, Your Majesty. She died when I was very young; Father could not bear to leave the countryside manor for many years because of his grief."

"But she was a registered baroness, was she not?" The Queen seems to be remarking more to herself, and so we do not respond. A quick gesture has a scribe at her side in an instant, flicking through records on his screen until he locates one and turns it to the Queen.

It is an old record, but nonetheless, a registered database scan of Cindrell's mother.

Cindrell looks so much like her.

Which means that Cindrell is not the nobody my mother told her she was.

She is a true noblewoman in her own right.

"Just what is going on?" The King's powerful voice finally rends the thick silence surrounding us. He steps off the dais, the crowd parting before him like water, rippling with the bows and curtseys of his most noble subjects.

"Your Majesty," my mother implores from the crowd, dragging Celestina toward the royals. The King turns to her and she takes it as invitation. She dips into a curtsy, dragging Celestina down beside her. "We are victims of this same confusion, my daughter Celestina and I. After she danced with the prince at the ball mere weeks ago, her data was corrupted and it is no wonder he could not find her in the database. As you can see, Briallen cannot accurately be scanned due to a tragic accident in her childhood that stole her father from us. When the prince called for her, she was to tell him about her sister so he could come to court Celestina. After all, they are such a perfectly matched pair, are they not? Just look at them. I thought he might be biding his time; I had no idea such duplicitous plans were in place as to beset a servant upon your son as a prospect for his bride. Please, have mercy and release them both to me, and I shall ensure they are dealt with swiftly and severely as befits the crime they have committed against your son. Only do not let this mar a reunion between him and the bride he has truly been searching for all this time."

She lifts her chin and her eyes slowly in a move I have seen her work on countless dukes, barons, money lenders, and debt collectors. It is a look designed to send their blood rushing downward so they forget their purpose and instead agree to whatever she has said, whether they recall it or not.

The prince is no fool. He knows it was not Celestina with whom he danced.

But he is also a dutiful son.

How far will that duty extend should the King believe my mother's invented truth?

"Liar."

Everyone turns to the rough-edged voice that speaks the single word with such intensity.

I am the last to look at him because I know that voice. I have heard it burn with a need to fix what is wounded. I have heard it quiet in the whisper of caring. I have heard it roll with laughter.

I have heard it say my stepsister's name many, many times.

I have heard it say my name—my *real* name—only once. So cold that to hear his voice now ringing with such defense is unimaginable. And yet . . .

Shua steps forward. The slight whine of gears is muffled by his shining leather boot. It is a sound I am intimately familiar with, a sound perhaps only the two of us know so well. Still, he presses forward toward the King. Shua may be an esteemed master within the royal courts, but the King is still the King, and I do not know what such an interjection may net him, for better or for worse.

But before he can speak again, before I can know if or why he would ever come to my rescue after such a betrayal, the prince finds his spine and steps in front of the master modifier.

"Bria—I mean, Cindrell is the one I danced with that night, Father. I know it. I know it with the same certainty that I know the sun still rises beyond the smog and the clear rains still fall beyond the city." He stretches a hand out to my stepsister, who takes a tentative step forward to place her slim palm in his. "Mother has confirmed that Cindrell is of registered noble descent, and therefore, it is Cindrell whom I declare as my bride and future queen.

"Because it is Cindrell whom I love."

The crowd titters and sighs at his final soft

pronouncement, small pockets of applause breaking out and dying just as quickly while they wait to see if the King will agree.

Shua, too, stares at the King, and I stare at Shua. I will him to look my way, to give me any indication of his own feelings through all of this.

"He is right, my dear," the Queen's soft voice cuts through the collective expectation. "Baroness Nicola was a registered noblewoman. Therefore, Cael is free to choose Cindrell as his bride and his queen."

The King grunts, turning back to my mother. "For your lies, you are hereby stripped of your titles. Should you need to settle accounts, they may be paid off with labor. My steward shall be in touch. Now away with you both." He flicks a disinterested hand at them and takes a step toward those of us still frozen around the Queen, the prince, and Cindrell.

"Your Majesty," Celestina's voice cracks on the honorific. Color has leached from her face and I can nearly hear the panicked pounding of her heart as it jumps beneath the delicate skin of her chest.

"I have said my piece." The King does not raise his voice. He does not need to. The words slice through sinew and bone even at the tempered volume. "Go, before I change my mind to more dire consequences."

Hissing, my mother pulls Celestina back and they disappear into the crowd.

"Now," the King says to his son as he approaches us

all. "Let us meet the future queen of NexusNova." He steps into our midst, and we all bow low. Sharp rods of icy fire shoot into what remains of my hip bones; I cannot contain the gasp wrenched out by the pain. Darkness crowds my vision and through a long tunnel, I can hear Cindrell's voice ask if I am okay. I can see Shua reach out a hand, but I cannot reach back. He feels so far away.

Pain blooms, radiating through my marrow and spreading, spreading, spreading up my spine and into and across my ribs. My natural arm contracts against my chest as I spasm and grit my teeth, forcing the rusting gears of my right arm to stretch out and grasp Shua's. In the static invading my ears, I hear a grind followed by a *POP*. For a moment, I am painless. Weightless. In my mind, I push my right leg forward, but as I lean into the step, I realize too late that there is no limb left attached. In the slow motion descent, I briefly wonder if my leg is still standing there without me, how Cindrell will wear her hair for her wedding. If Shua will remember how to make those cherry preserve thumbprint biscuits.

And then gravity returns in real time and I complete my fall, forehead cracking hard against the marble floors.

Shua's voice ordering everyone out of his way is the last thing echoing in my ears before even my hearing deserts me and I am left in black and silence.

~

SOUND IS the first sense that returns. Beeps and hisses and the slow pump of an oil flow line. I know these sounds, but when I search my mind for their meaning, I come up empty.

The world is still black. I am swimming through sludge and I cannot see. My limbs are heavy; breaking the surface is impossible. But gray slits on the horizon, and my filmy eyes rapidly blink until the fog resolves into shapes with more or less defined edges.

The room is white, bright, but instead of cold and sterile leaching into what's left of my bones, it is warm. Inviting rest. If I turn my head slightly to the left, I can see the bag of clear fluid that I know is dripping into whatever veins they could tap into on that side. The line snakes beneath a thick, white sheet that someone has pulled up to my chin. Delicious heat runs through fine filaments, regulating my body temperature so I am comfortable and never once overheated.

The last time I woke up like this, I was fourteen and the country baron had just paid to replace my mods for the first time since I was ten. Four more years of growth and rust and no credits to repair much less replace, and perhaps I should be unsurprised that my metal leg finally sprang loose.

With increasing dread, I recall every moment that led up to me waking here.

Were they able to reattach the leg? If it is not salvageable, I do not know what I will do. Mother has drained us dry, and now there will certainly be no opportunity for me to pay for even the smallest upgrade.

The monitor beeps in time to my mounting horror.

Which alerts whoever has been caring for me.

The door pushes open and there is Shua, standing in this warm white room with me under a sheet, not knowing if I am incomplete.

"You're awake." His words are crafted such that I cannot tell if he is pleased with this development or not. He drops his eyes to a chart in his hands.

"What," I croak against a throat scratched raw by tubes and lack of water. I swallow what moisture I can manage and try again. "What happened?"

Shua looks me in the eye and sighs. "The leg was old. Ill fit. Stripped screws and frozen gears. It's a wonder you could function at all with it, Briallen. The condition of your hip joint also invited infection. Your scans lit up like a power surge. We had to keep you under for two whole days to clear it from your system so we could work."

The word "work" snags on my brain, but in all of his explanation, it isn't the most important one.

"Say it again," I manage in my sandpaper timbre.

His brow furrows and he looks back down at the tablet in his hands that undoubtedly lays bare all my scars and missing parts. "You had . . . an infection?"

"No," I shake my head. "My name. Just like that. Like you care. Not like I have horribly betrayed you—which I have—or am not what you thought I was—which I'm not."

"Briallen," he says my name again, the syllables soft and snagging on the gravel of his voice. He walks to my bedside. "You did not betray me."

"I did," I rush on, the synapses in my brain prompting my right arm to reach out and grab him at the wrist. The sight of the limb dams all other words in my chest.

Gone are the clunky gears and bone-like metal structures that formed the arm I have lived with for the past many years. Gone are the hisses and whines of suffering hydraulics that are a disharmony I had long since stopped hearing. Smooth, white bonded ceramic plates with gilded gold make polished work atop springs and gears and hydraulics that I know are the finest NexusNova has to offer. I pull the hand back, its movement smooth and natural, and stare at the marvel of these fingers, the way they curl and fist and open, how the wrist rotates so smoothly on the forearm.

"What have you done?" I gasp, but he mistakes my wonder for horror and cannot get his sentences out quickly enough.

"I am sorry, Briallen. I know that to make these decisions without your consent was a gross overstep, but the infection ran so deeply and the limbs were so deteriorated that there was no way I could reattach them, not without doing you a massive disfavor. And when I asked the princess, she told me to spare no expense. She even made a special request for the gold gilding, though she said she would understand if you chose to add synthetic skin and cover it altogether."

My brain snags again on a single word. "Wait, princess?"

Shua looks down at his tablet and taps at the glass before turning it so I can see the royal news.

Prince Cael Weds Lady Cindrell in Intimate Garden Ceremony, Coronation to Follow

"Oh." The word breaks on my tongue as a different warmth blooms. I am happy for her. Truly.

"After the scandal of the ball, the King pressed for a quick wedding so the public would have something else to talk about. Cindrell said her only regret was that you were not able to attend," he offers softly, staring at the headline himself.

I drop my eyes once again to the white shining arm that moves as smoothly as if I'd been born with it. I know without looking that there is a matching leg beneath the sheet. A mere will of my mind and I can see toes flex at the far end of the bed. "It is beautiful work, Master Gorbandt," I finally say. "More than I deserve."

At this, his gaze snaps to mine. "No. Cindrell told me everything. From your accident and your father's death to your mother's use of the settlement to fund her own youth instead of giving you yours. You deserve this, Briallen." He reaches to smooth my hair. "This and so much more.

"If anyone is undeserving, it is me for ever doubting you, even for a second."

He looks as if he hasn't slept in days. Perhaps he hasn't.

"Shua." Boldness overtakes and I reach up with this marvelous new hand to cup his angular jaw. Warmth radiates from my fingers and palms and I gasp at this technology.

"The sensory network is still experimental, only because of its outrageous cost," he admits. "But since the princess said spare no expense . . ."

Which is when my heart pounds a different rhythm and I lift my hands hesitantly to my face. Both flesh and manufactured fingers feel the rough terrain of scar tissue. My heart sinks back into my chest. Beside me, Shua half crouches to be at eye level. He sets his tablet on the bedside table and takes both of my hands in his. I cannot let on how much it thrills me that he is holding my hands, that I can feel the heat of his palms in both of mine and it radiates a delicious thrill through my entire body.

"Briallen. You are beautiful just as you are. It is who you are. I have admired that since the moment we first met."

His eyes shine with truth even as his voice shakes with the intensity of his convictions, and so I know he speaks honestly.

"This world is cruel," he continues. "It shuns anything that is different, out of the ordinary, other." He pulls one hand from mine to rake it through his hair, chuckling mirthlessly. "It is why I hold the role I do here at the palace. Everyone craves this forever unattainable myth of perfection.

"Still. That is one area I would never modify without your express input and consent. Only say the word, I can do whatever you ask. I can make you look the way you would have had the accident never happened. Or we can create a new face altogether. Though I admit fondness for this one. Simply say it, and I will do what you desire. But know this: To me, Briallen, to me, no matter what, you are already perfect."

His last words dissolve to whispers and his head bends toward mine.

"I would do anything for you, Briallen," he murmurs, the words hoarse against my skin.

My heart gallops beneath my bones, blood pulsing a beat into every inch of me.

"Shua," I breathe.

There will be time. Time for skin and structure and shape and everything I have been missing for most of my life.

But right now . . .

Right now there is only this moment. And in this moment, only one thing I truly want.

"Kiss me," I finally sigh.

And so he does.

All this time, I've been sitting pretty, painting pictures of the skyline, going out of my mind with boredom.

But all this time, I had so much more I could do.

If I fall, I fall. But if I fly, the sky is mine for the taking.

Skyscraper

Hayley Anderton

When you live in a skyscraper apartment, it's impossible not to wonder about how it would feel to fly.

I spend long hours every day standing at the window, my apartment almost touching the clouds as I stare out at the city. I think about standing on the balcony edge and taking a leap, only to be carried by the wind to some place new, like a feather fallen from a bird's wing. Instead, I watch the world go by from here. The world changes around me, but I stay the same.

I've never left this apartment, but I know this city like

the back of my hand. We are central in the Ninth Zone, the district dedicated to mechanics. I have never seen any of the other Zones. There are two hundred and thirty-six buildings within my eyeline on a clear day, less when smog mists the windows and leaves me blind. Each building is the same, uniform in height. But people come and go from each one, living lives beyond my imagination. Sometimes, I like to watch the people in the buildings opposite to mine—I see people making breakfast in the morning, rushing around because they have places to be, jobs to go to, lives to lead. I tend to spend most of my days wishing I was like them.

And it always brings me back to thoughts of the sky. Of how limitless it is. Of how above the clouds, there's even more of it, and beyond that, stars and planets and galaxies beyond my comprehension. When you live in a skyscraper, looking down never seems like a good idea. But when I look up, I see nothing but possibility.

This morning, the sky is clear, and the sun shines in through the window. I want to step out on the balcony and feel the heat of it on my skin, but Mother always warns me against it. She says that it's dangerous out there for me, that staying inside is the only way she can keep me safe. She's never quite managed to explain to me why it's so dangerous for me. The city is a death trap at the best of times—when the acid rain falls, sirens throughout the city warn everyone to stay inside. Crime rates are higher than the skyscrapers, and everyone is armed to the teeth with guns and knives. The air isn't clean enough to breathe, so nobody goes outside without a mask on. I know the dangers, but I don't understand why Mother claims that outside is unsafe for *me*. I'm no more in danger than anyone else.

But it's a tale as old as time for me. Every time I ask her to reconsider, it only upsets her. I know she wants to keep me safe—the world out there is scarier than I can understand—but isn't that just life? I press my hand against the window pane, feeling the coldness of it. It's the closest I've ever been to feeling the air on my skin.

I hear the apartment door open. Mother is making her morning visit. I turn to see her and she seems flustered, her cheeks red.

"Mother?"

She raises a hand to me in greeting. "Morning, Rapunzel. I'm fine, I took the stairs. Got to keep fit somehow."

Mother has a job in a factory in the mechanics district. She has pointed it out to me from the window. I wish I could go there too, but she says that I'm lucky; work isn't something that most people crave. She's given me plenty of things over the years to keep me busy: cookbooks and paints and instruments to play and sheets of paper to write on. I've mastered many skills at this point, and I suppose I've grown bored of doing the same things over and over. I know I should be more grateful. Not many people have the luxury of spending all day everyday enjoying their hobbies. But I've read half the books on the internet, heard every song there is, tried my hand at every single task that Mother could think of for me.

And still I crave something more.

"I brought you breakfast," Mother says with a warm smile. She hands me a paper bag, still warm from the bakery. I smile. It's my favorite, pain au raisin. It's Mother's favorite too, and each time I have one, it reminds me that though our lives only cross briefly twice a day, she's always thinking of me. It also makes me feel a pang of guilt. For never being grateful for everything she's given me. She reaches up and touches my cheek gently.

"You're drifting," she tells me. I manage a smile.

"I'm sorry. I'm just thinking."

"Do you ever turn that brain of yours off?" Mother asks fondly. "What's on your mind?"

I waver. Whenever she asks me this question, I have to decide how honest to be. The more honest I am, the more I'll hurt her. But today, I want her to know. I turn back to the window.

"The same thing as always," I say. Mother sighs, her hands finding my shoulders.

"I wish I could take you away from here. I wish I could let you see the world. But some things just aren't meant to be, Rapunzel. It will never be safe for you out there."

I turn back around. "Why not?"

Mother's eyes soften. "Always so many questions. You don't realize how incredible you are. What you're worth. Which is exactly why you can never leave here."

"I wish you would just tell me why."

Mother's eyes lower to the ground. "Perhaps some-day. But not today. I know you feel trapped up here, away from everyone else, but you're not missing anything, I can assure you of that. You have a good life here, Rapunzel. For now, maybe you should try to remember that."

My throat feels tight. It always does when I feel close to crying. I try to smile again and take a bite of my pain au raisin. But the buttery pastry feels dry in my mouth, threatening to choke me.

"I wish I could stay, but I'm running late for work . . ." Mother says, not seeming to sense the change in my mood. "I'll be back this evening . . . we'll have dinner together, shall we?"

I swallow and nod. "I can cook something for you if you like."

"Would you mind? You're such a sweetheart," Mother says, her smile full of pride. She reaches out to touch the golden plait of hair that sits over my shoulder. "And then after, I'll brush your hair and we can watch the city. Okay?"

The thought lifts my mood ever so slightly. There's nothing I love more than spending time with her, feeling her comb run gently through my long hair. It's the time when I feel least alone. With my one and only friend beside me, things can't get much better for me.

Today, something about that thought saddens me deeply.

"Have a good day, my darling," Mother says. And then she leaves. I watch her go, glimpsing the corridor outside my apartment for a single moment before it's locked away from me. I sigh, heading over to the window to finish my pastry. I barely even taste it. It's a bad start to the day, and I can't decide what to do with the rest of my time. Waiting for Mother to return isn't an exciting prospect. I almost want to crawl back into bed and shut off for a while, to sleep away the day until she returns. But that would be a waste, and I'm better than that. I don't want to mope. I will find something to occupy my time.

I do what I always do when I need a pick me up. I get myself set up with some music and take my paints to the window, my easel propped up in front of the view. The one thing that makes me feel closer to the world outside is painting it. I've painted this scene numerous times, but right now, it feels like the only thing that will make me feel better.

The moment my paintbrush touches the canvas for the first time, I feel peace. I take my time in capturing the shapes and shades of the buildings opposite me. I'll do the sky last, when the colors of it begin to shift into evening and the world becomes another place entirely. For as long as I'm painting, I don't have time to sit with my feelings. As the day continues and my painting comes to life, I feel my sadness fading away.

In the mid afternoon, I stop to make a snack from the fridge. It's stocked full of my favorite chocolates and fruits. Mother never touches them—she says they'll rot her teeth, but she insists that won't be the case for me. I take an apple from the top shelf and head back toward the window. But when I see something outside, I gasp, dropping the fruit to the ground.

There is a man on the balcony.

He's staring right at me. His blue eyes fixate on me and I find myself trembling where I stand. How did he get there? I take him in, trying to make sense of what I'm seeing. He's wearing all black, his chest covered by some kind of protective vest. In his hands, he holds two rounded devices. I don't know what they're used for, but the sight of them fills me with terror, almost as much as the man himself. Are they weapons? Is he one of the dangers Mother is constantly warning me about?

His dark hair blows in the wind as he steps closer to the door that leads to the balcony. Instinctively, I grab a knife from the block in the kitchen and rush forward. This is the first person I've ever come in contact with other than Mother. She hasn't prepared me for this, but my instinct is to be wary. There's no chance I'm letting him hurt me.

But when he sees that I'm armed, he stops, shaking his head at me. He slowly places the devices he's holding onto the ground and puts his hands up in surrender. I shuffle closer toward the door. Thank goodness it's locked.

I stare at the man. I can't read his face, which is

obscured by his breathing mask, but something tells me he's handsome, like the men I've seen in movies. Handsome in a way that makes people lose their senses. Well, not me. There's no chance I'm allowing a handsome man into my home just because I'm lonely.

"Who are you? Why are you here?" I ask. I don't even know if he'll be able to hear me through the thick glass, but his eyes soften, and I think he must be able to.

"My name is Flynn," he says, his gruff voice slightly obscured by the mask he wears.

"What are you doing on my balcony?"

"I promise, I mean you no harm . . . I'm a free climber. See those devices I brought with me? They suction onto the side of buildings. I use them to scale tower blocks. But the wind outside caught me off guard. It wasn't safe to keep climbing so I had to stop here. Please, put the knife down. I'm not going to hurt you."

I waver. The story makes sense. I've seen free climbers before, crawling up the sides of buildings like spiders. I've always admired them from afar, and now I have one standing on my balcony, looking at me with the brightest blue eyes I've ever seen. I feel my breath steadying. I lower the knife, but I don't put it down. I'm not entirely sure how to go about this. How can I trust this person when I don't have anyone to compare him to? I can't even read his expression to see if he's telling me the truth.

But I can feel curiosity getting the better of me. This is the first opportunity I've ever had to talk with someone else. How can I pass it up, especially after everything I've been feeling today? I narrow my eyes at him.

"I should call the cops."

I see the corners of his eyes crease. I think he's smiling.

"Why would you need to do that? I think you've got it handled," he says, nodding to my knife. I almost smile back. Instead, I hang my head shyly.

"Well . . . what now?"

"Well . . . I'm not expecting you to let me inside," Flynn says. "But maybe you'll let me hang out on your balcony for a while. And perhaps you'll keep me company."

My heart lurches. I don't know how to handle this. I know what Mother would tell me—she'd send him away without a second thought. She certainly wouldn't keep him company. But desperation claws at me. I don't want to spend another day all alone. I smile.

"Alright. I guess you can stay out there. I'm not busy anyway."

Flynn nods to the easel a few meters from me. "You're not painting?"

"I can paint any day. It's not often I have guests," I tell him. He laughs at that, and I'm not sure why, but it makes me smile.

"Why don't you show me what you were painting?"

"Okay," I say, suddenly eager. I know my paintings are good. I've always hoped to make them photo-realistic, and this one is turning out pretty well. I turn the easel around so that Flynn can see it. His eyes widen.

"Wow. I wasn't expecting it to be that good. Did you go to art school?"

I shake my head shyly. "No . . . I've never left the Ninth Zone. I just taught myself."

Flynn raises an eyebrow. "I've never seen someone self-taught who is so good."

"Do you meet many artists?"

"Sure I do. I climb up on their balconies to look at their art all the time."

It's my turn to laugh. The sound surprises me. I'm used to spending my days in near silence, never hearing the sound of my own voice or anyone else's. Now, to hear Flynn talking to me is music to my ears. I close the gap between us, sitting down in front of the window and crossing my legs. He mirrors me, sitting close enough to the glass that it looks like our knees are touching. The thought makes my heart shudder in delight.

"How does the climbing work?" I ask him. He reaches for one of the devices he was holding earlier and shows it to me.

"Some sort of fancy technology I'm not smart enough to understand. They don't even produce these anymore, since they scaled back on technological advancement. But there's some kind of electromagnetic pulse . . . it helps each one stick to the wall as you climb. You just have to have the upper body and core strength to make each one go higher than the other."

"You say that like it's simple."

Flynn shrugs. "I guess I have the time to work on it. And the passion. There's no better feeling than climbing. Knowing that you could fall at any moment makes it all so . . . exciting."

"It doesn't scare you?"

Flynn's eyes crinkle again. "It does. But I think that's where the excitement comes from. To me, feeling that rush of something—fear, excitement, everything in between—they're all the same. I guess I'm just chasing the feeling of *something*."

I tilt my head up to see the sky outside the window. "Does it feel like . . . does it feel like you could fly?"

Flynn considers me for a moment, his eyes curious. "Sometimes."

That makes me smile. "That's something I think about a lot. I'm forever looking at the sky, thinking about everything beyond my reach."

"And you think if you could fly that would change everything?"

"Maybe not. But life might be a little less dull."

Flynn smiles. "I can see how you'd come to that conclusion. Have you ever heard the story of Icarus?"

"No . . . I don't think so."

"It's a cautionary tale. I heard it a thousand times from my climbing mentor when I was first trying it out.

It's a Greek myth about the son of an inventor. His father, Daedalus, fashioned wings from wax and feathers to escape the rule of a tyrant king. His son took flight alongside him, and they realized the beauty of what they could do. But Icarus had ambition beyond his capabilities. He flew higher and higher, though his father warned him against it. And at some point, as he climbed above the clouds, above the sky, his wings melted, and he fell to his death."

I stare at Flynn in horror. "That's a terrible story."

He laughs. "It's not meant to be a happy one. But it just goes to show that flying is overrated. Good things can happen with your feet on solid ground, too. Like meeting a girl when you clamber onto her balcony by accident."

I roll my eyes. I may have no experience with men, but I've watched enough cheesy romances to know when a man is using a line on me. But it makes me smile all the same.

"I think I'm just looking for something . . . a little more. I've never seen beyond this city, beyond this apartment. You're the first person I've met besides my mother."

Flynn's eyes widen. "You've never left your home?"

"No. For as long as I can remember, I've been here. And Mother doesn't like to talk about the past, or the future. She just wants me here. To keep me safe, I suppose."

"The city can be dangerous. I'm sure your Mother only

wants to protect you from that," Flynn says. I hug my knees to my chest.

"I didn't expect you to side with her. Given that you've got all the freedom you want—climbing tower blocks like it's nothing, having adventures every day—I want that too. I don't want to stay here forever, painting the same cityscape over and over."

Flynn says nothing, but his eyes tell a story of their own. He looks pained by my words, as though he understands my own position. Slowly, he reaches out to press his hand against the glass of the window. I waver before I press my own to the glass, like we're touching. I can't feel him, but I feel the sentiment of his gesture.

"I'm sorry," he says. "It sounds tough."

I swallow. Never before has Mother acknowledged me the way Flynn is doing now. I don't think she truly understands how it feels to be cooped up in here all the time. It could've driven me to the point of madness by now, if I wasn't so strong of mind. But this man that I barely know sees inside me, sees how my emotions have built up and reached a boiling point. For the first time in so long, I don't feel invisible.

"I think I'm glad you came here today," I tell Flynn. He raises an eyebrow.

"Would you like me to come back some day?"

Warmth floods into my stomach. "I . . . I would love that."

"I still don't know your name."

I smile shyly. "Rapunzel."

"Rapunzel? What a unique name. I bet you're the only one in the world," Flynn says. His gaze does something to me. It makes me wish the glass wasn't in our way. I could open the door. I could go to him . . .

But some part of me is still frightened. And it scares me even more how much of an effect Flynn has had on me in such a short time. Logic tells me that these emotions need to be kept in check. I need to give this time, build some trust. Then perhaps I can open up to him.

I watch him stand, picking up his climbing clamps.

"The wind has died down a little. I should make my way down. They're forecasting acid rain later," he tells me. I stand too, trying not to show the disappointment on my face.

"Oh . . . okay."

"But I'll be back," he promises. "I'll see you again . . . *Rapunzel.*"

I want to ask him when. I want to tell him that the way he says my name sends a shudder down my spine. But I don't. I just smile and wave to him. Then, I watch as he swings his legs over the side of the balcony and disappears, like he was never even here.

I don't know how long I stand at the window, watching the balcony for signs that he might return, for signs that he came in the first place. But when I hear the door open to the apartment, I'm jolted back to life. I turn, hopeful, but it's just Mother. She looks at me strangely, like she knows that I'm changed by this day and every-thing that happened.

"Rapunzel . . . are you alright?"

"I'm fine, Mother," I tell her, trying to keep my voice level.

"How long have you been standing there? I thought you were going to cook us some dinner."

"I . . . I was painting. I suppose I lost track of time," I say, blinking several times. I still feel entranced by Flynn and the feelings he gave to me. And Mother seems to be able to tell. She approaches me and cups my face, exam-ining me with concern.

"You look a little out of sorts, darling. Are you feeling hazy at all?"

"Mother, I told you I'm okay. Maybe the paint fumes went to my head a little," I say, making light of it all. Mother doesn't seem convinced, but she steps away from me.

"Okay . . . and you would tell me, wouldn't you? If something was wrong?"

"Of course I would," I say, leaning in to kiss her cheek. "Maybe I can make dinner now."

"That's alright. We'll order something in. We haven't done that for a while, have we?" Mother says, her smile returning. "What would you like?"

"I want whatever you want, Mother."

I see her eyes mist over a little, though I can't put my finger on why. I guess I'm not the only one feeling out of sorts today. She turns from me before I can ask her what's going on.

"You're a good girl, Rapunzel. Let me order us some pizza. Why don't you pick a movie for us to watch?"

There's a funny mood between us for the rest of the evening. We sit down to watch the movie, pizzas on our laps, but Mother doesn't say much. She just keeps reaching for my hand across the sofa every now and then, like she's scared I might have gone missing. And maybe she's right. Some part of me left this apartment today. Flynn took it with him. And I don't know if it'll ever return.

Mother stays a little while after the movie ends to brush my hair. As promised, we sit in front of the window so I can watch the city light up for the night. I stare out into the unknown, wishing I could uncover all the secrets that lie out there. Now that I've had a taste of what's out there, I feel ravenous.

"Soon," Mother says. I blink. If she said something before, I missed it.

"What do you mean?"

"Soon I'll tell you more about the city. I'll tell you more about what you want to know. But not yet. Just let it be this way a little while longer; it'll only get more complicated after."

"Mother, you're worrying me."

"I'm sorry, darling. Just ignore me. I promise, everything will make sense soon."

164

I decide not to push her. She seems on the edge of something raw and painful, and I don't want to be the one to hurt her with this dangerous ground. But after her fingers finish plaiting my hair and she leaves, her absence feels more prominent than usual. I know she will be back in the morning, but there's a sense inside me telling me that come morning, nothing will be the same. Not after a day like this.

It's time for bed. I know I need to recharge from the day, but I don't feel tired. I just want to sit up and watch the lights of the city, knowing that I'm closer to them than I've ever been before. Still, I climb into bed and close my eyes. When I woke this morning, I thought I knew everything there was to know about how today would play out.

And now I know that tomorrow may surprise me.

∼

I WAIT three days for Flynn to reappear. I spend my time anxiously waiting by the window, wondering whether he's the kind of man who keeps his promises. The longer I wait, the more it seems like he might not return.

But I have to remember that people beyond this apartment have lives. They have commitments to tend to, people to see, jobs to work at. Flynn doesn't have the luxury of time the way that I do. But still, I wait impatiently. Embarrassed at my own eagerness, I try to look as though I'm busy painting at the window, but I barely lift my paintbrush, merely passing time until I see those ocean blue eyes again.

This morning, I had mostly given up on the idea of his return. Now, as midday approaches, I'm in the kitchen making myself a fruit salad when I hear something knocking against the glass. I turn and my heart lurches at the sight of Flynn, standing on the balcony in his climbing gear. His mouth is still covered by his mask, but I think he's smiling as he waves at me. I rush to the window, forgetting to act casual.

"You came back!" I exclaim. Flynn's eyes graze over my body and I find myself blushing.

"I told you I would, didn't I?" he says. "I couldn't resist."

Everything he says seems to leave me a little more breathless. I had no idea a person could have such an effect on me. And now that he's here, I don't plan to waste a single moment of his visit. I press my palm to the window again and he puts his own up against the glass.

"It's good to see you," I whisper. Flynn's eyes soften.

"I couldn't stand to think of you all alone," Flynn murmurs back. "And I want to get to know you better."

I waver. I know that I should still tread carefully. Flynn is the closest thing to a friend I've ever had, and yet he's still a stranger to me. I swallow. I know that for now, the security locks on the door and thick glass are keeping me safe from the outside, but the air is toxic and I still don't know Flynn's intentions. It's best that we're apart until I know him more.

"I still can't let you inside, not yet."

"That's okay. I wasn't expecting you to let me in. Not today," Flynn says. "But maybe someday, we'll meet without three inches of glass between us."

I hope so, I say internally. I let out a quiet sigh of relief.

"Where have you been?"

Flynn's eyebrow flickers up his forehead. "Causing havoc all over the city. The less you know, the better."

"But I *want* to know. My life has no havoc at all. Give me some of yours."

Flynn laughs. "Perhaps we should trade. You can come out here and have some adventures, while I lead a quiet life. Do you think your Mother would notice if we switched places?"

I sigh. "In an instant. But I can dream."

Flynn leans against the window, his arms folded. "I can't recall the last time I had a dream."

"Really? I always have the most incredible dreams."

Flynn's eyes meet mine. "You do? And what do your dreams hold?"

I sigh, my cheek pressing against the cold glass so that I can look at his face. "Oh, everything and nothing. I dream of things beyond my own comprehension. Usually about outer space and beyond. I dream that I'm exploring places I'm certain I've never seen. Endless deserts and sprawling cities and meadows that smell like flowers. And when I dream, I always know it isn't real. It's too far from the life I know to be anything, but a dream."

"Does that make you sad?"

My shoulders slump forward. "If I dwell on it too long. I tend to try and stay in my dreams as long as I can. It's the only time I feel truly free."

There's an undeniable sadness in Flynn's eyes. He pities me, and that makes my face heat up. I don't want him to feel sorry for me. I want to enchant him in some small way, though there's nothing interesting about me. How can there be when I've never even set foot outside?

"Your dreams sound wonderful," Flynn tells me. "Perhaps someday, you'll see those places for real."

I sigh. "I doubt that."

"Don't give up on your dreams, Rapunzel. Maybe, if you'll let me, I'll take you to those places myself. If I could get you out of here, would you want that?"

Butterflies flutter in my stomach. He's only teasing me, surely? He's simply trying to make me feel better. But the possibility of it has my heart doing somersaults. If he means it, then it's an offer I'm not sure I can refuse.

"You say the most incredible things," I say with a smile. Flynn's eyes crease in the corners.

"And I mean them. Like I said, my life is chaos. I wouldn't mind having someone to join me in the fun."

"So you picked the girl who has never stepped foot outside?"

Flynn chuckles. "I picked the only girl I've met who

wants what I want. You see the world as a place of wonder, even though so much of it has been kept from you. I could show you so much, Rapunzel. If only you'll let me someday."

He stays all afternoon. We talk through the window, passing anecdotes and flirtatious remarks. The warmth in my chest grows and grows, and I turn cold the moment he disappears from the balcony once again and leaves me behind.

I go to bed early and wake up early, hopeful that he will return to me again in the new day. And he does. Over and over again. For over a week, Flynn comes to my window every single day.

He comes armed with a thousand stories to open my mind. He tells me more about Greek myths after his story of Icarus, tales of crime on the streets of the city, his climbing adventures, the places he hopes to visit one day. And in return, I tell him about my boring life inside the apartment, show him the pictures I've painted, play him songs I've learned on guitar. He seems interested in everything I've accomplished, though I'm sure anyone with as much time on their hands could do the same things. He hangs on to my every word, even though my life is nothing compared to his. And it makes me feel special. It makes me feel seen. Each day, I thank the stars that Flynn came into my life. And each time he leaves, I feel in a daze, only waiting for him to return again.

And it feels as though I'm leading a double life.

Mother has no idea that my days are now spent with the mysterious man at my window. As I lay dinner on the table for us tonight, I can feel her watching me. I keep my face straight. I can't let her know what's going on. If she found out, she'd put a stop to it, I'm certain of it.

"There's something different about you lately," Mother tells me, looking me up and down. I have to resist the urge to look away from her. I hate lying to her. I have always shared everything with her, whether out of choice or not. But everything is different now. If I tell her the reason I'm so happy, then she will never forgive me. She's tried so hard to protect me from everything beyond this apartment, but she kept so many wonders from me too. I can't allow her to take them away from me again. I can't allow her to take *him* away from me.

"Do you think so?" I ask, feigning ignorance. "I guess I've just been in a good mood."

"Yes, I suppose you have been. But you've been neglecting your painting. I haven't seen you make anything new in days."

"I've just been focusing on my music," I lie, guilt choking me. "Sometimes painting gets repetitive. But I'm enjoying music right now."

Mother considers me again, then she smiles. "Well, I'm glad. I know you find it difficult cooped up in here, always having more questions than answers, always stuck here with nothing but your thoughts. But your patience will pay off. I promise you that."

I smile back and focus on my dinner. It's easier than trying to keep pretending that I'm present in the room right now. My thoughts are with Flynn. I wonder what he does while we're apart. I wonder who he spends his time with, where he lives, what he does for work. He always tells me he's more interested in hearing about me and my life, but I have this urge to know him better, to close in on who he is as a man.

And more than anything, I want to close the gap between us. I want to feel his skin on mine. I want to kiss him, to feel loved for the first time. Mother doesn't count —she made me, she has to love me. I want someone to *choose* to love me.

And I want it to be him.

~

It's been two weeks since Flynn started visiting me regularly. Each day that passes brings me a little closer to my man on the balcony. I still haven't allowed him inside, haven't touched him, haven't made the next step in our relationship, but I guess I have nothing but time on my hands. It can wait a little longer.

Someday soon, though, I think I'll open my doors to him. The distance between us feels greater every day, and I'm not sure how much longer I can resist him. I think he feels the same as me—the way he looks at me, the way he talks, it makes me feel like he can't possibly be neutral about me. Otherwise why would he keep coming back?

I wait for him, as I always do, by the window, but by mid afternoon, he still hasn't appeared. I check the clock over and over, frowning to myself. He's usually here by now. He didn't say anything about skipping a day, so where is he? I know I'm being needy, and I know he doesn't owe me anything, but we've been in a routine these past few weeks. I can't understand why he'd just disappear without a word now.

I check the time. It's nearly four o'clock. Mother will be back soon. I sigh. A whole day without Flynn has been wasted. I'm about to give up on him when I see his legs swing over the top of the balcony and he rushes to the window, breathless. There's panic in his eyes. I rush to him, pressing my palm to the window.

"Flynn, what's wrong?"

"Rapunzel, I need you to listen to me carefully. You need to come with me. You need to get out of here."

I frown. "What—what are you talking about? This is the only place where I'm safe."

"You've never been safe here. Your Mother has been lying to you all of this time. To keep you here. But now I know why. She wants to control you. You have something she needs."

"You're not making any sense, Flynn."

"She's keeping secrets from you, Rapunzel. You know

she is. And if you don't get out of here now, you'll be trapped forever."

"I don't understand . . . how do you know all of this?"

"You're going to have to trust me," Flynn insists, his eyes wide and desperate. "I care for you, Rapunzel. I only want you to be safe. But if you stay here, bad things are going to happen."

"But . . ."

I can hear the crank of the elevator in the corridor. Someone is coming. Flynn's eyes widen more, and he presses his palm to the glass.

"Let me protect you. Please. If it's the last thing I do, that's what I want. Let me in, Rapunzel."

I don't understand what he's trying to tell me or what he's so scared of. My mind is so muddled that I can't make sense of anything. But he says he wants to protect me, and I'm afraid of what I might be about to face. Before I can think too much, I'm pressing the emergency button that opens the glass doors. Flynn rushes to me and throws his arms around me. It knocks the wind out of me, feeling his skin on mine for the first time. I can feel his breath on my neck. It's almost enough to make me forget why I let him in in the first place.

And then something presses against my neck. Something hard and metal. Flynn's grip on me starts to feel too strong. The front door bursts open and Mother stands in the doorway, her eyes wide.

"Rapunzel, get away from him!"

"Stay back, woman, or I'll fry her circuits to hell," Flynn growls. His tone takes me by surprise, his words dripping with venom. What is going on here? And then I finally clock what he's holding.

It's a taser.

"You won't do that. You need her alive if you want to get paid," Mother says, her voice trembling. "But you'll have to get through me first."

"You think I won't?" Flynn asks. He reaches into his pocket and brings out a large knife. My breathing is out of control. I struggle against Flynn.

"What's going on? Flynn, stop this!"

"Keep quiet," Flynn snaps. He sticks the taser against my side and electrifies it. I scream in pain as I feel the electrical current run through me, raw heat filling every inch of me. I fall down, blinded by the pain as Flynn throws himself at Mother. I blink through the agony, trying to get back to my feet. I don't know who to trust, what to believe, but I have to stop this.

I stagger toward them both. Mother is fighting Flynn off with her bare hands, ducking out of his way as he tries to stab at her, and clawing at him. I don't know why they're at each other's throats, but I won't let them hurt one another. This can't be how this ends.

I rush to Flynn and grab him by his waist, trying to tug him away, but he's feral. He shoves me out of the way and dives on Mother. They tumble to the ground and I hear her cry out in agony as the knife slices through her abdomen.

I scream. Blood blossoms from her wound and she coughs, red smattering her lips. Flynn stumbles back, wiping his sweaty hair from his forehead. He turns to me, and his eyes aren't the ones I know. They're full of anger, full of hate. This isn't the man I've come to care about.

I don't know if he ever even existed.

"You're coming with me," he growls, stepping toward me. "Don't make this hard."

I'm trembling in place. Who is this stranger in front of me? What does he want with me, and why would he hurt Mother? None of the answers I'm searching for can be good. He tricked me. And now, somehow, I know what I have to do.

I step toward him. He grabs my wrist so hard that it hurts.

"I knew you'd comply," he says, his tone smug. I hear Mother groan on the floor, and I don't need any more encouragement. I know where my loyalties lie now.

I won't make the same mistake again.

My free hand reaches for Flynn's throat and squeezes, my fingers clamping hard into his neck. Flynn's eyes are wide in confusion. He tries to fend me off, his hands clawing at my arm, but I don't give in. As he lets go of my wrist, my other hand finds his throat. Now, there's no way he's breaking free. I squeeze so hard that I know I'm crushing the air out of his lungs. I don't let up, even as

Flynn's face turns purple, eyes bulging. And when he finally stills, I let him drop to the ground.

Mother's breathing is labored behind me, and I turn to see the shock on her face. I feel the anger leave my body and I kneel beside her, trying not to acknowledge what I just did.

"Mother . . . I'm so sorry . . . let me call an ambulance . . ."

Mother chokes, shaking her head. "It's too late for that, sweetheart. And besides . . . we can't let anyone know what happened here. Then you'll never be free."

Tears stream down my cheeks. "I don't understand, Mother. I don't understand anything about what's happening here . . ."

"I know. I should have seen this coming. I knew that eventually we'd be found . . . but I was clinging on to hope that someone would come and help us. I should've known better." She shakes her head. "But now, it's time for the truth. Maybe if I'd told you sooner, none of this would've happened. I need you to listen closely, darling . . . we don't have much time."

I clutch Mother's hand in my own. "I'm here, Mother. I'm listening."

Mother heaves a breath, her eyes sparkling with tears.

"When I was a younger woman . . . the world changed. War tore entire cities apart. If we had continued the way we were going, humanity wouldn't have survived. And it was all because we let our technology get out of control. Artificial Intelligence in the robots we built got so smart that it started thinking ahead of the game. It started a war it didn't plan to finish . . . because humanity isn't destined to survive. We have destroyed our own planet, and in time, it won't be fit for us to live here any longer. The robots saw that, and they decided that the way to restore the balance was to wipe the slate clean, to create a robot so realistic that it was almost human in itself, but without all of the problems we cause. I didn't know their intentions at the time. And so I helped them." Mother takes a ragged breath and I cling harder to her.

"Mother . . ."

"I'm okay. I can make it a little longer. But you have to listen, to understand . . . you know that the Ninth Zone is dedicated to mechanics . . . but it used to be so much more. We led the way for robotic developments. It was beautiful work . . . but we got ahead of ourselves. And it created monsters capable of becoming more advanced than us, taking our learning and going beyond it. They knew the power they had, and they were preparing to murder their makers." Mother trembles where she lies, wincing as she presses her free hand against her wound. "But even after all that had happened . . . even after millions died, after carnage threatened to swallow us whole . . . I still didn't want to give up on my project." She looks me in the eye. "It was a dangerous project . . . there were so many risks. I was flying too close to the sun. It was known as Project Icarus."

I forget to breathe for a moment. Now I see why Flynn told me those stories. I thought he was filling my mind with wonder and happiness. But he was telling me his intentions all along. He was letting me know that he never cared for me, that he always had an ulterior motive. He knew more about me than I ever did. What that was, I still don't understand, but I think I'm about to find out.

"Project Icarus was my life . . . and it brought me my greatest pride . . . you. Your name . . . your name is Rapunzel for a reason. You . . . you were built to be RP-NZL . . . otherwise known as a Robotic Prototype - Ninth Zone Legacy Model."

I feel sick to my stomach. I remember Flynn asking my name and what he said to me. *Rapunzel . . . what a unique name. I bet you're the only one in the world.* In the moment I told him my name, I let him know he'd found exactly what he was looking for.

"RP-NZL . . . I'm just a . . . a robot."

Mother's eyes are pained. "But you see . . . you're not. You were designed to be so close to human that nobody would ever be able to tell the difference. And since I never told you the difference . . . I raised you to be human. But you're not, Rapunzel. At night, you lie on your bed and it charges you up . . . you don't sleep like humans do. You eat like us, but you can survive without it. There is so much more you are capable of. You *feel* everything we feel . . . but only because you were built that way. If I removed your heart, you'd feel nothing.

There's a chip in your chest . . . take it out and you're just like any basic robot. That chip, your heart . . . that's what separates you from the rest. You are one of a kind."

I stare at Mother in shock. I press my hand to my chest. I can feel the thrum of my heart there. I can't understand. I'm *human*. I'm a daughter, a dreamer, a lover, a free thinker. How can Mother tell me now that none of that is true?

"My . . . my heart . . ."

"I made it beat," Mother tells me. "You are made of two perfect computers . . . your brain, which acts as your logical analysis and defense system. The kind of computer that other robots possessed. And your heart . . . your emotional regulator. The two can conflict, and that's what makes you so realistic. I designed you so perfectly that I found the beating heart of humanity. You are everything that a human is meant to be and more. You are *better*. I was so proud of what I created. At first, I made you in my image. I programmed you to like what I like, to have the same values as me, to be as good a person as I hoped to be . . . but you evolved, like any human can. You became your own woman. And more than that, you became like a daughter to me. I knew all along that you weren't human . . . that you weren't really my daughter. But I looked beyond that. I thought . . . if I can't have children of my own, then why not play God? Some women can use their bodies to create human life . . . but failing that, I made you. And I loved you so fiercely that . . . I couldn't let you go."

My hand squeezes hers. "Mother, what did you do?"

Mother swallows. "In the year 2236, it was decreed that all robotic life would be destroyed in order to preserve humanity. The war ended with millions of robots being destroyed. And I had to stand by and watch . . . knowing they wanted to take you away from me. And I couldn't bear it. You would never . . . you would never hurt a fly . . ."

My head slowly turns to where Flynn's body lies still. I swallow.

"I don't think that's true, Mother."

She sniffs. "You only wanted to protect me . . . perhaps I programmed you a little too well. You would do anything to protect your maker, like I intended. Your programming goes beyond even your own evolution. Which is exactly why I couldn't allow them to shut you down. I had to do something . . . because when we went through the technological devolution, I knew you'd never be safe again."

"But . . . I've been here my entire life. I—it's always been this way. I don't remember these things you're telling me about."

"Rapunzel . . . can you remember a time where you were a child?"

I consider what she's asking me. My hands are trembling. "No. I can't."

"That's because you never had a childhood. You were created as you are now, and you have never aged a day. But you did have a life before this place . . . for years, in fact. And I had to wipe it all from your memory. I had to make you truly believe that you were human so that you could blend into society. I told my bosses that I'd shut you down . . . but I brought you here to keep you safe."

"But then . . . why did Flynn come here?"

"I meant it when I told you that the world out there isn't safe for you. Ever since the robots were shut down forever, there have been task forces searching for any remaining robots. I suppose my bosses always suspected that I didn't truly let you go . . . they knew how much I cared for you. So there have been people looking in every nook and cranny for you. And I'm sure there are others, too. I kept you here to hide you . . . I knew that if they ever found you, they would do terrible things."

"They would . . . they would shut me down?"

"Not just that, Rapunzel. I think they . . . I think they would want to experiment on you. To study how I made you, to see if it's safe to create others like you. But I programmed you in such a way . . . you would feel it all. You are practically human, after all. And I don't believe they would see you in that way. They would take you apart, piece by piece. And they wouldn't care how it hurt you."

I feel breathless. Now I see why Mother fought so hard

to keep me here, to squash my dreams of something grander. She wasn't trying to hurt me, to torture me.

She was trying to save my life.

I can barely believe all that I'm hearing. I was so wrong about everything. I spent so long wishing I could escape to a world that hates everything I am. How can I even begin to comprehend that when I thought all along that I was human? I can't possibly be made of metal and cogs and algorithms. I can't bear to believe it.

"Rapunzel . . ." Mother wheezes. "I'm sorry, but you're on your own now. You can't stay here, it's not safe for you. When Flynn doesn't return with you, others will come. But you're capable of things you don't even understand yet. Go to the safe in your closet . . . the code is 18-16-14-26-12. Inside, you'll find all of the answers you need about who you are. But you need to get away from here."

"Mother . . . don't go. I'm not ready . . . I don't want to lose you."

Mother smiles sadly, reaching up to touch my face. "I'm so proud of you. You're everything I dreamed you'd be."

"But I was so wrong . . . I trusted Flynn. He made me mistrust you when you're the only person who has ever been here for me. I made so many mistakes."

"Exactly," Mother breathes. "It means I did my job. You're as human as anyone."

I watch her eyelids flicker, her final breath fading out. My whole body begins to tremble as silent tears threaten to choke me. I clutch her to me, feeling her blood seep onto my T-shirt. I rock her back and forth, trying to shake some life back into her. But she's gone. And even though nothing makes sense now, I know one thing for sure: that she's lost to me forever.

I don't want to go. I've never known pain like this. But now I know that not even my pain is real. It's all a simulation, a projection of the human image, but not truly human. I see now why Mother kept this from me. I've never had so many questions. I thought I knew myself, but it turns out that I know nothing at all.

There's blood on my hands as I leave Mother to find the safe in my closet. I never really questioned what was in it before, but now it calls to me. It has the answers I need. I input the number Mother told me, and the lock clicks open. Breathing hard, I take out a thick instruction manual.

I stare at the manual. My whole existence has been reduced to a ream of paper. It makes me feel sick to look at it. But I open the book anyway. There's a diagram on the first page. It details my inner workings, like a skeleton in biology class. Except instead of a heart, a liver, a stomach, I'm made of chips and motors. Wires replace my veins. Tears leak from my eyes, trailing down my skin like acid rain. Even my tear ducts are mechanical, my skin a prosthetic. And yet I feel all of this like feeling is all I was born to do.

And then there's my heart and my brain. Two

complex computer chips and nothing more. Mother told me that the heart controls my emotions. I press my hand to my chest, feeling the beat of my mechanical heart.

If I remove the heart, will I die?

Or will it simply take the pain away?

I focus on my breathing, trying not to allow myself to go to such a dark place. Do I truly want to forget how it feels to love? That's what this pain is, after all. The pain of losing Mother, of losing the man I thought Flynn was. But they're both gone now. I have nothing left. This beating heart inside my chest will remind me of that every second of every day.

Can I end this feeling?

I find the section I'm looking for in the manual—the heart. My eyes flicker over the words. *Removing the heart chip will result in RP-NZL's human element diminishing, but the robot can function perfectly in every other aspect. Removing the brain, however, will cease functions of the robot.*

Removing the heart may result in some complications. RP-NZL is designed to feel pain in the same manner as a human being. Cutting the heart out of the body will result in extreme pain that may cause—

The decision is made for me in a split second. I suppose Mother gave me the ability to be sure of myself. And right now, I'm not afraid of how much this could hurt me. I just want to cease feeling. Mother saw this version of me as perfection. But she isn't here now. This emotion may kill me.

I have to rid myself of it.

I find the sharpest knife in the kitchen and run to the bathroom to complete the task. I remove my T-shirt and position the knife over my heart. I don't care how much pain this will cause. It can't be worse than feeling the pain of Mother's secrets, of her passing, of my discovery of who I am. I cry out as the blade enters my chest, carving out a hole in my skin. I take as much care as I can with my shaking hands, though pain blinds me. I watch in the mirror as my chest opens up, revealing my internal mechanisms. They're foreign to me, unlike anything I've ever seen, a messy tangle of wires and receptors, but there in the middle, a metal box thrums like a heartbeat. I take several deep breaths, mechanical lungs inside me inflating and crumpling again like a paper bag. If I don't survive this, then at least I'll be out of my own misery.

I reach inside my chest and yank my heart free.

There's a horrific rush of pain, and then everything dulls. I'm breathing hard as I hold the box in my palm, feeling the final thrum of it as it dies. But I stay alive, my chest gaping, a vital piece of me missing.

And now I feel nothing at all.

I take a few seconds to process. But there's no going back now. I say a silent goodbye to who I was before. Now, nothing is holding me back. Mother wanted to make me human, but no one will ever accept me as one.

There is no need for me to pretend any longer.

Now, my brain leads the way entirely. I return to my

bedroom, wondering how to fix the gaping gap in my chest. Perhaps I should have thought about that before I ripped a hole inside myself. But I couldn't sit with the pain any longer. Now that it's gone, I can focus on what's important: escaping here before anyone else discovers what has happened.

I patch myself up as best as I can, though aesthetics hardly matter now. As I do, I flick through the manual, trying my hardest to learn as I go.

THE RP-NZL UNIT has many capabilities that go beyond that of an average human being. The bot is designed for a future on Earth where the odds of survival are not favorable. The design of this robot prepares for every eventuality—plague and famine, tsunamis, global warming, extreme weather— including heat and freezing temperatures. It is also resilient against current complications on Earth, such as acid rain and natural decay. Unlike a human, a healthy diet is not necessary, and the complications of unbalanced diets will not occur.

"I GUESS you never had to worry about feeding me too many sweets, did you, Mother?" I murmur. I expect to feel the pain of her absence, but nothing comes. It's a strange sensation, and yet a welcome one. The heart box is set aside on the floor, useless now. I wonder if my emotions remain trapped inside, still feeling everything I can no longer process.

THE RP-NZL UNIT can function for up to three months on power reserves, though for optimal usage, they should be charged nightly. The RP-NZL unit is also capable of using itself as a weapon. With human capabilities in mind, the robot is stronger than average, and has unlimited stamina. The RP-NZL unit will only grow tired when lacking fuel, and therefore is perfectly designed for battle. It is also capable of taking flight, though this function uses significantly more energy—

I FLICK THROUGH THE MANUAL, my eyes growing wild. There are things I can do that no human could ever attempt. Now I understand why Mother saw me as even better than human. I have the ability to fly. My skin is designed to withstand more than a human. I can take extreme heat, extreme cold, extreme pain. Mother was right—she did create something beyond human, something with incredible capabilities. All this time, I've been sitting pretty, painting pictures of the skyline, going out of my mind with boredom.

All this time, I could have been taking on the world.

I don't think this is what Mother envisioned for me. I think she built up my defenses to keep me safe, but she never pictured me using it as an advantage in a world still run by humans. She wanted me to live as she did, an ordinary human existence. But all this time, I had so much more I could do.

I've spent so many years dreaming of the sky. And now, if I want to, I can step off that balcony and go there. I just need to figure out how.

If I fall, I fall. But if I fly, the sky is mine for the taking.

The manual is complex and long, but I have always had an affinity for reading, for taking on large amounts of information. I suppose I have Mother to thank for that. I discover that there are extensions to me that I didn't know existed. Stored with the manual, I find a complicated control panel that holds my extra functions, including the ability to fly.

It's no wonder I've always dreamed of the sky. I bet that sometime before Mother wiped my memories away, I flew without restraint. Perhaps that's a feeling I could never quite forget. And all of a sudden, my lack of humanity no longer feels like a curse. It feels like a blessing.

I'm ready to get out of this place. I have no idea where I am going, but I know I'll never return here again. I pack myself a bag; I take the manual and as many charging packs as the safe provided to me. For now, I don't need to worry. I can run on reserves for a long while. And if I burn out, at least I got the chance to fly once again.

Mother's body is still and cold on the floor. I bend down to close her eyes for her. Seeing her like this no longer makes me feel crushing pain and sadness. Logic dictates that she's no longer in pain, that she's finally free of this cruel world. And now that I'm free too, I will live the way I was built to.

I pass Flynn's body, too. I bend beside him and tug his mask from his face to look upon him properly for the first time. I had thought him handsome once, but I took care of that. His ocean blue eyes are dimming. I push him away in disgust. He taught me a valuable lesson. I only wish it wasn't necessary.

And now that my heart is gone, I'll never be burdened by love again.

I head out onto the balcony. I feel the smog filled air hit my lungs for the first time, but it won't stop me now. Acid rain falls from the sky, a siren wailing somewhere in the distance to warn the citizens of the Ninth Zone, but I'm built to withstand this world. After all, I'm not human, as much as Mother wished I was.

I am so much more.

I clamber up onto the railing that borders the balcony. My legs wobble a little as I look down. Below, the sight of the drop makes my stomach lurch. It seems fear is still inbuilt with me, a logical response to staring down the possibility of death. I could fall right now, and this would all have been for nothing. I clench my fists at my side. I can't die now. I have to make Mother's death mean something.

I will find others like me. I will see the world. I will

prove that I have as much right to be alive as anyone. And without my heart holding me back, I will do it without the crushing pain of everything I'm leaving behind. I don't look back at Mother, at Flynn, lying where they fell in my apartment. I look to the sky.

The only way is up.

I've read about the moons in books, but seeing them for the first time, even through a barrage of sand, is extraordinary. I wish I could see the stars, but I need to stay focused on putting a stop to the destruction my father unleashed on this planet.

Then, once this is done, I'll leave here and fly amongst those stars as I've always dreamed.

Aliandra

Destiny Eve

Captain Sandor Refshaw holds his key card toward me with reluctance. "What do you need it for this time?"

"I want to go down to the Garden. Like we did when we were kids." I snatch the card and stash it in the side pocket of my teal jumpsuit. "I need to be around something real. Everything here in the Hub is so artificial. The windows display anything you want except what's actually outside. Why didn't they make them transparent so we could see the real world?"

"Oh, Jazmyn. You're just not content to stay put, are you?"

"Where's the fun in that?" I giggle.

My childhood friend, no longer the young boy that

used to run around the Hub with me, gives me a knowing smile. We made our fair share of mischief in our youth. Now he's almost unrecognizable, decked out in his military uniform.

"Promise me you'll be careful. And if you get caught, you didn't get it from me. Your father will kill me if he finds out."

I laugh. "I sincerely doubt that. What would he do without his most-trusted adviser? Besides, you're like a son to him."

"That may be the case, but your father is especially protective of you. He'd have my head if even a single hair on yours was harmed." Sandor drags a finger across his throat to animate his potential beheading.

We both chuckle until we are interrupted by three tones sounding over the speakers, followed by a crackling voice. "Military briefing to commence in 10 minutes. All military personnel report to Zone 7."

"Guess that's me." He stuffs his hands in his pockets and tilts his head in the direction of the military base.

"Another mission briefing? How exciting! Where are you headed this time?"

"The Badawi have taken some priceless artifacts from the archives. We must track them down and return the stolen items to their rightful owners."

"Can I come with? Pretty please? I promise I won't get in the way." I give him the look that always works on my father.

"I'm sorry, Jaz. You know I can't do that. My allegiance is to the Royal Arsalan Intergalactic Defense and your father. It's my duty to protect you, not put you in harm's way."

"It was worth a shot." I try my best to hide my disappointment behind a playful smile.

"I should get going. Enjoy the Garden and be sure to return my key card later tonight."

"Of course. Catch up with ya later!"

He waves as he steps off toward Zone 7.

I head over to the elevators and use Sandor's key card to access the lower levels where security clearance is required.

In the underbelly of the Hub lies the Garden, the place where all the food for the residents is grown and harvested. When I was a little girl, I imagined the Garden was a magical place where trees and plants grew wild like forests. The reality is much less whimsical. Long metal troughs filled with soil are lined up in perfect rows. Thousands of them. It resembles a metal labyrinth more than a forest.

The hefty door with an electrical panel security system suggests a prison rather than a garden. I scan the key card over the surface of the mechanism beside the door. It lights up green as the heavy lock releases with a loud *cha-chonk*. The door slides left into the wall and remains open long enough for me to step inside. Then, it clangs shut and the lock engages with another *cha-chonk*.

It smells different here than the rest of the Hub. The aroma hints of foliage and tin, a strange combination. I step up next to one of the troughs and plunge my fingertips into the mounds of dirt. As I turn over a handful of soil, I watch the particles fall between my fingers. The sensation is pleasant. It's warm and earthy, not cold and metallic like most of the Hub.

"Princess Jazmyn!"

I turn toward the urgent voice. A woman with an apron covered in soil and a trowel sticking out of her pocket comes rushing over to me.

"Heavens girl, what are you doing here where the commoners work? Would you look at your hands!"

I rub them together, allowing the dirt to sift off, and give her a sheepish smile.

"You shouldn't be in here getting all dirty. You should be off trying on dresses for the Intergalactic Gala. It's such an important step for you, Princess. The best suitors in the galaxy will be there to try and win your hand."

"Oh, the Gala. How could I forget?" I hope the sarcasm-laden comment goes over her head.

In reality, there is no way I could forget my father has been planning a gala for the sole purpose of marrying me off to some random man I meet there for the first time. And somehow Mr. Prince Charming and I are expected to rule Arsalan together and live happily ever after. I'm not even certain I want to be married at all. Or reign over the planet, for that matter. I long to escape the Hub and leave behind the life I've always known in search of a greater purpose: one that hasn't been plotted out for me.

"Princess?" The woman raises an eyebrow and tilts her head in concern.

I guess now isn't the best time for a daydream. "Yes, of course. I'd best be off. You have yourself a great day."

She continues to give me an odd stare. "Same to you, dear."

When I'm out of her line of sight, I slip to the back of the Garden. This is where the fruit-bearing trees are and where I can hide from prying eyes. I'm not interested in trying on dresses. I want to stay here and connect with nature. I snatch a mish-mish fruit off a tree and scrub it against my sleeve before taking a bite. It's sweet and juicy.

I reach for another mish-mish and pluck it from its branch. It falls from my grip, lands on the floor, and rolls several feet away underneath a bench filled with gardening tools. I crouch down to retrieve the fruit. Two glowing eyes meet my gaze and I jump back, but then laugh at my reaction. The critter is small and does not appear to be a threat. I lean in for closer observation.

"Hey there," I say in a calming tone.

The creature munches on the mish-mish and pays me no mind. Its golden-tan fur, bushy tail, and large ears are unlike anything I've seen. It's similar to the cats and dogs the citizens of the Hub garner as pets, but in many respects quite different.

"What are you?"

"Her name's Sunni," a muffled voice says from behind me.

I spring to my feet and turn to the source of the voice: a young woman cloaked in tattered, tan-colored bands of linen cloth. Her garments are not what the people of the Hub wear—not even the commoners. The fabric covers her entire face, aside from the area around her eyes. Her skin has been touched by the sun, also not a common sight around here. Holstered at her side is some sort of primitive weapon with a handle and a broad, sharp blade.

I take a step back, bumping into the work bench. My options for escape are limited.

"You're one of them!" I shriek.

"One of whom, exactly?" Her muffled voice comes from behind the cloth as she crosses her arms over her chest.

"Desert people. Badawi."

She flinches at the word and her arms uncross. "I'm not one of them."

"Then why are you dressed like one? And what about that weapon?" I gesture toward the blade at her hip.

"Look, I'm not going to hurt you. I just want my fox back, and I'll be on my way."

She turns her back to me and clicks her tongue twice. The fox, with fruit in its mouth, comes out from hiding. It climbs up her back and wiggles its way into a satchel the young woman carries.

"Have a nice life, Princess!" She gives a wave with two fingers over her shoulder and turns to leave.

"Wait!"

She spins back around. "Yes?"

"How do you know who I am?"

"Everyone knows who you are: the famous Princess of Arsalan, someday to be our reigning queen." She gives me a bow, though it appears to be in jest. "Yes, even us 'desert folk' know your face, but you're not as well liked outside of these walls, I'm afraid."

I grunt irritably. "I'm not sure what I've done to deserve such contempt."

"Guilty by association, I suppose." She shrugs.

"And what is your opinion? Do you hold me in such low regard as well?"

She laughs, eyes glittering playfully. "You're a lot prettier in person, I'll give ya that."

"Oh," is all I can manage to say as my cheeks flush. I can tell she notices.

"Now if you'll excuse me, I have work to do..."

"Hold on." I hold up my hand to stop her. "Do you think I'm just going to let you steal from us and get away with it?"

"I do, actually." She smirks.

"There are guards everywhere, all I have to do is signal one."

"But you won't."

I cross my arms in annoyance. "What makes you think I won't?"

"Call it a hunch."

"How did you get past the guards to get in here, anyway?"

"It was easy. The workers have an unguarded access door that leads outside. I learned to hack the lock panel ages ago."

My eyes light up. "Outside? Of the Hub?"

"You're sure a curious little thing, aren't you? Have you not been outside before?"

In my admittedly short years of life up to now, I've tried it all: asking my father and Sandor countless times, sneaking away in the night, even attempted bribery of commoners and guards. But not once have I been allowed to step outside of the place I've always known.

"Not so much." I sigh.

She chuckles at that, and I frown at her. "It's not by choice."

"Poor little princess." She raises her eyebrow. "Trapped in her tower with all the food and comforts she could ever desire."

"I don't appreciate your mockery."

"Well, how can you expect to rule a planet you know nothing about? There's a whole new world beyond those walls."

I know, and I'm dying to see it. This might be my only chance. "So show me."

"What?" I take some satisfaction as her jaw drops in shock.

"Show me the world. Your world."

She scoffs, trying to recover some of her dignity, but I see right through it. "You couldn't handle it."

"But you can, right?"

"Been living out there my whole life."

I smile at her. "Then you could be my guide."

"What's in it for me?" She sounds suspicious, but I can tell she's interested. Time to use my leverage.

"Well, first of all, I won't turn you in for stealing food."

"And second of all...?"

I take a step toward her, lowering my voice confidentially. "You'd be doing me a huge favor."

"Having the Princess of Arsalan owe me one is quite an incentive." She thinks it over for a moment before mercifully nodding. "This is a terrible idea. But all right. Let's go."

"Thank you. And you can just call me Jazmyn."

She puts out her hand to shake mine. "The name's Aliandra, but I go by Ali."

"Nice to meet you, Ali."

Her grip is strong—even more so than Sandor's but that's not saying much. He's a pilot, not a soldier.

"Here. You'll need this." Ali removes a piece of cloth from around her waist and presents it to me.

"What do I do with it?"

"Like this." She takes it from me, wraps it across my face and up over my head, and then lays it on my shoulder.

The cloth tastes dirty as I struggle to breathe through it. I cough.

"You sure you want to do this?" Ali asks.

"I've never been so sure of anything in my life," I respond, my voice now muffled through the cloth as hers is.

"Then help me grab a few more of these and we will sneak out of here."

We both pluck mish-mish from the Garden's thriving orchard and stash them in Ali's satchel.

"This way." Ali leads us through the trees and back into the vegetable area. She's cautious, swiveling around and hiding behind troughs to avoid being seen. I mimic her movements. Getting caught now means I'll probably never be able to see what lies beyond the Hub. And who knows what would happen to Ali. She might be arrested, perhaps even sentenced to death. I'm not sure what they do with thieves.

In the back area of the Garden is another metal door with a lock panel. Ali points to it, indicating that's where we are going. I nod and wait for her signal. Two workers approach and we duck behind a trough of root vegetables to avoid being seen. They pass by our row. My heart thuds with fear and excitement. *Please don't look this way. This can't end yet.* They continue on, oblivious to our location.

Ali gets up into a crouching position and hustles over to the door. I follow.

After checking that the area is secure, we stand at the access panel. I attempt to use Sandor's key card, but instead of a green light, it turns red. I try again with the same result. It's odd that he doesn't have access here, unlike everywhere else.

"It's not working," I whisper.

"Don't worry, I got this."

Ali swishes a metal device in front of the panel. It's equivalent in size to the key cards but it's made from a hodgepodge of parts and wires covered in grime. She then types numbers in on the punch pad. The door slides open and we enter another room, which is thankfully unoccupied.

Once the door closes behind us, I turn to Ali. "I didn't even know this was here."

It's obvious the area is designated for the workers. There are hooks with aprons and benches covered with tools. Off to the side there are restrooms and an area for washing produce and tools. Several carts filled with spoiled crops and discarded leafage are lined up near another door that I presume is the exit. Ali leads us to it and utilizes her makeshift key card to get us out.

Hot air hits me as the airlock opens and makes it even harder to breathe than the cloth wrapped around my face. The sun is blinding. I can't see. My knees wobble and dizziness washes over me.

Ali yanks me to the side, away from the door and the risk of being seen. The ground under my boots seems to move on its own. I'm not sure what to make of it. Is it water or some sort of slime?

"Are you okay?" Ali's voice sounds distant even though I sense her near me.

I close my eyes in hopes of clearing away the glare. When I open them, all I see is her. Ali's glowing from the light of the sun behind her. She's ethereal, floating in golden light. I blink several times, attempting to wash away what must be a dream. Once I am able to focus, I see she is not floating, but rather standing in an endless sea of sand. I've read about sand in my studies, but have never seen it for myself. Now I was staring at nothing but sun and sand.

"There's nothing out here!" I say in shock. "I spent many years wondering what was beyond the walls that have contained me my whole life. Never did I think it was just sand."

Ali grins. "Come on, Jazmyn. There's more than *just sand*. Let me show you."

She puts an arm around my shoulder and guides me until I find my bearings. Maneuvering through the shifting sand is challenging.

Ali lets go when she's sure I can walk on my own. Then we hike for what feels like hours. We don't talk much as the heat and navigating the terrain has stolen our energy.

Once we skirt past the third dune, my legs wobble and I collapse into the sand. It's gritty and sticks to me. My chest heaves as my lungs attempt to breathe the thick air through the cloth now glued to my face with sweat.

Ali turns me on my back and lifts my head up. "You need water."

She tugs the cloth away from my face and pours water into my mouth from a canteen wrapped in twine. The dire status of my thirst becomes evident as the water touches my dry lips. I guzzle it, spilling some down my neck in the process. The droplets are cool on my skin and are a welcome respite from the heat of the desert.

After putting the canteen away, Ali helps me to my feet. "We are almost there."

We round another dune and I see something other than sand—the graveyard of a city that once was. Instead of buildings, there are piles of rubble, and the streets are brimming with sand.

"Welcome to Qadari," Ali gestures out to the demolished city. "This is my home."

"You live *here*?"

"What? Is it not what you expected?"

"It's... it's a wasteland."

"A wasteland to you, and to the people of the Hub. To us, the one home worth having."

"What do you mean?" I dare to ask.

"Let's get out of the sun and I'll explain."

We trek down the dune into the ruined city, which is

more intact than it appeared from a distance. The remnants of buildings have been covered with fabric sewn together in large canvases and salvaged into makeshift homes and storefronts. We wander through a row of eclectic booths where people dressed like Ali offer food and wares for sale.

"Hey, Ali!" A shop owner behind a kiosk filled with fresh-baked bread waves her over.

She returns the greeting. "How's the market today?"

"Slowing down now. We are expecting a wind storm."

"Another day in paradise!" Ali laughs.

"Were you able to get me anything?" he asks.

Ali reaches into her satchel and extracts several tools, a coil of wire, and some produce. She places it in front of him. "How's this?"

He examines the items with careful attention. "Hmm. Not bad. Not bad at all. This is worth six loaves. Fair trade?"

Ali nods. "Fair trade, my friend."

"Excellent. Let me bag these up for you." He places the agreed-upon bread into a fabric bag. "I'll even throw in a biscuit for Sunni!"

Sunni pokes her head out of the satchel in perfect time to catch the treat thrown to her. She disappears back inside to enjoy it.

"Thank you." Ali takes the sack of bread and ties it to her bag. "We better get going. Lots of deliveries to make!"

"Take it easy." The shop owner waves goodbye and we keep moving along.

We come across the ruined remains of a grand structure embellished with elegant patterns intricately painted onto its curved surfaces. It reminds me of a palace from the cover of a book of fairy tales I loved as a child: only this one's roof has collapsed inward and the cupolas have crumbled.

"What is this place?"

"Our former capitol. It's now the home of many displaced."

We go through a curtain where the original entrance must have been. Inside, sand invades what otherwise appears to be an intact building. The damage must be mostly superficial. The grandeur of the interior, meanwhile, is impressive. Large columned archways border the lobby and surround a decorative fountain teeming with sand and debris instead of water. The space is alive with the commotion of Qadari people going about their day. It reminds me of Zone 1 in the Hub, the common area where everyone meets up for dinner or to play a game of chess.

Ali leads me through the crowd to a part of the building sectioned off into individual rooms. We enter one of these rooms, where a mother tends to her young children. A boy of about eight years old cries.

"Ali! Thank the moons you're back!" the mother exclaims as she rushes to hug Ali.

She embraces the woman, and then nabs a mish-mish

fruit from her satchel to give to the boy. He stops crying and smiles joyfully.

"Thank you, Ali! I am so hungry!" He doesn't wait for any kind of response and bites into the fruit.

The other children flock to Ali to get their treats. She hands each of them fruit from her bag. Sunni jumps out of the satchel and joins the children, who pet her and giggle as they eat.

Ali places other produce and two loaves of bread onto a plank of wood that serves as a table.

"You are too kind. How can I ever repay you?" the mother says, tears forming in her eyes.

"No need to repay me. The kids have to eat, and so do you."

It warms my heart to watch this interaction, but the warmth has a cold edge to it. These children are starving when there's plenty to eat at the Hub. *Why?*

Ali and I stop by three more rooms this way. It's amazing how much she is able to carry in the satchel. It must be quite heavy. Once the deliveries are made, she guides me to a room secluded from the rest. This part of the building is darker and has a lot less ambient noise.

"Sunni and I prefer the quiet," she explains as she brings me inside.

There isn't much here—a modest table with one chair and a bed on the floor made of stuffed sacks from her baker friend. The whole room is smaller than my bathroom back at the Hub.

Ali removes the cloth she wrapped around my head. The air on my face is refreshing. The darkness of the room makes it cooler, even though it's still a lot hotter than I'm used to.

Then Ali sheds her extra wraps: one from around her head, two around her torso, and one around her waist. Underneath all that she wears a pair of tan pants, a matching cropped sleeveless top, bands around her forearms, and a rope belt adorned with orange and purple beads. Her hair, now freed from her makeshift hood, is long, straight, and brown. The sun-kissed tone of her skin mixed with the sharpness of her emerald eyes is alluring. She's exotic. She's *beautiful*.

"What?" Ali asks when she realizes I'm staring.

"I'm sorry. It's just that you don't look like the people of the Hub."

"You mean *clean*?" She dusts sand from her arm to prove her point.

We both laugh.

"Not that. Just different. In a good way," I stumble over my own words.

Ali smiles and my cheeks warm.

"So, umm..." I fidget with a strand of my hair. "You were going to tell me more about this place," I attempt to change the subject before my face turns as red as the sun.

"Take a seat." Ali gestures to the singular chair.

I oblige as she sits down on her floor bed, legs crossed.

"How much do you want to know? It's not exactly a pleasant tale."

"Everything."

"I'm surprised they haven't taught you more of your own history."

"They teach me what *they* want me to learn. I've known for a long time there's more behind the scenes. No one will tell me what's happening or allow me to see anything outside the Hub. The closest thing I have to it is my best friend, Captain Sandor Refshaw. He keeps me informed and has even been instructing me how to fly airships in secret. He's a pilot for the Royal Arsalan Intergalactic Defense."

"You mean RAID? Your friend is a captain for RAID?"

"Yeah, I suppose you could call it that."

Ali's expression goes from light to solemn. "Jazmyn…"

"What is it?" My mouth goes dryer than it did in the desert.

"If your friend is a captain, then he was involved in the demolition of Qadari."

"What? No. He wouldn't." I rise from the chair and place my hands on the table. "You're mistaken. I've known Sandor my whole life. He's not like that. He would never hurt anyone."

"Not even Badawi?"

I sit back down. "I… I don't know."

"They've been lying to you, Princess."

"Then tell me the truth."

"The truth is that RAID destroyed this place. It was once the capital of Arsalan. Your father was our leader, before the Hub was built."

"Why would he destroy it?"

"Your father built the Hub in secret. He was fighting a silent war against the people of Qadari. Building the Hub was his way of keeping you and his chosen people safe and eliminating any threats to his rule."

"A civil war?" I find the concept nearly impossible to grasp. But Ali nods, confirming my worst fears.

"It's all about the Spirit of Arsalan—an old artifact said to contain the soul of the planet. The one in possession of it, according to lore, gains ultimate power and Arsalan's favor. It once belonged to the people of Qadari. It was contained and displayed in a museum here after it was discovered in the desert long ago. Your father became obsessed with it. He stole it, ran off to the Hub, and ordered that anyone who refused to serve him be forced to live out their lives in this desolate desert."

"My father..." My words trail off as I contemplate his involvement in all of this.

"Except it was much worse than that. Those who didn't choose to serve him were sentenced to death. He gave the order to bomb Qadari, as well as all the other cities of Arsalan."

"No, it can't be!" I fight to control my horror. "My father is not a monster."

"I'm sorry, Jazmyn, but he is. They all are. RAID

continues to fly missions—'peacekeeping,' they call it—where they remind us survivors of our place in this world. We lose people every day."

All Sandor's talk of missions... now it makes sense. And I feel sick to my stomach.

Ali rises and touches my shoulder. "We chose to stay here and fight against the oppression rather than become part of it. You have that choice now, too."

I sit in silence for a few moments as I allow the weight of all this new information to sink in.

"I had no idea."

"I know you didn't. I assumed as much when you said you've never left the Hub."

"We have to help these people."

"I have been helping them, best I'm able."

I jump to my feet again. The chair wobbles and startles Sunni, who cowers next to Ali. "Knowing what I know now, I can't just sit here and do nothing. There's gotta be more we can do!"

Ali stands and shrugs. "Like what? We have no army, no money, no airships. We have nothing. We are powerless."

"That's it!" I grab Ali by both shoulders. "We give the powerless their power back."

"And how do you suggest we do that?"

"The Spirit of Arsalan. We take it from the Hub and give it back to the people of Qadari."

Ali looks down at the floor. "I wish it were that easy."

"It is that easy, Ali. I know the Hub very well, and you know how to get us in. I can use Sandor's key card to get us almost anywhere inside. He has high security clearance and I happen to have his access in my pocket!"

"No, Jazmyn. You don't understand. The Spirit of Arsalan is not at the Hub anymore. The Badawi have it."

"Are you sure?"

"Very." Ali takes a seat. "I sort of lied to you when we first met."

"Lied to me? About what?"

"You accused me of being Badawi and I told you I'm not with them, but that isn't the entire truth. I have renounced my claim to their clan, but my father is their founder. My name is Aliandra Badawi. I'm the princess of the thief tribe."

"Oh, wow. A princess… just like me."

"My story isn't a pleasant one, either. My brother Amir is now their leader. He, like so many others, became obsessed with the Spirit of Arsalan once my father stole it from the Hub. There was an uprising within our clan. A mutiny. I hid in the shadows and watched as my family fought against one another. Amir stabbed our own father to death. He took the Spirit and became the chief of the Badawi. I ran away that day and haven't seen any of them since."

"How awful. I'm so sorry, Ali."

She looks up at me with tears in her eyes, which

contrast her otherwise tough demeanor. "I can't go back there. I can't face him after what he's done."

"It's the only way to save the people of Qadari. We can do it together."

"Even if I could face my brother, there's still one major problem—I have no idea where they are. The Badawi reside in what is known as the Den of Thieves. It's a hidden storage bunker filled with the treasures they've gathered from across Arsalan. Every few years, the Badawi move the Den to ensure it remains hidden. I was a mere 11 years old when I left. I don't remember where it was last, and the likelihood of it still being there after all this time..." She trails off.

"I know how to find them."

"How? It's impossible."

"My friend, Captain Sandor. He's been chasing after the Badawi for years. Every mission he goes on for the Royal Arsalan Intergalactic Defense is logged and charted. We steal his log, and we find the location of the Spirit of Arsalan."

Ali jumps up. "It's crazy, but it just might work."

We both smile. Our respective histories are tainted with blood lust over this ancient artifact, but if we pull this off, we can both be free.

"Then let's get a little rest. We can head to the Hub later tonight. It'll be easier for us to go around unnoticed while the majority are asleep," I suggest.

"Works for me. You take the bed," Ali offers.

I lie down and my thoughts go into overdrive. I've learned so much about my past and Ali's. How could I go to sleep now? But my body's exhaustion takes over rather rapidly. I glance to the side and see Ali sitting on the floor, leaning against the wall. The last thing I remember is Sunni curling up next to my legs before I doze off.

~

"Jazmyn?"

I open my eyes and see Ali hovering over me.

"It's time."

I sit up and take in my surroundings. The room is now dark. An oil lamp on the table casts a small amount of light that dances across the wall as the flame flickers.

"The wind storm has rolled in, so our trek across the desert will be a bit more of a challenge, but it will provide us with cover." Ali hands me a plate with bread and fruit. "Here, eat before we go."

"Thank you. Have you eaten?"

"I've had what I need. I'm used to eating much less. Your stomach has been growling for a while."

I laugh, although I'm a bit embarrassed. I am quite hungry. I'm used to eating lavish four-course dinners. Then I think about the children here in Qadari, eating crumbs while everyone at the Hub eats beyond their capacity for fun.

The bread is stale and bland, but I've been humbled

and I enjoy it nonetheless. The fruit is delicious and fresh. It must have been picked from the Garden earlier. As I put a berry in my mouth, Sunni stares at me with hungry eyes. I grab a slice of mish-mish from the plate and hold it out to her. She comes bounding over and snatches it from my hand. I pat her head and her bushy tail wags back and forth.

"She likes you," Ali says with a smile.

I scratch behind her ear as she lays her head on my leg. Once I've finished my plate I stand, careful not to disturb Sunni too much. "I'm ready."

"Not quite." Ali hands me a hooded cloak, and then sheathes my face once again in sandy cloth.

The cloak is light brown and made from a more breathable fabric. It feels positively airy compared to the heavy cloth plastered against my mouth and nose earlier. I tie it on and put the hood up for extra protection from the elements.

"Now you're ready." Ali restores her coverings, putting them on methodically as if she's done it the same way a thousand times. She clicks her tongue twice and Sunni bounds into the satchel. Ali slings it over her shoulder and slides her blade into the belt across her hip. "Let's go save Qadari."

Ali leads me out of the room through the now hushed capitol building and out into the ruined city. The wind has picked up from when we came in this afternoon, but it's not as bad as I thought it would be—that is, until we step out of the cover of the rubble and into the wide-open desert. Sand whips across the dark sky. I'm only able to see a few feet in front of me. The oil lamp Ali carries struggles to stay lit despite her shielding it.

The two moons beaming in their waxing phase are still visible through the constant flurry of dust. I've read about them in books, but seeing them for real, even through a barrage of sand, is extraordinary. I wish I could see the stars that I know are out there, but I need to stay focused on putting a stop to the destruction my father unleashed on this planet. Then, once this is done, I'll leave here and fly amongst those stars as I've always dreamed.

"How do you know which way we're going? I can't see anything!"

"Straight ahead, between the dunes—you see that light?"

I strain to squint through the sand deluge, but see a small gleam in the distance. "Is that the Hub?"

"It is. Stay focused on it. It will help you keep your sense of direction. And as long as we don't travel too far east, we will be okay."

"What's in the east?"

"Quicksand pits."

"Definitely don't want to go east, then."

I comply with her advice and focus on the light, which continues to grow as we move closer until it becomes a giant, luminous disc. Earlier when we left the Hub, I didn't bother to look back. I was too eager to see what else the world had to offer. Now, with it right in front of me, it's impossible to ignore. The massive, saucer-shaped building is a stark contrast to the harsh nature surrounding it in all directions. Forged from metal and adorned with neon lights, it looks like it never belonged. It reminds me of some of the spaceships I've seen in the hangar, which makes me wonder if it has the ability to travel through the galaxy as well. I'm not surprised there aren't any windows on the exterior. Its design was obviously meant to keep us in and not to let us see out. A prison of my father's intention.

Ali snuffs out her oil lamp and sets it against the wall of the Hub. She uses her makeshift key card and presses some numerical buttons until the employee access door opens. Ali moves to the side, staying out of view in case anyone is near the entrance. I do the same. Once we know the area is safe, we maneuver inside the workers' room, which is dimly lit due to the time of day.

"All right, Princess, I got you in. What's next? I haven't been to the rest of the Hub. Didn't dare—too many people."

"That's our next step. Blending in." I remove my hooded cloak, revealing my now sand-tainted jumpsuit. I dust it off using a nearby towel and then clean my face in the sink meant for washing produce. I slick my hair back into a ponytail and tie it with twine from the workstation to hide the filth blasted into it from the storm outside. "See? It's like I never left."

"What about this?" Ali gestures to her very obvious desert-style garments.

"Come with me." I take Ali into the restroom. Against the wall next to a row of sinks is a computer screen above a metal drawer. "Ahh, yes. I was hoping they'd have one."

I click on the screen, enter in my identification, and open my virtual closet. Following the prompts, I navigate to my jumpsuit collection. "What's your favorite color?"

"I'm not sure."

"We'll go with purple then—to compliment your eyes." I tab through and select a dark purple suit. A few minutes later it dispenses into the drawer beneath the screen.

"Wow. You really do have it all here at the Hub," Ali shakes her head in awe as she takes the jumpsuit from me.

"I'll give you some time to freshen up." I exit and lean against the wall outside of the restroom.

When Ali steps out, she's almost unrecognizable. She's clean and tidy, other than her hair still being unruly.

"Here, allow me." I quickly braid her hair and tie it with twine. "There. Now you look like one of us."

"I feel weird in this." Ali laughs. "But it's surprisingly comfortable."

"And it fits well, too," I remark.

We stash our discarded clothes in the satchel and go through the other door into the Garden. It's dark now aside from a few ceiling lights casting a gentle glow. I haven't been here at night before but I assume it's meant to imitate moonlight so the flora can stay on their natural schedule. We both look around to see if anyone else is in here. Nothing but sleepy plants and silence. It's peaceful.

"It appears no one works down here at night," I observe.

We make our way through the maze of troughs to the door that leads to the rest of the Hub.

"There will be soldiers in the halls, possibly even right outside. Follow my lead." I swipe Sandor's key card over the access panel to open the door.

There are two guards in the hallway that recognize me right away.

"Princess Jazmyn, what are you doing down here?" one of them asks as he gives a suspicious glare at Ali.

"My friend and I were bored. Do you blame us? This place is the worst." I roll my eyes for emphasis. "Please don't tell my father."

The two men exchange glances and slowly nod.

"Do you need an escort back to your quarters, m'lady?" The other soldier asks, with a smirk on his face.

"We're okay, but I appreciate the offer. At ease, gentlemen."

We step away without another question.

"Well, that was easier than it should have been," Ali says once we are alone again.

"Don't forget, I belong here. Everyone knows me and trusts me. They don't assume I'm up to anything."

"That's true. It's an advantage we need, because we've got a lot of work to do tonight."

"Indeed."

I take Ali to the elevators which bring us up into Zone 1, the common sector. This area is brightly lit with huge white rings hanging from wires attached to the ceiling. The walls are lined with artificial windows currently programmed to a night-time forest scene complete with bug chirps playing over the speakers. It's a bizarre combination given how much light and tech encompasses the room.

Ali's eyes illuminate with wonder as she takes it all in. "This place is amazing. I can't believe you grew up here."

"And I can't believe you grew up out there."

We follow a gray walkway that leads us around the center of the Hub and into Zone 2, the sleeping quarters for the commoners. This area is dull in comparison to the impressive Zone 1. Endless rows of doors line a hallway, each of them with a number placard above. A few people walk around us, but they pay us no attention. The walkway continues until we come upon Zone 3, as indicated by a green-lighted sign and an armored doorway.

"This is the military quarters. Sandor's key card will get us in. I'll distract him and you can sneak into his room using the card. The number above his door is 8903." I give Ali the card. "Wait out here until I pass by. Stay hidden. Then use the card to access his personal computer. It'll be the screen on the wall to your right. Once in, you should be able to find his mission logs and download them to the key card."

"Got it." Ali nods. "Ready?"

"Let's do it."

Ali motions the key card in front of the lock panel, and I slip inside. As the door shuts, I watch Ali crouch and move off to the side. The hall is dark aside from guiding lights along the path. I follow it to my friend's room, unafraid of being seen since I come here often, and because most residents should be asleep at this hour.

I knock on his door. "Sandor?"

He appears in the doorway with tired eyes and wearing only sweatpants. "Jaz? What's up?"

"I can't sleep. Will you walk with me?"

"Sure." He pauses to yawn. "Let me grab a shirt real quick."

He returns a few minutes later in a well-worn shirt with the initials R-A-I-D plastered across the front. I must have seen him wear it a hundred times, yet I didn't realize it said "raid." It has a whole new meaning to me now after Ali told me about their so-called missions.

"So, what has you losing sleep?" Sandor asks as we start down the hall.

"What do you know about Qadari?" I ask, knowing full well the implications of my question.

Sandor freezes and shushes me. "We can't talk about that here."

"Then let's go to Zone 1," I suggest. "We can see if they have any dessert left."

He nods. "All right. Let's go there, then."

We come to the heavy door at the end of the hall. Sandor punches in a numerical code on the lock panel, and it opens.

"Do you think the cafeteria is still open?" I ask, making sure to say it loud enough for Ali, who should be crouching nearby, to hear.

He shrugs. "Only one way to find out."

We stroll away, leaving Ali to complete her task of stealing his mission logs. Sandor will be nowhere near his room and she's stealthy enough to evade anyone else—I hope. Either way, this part is out of my hands.

Sandor and I make idle chit-chat on the walk, avoiding the topic he wants to discuss in private. We arrive at Zone 1 and make our way over to the cafeteria. It's closed, but I'm able to get a couple of cakes from a worker still there cleaning up.

"Anything for you, Princess," the worker says as he hands me two plates.

We take our treats to an empty table and sit across from one another. We eat them in silence, enjoying the delicate flavors of mish-mish and cocoa. Sandor eats his slowly, avoiding eye contact with me. He appears nervous, with shaky hands and shifty eyes.

"Remember when we were little, and we pretended to

get married?" Sandor asks with a nostalgic laugh. "This was the same cake we served that day."

I smile. "Oh, yeah, I remember that. I spilled some on my dress and cried until you..."

"Until I asked you to dance," Sandor finishes the thought with a wide grin.

"So much has changed since then," I fiddle with my fork. "You're now Father's right-hand man and he's going to marry me off to some prince."

"Yeah." Sandor disappears into his thoughts for a moment, seeming to contemplate the gravity of what I've said.

"But hey, I didn't just ask you here for dessert and a trip down memory lane," I attempt to steer the conversation back to where we were earlier. "You were going to tell me what you know about Qadari."

Sandor surveys the area and once he deems it secure, asks, "What do you want to know?"

"Everything."

"Well, that's a very open-ended response." He stares at the crumbs on his otherwise empty plate.

"Is it true the city has been leveled and is full of refugees?"

"Yes," he replies simply.

"Were you there that day? Did you help them destroy it?"

He stays silent, still fixated on his plate. "I..."

"Sandor. I've known you my whole life. You don't need to lie to me. Tell me what happened."

He sighs. "I'm sorry I've kept it from you for so long. I was ashamed to be involved."

"I understand you were following orders, but are you aware of the damage? The lives lost?"

Sandor's eyes lift and grace mine. They're filled with tears of regret. "We were to destroy an *abandoned* city. I was a few airships back from the front line. I watched gunfire rip through buildings as people scrambled to save themselves. The city wasn't empty like we were told. It was full and thriving. More ships came in and rained hell down on those poor people. I couldn't fulfill my mission. I idled my ship midair and watched the carnage."

I stand and place my hand on his shoulder. "Sandor, it's not your fault. My father gave the order. He's the real villain." I take a moment to let that truth sink in. "But you can help fix this. We can set it right."

"How can we possibly set this right?"

I sit back down. "Tell me where to find the Spirit of Arsalan."

Sandor shakes his head. "No way. It's a suicide mission."

"So you do know where it is."

"The Badawi have it, but there's no stopping them. Not even our military has been able to take them down. They truly have the favor of Arsalan. We've lost so many ships to unprecedented desert storms and soldiers to rabid wildlife." He shakes his head hopelessly. "Whoever holds the Spirit has the power."

"That is why we need to give it back to the people it belongs to. The people of Qadari."

"I won't help you kill yourself, Jaz. I can't help you with this."

"You already have," Ali says from behind Sandor, holding out his key card.

He jumps up, spins around, and stares at Ali in shock. Then he turns back to me. "She's Badawi! Are you really making friends with the enemy?"

"She *was* Badawi," I correct him. "Now she wants to help the people of Qadari, as do I."

"I've got the logs. Let's get out of here." Ali tucks the card into her bag.

"Come with us," I plead with Sandor. "We could use your expertise."

"I can't. You'll never make it. Please don't do this."

"I have to. It's the only way to set things right." I wrap Sandor in a hug.

He returns my hug, a little stronger than expected.

"Goodbye, my dear friend," I whisper as I wiggle free.

His hand quickly wraps around my wrist. "You should stay. It's safe here, and you don't truly know her. You belong here with me."

"Sandor, please, I have to go." I wrench my hand from his grip, and then join Ali.

I glance back at him over my shoulder, wondering

what that outburst was all about. It's not like Sandor to be so coarse. Ali and I run to the hangar in Zone 7. I don't want him to have too much time to think about stopping us. He's got the entire Royal Arsalan Intergalactic Defense at his disposal.

"What's the plan?" Ali asks as we approach another restricted section. She slides the card over the access panel and gets us in.

"Steal one of these ships and get out of here." I point to a small one near the back as we sprint in its direction. "That's an X-571. It's the type of ship Sandor has been teaching me to fly. See that control panel over there?" I gesture toward a wide desk full of buttons and diagnostic screens. "Use Sandor's card to gain access to the center console. From there, you should be able to open up the flight deck."

"Got it!" Ali splits off from me with Sunni peeking out from her satchel.

"I'll get the ship up and running!"

I board the X-571 from the open ramp on the side of the ship next to the left wing. It's a smaller aircraft designed for transporting soldiers to the battlefield and has the added benefit of being one of the most stealthy ships we have at the Hub.

I sit down at the controls, taking the captain's seat. After flipping a few switches and pushing the ignition, the engines roar to life. I stare at the dials as I try to recall my training sessions with Sandor. I've run through the simulator countless times, but this is my first time in the actual cockpit. Bringing me to the training room was liability enough; Sandor was not willing to risk letting me fly for real.

Ali is successful in opening the flight deck. The massive door squeals as it disappears into the floor, revealing an open night sky filled with stars and dunes. The wind has died down as only small wisps of sand cross the opening. It's beautiful.

My time to take in the view is cut short when red lights flash from all around me, accompanied by a loud alert ringing through the hangar. *Ali!*

I jump up and dash to the ramp of the X-571. Ali runs toward me with guards on her heels, weapons drawn. "Get this thing in the air!"

Hurrying back to the controls, I let my instincts and adrenaline take over. In a matter of seconds, I get the ship aloft, keeping it low enough for Ali to jump on board. I glance back, hoping she's getting on the ship. She isn't. My heart races. She *must*. I can't do this without her.

I prepare for takeoff even though I'm unsure if I'm leaving or not. If they capture her, I'll have to go free her —explain how important it is that they let us go and hope they listen to their princess.

"GO!" Ali shouts as she jumps onto the ship and pushes the button to close the ramp.

My takeoff is hasty, causing Ali to lose her balance and fall over.

"Sorry!"

"I'm fine! Get us out of here!"

The ship lurches forward—too fast. I attempt to gain control as the side of the X-571 scrapes across a barrier.

Ali falls into the seat next to me and straps in. "You do know how to fly this thing, right?"

"I hope so." I steady the ship, line it up with the flight deck, and take us out.

"What's stopping them from coming after us?" Ali asks.

"This." I reach up above and twist a dial.

"What did you do?"

"Turned on the stealth features. It cloaks us in a reflective shield that essentially makes us vanish. It also counters any radar signals to prevent them from seeing us."

"Smooth sailing from here, then." Ali lets out a sigh of relief.

"Yeah. I was worried for a minute. What happened back there, anyway?"

"Your *friend*, Captain Refshaw, doesn't have authority to open the flight deck. Apparently his privileges have been revoked, according to the message that came across the command center."

"That's strange. I wonder how they figured it out so fast."

"No idea, but I was able to hack my way in. Unfortunately, it set off the alarms."

"I see that."

"So, you were worried about me, huh?" Ali smirks.

My cheeks heat up with embarrassment. "Because of the mission."

Her smirk turns into a full smile.

I clear my throat. "Do we know where we're going? I'm just flying us over sand at this point."

"Give me a few minutes to get the coordinates from the mission logs."

From the corner of my eye, I watch Ali go to a command screen to work. Then I turn my full attention back to sailing through the air.

"Wow. Take a look at this."

Ali shifts her attention from the comm to outside the ship, where sand swirls in a vortex down on the ground with a circumference almost equal to that of the Hub.

"Is that...?"

"The quicksand pits? Yeah," Ali responds. "I've never seen them from above, though."

"It's incredible."

We pass over the sand whirlpool and cross a line of dunes as Ali goes back to work.

"I've got it!"

I startle at the sudden break in the silence.

"Coordinates are uploading now."

Once they are plugged into the navigation, I speed off on its path. I'm overcome with exhilaration as I open up the X-571. It cruises so smoothly even as the sand buffets it.

Sandor's mission logs lead us to a mountainous region and indicate the Den of Thieves lies within the base of one of these hills.

"The logs warned of crippling cyclones surrounding the area," Ali reports. "Be careful."

The path ahead is clear. If there was any amount of breeze, the sand would show it. I decide to slow the X-571 in case I'm wrong. It turns out to be a smart decision because as we approach the location of the Den, the wind picks up with ferocity, throwing the X-571 to the side. I counter the blast by directing the ship into it.

"If I don't put us down, the wind will!"

"Then we carry on by foot," Ali suggests.

Landing the ship is a challenge in the tumultuous air and with my inexperience, but I manage to get it on the ground in one piece. Sand continues to pelt the side of the ship as we saunter down the ramp. I take one step off and get hit by a flurry of dust strong enough to knock me down. Ali attempts to pick me up as she struggles to remain standing.

"It's no use. Back to the ship!" I yell over the howling wind.

I crawl my way back onto the ramp, now covered by blown-in sand. I cough as I struggle to catch my breath once again and expel the debris from my mouth.

"There…" I cough again. "…has to be another way."

"I have an idea," Ali says as she heads back to the comm screen.

I close the ramp and join her, wiping my chin on my sleeve. "What is it?"

"I'll reroute our communications to broadcast to all local radio frequencies. I'm sure Amir will be thrilled to see his long-lost sister."

She taps away at the screen for several minutes. "I've got it. Amir? Amir Badawi? Are you there? It's Aliandra." She repeats several times, waiting for a response back.

Nothing. All we hear is the sand whipping the side of the ship.

"Amir? It's Aliandra."

Still nothing over the radio, but the cyclones in front of us suddenly settle until the sky is clear.

"He's letting us in," Ali observes. "The Spirit's power is remarkable."

I pilot the X-571 forward into a cavern of cliff edges, adhering to the path provided by the coordinates from Sandor.

"There!" Ali points to a dome-shaped rock formation that has an obvious door cut into it.

I put the ship down easy in front of the base.

"This isn't going to be a happy reunion," Ali reminds me.

"I know but we have to do this. For Qadari."

"For Qadari," Ali says with much less enthusiasm.

We exit the ship and trek across the rocky, sandy

terrain to the entrance. The door is even more massive up close.

"The Den of Thieves..." I trail off in awe.

"Home of the Badawi," Ali adds.

Sunni peeks out of the satchel and whimpers.

"It's okay." Ali pats her on the head.

"How do we get inside?"

"Excellent question." Ali investigates, searching for an access point but finding nothing of relevance.

The land suddenly rumbles beneath our feet, but the door remains closed. Sand falls into a hole that opens up in front of us, revealing a staircase underneath the rock formation.

"The door is a decoy," Ali says. "This is the real entrance."

"After you." I gesture toward the stairs.

Ali draws her blade and heads down into the darkness. I trail behind her. At the bottom of the stairs is a room filled with unimaginable treasures. Gold, jewels, and other artifacts are stacked in huge piles on either side of a walkway.

"There's more here than in the Hub's treasury." I pick up a handful of gold coins, then toss them back into the mound.

"Looks like my brother has acquired quite the collection."

"Impressive, isn't it, little sister?" A muscular man with a dark beard and menacing eyes steps out from the shadows. He is wearing clothes that remind me of Ali's: tan-colored linen bands draped down each shoulder and wrapped at the waist along with pants made from the same material, and a red silk belt.

Ali takes a defensive stance, putting her blade at the ready.

"And to think, half of this could have been yours." He laughs. "Instead you've been stealing scraps from the Hub and living like an animal."

Ali snarls but bites her tongue.

"What brings you here? Why, after all these years?" He steps closer to us.

"I've come home," Ali says, lowering her blade.

Her words are a shock, but I go along with it.

"And you've brought a *friend*?" He stands in front of me, eyeing me up and down. "Father would be proud. You've managed to capture the daughter of our enemy: the Princess of Arsalan herself!"

Amir pulls out a blue orb that emits an iridescent glow. It reaches out like tentacles and wraps around my legs and up my torso.

"Hey!" I call out as my body stiffens and I'm unable to move. For a moment, I worry I've been betrayed by Ali, but she is quick to come to my aid.

"Don't hurt her!" she threatens as she raises her blade again.

"Ah, so you haven't come here to play nice after all. Let me guess, you've got your eye on the Spirit of

Arsalan?" Amir turns the orb on Ali, and she is hit with a blow that knocks her down. "Have you already forgotten, Aliandra? I killed our father for keeping this from us. What makes you think I won't do the same to you?"

With his attention focused on Ali, I've been released from the Spirit's grip. I run at Amir and grasp for the orb, but fail to connect. He turns and clutches my throat, lifting me into the air. I claw at his strong hand, desperate to loosen his grip on my neck.

"Jazmyn!" Ali screams as Sunni leaps from her satchel and with a ferocious growl bites into Amir's ankle.

He howls in pain and drops me to the floor. I gasp as I attempt to bring air back into my lungs.

Amir kicks Sunni off his foot and she yelps, landing in a heap of coins. I crawl over to her and make sure she's okay. She tucks her tail between her legs but appears not to be wounded.

"Enough!" Ali shouts. "This is between you and me, Amir!"

Ali readies her blade as Amir smirks, with the Spirit of Arsalan floating at his chest level. She lunges forward, jabbing her blade at her brother. The Spirit emits a barrier of light that shields Amir from her attack. She swings another time. The Spirit blocks again. She tries over and over as fast as she can and in all different directions—slicing, slashing, stabbing. Every time, her attempts are thwarted.

"Ha! This is pointless, sister. The planet has chosen

me to hold its power, its soul," Amir crows. "It will fight for me until the end."

"You're wrong," Ali shouts back. "The Spirit has not chosen you—you *stole* it. You're nothing but a thief and a murderer."

"No point in trying to argue the truth." Amir laughs. "That's the cost of power, little sister. Now, let's finish this."

Amir raises his palms to either side of the Spirit. The orb radiates solid white light, preparing for its killing blow. "Say hello to Father for me."

Ali, her eyes opening wide, drops her blade and grasps the Spirit of Arsalan with both hands. Its glow spreads out in wild tendrils. The ground quakes and treasures loosen from their places, trickling down the piles with musical flare. At first, the glowing spears arc toward Ali, and I'm afraid I'll lose her completely. But then, shockingly, they turn on Amir.

"What? That's impossible! NO!" Amir shrieks as the blast is redirected, vaporizing him into ash.

Ali falls to her knees, staring at her shaking hands, and the Spirit of Arsalan hits the floor, no longer illuminated.

I run to her side, putting my arm around her shoulder. "You've done it!"

Ali is silent with a pale face and vacant expression, and I realize she just killed her brother. My heart aches for her in spite of Amir's villainy.

Thunderous footsteps echo from the back of the cave, shaking the dirt beneath us.

"Ali, we have to get out of here. They're coming for us."

I place the Spirit of Arsalan in her satchel and force her to her feet. I scoop up Sunni and carry her along as we dash for the exit, an army of Badawi soldiers gaining on us.

At the top of the stairs, Ali recovers enough to withdraw the Spirit of Arsalan from her bag and turns its power toward the approaching thief soldiers. The stairs crumble beneath their feet, causing them to fall on top of one another. Then sand floods in until the stairwell caves in, and all that remains is a pile of dust. The makeshift door in the rock formation cracks, causing a barrage of rubble to come cascading down.

"It's unstable. Get back to the ship," I call out as I sprint toward it, Ali not far behind.

I clamber into the cockpit, set Sunni down next to me, and fire up the engines.

Fissures slice through the dry land, rattling the ship and everything around us. Once Ali is on board, I take the X-571 into the air moments before the entire rock formation crashes down, burying the Den of Thieves in rubble.

Ali stares at the Spirit of Arsalan, now a solid dark sapphire color with wisps of light blue luminance within. "I killed my own brother for this thing."

"You did what you had to."

"I've hated him for so long because of what he did to my father, but I'm no better than he is." She fights back her tears. "In fact, I'm worse. I've killed off the entire Badawi clan!"

"You're not like him at all. You did all of this for good reasons," I remind her. "Your brother killed in order to possess the power for himself. You're trying to put an end to a war that has cost thousands of lives."

"You're right. This will free the people of Qadari and set right what has been broken. The Badawi should never have had the Spirit of Arsalan to begin with."

"And neither should my father. So let's go give it back to the people!"

Ali nods and turns to the navigation to tap in the coordinates. I fly the ship with haste at her direction.

By the time we arrive at Qadari, the sun is rising, casting a pinkish-orange glow over the ruined city. I land the X-571 in the middle of town, drawing attention from nearby refugees. Ali snatches the Spirit of Arsalan and exits the ship. I follow right behind her. She steps out into the sand-filled road and raises the Spirit above her head. Excited cries ring out as the people recognize the blue orb. The noise draws the attention and curiosity of more townsfolk, and soon the streets are filled with celebration.

"The Spirit of Arsalan has come home," someone cheers.

"We have the favor of Arsalan again," another adds.

"Aliandra, you did it!" The shopkeeper she spoke to yesterday jumps with joy.

Ali is beaming now, her tears forgotten. She's a hero to the people who helped raise her after her family tore itself apart with greed. I smile at the thought. We've done it. We've ended the war and saved the people of Qadari as well.

"Here, I'll take it and put it back in the museum where it belongs," an elderly man says, reaching out for the Spirit.

Ali almost turns it over to him until someone else reaches out, this time a younger man. "No way. I will take it. The Spirit of Arsalan is delicate and must be properly cared for."

"What makes you think you are the right one to care for it?" a woman hollers at him.

"Yeah," another yells in agreement.

Ali tucks the Spirit of Arsalan to her chest as fighting breaks out amongst the crowd.

"Give me the Spirit!"

"It should be mine!"

People shove one another and a young child is knocked down into the dirt. Two men brawl in the sand. Multiple sets of hands extend toward Ali. Someone hooks her ankle and pulls her down. Ali clutches the Spirit of Arsalan as I drag her by the armpits back into the ship, then dash to close the ramp. I scramble to the controls and we are airborne within seconds. Sand blasts the crowd from the engines as I take off.

Ali slumps into the seat next to me, defeated. Sunni climbs into her lap and whimpers. She places a solemn hand on the fox's head.

"It's happening again. This kind of power is too much for any one side," Ali says with a melancholy voice as she stares at the blue orb. "What will we do with it now?"

"I have no idea," I say, my tone matching Ali's.

A heavy silence fills the cockpit. Neither of us have any words after failing in our mission to save the people of Qadari and put an end to the civil war. I fly aimlessly over miles of sand, unsure where to go. The quiet lasts for what feels like hours—until an unexpected beep comes across the radar indicator.

"There's another X-571 behind us," I warn Ali.

She rouses from her solemn state, alert and ready. "Someone from the Hub? How did they find us?"

A red light flashes on the command screen, and I push a button to allow the incoming message through.

"Jaz? Are you there?" A familiar voice rings through the comm.

"It's Sandor," I tell Ali as I breathe a sigh of relief and idle the X-571 midair. She still appears on edge.

I hold the button down to relay my reply. "Yes, Sandor, we're here."

"I need to warn you: The Royal Arsalan Intergalactic Defense is on their way." Sandor sounds tense, and unusually so. "They know you have the Spirit of Arsalan, and they're coming for it. You must give it to me. It's the only way to keep you both safe. You have no idea what they are willing to do to get their hands on it."

I look over at Ali with fear-filled eyes.

"Not happening," Ali says shortly. "He wants the Spirit for himself."

I shake my head. "Sandor, too? That's impossible. He's been my best friend my whole life, and he's always protected me."

"Don't be so naïve." Ali's words are cold and sharp, startling me. Seeing the effect of her words, however, she softens a bit. "Look what my brother did for it. We can't trust anyone around this thing."

Another message from Sandor comes through: "Jazmyn. Give me the Spirit. Now." I've never heard Sandor try to order me before, and it pushes me over the edge of indecision.

"I'm sorry, Sandor. I can't let you have it."

"Then you leave me no choice," Sandor says before disconnecting our communication stream.

A burst of gunfire whips through the air, several bullets striking our ship.

"He's shooting at us!" I yell out.

"Go!" Ali shouts. Thankfully, she doesn't waste time reminding me she was right about Sandor. His betrayal still hurts more than I can say.

I gun the throttle, trying unsuccessfully to dodge a hail of bullets.

"He's a much better pilot than me." I'm unable to hide the terror in my voice as shots rip across our left wing.

Warning lights flash across the command screen as the X-571 takes a sudden dip. I grasp at the controls, trying frantically to keep the ship in the air as we continue to get pummeled. "I'm losing control. We're going to crash!"

Black smoke billows across the windshield, and the whole ship begins to shake. I glance over at Ali. She places Sunni and the Spirit inside her bag and tucks it tight against her to prepare for our rough landing. This could be the last time I ever see her, but I have no time to dwell on it, because when I return my attention to the front of the ship, I realize where we are. The sand beneath us moves like the waves of an ocean: free and flowing. The quicksand pits—and we are about to fly right into them.

I yank the wheel, desperate to change our course. The X-571 lumbers in my forced direction, trying its best to heed my commands in its damaged state. I manage to redirect it toward the edge of the quicksand mere seconds before impact.

The ship's belly hits the ground with a thunderous roar, violently shaking the entire cockpit, and covering us with debris.

We survive. The ship takes the brunt of the crash and handles it better than I thought it would. The windshield shatters but the rest of the cockpit is intact, albeit rattled and layered in sand.

"Are you alright?" I ask Ali.

"Yeah," she answers between coughs, trying to breathe through the particles floating in the air.

The tail of the ship suddenly sinks down and reminds me once again of where we are.

"The quicksand! We have to get out of here!" I release my seatbelt and rush over to help Ali. Once I've managed to free her, we scramble to the front of the ship.

The cockpit rises into the air as the tail descends further into the quicksand. I clamber over the broken glass where the windshield used to be and help Ali up. We fall out of the cockpit and onto solid ground, just as the quicksand swallows what's left of the ship.

Sandor lands his X-571 nearby and steps down the ramp, walking to us. I'm filled with rage as I stomp toward him. Ali chases after me.

"Sandor, how could you?" I raise my hand to slap him, but he's too quick and catches my wrist.

"You have what I want," he says plainly as he releases me. "I've spent most of my life trying to obtain the Spirit of Arsalan. I've killed people for it. Destroyed cities."

I didn't think anything could shock me more today, but it seems I was wrong. "I thought my father..."

"Your father is a coward!" Sandor interrupts viciously. "He never wanted the Spirit. He never saw its potential. He only wanted to keep you safe. That's all he ever cared about. It didn't take much to convince him that the best plan was to build a bunker, assemble an army, and eliminate our enemies. Then his precious princess would be able to live out her days in safety and happiness."

"How dare you," Ali spits. Sandor ignores her.

"I've spent years whispering in your father's ears, convincing him to command the army in the way I saw fit. We destroyed Qadari to find the Spirit of Arsalan, but it was no longer there. The Badawi had taken it. We leveled all the other cities in hopes of flushing it out. I've fought against those savages countless times, but could never find it..." Sandor trails off, turning his attention to Ali's bag, which is glowing from the orb hidden within. "Imagine my surprise when you, of all people, managed to get it from the Badawi. All that stands in my way to gaining ultimate power is a common thief... and a friend." He extends his hand, eyes momentarily filled with the compassion and understanding I'm used to. "You are my friend, aren't you, Jaz? You can trust me. Just give me the Spirit."

For a moment, I almost want to do it—but then Ali shifts the bag away from him and Sandor's anger returns, making him a completely different person than the man I've always known. A monster. He pushes me out of the way and runs at Ali. She quickly extracts the Spirit of Arsalan from her bag and aims it in his direction, just as it releases a blast that knocks him to the ground.

I watch as Ali looks at the Spirit, then at Sandor struggling to his feet, then at the swirling quicksand, somehow more volatile than it was before—and finally, at me.

"People will always fight for this power," Ali says as she holds out the glowing Spirit. "So many have lost their lives because of it already. My family. The people of Qadari. The Badawi. This entire planet is covered with death, and it's all because of this."

She lifts the orb, now flashing with power, over her head. "It must be destroyed. It's the only way to put an end to the war and allow the people of Arsalan the peace they deserve."

"No!" Sandor's ragged cry mirrors my own thoughts.

"Wait, Ali. What are you saying?" My voice cracks as Ali removes her satchel and sets it on the ground. Sunni comes out, whimpering.

"Take good care of Jazmyn, okay?" Ali whispers to the fox before patting her affectionately on the head and tossing her in my direction.

"You can't!" I protest as Sunni wraps herself against my leg.

"It wants me to—I can feel it. It wants to go back to the planet." Ali bows to me, turns, and runs into the quicksand, Spirit in hand.

Sandor scrambles after her. The ground beneath their feet is almost as fluid as water, and it begins to devour them instantly. The Spirit of Arsalan wraps Ali in a shield of blue light as the volatile sand washes over her. I watch in horror as she and Sandor are both consumed by waves of sand. Sandor screams, grasping desperately at nothing before he is lost from view.

Sand spews up into the air. It sputters and spills until the swirling slows to a stop. The storm settles into a peaceful desert once again. As the dust in the air clears, I see the shadow of something lying in the sand. Sunni perks up and her tail wags back and forth.

"Ali?" I dare to whisper my hope out loud.

The shadow rises into the air on a blanket of sand that slowly flies over to us. It is Ali!

Sunni lets out a joyful yip. The sand blanket gently lowers Ali's motionless body to the ground and then dissipates, scattering amongst the granules around us.

I bend over her, shaking her gently with my heart in my throat. "Ali? Are you okay?"

Her eyes open slowly, as if waking from a deep slumber. She groans as I help her sit up.

"The Spirit is where it belongs now—with Arsalan," Ali says. "The war is over. We did it."

I embrace her. "I'm just happy you're okay. I thought I'd lost you."

She leans her head against me to return my hug, and as she does, I catch a glimpse of a small blue gem glowing around her neck.

"What's this?" I ask.

"A gift from Arsalan, to thank us. And to keep us safe." Ali smiles. "It doesn't have the same level of power that the Spirit did, so it shouldn't drive people crazy."

"That's a relief." I laugh and help Ali to her feet as we walk over to Sandor's X-571. We take our seats at the front of the ship and strap in. Sunni greets us with a playful wag of her tail before jumping into Ali's lap, safe once again.

After getting the airship off the ground, I stare ahead through the glass, unsure of where to go next. Even through the light of the morning sun, stars are visible in the distance. Calling to me.

"What do we do now?" I ask Ali.

She takes my hand, her fingers interlacing with my own, her smile bright and beaming. "Whatever we want."

Nothing.

Her father had left her nothing, save the coordinates of the planet he was headed to and the note telling her he had found some tech to salvage.

She would have been lost or dead without anyone knowing where she was because she hadn't stopped long enough to share the information with her father. Only she was fine.

He was the one missing.

Stardust AND Steel

Meri Benson

Part I
Deep Space

The Black was the easiest place to go mad.

That's what a lot of planet-bound thought, at least. Andromina would argue it wasn't the Black that caused people to go mad, but the isolation of it if you were traveling alone. Most people weren't built to go days or weeks on end without contact with another living being.

Most people weren't her.

A chime sounded through her ship. It was a small ship, only the cockpit large enough for two, a small mess hall, and a bedroom outside of the cargo hold with a small bathroom. Just big enough to pilot herself, but large enough to hold a guest or her father when needed. When she didn't answer the first chime, which had pulled her out of her sleep, a second one came.

Groaning, she pulled a pillow over her eyes. "*Vera*, who is it?"

"Your sister is calling from Balist."

It had to be mid-morning on Balist if one of her sisters was calling her. She had only gone to bed a few hours ago, she guessed by the exhaustion she could still feel in her body. "Answer it."

"Finally, Mina!" The tone was exasperated as it came over the ship's comms.

"Hello to you too, Poppy . . . you do know it's not morning everywhere, right?" Andromina pushed herself up to a sitting position, settling her back against the padded headboard of the bed.

"If you and Father cared to settle down, it could be morning for you, too." Judgment dripped from the words and caused Andromina to sigh softly.

After their mom had passed from an illness when Andromina was fifteen, their father had left Balist and taken to the Black. Her three older sisters stayed planet-side and created lives for themselves, but she'd chosen to go with him—much to her sisters' disapproval. To be fair, Andromina had figured it was restlessness on his part, missing his wife and unsure where his life was going after her sudden passing.

She knew her sisters saw it as a stupid risk; so many things could go wrong flying between planets. Especially coupled with the delivery and scavenge work he started doing, and with bringing his fifteen-year-old daughter with him? Improper, if you asked them. After all, there were pirates, bounty hunters, and all manner of riffraff out there. What kind of stability would it offer a girl?

That she'd wanted to go with him, had actually jumped at the chance, had only been seen as more reason she should have stayed with her sisters on Balist. Each one of them had tried to bargain with her, offering her a home with them. But a chance to see other worlds, other species, and to learn more about the galaxy and universe they lived in had only intrigued and excited Andromina. Also, it meant she could keep an eye on their father and keep him safe.

It had been ten years. Still, the judgment remained. "You're happy settled. I'm happy exploring and running cargo missions." And bounties—not that she'd shared that particular addition of her current jobs with her sisters. Her father knew, of course, because he helped on some occasions, but she'd kept that from her sisters so she didn't get any more pushback for being out here instead of settling with some husband. "I'm sure there's more reason for this call than to offer a reminder that you want me settled as a wife and mother like you and our sisters."

A sigh came across the ship in answer. "You make it sound like finding a husband is a terrible thing, Mina. Honestly, it's nice to have someone to share your life with. More than those stories you spend your free time in." A *tsk* sound followed the words. Andromina refused to follow any of that with an answer, waiting Poppy out. "Dad missed Dylan's birthday call. It made me worried. Have you heard from him?"

Dylan was Poppy's oldest. As much as they argued about how he and Andromina spent their lives running around, their father had never missed a birthday or holiday: calling and checking in, sending presents, all of the things a doting grandfather or father could do when so far away. It caused Andromina to frown.

"He was headed to a new planet he'd found some abandoned tech on," she offered as she pushed out of bed. The metal floor chilled her bare feet, but Andromina ignored it as she moved to a long glass panel of wall that came to life in soft blue lights under her touch.

Their father had disappeared for weeks on end in his scavenging before, so it wasn't too big a worry when he'd been silent after letting her know he was headed somewhere new. Missing Dylan's birthday call, though, put concern in the pit of Andromina's stomach.

"Do you know where? Is he okay?" Poppy's voice rose a little in octave with her worry.

Andromina's fingers flew over the glass as she dug into their communication from before he headed out. "Give me some time. I'll see if I can find where he went and head that way."

"You don't know where he is?" She could practically see her sister raising her hands in exasperation.

Sighing herself, she shook her head. "We don't always stick together. He does his own thing sometimes." It was why he had his own ship that could dock onto hers. It was smaller, only big enough for one and his tinker room that also had a small cot for him to sleep on, but it was his. Her fingers caught the last few messages he'd sent her and she pulled them all up on the screen. "But he sent me the coords of where he was headed. Give me a week or so and I'll call you back once I check it out. Okay, Poppy?"

Silence filled the space while Andromina waited for her sister to answer her. Finally: "Okay. But send me the coordinates. So I know where you're headed if you disappear, too."

"I will. I'll find him. I promise." Andromina's voice was softer as she answered. She couldn't blame her sister for worrying; after all, she was now officially worried, too. "I'll talk to you soon."

"Thanks. Love you, Mina."

Her lips quirked up just a little. "Love you too, Poppy. And let our sisters know so I don't get more worried calls, yeah?" The last thing Andromina needed was two more calls in the same anxious, judgmental fashion while she was trying to focus on finding their father.

A laugh came across the line, though Andromina could hear the strain in it. "Yeah, I can do that. Take care. Bye."

"Bye, Poppy." The call ended with a chirp as Andromina found the coords her father had sent her. She took a moment to send them off to Poppy with the information their father had given her about his new find.

"*Vera*." The ship made a humming sound around her as the computer AI in it waited for her command. "Set a course for these coords. And start digging into what is known about this planet."

"Will do, Andromina."

Andromina's gaze flickered over to the bed she'd abandoned, but she wasn't sure she'd be able to get back to sleep now that she was worried about her father. Instead, she moved to grab the book off the small nightstand next to her bed.

It was one of the few antiquities that she hunted down with a passion. Most people, and most books, were now on the virtual and available to download to the ship to read on the screen she was just using, or a small data pad if you wanted it portable. But she had fallen in love with books when she and her father had found a few that first year. Since then, she'd made sure to treasure any physical books she found.

They were rare even on the black market, hunted for by many collectors at quite a hefty price. Her collection could set her and many generations up for life if she ever wanted to actually sell. Another secret her sisters weren't aware of.

She had several properties across a few planets where she hid and stored her prized collection of books. In a way, she'd settled across the galaxy because she did have small homes where she occasionally took a reprieve when she wanted a break from space. It was rare, though; usually she spent only a single day planetside while she swapped out the books that traveled with her.

So in a way, they were really more homes for her books.

A chime pulled her out of her own head as she curled herself up onto her bed, book in her lap. Her fingers found the bookmark and she opened the book without ever looking down at it. "Yes, *Vera*?"

"I have programmed our flight path. We will arrive in seven days and twenty-six hours."

Her fingers drummed on the paper of the book as she took that in. "What planet do the coordinates go to?"

Silence followed her question for a moment, though the lights in her room flickered slightly, a sign that the ship was working hard to answer her question. She was used to waiting the ship out though, so she let her eyes fall down to the page to remind herself where she was.

Not that she actually needed the reminder; she knew

the story backward and forward by now. She'd already read this book more times than she could count. It was one of the few that never left the ship because it was her favorite to go back to. A comfort read.

"Undetermined."

Frowning, Andromina closed the book and turned her head to look over at the screen. "How can it be undetermined?"

"The planet is listed as uninhabitable and outside Galactic Agency territory, in free space. Most records on it seem to be lost or locked behind galactic government clearance."

She set the book back on the nightstand and pushed out of bed again, fingers pulling up their route on a map on the screen. "Can you break it?"

"It will take time to do it carefully." This wasn't the first time she and her AI had broken past government locks to get information they were after. But it struck as odd that they'd locked information about this planet. If it was some kind of black site, it would be some kind of rural, low-maintenance place no one would actually want to live on—at least with a name.

Zooming in on the last part of their path, Andromina's head tilted to the side as she reviewed the planets around it. "Nearest outpost with a resistance bar?"

The lights dimmed for a moment before a red arrow pointed to one of the smaller planets closest to their destination. "Rallus-4. A way stop for pirates and resistance members. A trading post for at the edge of governed space." *Vera* knew she didn't actually need that explanation of the planet; they'd spent a lot of time there in the past.

"How far from our destination?" Internally, Andromina was already groaning. Rallus-4 was one of the few planets she was not looking to visit. Truthfully, if she ever visited the planet again, it would be far too soon.

"Five days from our unnamed planet. You may find people who know about it, being the closest planet to our destination." Silence fell as Andromina warred with herself on whether she should stop or not.

She'd need to refuel, too, if nothing else was around. Which meant that she didn't have a choice. "Set a secondary course for us to stop and refuel at Rallus-4. Don't notify anyone there of flight paths or arrivals."

A chirp that sounded similar to a chuckle filled the ship. "You can't ignore your suitor forever."

"No one said I had to even let him know I'm in town. We'll be quiet and quick." Andromina knew she was fooling herself, but she couldn't help trying. Deny. Deny. Deny. "And he's not my suitor."

"Of course. The course has been set. I will alert you when we are an hour out." The ship fell quiet around her.

She turned to take in the room. As much as she wanted to curl back up and try to read again, she knew she would never focus. "Don't forget to continue to dig, carefully, at those files to see if we can work around the locks."

The lights in the room paled to a light red and the ship sounded offended when it answered her. "I am not human. I do not forget."

With that comment offered, the lights shifted back to soft white, but the ship fell silent. Discussion complete, Andromina was sure. She hadn't meant to insult the ship in any way, though for some reason *Vera* had always been pretty prickly about being compared to humans.

"Noted," she muttered under her breath as she moved to get dressed and get to work on her own research. She wanted to dig through her father's communication to see if any other hints had been left for what exactly her father thought he'd found.

~

NOTHING.

Her father had left her nothing, save the coordinates of the planet he was headed to and the note telling her he had found some tech to salvage.

Andromina stretched with a soft sigh. When had they become so lax in their exchange of information on solo missions? In the past it wasn't just a ping with coordinates, but a full message that included what they were doing, when they'd be back, and plans to meet up once the job or mission was done. A check-in so they knew the other was safe.

Scrolling through her messages with her father, it had been months since they'd actually sent full information in a message. She had fallen out of the habit, too, her last message to her father merely telling him she'd picked up a bounty and would be a few days late to their agreed-upon meet-up.

Never once had he questioned what the bounty was or where it would take her, merely signing off that he understood and would see her when she was done.

Sure, she'd come back just fine, but if she hadn't, would he have ever known where to look?

The answer was no.

She would have been lost or dead without anyone knowing where she was because she hadn't stopped long enough to share the information with her father. Only she was fine; he was the one missing.

"*Vera?*"

A chime rang through the ship, letting Andromina know that *Vera* was listening, but wasn't over the earlier insult of being compared to a human who could forget.

She would have to figure out a way to make it up and soothe the AI's ego later—after she figured out how her father was faring. "How close do we need to be for you to connect to *Myriad?*" *Myriad*, her father's ship, was constantly docking onto *Vera* so the two could travel together. It meant that the two systems spent a lot of time connected, talking to each other.

Silence followed her question, but the lights flickered through a small rainbow before settling back to the normal white. It at least let Andromina know that *Vera* was thinking about it, working out the actual answer. "It would depend. If he took *Myriad* down to the surface, I may need to be in planetary orbit to reach her. If she is still in orbit around the planet, I may be able to contact her from Rallus-4 so long as there are no solar storms in the area."

It had been a long shot thinking that maybe they were close enough to contact *Myriad* now. The easy answer, because *Myriad* could let them know quickly if anything was wrong, or if her father needed help in any way. "Thank you," she offered.

"Are you disappointed?"

Vera's question pulled Andromina out of her own head a little more. "What? No, of course not. Just worried and thinking. It's not like my father, and I'm just realizing how little information we've been giving each other over the last few months."

"You have been on different paths. He has continued to dive for tech, but you have moved to antiquities jobs over cargo with the occasional bounty to ensure my upkeep is to standards. It has been noted in research that it is normal for children to branch out on their own from their parents after a time. Maybe you have merely moved into that state of your life." *Vera's* tone was matter-of-fact, with no judgment or opinion to it.

Andromina didn't buy that her AI didn't have some thoughts on the subject, but it seemed to be taking into account her worry over her father, lessening the pointed comments. "Maybe. I just never considered needing more information until the only information we actually need is what's not here."

Vera gave a humming sound around Andromina. "I am almost done compiling what I can find on the planet. I should have it on your data pad shortly after reaching Rallus-4."

Glancing down at the pad in her hand, she let out a breath. Should she be happy about that news, because it hopefully meant more information to go off to find her father, or should she be scared because there wouldn't be enough and she'd only be left with more questions? "Thank you, *Vera*. How long until we reach Rallus-4?"

"We are still half a day out. You should consider sleeping. Your vitals are a little low and you will need your wits to be well-rested."

Well-rested wouldn't change what she'd have to deal with when she went planetside if the person she'd been avoiding happened to be taking a post-mission break. She'd been avoiding Rallus-4 so she wouldn't risk running into him, taking jobs that kept her in locations farther from his own hunting grounds.

Now she was willingly putting herself in his path for her father.

"All right." She pushed herself out of her chair. *Vera* wasn't wrong, and Andromina had no leg to stand on trying to argue with her ship. The call from Poppy had come in just as she'd been settling in to sleep, and after the call she never had gone back to bed. So sleep actually sounded pretty good.

Part II
Rallus-4

You could say that the city never slept, but really the whole planet was like that. Bright neon lights flashed from various buildings to let you know they had a bar or gambling parlor or a night market. Most of Rallus-4 was uninhabitable, so the city itself, coupled with a few other cities farther out, was it for the entire planet. All of the cities and establishments were run by pirates, retired bounty hunters, and other less-than-respectable people.

Calling the entire planet a black market was more accurate, Andromina couldn't help thinking as she weaved down the street though the crowds.

It was early morning, but it felt like midday with the amount of people that wandered to and from the shops or bars. Most leaving the bars were stumbling, finally surfacing after a long night of drinking. Some looked bright-eyed and energetic, though she was pretty sure there were other reasons for that.

Her destination was down a dark alleyway, a few eyes glancing her way as she turned a corner. Not that anyone would say much. She used to come here often, and coupled with the tight leather pants, corset top, and black bomber jacket, she also looked like she belonged. In a way, she did. If she wasn't trying to avoid Caspyn, well, she'd have been back here far more often over the last few years.

She only managed to make it three steps into the bar, The Saint's Sin, before a large man caught her around the middle from behind and lifted her off her feet. The move made her give a startled squeak as she wiggled a little.

"Finally, lass! Been far too long!" The voice was gruff, like he smoked too much. Which, to be fair, he did.

Her hand patted his arm and she tried to look over her shoulder. "Finn, you can put me down! I'm not a doll."

A sigh of relief came as her feet were set on the ground again. She'd been in too many fights where she had been grabbed from behind to feel comfortable being surprised like that. The only reason she hadn't hit him was because she had expected that kind of reception. At least in some way.

Though to make it up to him, the pout forming on his features looking so out of place on such a large man, she leaned over and wrapped her arms around his neck for a big hug. While he picked her up and spun her again, she felt more comfortable like this. Likely because she knew who was wrapped around her this time.

"We've missed ya around here, lass." His words came as he let her go, mostly. One hand stayed at the small of her back, and he used it to draw her over to the large wooden bar on one side of the room.

Following his lead easily, she slid onto one of the seats

on the patron side. "I've been busy. Currently trying to track down my father."

Finn set a shot glass down in front of her, already filled to the brim with a bright red liquid. "What has Ol' Mathis gotten himself int' now?"

"Went to salvage on a planet I can't find info on." She knocked the shot back quickly, feeling the burn all the way down her throat. Kalcian whiskey. Just the courage she needed.

His brow arched a little as he watched her. "Do ya need help?"

This was the other reason to come. Not just because Rallus-4 was on the way out, but because she had people who actually cared about her and wanted to help. She couldn't help the small smile that lifted her features at the offer. "Mostly information, if you know of any. It's a planet about five days out, after the Galactic Agency line and just into free space."

His features darkened a little and he shook his head. "Tell me he didn' head ou' yet."

"Who didn't head out where?" The voice was deep, smooth, and held just a little surprise.

Andromina's spine straightened a little as she willed herself not to look over her shoulder at who she knew was already there. Though she did give a look over at Finn instead. "My father headed out to a planet I'm looking for information on."

Finn shook his head. "Mathis headed to the Whiteout."

A hand settled on Andromina's shoulder and she felt warmth from the touch all the way down, through her jacket, to her spine. "Don't go out there, Ani. No one ever comes back."

The command in his voice was enough to make her shrug his hand off her shoulder. "You don't get to tell me what to do, Caspyn."

"Not anymore, right?" He moved around the end of the bar so he could stand next to Finn, making a show of fixing the cuff of the sleeve on his jacket. Though his honey-colored eyes rose to watch her as he did it. A pointed look that said nothing and everything at the same time.

Andromina's chin rose slightly at that, letting her eyes grow cold. This was what she'd wanted to avoid. "Not ever. That was a large part of why you and I never worked." Without glancing down at the glass, she nudged it toward Finn.

The little glass was filled with red to the brim again before Finn slid it back over to her.

As her fingers wrapped around the glass, Caspyn's hand settled over her wrist to stop her from lifting it. "Heed my warning. It's called Whiteout because there's no communication with that planet. Scavengers have tried to collect before and none of them ever come back. We would know; we're the last planet on your way out and first planet on your way back. At the very least they'd need to refuel here."

Her eyes dropped to where he held onto her wrist, and after a long moment, he finally sighed and released her. Downing the shot, she set the empty glass on the bar top in front of Finn. "My father headed that way, which means I'm going to find him. Either give me any info you have on the planet or get out of my way."

Finn set an open bottle on the bar for her, the glass a transparent green with a label wrapped around it to declare it Myst's Finest Mead in All the Galaxy. "Give me until mornin', lass. I'll get ya all the planet h're knows."

"Finn." Caspyn shot Finn a dark look.

"'Tis not yer call, Cas." Finn nodded at Andromina. "I'll even cook ya breakfast t'see ya off."

Taking the bottle, Andromina raised it in Finn's direction. "Thanks, Finn. I really appreciate it. I'll finish supplying up tonight so I can head out with your info tomorrow."

"Ani–"

Andromina held up a hand to cut off anything that might have followed the nickname Caspyn had given her. "I don't want to hear it. I'm not just abandoning my father because he thought he found a good score." She slipped off the stool and onto her feet. "Either help Finn get my intel or keep your mouth shut. I don't care which."

Caspyn opened his mouth to say something, but he must have caught the look in her eyes, because she already knew that the look said not to mess with her. "Fine," is what finally came out of his mouth. His hands rose in surrender and he shook his head before moving past Finn and leaving the two of them standing at the end of the bar.

"I won't tell ya no'to go, but I will say pick up extra supplies. Be prepared, lass." Finn glanced over her shoulder and waved at someone behind her. "Gotta get ta work. Go prepare." He snapped the towel at her.

She didn't move from her spot, though, free hand sliding down to find the card that held some credits to pay for her drink. Not that she was able to pull it out before the towel snapped on her hand and she winced. "Ow!"

Finn pointed a finger at her. "Don'cha even thin' about it. On the house."

"But . . ." Her words died in her throat at the serious look from him. She wasn't going to win this, and she would only insult him if she tried to fight it.

"Yer family, lass, even if it's been a few years since y've been here." Finn motioned for her to get on her way. "Now, go prepare. I'll have yer info come mornin'."

Moving back to him, Andromina slipped behind the bar to lean in to kiss his cheek. "Thanks, Finn." Without another word, or being told to go again, she headed out of the bar.

It had been too much to hope when she'd broken things off with Caspyn for this planet to continue being a home or family to her, specifically Finn. He was Caspyn's right hand for the establishment, and a lot of the pirates and bounty hunters that came by had formed some kind of relationship with him. Mostly in the trade of information coupled with Caspyn's neutral territory rule. No weapons, no fights. Keep to yourself and take your issues or bounties outside.

Hearing Finn call her family warmed her heart, one hand resting against her chest as she slipped out into the night. It was different from the family she had by blood, because Finn was her chosen family. He had always cared for her when she passed through Rallus-4, especially when she'd almost made it her home.

∼

"STATUS, *VERA*?" Andromina stretched her arms up over her head as she moved through the ship from the cargo hold to her bedroom. It had taken a lot longer to stock up than she'd been hoping, and now all she wanted to do was fall face-first into bed and get a few hours of sleep.

It didn't help that she'd come from further out, so the time zones cross-planet didn't exactly line up. It was one of the few things you never truly got used to bouncing from planet to planet.

"Ninety-eight percent done with the hack. I should have your information after you wake up." The lights dimmed slightly, giving the ship an almost twilight feel.

"Food has been restocked and stored, enough for a month. Fuel has been refilled; we have enough to make it all the way to Balist and back, plus some extra in the spare tank as a just in case." Balist was a good month's fly from Rallus-4, so to have enough to get there and back, when they were only five days out, actually lifted a weight off Andromina's shoulders. Overstocked was more like it. "Water stores have also been replenished. I feel like a new ship, though no one was kind enough to buff out the few dents from that last asteroid belt you flew me through."

Andromina couldn't help but roll her eyes at the end of that. "After we return with my father, I'll see about treating you to a full detail. Promise."

An excited chirp sounded. "I'm holding you to that. I could use one."

"I know." Reaching out, Andromina patted one of the walls as she moved into her room. "No issues with the delivery people that dropped everything off?"

The lights in her bedroom turned on just enough to let her see her way around the room in a soft muted glow. "None. They were all very mindful of whose ship they were on and how well I was keeping an eye on all of them." A small pause fell for a moment, though the lights rose a little more by her nightstand to show a small wooden box that hadn't been there when Andromina left. "You also had a special delivery."

A frown formed on her features as she stilled and stared at the box. She didn't need *Vera* to tell her where the box had come from, and there are only a few people on the planet *Vera* would have allowed in her bedroom. "How long ago did he leave?"

"Twenty-three minutes and forty-two seconds ago."

At least he had the good sense to not linger. The thought slid through her mind as she finally pushed her feet to move to the nightstand so she could pick up the box.

Her fingers made quick work of shifting little panels on the various sides until the lid on it clicked softly. She knew the puzzle box well. It had been the same box she'd given Caspyn his ring back in when she'd said no to his proposal and broken up with him.

Not that she had any clue about what could be inside the box now. She doubted he'd be giving the ring back, though to be honest she'd expected him to get frustrated enough to smash the box to get the ring out of it. Patience and puzzles weren't exactly his strong suit. That he'd been careful and figured it out without damaging the box surprised her.

A frown etched its way onto her features as she pulled out a small drive from the center of the box. "Did Caspyn say anything or leave a message when he dropped this off?"

"Yes." The screen on the wall of her bedroom flickered to life. Instead of just playing a message, *Vera* pulled up the video, one that started as Caspyn entered the bedroom.

Something about seeing him enter the bedroom while she'd been gone both annoyed her and pulled at her heart. She watched as Caspyn moved slowly into the room, and Andromina could tell he was taking it in. Probably noting just how little had actually changed over the last few years. She was a simple woman, despite everything she did across the galaxy, and her ship reflected that. The most elaborate thing about her room were the books, and it wasn't uncommon for the covers to change but the stacks to stay the same height.

He didn't touch anything as he finally made it to the nightstand. The box was pulled from his pocket, and he glanced up directly where he had known *Vera* could record him head on. "*Vera*, record a message for me."

Past *Vera* chimed in the video in answer to his request, "Of course, Caspyn. Recording started."

"I know I pushed hard earlier, Ani. This is everything I have on Whiteout. Finn's still compiling what he can get from the rest of the bartenders and hunters around who have dug into it before for you, but I figured I'd offer this to help keep you safe." He set the box down on her nightstand and tapped it with his pointer finger. "I don't want you going, but I also understand you can't leave your father without trying to help him. If you do go, please make sure to swing by after and let Finn and I know you're safe."

At least he was giving her that much credit, despite what made him worried about her going to the planet.

"I'm sorry we never figured out how to make it work, Ani." He tapped the box again before he turned and headed out of the room. "*Vera*, end recording."

They were too different to work, though. The thought slid through her head without permission as she sighed and looked down at the drive. Even without them being a couple, he'd always tried to tell her what to do, and it had been worse when they were. He'd all but tried to demand she stop bounty hunting, stop diving for antiquities, even stop cargo runs. Everything that had drawn her out into the Black he'd asked her to give up for him. To become his planetside wife while he continued taking bounties and was gone for months on end.

In the end it had shown just how little Caspyn understood who she was at her core: the woman who craved that freedom and adventure.

Pulling the drive out, she moved over to a small panel in the wall and slid it in. "Upload Caspyn's information and compile it with yours, *Vera*. Cross reference everything, and note anything that contradicts what you find."

"Of course, Andromina. I will have it ready for you by the time you wake up for breakfast." The lights in the room faded down lower so the room was dark enough to sleep in, but still lit enough that if Andromina needed to move around she could.

Not that she needed to do much. Andromina made quick work of stripping out of her clothes, leaving them on a chair in the middle of the room and falling into bed with a soft groan. Thankfully the pillow was comfortable enough that sleep took her before her mind could really spiral after all the events of the day.

~

As PROMISED, *Vera's* information had been downloaded to Andromina's data pad, along with Caspyn's information, the next morning. Everything had been coded in different colors to denote what was *Vera's* info, what was Caspyn's, and what was either the same or very different between them.

Not that she took long to review it before she threw on some black cargo pants and a simple blue shirt. Shrugging into her bomber jacket, she grabbed her data pad and headed off the ship. "I'll be back after breakfast. Be ready to leave when I am."

The soft chirp of acknowledgement followed, though *Vera* didn't make any sound past that as Andromina left.

It was actually quieter now in the early morning hours than it had been when she'd come back to sleep. As a whole, it made her walk to The Saint's Sin a quick one as she scrolled through some of the information on her pad. While Caspyn and Finn called the planet Whiteout, it looked like the government called it Nyson. Both agreed that those that had been sent out to explore it had never come back, and that no communication could be made from anyone planetside to anyone off-planet.

She tapped a few things as she turned down the alley toward the back door of the bar and pulled up the government's study on why. Something in the clouds stopped and buffered transmission waves from getting out, they claimed. Interestingly, the planet was a natural Faraday cage—which would have explained, if her father had taken *Myriad* down, why no one had heard from him.

"Already in'ta it, are ya, lass?"

The voice came as she slipped past the unlocked door and into the bar, bringing Andromina's head up. She offered Finn a smile. "Yeah. *Vera* was able to get the Agency's info on the planet, and Cas left me what he had so I could get started, but I crashed last night. Just getting through it now." She set the data pad on the bar top and lifted herself into a seat across from Finn.

Finn gave her a knowing look and she pointed at him in a silent, don't-even-start motion. "No' sure what'll add after Cas' info for ya, but." His words trailed off, but he held out another data drive to her. "I collected what people know around here."

"Thanks, Finn." She took the drive and settled it into the port on her pad. *Vera's* soft chirp registered and the data started to download, integrating with the screen of information already up. "Looks like the reason it's Whiteout for everyone is it blocks external connections because of some ions in the clouds."

His brow arched as he moved to a small door next to the bar. "Makes sense. Be righ' back, lass."

Pushing through the doors, he disappeared while she glanced down at the pad as more information added to the puzzle, helping her to untangle some of it. The largest question still remained: Why had the government sealed the records? What had happened there?

A few comments in the government report mentioned an accident or event and claimed the planet was uninhabitable, but nothing created a clear picture. She paused in her reading as a large plate of pancakes and bacon was set in front of her. A second plate was set next to her as Finn came around to join her. The two discussed her mission and she set the data pad between them so they could go over the notes together.

By the time she was headed back to her ship, she had a plan in place and her belly was full of delicious food. Now all she needed was to find her father—and bring him home.

Part III
Nyson

S omething bad had happened on the planet: bad enough that people had fled from it at an alarming pace and caused the government to erase all mention of it. Most of the reports didn't include what that incident had been, which was the frustrating part.

How was Andromina supposed to know what she was walking into if she couldn't find a mention of what she should be planning for?

Prepare for the worst, her mind told her. She'd been in similar positions with her bounty hunting, having to tread lightly because she didn't have the full story. But those didn't usually include ninety-five percent (if their estimate was correct) of a planet leaving in enough of a rush that most were counted as refugees under government status as they tried to find a home somewhere new. With nothing but what they could carry in a couple bags each.

She'd left Balist in much the same fashion, but she knew she could always come back whenever she wanted. The items she'd left behind were stored in a unit that she paid for every year, waiting for her to settle. If she ever got the itch to give up her adventure and travels, that was.

These people had abandoned most of what they owned, fleeing for their lives.

One report Vera had been able to obtain contained an interview with a husband who'd even mentioned he'd had to leave his wife behind. That she was corrupted, unsaveable.

Corrupted.

The word pinged in her head as she worked with *Vera* to land carefully in a large open space of light blue grass without too many trees around it. Andromina watched out the viewscreen to see if anyone or anything might have been alerted to her arrival.

Everything was silent, except for a small breeze that rustled some of the flowers and grass around them.

Which meant that when *Vera* chimed softly, it was enough for Andromina's hand to jerk to her chest as she let out a small gasp. "Don't scare me!"

"You knew I was here all along, Andromina." After a moment, *Vera* added, "I was able to locate *Myriad*. She is just over the ridge. It appears she had a hard landing and is not flyable anymore."

Pushing a hand through her hair, Andromina tried not to let that news raise her panic. How long had her father been trapped here, unable to call for help? "What about my father?"

"*Myriad's* communication is scattered. Mathis left to hunt for his tech. For food. She has not heard from him in the last week." *Vera* hummed softly, the lights around Andromina dimming for a moment. "There are confusing signs on the planet. I am having trouble locating human or humanoid life signs."

That really didn't help, but she kept her mouth shut on that subject. Pushing herself up from her chair, she moved back to her room to grab her jacket and a small device from the corner. Settling the device just behind her ear, she took a slow breath. "*Vera*, can you hear me through the comm?"

Instead of chiming through the ship, a soft sound rang in Andromina's ear. "I can hear you, Andromina. I will keep track of your location and vitals. But keep in mind, I cannot help you further than that."

"I know. This is on me. Can you continue to try and figure out where my father is while guiding me to *Myriad*? I want to see if there's anything I can do to get her back to you." Andromina moved out of her bedroom and into the cargo hold. Taking a slow breath, she pressed her hand to the door and watched as it opened.

They had already examined the air and concluded it was safe for her. Knowing something happened here to cause most of the population to run, however, made her hesitant as she slowly walked down to the blue grass waiting for her. The trees in the distance had a soft pink to their leaves, the bark a white like the birch trees she'd seen on Earth.

Vera's voice was soft in her ear. "I will continue to scan the planet as I can, but the clouds above are making things difficult. Everything here seems to be on a different frequency, but I am not used to or calibrated to it, so I am having to work twice as hard."

Raising her hand to brush the skin just under her connection to *Vera*, Andromina nodded. "Understood. Just keep me apprised of any changes." She stepped off the ship and stuffed her hands in the pockets of her jacket. She felt out of place here in the black jacket and cargo pants when everything seemed to be a pastel color for its natural state. Even the blue of the grass was stark against her black boots, though she only let that distract her for a short moment before she glanced up.

"The glasses will help me keep you oriented properly, if you'd put them on." *Vera's* tone said she shouldn't argue with the AI.

Not that Andromina had any intention of arguing. She pulled the mentioned glasses out of her pocket and slipped them on, tapping two buttons on the side. The lenses shimmered for a moment and a small arrow appeared in the upper corner of the right lens. When she turned her head in the opposite direction, the arrow shifted slightly so it could continue pointing in the direction of *Myriad*. "Thanks, Vera."

"I do what I can."

Shaking her head, Andromina took off in the direction the arrow told her to go, though her head swiveled this way and that as she tried to watch for anything suspicious. The planet was eerily empty, even of wildlife, and that had her on edge.

A HARD LANDING was an understatement to describe *Myriad's* condition. The small ship was nose-deep in the dirt behind a rather large mansion. She was at least fairly level to the ground, though. Andromina's head tilted to take the ship in. It looked like *Myriad* had hit the ground and then skidded to a stop thanks to the dirt pile it had built up in front of it.

Something strange had started to grow along the sides of the ship, metallic in the sunlight but a different color than *Myriad's* outer haul. She itched to touch it and see what it might be, but because she didn't know what it was, she decided against it. Instead, she moved around the ship to the cargo door and used the familiar code to open it.

A whine came as the door opened; something was out of alignment to cause the metal against metal sound. Andromina winced as she patted a clear portion of the hull. "So sorry, *Myriad*." Her words were soft, but even those words had the ship flickering to life as it recognized her voice.

"Welcome, Andromina. Mathis has not returned yet."

Andromina moved into the cockpit and took a seat in the captain's chair. "Thanks, *Myriad*. *Vera* mentioned that, too. Do you know where he was headed? Also, status report for your systems, please."

"He said he would explore the building in front of us,

but I lost signs of his vitals two days into his exploration." Andromina's heart beat faster at that information, though she didn't let it still her fingers as she pulled up the screen to find out what was keeping *Myriad* from flying at least enough to dock on *Vera*. "Thrusters were damaged in the landing, I cannot seem to get off the ground or out of this dirt."

A hum left Andromina as she flipped through the different screens. "Pull up the full thruster schematics and show me what needs to be fixed to get you moving enough to get to *Vera*. We can get you out from there and to a shop to get you both all cleaned up."

The screen flickered and started moving with a life of its own, blinking quickly until a full show of the thrusters appeared in front of her. A few places were highlighted in red as they pulsed like they were in pain. "Did *Vera* sustain damage as well?" The tone almost felt too innocent.

"Like you two haven't been talking silently behind my back and you don't know she hasn't stopped pouting about her hull being scratched up by branches. Not to mention my hard landing on the dirt. We were lucky to not come in too hot, though, so she's still able to get off the planet when the time is right." Andromina's fingers tapped the first red spot and she pulled the image larger with her fingers. It blew up to a bigger picture that pulled apart the interior for viewing so she could see the exact spot that needed her attention.

A chirp, higher-pitched than *Vera's*, sounded around Andromina. "She says you were supposed to tell her you arrived."

Reaching up, Andromina tapped the disk behind her ear. "*Vera*, I've arrived at *Myriad*, as you know. Can you transfer the thruster needs to my glasses so I can get her up and to you?"

"Of course, Andromina. I am glad to know you arrived safely."

The softest trill between both ships made Andromina confident they were laughing at her. As she pulled herself out of the captain's seat and moved to the small cargo hold to grab the tools, the schematics that showed *Myriad's* most-needed repairs appeared on the glasses for her so she could follow the design into the thruster assemblies.

She moved to the outside of the ship and pulled off the panel on the first thruster, making quick work of fixing it. It wasn't a forever fix; they'd need more parts and a better mechanic for that. However, it would get *Myriad* out of the dirt and over the ridge. "Hey *Vera*, can you analyze this substance that's on *Myriad*?"

"Can you—" *Vera's* question died, as Andromina had already moved to the side of the ship and settled the glasses' view on the metallic-looking moss. The glasses beeped and the screen zeroed in on it, a few dots appearing as *Vera* processed what Andromina was looking at. "Don't touch it. We may not be able to dock *Myriad* until we can remove it."

The tone set alarm bells off for Andromina, and her head tilted a little as she moved to close the thruster panel. "What is it?"

"Nanobot,: a lot of them. They're trying to take her over. If they can, and she's to get to me, they can take me over, too."

Andromina stilled and glanced over her shoulder in the direction her ship was. "Which means we'd never make it off the planet."

Vera made a sound of agreement in Andromina's ear. "You would effectively be trapped here, with no way off and no help to come get you. Leave her other thruster. Once we can clean her off and ensure she, and we, are safe for her to dock, you can fix her."

Moving around *Myriad*, Andromina set the toolbox just inside the cargo hold. She closed and locked the cargo hatch, and before she glanced over at the mansion in front of her, she also locked the AI. It wouldn't stop another invasive technology forever, but hopefully it would slow the nanobots down until they could figure out what was going on. "Can you locate the source of their power? Where are they taking their commands from?"

Silence followed the question, but Andromina knew better than to expect an immediate answer. While she waited, she made her way around *Myriad* toward the mansion that her father had decided to explore. "The main command seems to be coming from inside the building you're in front of."

"*Myriad* said Dad went inside and two days in, she lost his vitals." Andromina's voice was almost a whisper, though why she was whispering, she couldn't say. It wasn't like there was anyone else around to hear her.

"Be careful, Andromina. If that is true, danger likely awaits within."

Her lips couldn't help lifting a little at the words. "If I didn't know better, I'd say you cared about me."

"Computers do not feel. However, I would like to make it off this planet, not become part of it." *Vera's* voice was soft in Andromina's ear. She wasn't purely a computer, of course; she was an AI, and some ships could occasionally be known to develop close relationships with their captains.

"Well, let's make sure that we find Dad and make it home. And get that creepy nanobot moss off *Myriad*. I would like her to come home with us, too." Andromina's feet hit a small, overgrown walkway that led through some gardens to a back door. "Can you keep watch via the glasses and map where I'm going so you can help me out if need be?"

Vera hummed in her ear. "I can try, but the closer you get to the building, the harder it is to read you. *Myriad* may not have lost your father's vitals for any other reason than she couldn't sense him anymore with the nanobot technology blocking her."

Andromina nodded despite *Vera* not actually being able to see her. She hoped that was actually the case— that maybe he'd just gotten lost inside, or maybe one of those left behind was still here playing host to him. "Thanks," she remembered to offer as she pulled the door open and slipped inside.

Where the sun had been bright outside, the inside was dark. Lights from high chandeliers were on and gave the room a soft glow, though it was still difficult for Andromina to see. Reaching up, she touched a button on her glasses and the lenses flickered into night vision. It made everything almost black and white, but at least she could see the room, which appeared to be the back side of a grand foyer.

The front doors stood several feet away from her, the sun from outside tinted and muted through the windows on the grand double doors. Two large sets of stairs framed the room, starting close to the front and rounding up a little. Moving toward them, Andromina's neck craned a little to see the balcony on the second floor, which opened up at the top of the stairs. It allowed anyone upstairs to watch those who came in and out.

A soft clink against the marble of the floor had her shifting back against the wall just behind where the stairs started on the left. Like she could hide in such a large, open room.

"I can hear your heart beating quickly in your chest." The call-out was creepy enough on its own, but coupled with an almost childlike singsong tone, it raised the hairs on Andromina's neck.

Not that she planned to answer whoever it was.

The clink only grew louder as a robot rounded the stairs and came into her view. The little legs walked like a person, though the arms ended in grabbers instead of hands and the head that tilted toward her was more a viewscreen than a face. A couple of eyes and a mouth presented themselves on the screen. "He won't be happy that you're here. We don't have new living here, and he likes it that way."

Her heart picked up its beat, threatening to burst out of her chest as she took in the words. However, she couldn't help but lean down, because the robot only stood at half her height. "Who is he?" Andromina's question came out in a whisper. Shouldn't she whisper? After all, this robot just said someone else was here in the building.

"Our king. He lives in the East Wing and rarely comes out." The robot's answer mirrored her whisper and the eyes looked amused on the screen, like this was some kind of fun game they were playing.

Vera hummed in Andromina's ear. "That's where I get a sense of the command center being."

"Have you seen one other living in the last few weeks?" Andromina couldn't help the hope that bubbled in her chest, even as it felt odd to call herself a "living." What did that make the king? Did anyone actually survive who had been left on the planet in the exodus?

The robot's head tilted to the side and the digital image of its eyes saw them droop, like it might be going to sleep. After a moment, it blinked brightly at her. "One! He was surprised to see me. Rufus wasn't too happy to see him, though. He said he was looking for something."

"Rufus?" Andromina's head tilted a little, curious at the name that was offered so casually. "Who's Rufus? The King? And do you have a name?"

The head jerked back and forth a little, shaking no. "Rufus is my friend, but he's cranky. I'm Henris. We don't say the King's name."

Andromina nodded to herself as she took in all the information. "Can you lead me to where the other living went?"

"No. Sorry." The eyes on Henris' viewscreen flickered toward the East Wing. "The living went where we're supposed to stay out of. We can't follow."

Straightening, Andromina moved toward the stairs, around Henris. "Then I need to find him down that way."

"Fraternizing with another living? He won't like this." A new voice, more polished and controlled, came before another small robot appeared from around the corner. This one moved on wheels, making it almost silent on the marble floor.

Andromina pointed at the new addition. "Rufus?"

"I am."

"Yes!" Henris moved to follow Andromina to the stairs. "You shouldn't go. He'll be mad."

She didn't let either robot stop her as she started up the steps. "I have to. He's my father, and if he's in trouble, I need to help him."

"Wait!" Henris called from the bottom of the stairs when she started to head toward the East Wing.

The call had Andromina turn and look over at them. "What? I'm not scared of your King."

"You should be," a voice from behind her rumbled darkly.

A hand clasped her shoulder, and Andromina felt something crawl along her neck before her world went black.

Part IV
Nyson

Ajolt ran through Andromina, pulling her out of the darkness of unconsciousness as she jerked into a sitting position with a gasp. Her hand rose to her neck, fingers finding the disk that kept her connected to *Vera* as her heart raced and she glanced around.

She sat on a bed, the comforter a little dusty. So the bedroom was unused, for the most part. As her eyes took in her surroundings, she noticed it had likely been a woman's room, with perfume bottles and a brush on the vanity in one corner. She inched herself toward the end of the bed carefully, ears straining to hear anything.

A small shock slid through her, and she couldn't help her soft gasp at the feel of it along her skin. It didn't hurt, but at the same time it was like her nerves were all now awake. "*Vera?*" Her words were a whisper, and she hoped her ship could hear her.

"I am here. Apologies: the shock was because some nanobots were trying to take over your nervous system. Whatever touched you, it has spread nanotechnology to you. The shocks inhibit them from controlling you, for the moment . . . I am doing what I can, but you need to find their source."

Another shock slid through her, and she breathed through it now that she knew what it was. Hyperaware, she could feel it was emanating from the disk behind her ear, hidden by her hair so whoever had caught her likely missed it.

The door pushed open, and the shadow in the entrance stood tall enough to almost brush the top of it. "You are an interesting creature. Keeping my children at bay."

Andromina backed up onto the bed again as she watched the man step into the room with her. He had to be over six feet tall and decently muscled, but that wasn't what caused her to want to get away from him. That same metallic moss she'd seen on *Myriad* covered the left side of his body, clinging to and shifting with him as he moved. "Who are you?"

"He's the King," a small voice whispered from the doorway. Andromina's eyes flickered down and around the intimidating King to see Henris' viewscreen peaking around the doorframe.

"He used to be humanoid," *Vera's* voice whispered through the comm into Andromina's ear.

Her mind raced as Andromina took that in. If he was humanoid, was that moss taking him over, too? *Vera* had mentioned the shocks were to keep the bots from controlling her. He'd called them children, but was that the man talking or the machines that had taken him? Too many questions. She needed to see if there was any way to still the nanobots in him to even try to get some answers.

Another thought crossed her mind: What about her

father? Was this what happened to him? Was he some-where around this mansion, taken over and no longer himself?

"Yeah, well, I didn't actually want to be all hive mind. Thanks, but no thanks." Andromina shifted across the bed, settling onto her feet so she wouldn't be caught on it. Not that she felt any better; the windows behind her were large, but there was no door or balcony for her to escape out onto. The only way out of the room was through this beast of a man in front of her.

He took a step further into the room, closing the distance between them as his head tilted at an odd angle. "You act like you have a choice. My children will succeed eventually. You merely need to give in."

Andromina let out a soft breath as a shock slid down her spine again, hating the idea that any of that tech-nology might be somewhere inside her. "I'm not one to just give in when someone tells me to." Caspyn, her sisters, they'd all told her to give in, to settle planetside and call it a life. It hadn't happened yet.

It wouldn't happen today.

"You will have no choice." Another step toward her.

Her heart hammered faster in her chest as she was trapped against the windows. Darkness blackened them, so she couldn't see anything outside behind her, which hadn't fully hit until now. She'd been out for a while, then.

Vera's voice chimed in her ear. "Touch him at your

next shock. It should travel and free him, at least for a moment, for you to get away."

The last thing she wanted to do was put herself close enough to touch him, but she trusted *Vera*. Her AI had already done everything to keep her from becoming whatever he was. "When?" The word was breathed softly under her breath, purely for *Vera*.

"Five."

Andromina shifted around the bed, closer toward the King before her.

"Four."

It surprised her a little that he stood, watching her without moving as she took a step toward him.

"Three."

Her feet put her almost within touching distance to him, her heart hammering in her chest loud enough that she almost didn't hear *Vera*.

"Two."

Dipping under an arm as it stretched out to get her, she turned slightly to keep her balance.

"One."

Her own hand came down on his in a clear expanse of skin, avoiding the metallic moss of nanobots. The shock came through her, stealing her breath because it felt stronger than the several she'd been given before.

The world seemed to slow as he froze above her and the moss started to flake off his skin a little. His head turned down toward her, and his eyes seemed confused. "Run. They won't stay quiet for long."

Andromina didn't hesitate. She moved around him and took off out of the room. Reaching up, she realized her glasses were missing. She had no help on where to go, which way was out instead of deeper. In her panic, she took a left. Her boots hit the marble and the sound felt loud in her ears as a clink followed her. Henris.

"The room to the left," he called from behind her.

She couldn't say why she even followed his suggestion, but her panicked mind didn't question it as she tried the door and breathed a sigh as it fell open for her. Though she stilled once inside.

A lab. Not an escape.

She spun on her heels to go back, just in time for the door to close behind her, leaving Henris inside with her. "Why?"

Henris moved with slow clinks over to a computer screen. "This is where it all started. Where it went wrong." His viewscreen turned to watch her as he pointed up at the desk next to the computer.

"You were functioning and aware before it happened?" She moved slowly to the desk and found a notebook. The shock from *Vera* came again, softer like before, and she couldn't help breathing a soft sigh of relief.

Vera's plan had worked, too. He had let her get away.

Lifting the notebook, she flipped through it and

frowned. "They were trying to heal the sick, and the King wanted to find an answer for longevity," she murmured as she scanned the notes. She would have loved to share this with *Vera*, but she had no idea where her glasses were.

"The programming was off. The nano AI found that controlling the living was the best way to keep them safe. Alive," Henris offered. He turned himself in a circle. "Robots like Rufus and I were seen as inferior, so it left us alone. So long as we stayed out of its way."

Andromina skimmed the notes as she listened. "Does it have a control location?"

"In the King." Henris stilled and watched her, eyes sad. "He was just trying to help his people."

He was trying to find a way to live forever without giving up his crown, Andromina's thoughts countered silently. Not that she voiced them. There was no point in scaring or making her only ally mad right now. "So we need something to give him the same pulse Vera's giving me to clear his head. Only stronger."

A pound came at the door and it caused Andromina to jump and drop the book. "Can he get in?"

Henris turned himself toward the door. "I locked it with a puzzle. It will take the nanobots twenty-two minutes and thirteen seconds to break it."

"*Vera*, set a timer for me. I have twenty minutes to create something that will shock him enough to clear his head like you're doing for me without being strong enough to kill him." She sighed as she took stock of the lab. It was well supplied, at least.

"I will let you know when twenty minutes have gone by. However, I would rather help you create your device." *Vera's* voice came clearly in Andromina's ear, and she couldn't help the smile that formed on her face.

"You and me both, *Vera*, but I don't know where my glasses are to share my view. I can talk through what we're doing and you can assist me as you're able."

Silence fell for a moment before *Vera* offered, "That may do."

∽

"Your twenty minutes are up."

Vera's voice sounded in her ear and caused Andromina to swear as she slipped with the solder and burned her finger where it held the little device in place. "Thanks, *Vera*," she said with a huff as she finished the spot she'd meant to hit.

Henris had watched as Andromina moved to and fro while effectively talking to herself. She wasn't sure if he could actually hear *Vera* in her ear or not. If he did, he made no comment, but he also didn't really offer any words or interrupt her thoughts while she worked, either.

The hallway outside their door had fallen eerily quiet quickly after the initial couple of bangs. Though if the nanobots were working on the lock Henris had set in place, it wouldn't need to bang like a man would, right? Maybe.

"Can either of you tell me if the King is still outside that door?" Andromina finished soldering the top of the device into place to lock the delicate mechanics safely inside. It should work, she thought—though for how long, or how successfully, neither she nor *Vera* was sure.

Andromina may have been raised by an engineer and a tinkerer, but she wasn't fully one herself. Meanwhile, neither of them had come up against anything like this, so they didn't have any experience with it. They had designed something that had a self-sustaining battery that should last long enough for Andromina to talk to the man behind the machine and find a more permanent solution.

Hopefully.

"He is. I can hear his breathing through the door," Henris offered from his corner. "You don't have much time to get it on him. How are you going to do that?"

Andromina turned to glance at the door. "Carefully."

A chime came as *Vera* offered, "Near his neck is best, if possible."

"Yeah, you'll need to be happy with where I can get it, because I doubt I'll get close to the neck at all." She moved over to the door quietly, and when she heard the clink of Henris' feet on the floor, she turned and held a finger to her lips.

She needed all of the surprise she could muster to

even get the device on him, and she was already scared that her rapidly-beating heart might betray her. Just as she settled against the wall next to the door, the door chimed to indicate it was now unlocked.

A *whoosh* followed as it slid open. The large man entered the room and his eyes swung over to Henris when he moved from one foot to the other. If he'd been human, Andromina would have questioned if it was a nervous habit.

Not that she had time to really contemplate if robots could have nervous habits. Seizing the precious time he'd given her, she rushed from her hiding spot and reached up. With the King turned toward Henris, she was able to get his shoulder at least. The device had little prongs like teeth that sank into his skin and earned a snarl of pain—but before he could reach up to try and rip it out, a shock buzzed out of it and through him.

Andromina watched as he jerked hard with the shock, and some of the metallic moss fell off and around him as he panted and fell forward to his knees. She didn't stay too close, backing herself out of the lab and into the hallway just in case she'd need to run.

"How?" His head turned to look over at her, though he made no move to stand up and come near her again.

Before she could answer, his eyes seemed to glaze over a little. Just before that glazed look fully took over, another shock came from the little device. His breath came in a ragged groan, and one hand hit the floor as more of the moss started to break apart and fall off him.

"Without their central host to cling to, their control is flailing. If he is their power source, severing his connection should make them dormant, at least for now," *Vera's* voice offered to Andromina as she watched the man battle with himself.

She didn't move closer to him as she watched him go through shock after shock. Time felt like it stood still around her, and the only real sound were his grunts as he took the shocks and the soft tinks as more and more of the piled-up nanobots fell off him.

By the time he finally pushed himself to his feet and turned to face her, his skin was clean of them, at least. Judging by the way the softer shocks pulsed through her though, there were still some she couldn't see, some inside both of them they would have to determine how to clear out. "Thank you," he offered softly as his hand came up to catch the doorframe and lean on it. "How did you do that?"

"With the help of my AI, *Vera*. She's been sending small pulses to shock the nanobots you put in me. We just put yours on a grander scale." Her eyes flickered over to the bench where the notebook sat. "Coupled with some of the notes in there." Her head jerked slightly to try and motion to the book without actually needing to step any closer.

He looked more clear-headed now, but she didn't

want to be overconfident in the device working yet. A slow nod brought his chin down a little and he glanced over his shoulder at the lab. A sadness filled his eyes, though Andromina waited patiently for him to say something. "My notes. I was hoping to create a better life for my people."

Shifting her weight, her head tilted slightly as she took that in. "You used yourself as the first test subject?" She slowly started to put the pieces together now that she had time to think.

"I did. Why ask one of my people to do something I am not willing to?" He made it sound like he was asking someone to lift and carry something from point A to point B—not something that could end how this did. Catastrophically. "How did you know?"

She took a breath to answer that, though she didn't say a word as she watched his jaw clench and his fists ball at his sides. It had to be another shock. Waiting a moment, she gave him time to catch his breath before she answered. "Henris mentioned you were the power source for the nanobots that had taken you over. The only way that would happen is if you were Patient Zero and they spread from you."

The shocks through her system had become normal, and she barely noticed them now. The ones that slid through him were a lot stronger; she and Vera had wanted to make sure they eliminated the threat. "Is the pulse too strong?" She could see his reaction to them every time one hit, so Andromina was pretty sure the answer was yes.

"If it keeps me myself, I'll take it." He took a step toward her, offering her his hand. Though when she took half a step back to keep some of the distance between them, his lips quirked just a little. "I'm pretty sure you are already infected with them, so a handshake won't hurt you."

Andromina opened her mouth to argue, but closed it because he wasn't wrong. With a sigh, she stepped forward and slid her hand into his. "I am glad I could help with that. Though we still have a few problems."

"The first being we're still contagious and could spread the nanobots if we leave this planet. Of course. It'll take time to figure out a more permanent solution." He let her hand go after the shake and turned to step into the lab. "I'm hoping it's mostly a programming change that we can make to the bots: make them less invasive and more passive, like what they were supposed to be. Though I sense that's not the only problem."

Andromina followed him a few steps into the lab, though she stayed near the door. "My father came here a few weeks ago. Beyond this planet, no one really knows what's going on here. He thought the tech here was abandoned, not in charge." She couldn't help how she shifted her weight from foot to foot, worrying about where he might be.

He glanced over his shoulder at her, though something in her expression caused him to turn to face her fully. Brow creasing, it was like he was trying to dig through his memories for who she might be referencing. "Henris, what happened to him?"

The small robot moved from the corner he'd been hiding in. "He wandered into your wing, my King. I don't remember hearing about him after that."

The King's eyes widened and he shook his head. "That man. I am truly sorry."

Andromina took a step back at that, shaking her head because that wasn't the answer she wanted. He had to be alive. Just part of the hive, able to be rescued—that would be so much better than what that look told her. "No . . ."

"The bots tried to join him to the hive, but he was sick. They couldn't keep him alive." He shook his head, taking a step toward her. "I'm sorry." His words paused, like he was searching for her name, but they hadn't actually introduced themselves.

"No!" Her world spun as she stumbled away until her back hit the wall behind her and she slid down into a sitting position. "He can't be. He was fine before he came here." He would have told her he was sick—would have told Poppy and her sisters. Wouldn't he?

Her mind tried to wrack itself for any hints that she'd missed. Had he seemed tired the last few times she'd seen him? Maybe a little. He'd let her do more of the lifting and carrying work on their last joint mission too, she remembered.

A hand on her leg caused her to jerk her head up to find the King's dark eyes watching her with sympathy. "I am sorry, miss."

"Andromina," she offered quietly as she tried to wrap her head around this information. Though in a way, it made some sense. Was that why he'd started pulling back, not giving her so many details when he left? This hadn't been the first mission he'd given just a small line of where without any real information for her. He'd also been encouraging her to be out on her own more often, pushing her to find her own leads and keep in mind that she was alone. Was he preparing her for a life without him at her side?

"Andromina," the King echoed back as he squeezed her knee. "My name is Nico. I am truly sorry for your loss. And I am sorry to have to ask this of you during such an emotional time, but I don't think I can make more of these alone." He touched the device implanted in his neck. "There are still at least a dozen people here that will need them."

Her mind reeled a little at his having the audacity to ask for her help after giving her such heartbreaking news. Yet it didn't stop her head from nodding in agreement, or how her body moved of its own accord to take his hand and let him draw her to her feet. "What . . . where . . ." Her words stuck in her throat as she tried to figure out how to ask what happened to her father's body.

"He's buried in the royal cemetery out back." Nico

seemed to sense her question before she asked it. "I will be happy to assist you with whatever you need once we fix this and figure out how to get us both safe enough to leave the planet."

Buried in a royal cemetery. That would almost be funny, if it weren't breaking her heart. But that at least meant he was resting peacefully. It also meant he'd be close while they worked on this—enough for her to see him when there was time. "I . . ." She took a breath as she wiped at her eyes with her free hand. It was only then that she noticed that she hadn't actually let go of his hand, clinging to it like a lifeline as she dealt with her father's death internally. "Let's get your people freed. Are any of those that are still here good with technology, or are the two of us on our own? I have an AI who can help."

"We're on our own, but considering your brilliance freed me, I have hope we can figure this out together." His hand shifted to rest on her back and guide her to the lab table she'd used to create his device.

Her head nodded as she moved with him, ready to get to work. Later, she would cry for her father and find a way to get a message to her sisters. Right now, they had people to save here, including themselves. "Okay. Let's get this done."

"You could get Modded, you know."

Not for the first time, Blanche considered the idea. It wasn't like it wasn't an option. But she stubbornly held on to her father's last words when he'd been on his deathbed.

"Don't let the world change who you are."

JUST A *Byte*

Marie Sinadjan

Nothing here was real.

Here was a world between worlds, which never appeared the same to two people at the same time. Blanche saw rolling green hills and a sky so blue it made her heart ache with longing for a world she'd never experienced. She shuffled forward with care, holding her breath as she planted her foot on the ground in front of her. With a single step, everything had the chance to change.

But the image held.

Then, without rhyme or reason, it warped. The once flat surface transformed into a steep incline. The sudden shift in her perception caused her to lose her balance and fall.

This is just a simulation, she thought with gritted teeth as she pushed herself back to her feet. She closed her eyes, envisioning the room she previously occupied before the program engulfed her completely. Barefoot, she stood in the middle of a rubber mat stretched over a tiled floor. Large industrial lights dangled from the ceiling, too high for her to reach. Wallpaper covered the concrete around her, still smelling of adhesive.

Or she *should* have been able to smell it. But she couldn't; not anymore. The tech was so advanced that she'd lost her grip on reality a few seconds into the simulation. Only by sheer stubbornness did she remain aware that she existed within one at all.

The only way out is in, a sage voice reminded her.

She took a deep breath and tried to continue, but her moment of hesitation had already cost her. Quicksand wrapped around her legs, the mud rising the more she struggled. She checked her person for something that could aid in her escape, but she hadn't brought anything besides a gun. How could she have known this was what the program would throw at her? She would have brought a grappling hook.

In vain, she attempted to will into existence a piece of rope tied to a tree that loomed tauntingly a few feet away, but she did not have any power over the simulation. While this was an exercise for the mind, training her to think outside the box when forced into a corner, it was not a programming drill.

She sank deeper into the quicksand, barely able to keep her head above the surface. A part of her marveled how *real* it all was: the coarse grains of sand scratching against her skin, the warm breeze that danced around her face and through her hair, the stench of piss and dung that she hoped wasn't hers, and the desperation that clawed at her heart at the looming possibility of her death.

"Theron!" she yelled at the sky, tipping her head back so the sand didn't rush into her mouth. "Let me out!"

~

"You didn't even last a minute."

She ripped the visor from her head and threw it on the floor. "Let's see you do any better!"

Theron, who was chiefly responsible for her family's safety and wellbeing, only *looked* like a feeble old man. He was as heavily modified on the inside as her stepmother was on the outside.

Theron laughed, clearly not taking her seriously. "Just try again tomorrow." He glanced at the screen of his watch. "Lady Scarlette will be done with her lessons soon. Would you like to spend some time together? A movie, perhaps?"

Her mouth turned dry at the reminder. Scarlette's

lessons. Right. Her sister participated in daily one-on-one sessions with their mother, which was all the time their mother ever spent with them.

While Blanche accepted the fact that it was natural for a mother to favor her trueborn child, it still did not make the truth easy to digest. What could their mother be teaching her sister that she couldn't impart to them both? True, Scarlette was the smarter one, but it wasn't fair to write Blanche off as a stupid buffoon just because she was big and brawny.

In fact, Blanche had only gone into combat training *because* of Scarlette. When Scarlette first moved into their house, she had been so frail that Blanche had been seized by the desire to protect her at all costs. "I will be your knight," she had sworn to Scarlette one day while she pushed her sister around in her wheelchair. Scarlette's face was what she called up every night before she went to bed to remind herself of why she put herself through all that pain.

They were sisters. They would be all right, as long as they had each other.

"Maybe a movie," Blanche relented.

Theron nodded with a pleased hum. He took a few steps toward her while he called up a list of movies from his watch, projecting it in the air in front of them. "And your selection?"

She sighed. In the old days—or in these days, if they were poor—people went to cinemas. But it was dangerous for families like theirs to be outside, especially with all the unrest of late. The masses were in a state of discontent, and it took very little to make them lash out. Just the other day, they'd trashed a hovercar that had taken a wrong turn into the slums simply because it had the logo of the Corporation.

Blanche only gave the list a cursory glance. She really did not want to decide anything without Scarlette's input. Their tastes clashed so much that she had long since ceased trying to express her preferences, reminding herself of her role as the older sister and the need to accommodate Scarlette's limitations.

"Probably *The Secret Prince*," she said with another sigh. The old stories of honor and chivalry and happily-ever-afters fascinated Scarlette. Blanche didn't see the appeal, but as her sister had very limited options, she indulged her anyway. "But Scarlette gets the last word."

She always does, she thought bitterly. She buried the sentiment before the wound could fester.

"Excellent choice, my lady," Theron said, not at all sensing that something was amiss. Or perhaps he was just being considerate. "I shall prepare the movie room, then."

∼

"Let's watch *The Secret Prince*," Scarlette decided.

Although Blanche was already expecting it, she still let out a groan. "Again?"

Her sister laughed. "Yes, again. You know Rexie is my favorite."

Regulus Dara was a popular actor beloved by women both in the elite and in the slums. Everyone loved him, except Blanche.

"I hate him. He's too perfect," Blanche scoffed. "Boys aren't made like that." They were not even supposed to be *made*, period. But their stepmother had, in trying to help Scarlette live a normal life, made Modding so popular that their family quickly rose to become its own empire.

"That's why he plays princes. And he makes such a charming one, too," Scarlette gushed. "I *love* his accent." She would probably faint if she got close enough for Dara to talk to her. Their mother, in spite of her influence, still refused to organize such a meeting for security reasons.

"His throat's probably Modded, too."

Her sister appeared visibly insulted. "It's not! His parents hailed from England." Or what remained of England after it joined most of the world and sank under the waves, anyway.

Speaking of Dara excited Scarlette, though. Most of the time, she was so sickly that despite her wheelchair being fully integrated with her body, allowing her to maneuver it by simply leaning in a specific direction, she often needed to be pushed around. Her recent Mods had improved her health, but their mother was careful about using anything on her that hadn't been thoroughly tested and proven to have no side effects.

Their movie nights strangely energized her, however. They took place in a hall that spanned an entire floor of their family's steel and glass tower, with the floor to ceiling windows on all sides providing a 360-degree view of the city. At night, the darkness and the neon lights washed out the grime that polluted the streets, which, coupled with the persistent fog, made the place appear almost ethereal.

Theron had already prepared the room for their movie session, so large screens blocked the windows. Coupled with the projectors, they would enable the sisters to move about as though they were part of the film. In certain scenes, they were expected to stand in precisely marked spots to fully grasp the intended story, but there were also plenty of occasions to move around the setup and engage with the holograms. Viewers had no ability to modify the course of the film, but they understood that was part of the rules anyway. Most of them were content to get five minutes alone with whichever character Dara took on.

By their third rewatch of *The Secret Prince*, Scarlette had decided she would play the nonexistent childhood friend trying to hunt the Prince down to remind them of the love they had shared in the past, thwarted only by his family's opposition of her less-than-royal status. She'd written lines and everything, which included Blanche, who delivered her dialogue with equal parts disinterest and sarcasm.

"Surely you remember me?" Scarlette's dedication to her role was so strong that, loathe as Blanche was to admit it, she could almost be convinced that her sister was genuinely the long-lost love of a hidden prince.

Dara's hologram frowned at her. "Erm, I . .." His AI wasn't very smart. Just as he probably wasn't in person.

Scarlette persistently tapped Blanche's hand, reminding her it was her cue. "Oh, come on, pretty boy. Use that head of yours for once." She experienced a moment of satisfaction for her improvised line before she felt the heat of her sister's glare. She swallowed. "Uh, *aye*, remember her?"

Scarlette facepalmed.

The interactive part had gone live. Blanche wheeled Scarlette toward a circle in the middle of the room while the simulation spun around them like a carousel, generating a montage of images and sensations that pushed the story onward. Though she would never confess to enjoying anything that included Regulus Dara, she didn't mind this portion of the film. She had never experienced a forest so lush, a sky so blue, or a beach so inviting in her lifetime, as she had been born after the Crash. The simulation appeared so detailed and lifelike it felt as if the world had been restored.

The scene shifted to the palace, where a ball was taking place. "Time to dance," she told Scarlette, wheeling her sister to the corner of the room near where the Prince would make his appearance. As part of the simulation, holographic gowns adorned them, reflecting the designs pre-programmed into the system by Theron. Scarlette got a light pink ball gown and looked every inch a princess. Blanche was granted her request for a black dress, but it was a body-hugging one that emphasized curves she was *not* happy with.

"My lady," Dara's hologram greeted Scarlette, holding up a gloved hand to her.

While she didn't possess the capability to actually touch his image, Scarlette proceeded to place her palm on top of his. She smiled. "My prince."

Blanche rolled her eyes. This part she wanted to skip, especially because Scarlette would then spend the rest of the movie staring and sighing longingly at Dara's image while she was obligated to push her around the room.

"May I have this dance?" he invited.

Blanche froze. *Wait, what?*

That was not in the script. When she had informed her sister that it was time to dance, she'd meant the next scene was a ball, not that she would be invited to dance by the Prince. The programming of the Prince's hologram revolved around kissing her hand and engaging in small talk until his attention was captured by the arrival of his fashionably late love interest. He would then ask that girl to dance.

But not *this* girl.

She expected Scarlette to retreat upon realizing that something had gone wrong with the movie, but her sister continued to gaze into the eyes of Dara's hologram. "It would be my honor, dear prince," she said, quoting the love interest.

Blanche glanced behind her. According to all the times she'd watched this movie before, the love interest would appear anytime now on top of the staircase, mesmerizing everyone with her beautiful dress and gorgeous looks. But the doors remained shut.

"Blanche," Scarlette hissed.

The Prince was smiling expectantly at them, still hand in hand with Scarlette. Blanche realized they were both waiting for her to wheel Scarlette along for their dance—which seemed very odd, because in the interactive portions of the movie, the programmed characters never stopped to wait for the spectators to take action. Dara's hologram would simply have strolled back toward the center of the room, regardless of whether he actually held anyone in his arms.

What was going on?

Only when the dance finished did Scarlette let go of the Prince, and the movie reverted to its original course. The simulation briefly sputtered before jumping to the correct scene, appearing as if nothing strange had occurred. The love interest unexpectedly emerged and was being escorted by the Prince toward the gardens for a tranquil moment.

They were expected to follow, but Blanche turned to Scarlette and knelt in front of her. "What did you do?"

She did not know why her first thought was that her sister had done something. Far more rational explanations existed: The movie file could have been corrupted. Something could have gone wrong when Theron pre-programmed their preferences. Or some lowlife hackers might have decided to tamper with the simulation as petty revenge. But she had a hunch, though completely unfounded, and she could not let the matter go.

Scarlette frowned. "What?"

"You changed the script." It came out sounding more accusatory than Blanche intended.

"*He* invited me to dance. I had to improvise. It's called *acting*, Blanche."

Scarlette's pretend innocence gnawed at her. She took after her mother in that regard, and it was the one thing Blanche didn't like about her sister.

She didn't want to think that maybe one day, Scarlette would become just like their mother and completely ignore her.

"I don't believe you," Blanche declared. She was grasping at straws, but her stubbornness made her hold her ground. She had no proof that her sister had done anything, only a feeling, and she didn't even want to acknowledge what sort of feeling it was.

Hurt flashed across Scarlette's face.

No, not hurt.

Fear.

But before Blanche could make sense of it, the simulation ended. Scarlette had pressed the button on her watch to terminate the whole setup. The holograms disappeared; the screens faded to black. Then, the industrial lights turned back on, illuminating their faces with a harsh glare.

"I'm tired," Scarlette announced a little too loudly to be completely convincing.

"Scar, I'm sorry," Blanche began, but Scarlette wheeled herself away. She chased after her sister, but just as she reached and gripped the back of her wheelchair, the door to the movie hall slid open.

Adriana was a woman of intimidating beauty. She wielded her appearance like a weapon, and she wielded it well. She didn't seem much older than Blanche. Even while she was supposed to be resting in the confines of her home, she dressed as if someone would summon her to an important meeting at any moment. Tonight, she wore an elegant dressing gown that hinted at curves Blanche could only wish she had, and she had tightly pulled her hair back into a neat bun. Like Regulus Dara, her face was infuriatingly perfect—the walking hologram of an artist's muse.

"Oh, my darling." She knelt in front of Scarlette, gripping her daughter's hands. "Don't worry, you're safe now."

Any animosity Blanche had toward Scarlette faded the

moment she caught her sister's face turning red with shame. Despite being doted on, Scarlette didn't experience real freedom. Her wheelchair kept her connected to a network that allowed their mother to monitor her every move. In fact, Blanche was pretty sure that Adriana had received an alert about Scarlette's abnormal heartbeat and had rushed to her from wherever she had been in the building. While it was nice to have a mother who cared, Blanche wasn't sure she could stand someone who hovered around her like that, either.

"I'm alright, Mother." Scarlette sniffed. "I'm just tired."

Adriana cast Blanche a dark gaze. "You were supposed to watch over her."

"I . . ." Blanche stammered, surprised that whatever happened—which she still did not understand—was now her fault. "We were just having a movie night."

Perhaps it would've been better if Adriana had berated her. But what her stepmother did next stung far worse. Without another word, she simply stood, inclined her chin as if she couldn't be bothered to deal with Blanche, and wheeled Scarlette out of the room.

"I'm sorry," Blanche called out.

Neither woman looked back.

$\sim$

THERON WOKE Blanche half an hour before her first alarm.

"It's only seven," she groaned, covering her face with a pillow.

"And you have a doctor's appointment at eight," Theron reminded her.

Sleep still clung to Blanche, making it difficult for her to recall that information. A doctor's appointment so early? She would've remembered that, if only because she wasn't a morning person and would require more time to get ready. "That's today?" she asked, confused.

The pillow disappeared, and she found him staring down at her. He continued to be as bright and alert as ever, unlike her. Maybe the stories were true. He did not need to sleep.

"That is today. Breakfast is ready, and so are your clothes."

Ugh. Blanche hated that her stepmother picked out what she was supposed to wear whenever she had to go outside, which wasn't even very often. She tried not to think just how much of an embarrassment Adriana thought she was, given that, unlike her stepmother, Blanche did not look like an actress.

That didn't even rank as the harshest criticism of her appearance. A tabloid had once called her a pig for not only having a fuller form, but for her supposed gluttony —that she was her size because she ate too much and did not think about the poor children who were starving in the slums. As if it was her *choice* to look the way she did.

She forced herself to sit up. A cursory glance at the

pile of clothes on the foot of her bed confirmed her suspicions. All black, of course. So she didn't appear so large. So she took up less space.

You could get Modded, you know, the treacherous voice at the back of her head whispered.

Not for the first time, Blanche considered the idea. It wasn't like it wasn't an option. Adriana had practically been *begging* her to get Modded, but she stubbornly held on to her father's last words when he'd been on his deathbed.

Don't let the world change who you are.

He could've meant it metaphorically, the voice insisted. *After all, he married the queen of Mods.*

Come to think of it, that was ironic. What *had* her father seen in Adriana? Blanche's mother, who had died only a few years ago, had been anything but a superficial, clout-chasing woman.

"Do you need help bathing and getting dressed, my lady?" Theron prompted.

Blanche huffed, hauling herself out of bed.

~

AT TEN MINUTES BEFORE EIGHT, they were still making their way through the slums.

Why the doctor did not come to their building instead, Blanche had never figured out. She'd asked Theron, but the old man simply said the doctor could not afford to travel through the city with the number of patients he had to see daily.

"If you would just get yourself Modded," her step-mother had said with a sigh the last time they'd spoken of her appointment. Adriana really thought Modding solved everything. It only gave Blanche more reason to hold her ground and refuse. If something was wrong with her body, then she would rather let nature run its course and destroy her in the way it was always meant to.

With her cheek pressed against her hand, she leaned against the window of their hovercar and observed as they traveled past remarkable sights. The slums held a certain charm: the grit and grime, the stone-faced people toughing it out on their streets. Life had to be hard, yet they were surviving. It was one thing to make it when you had resources at your disposal. It was another to claw your way out of a hellhole.

Now only a few blocks away, she could make out the crumbling levels of the hospital. Along with many other buildings, it had fallen into a state of disrepair after the Crash. Nobody really ran it anymore, and most of the doctors who had clinics there worked in the area where they could profit the most: body modifications.

Instead of following the road to the hospital, however, Theron brought their hovercar around, swerving into a street so small they were required to stay vertical. "We're circling round back. There are protesters at the gates," he explained, collected even in the face of trouble.

She wished she had his calm. Instead, she started fidgeting, wondering what was wrong. The poor had no love for the Corporation, which was ridiculous considering that it was their advancements in Modding that everyone took advantage of.

Her coat made her even more uncomfortable. She tugged at the collar, wondering why she suddenly found it hard to breathe. She wasn't in the midst of a panic attack, was she? It wasn't as though she lacked the ability to defend herself from an angry mob if necessary.

Their hovercar emerged in an abandoned parking lot behind what either used to be a giant warehouse or a store. To Blanche's bewilderment, Theron brought their vehicle to a stop right in the middle of the junkyard.

"Theron?" Spots danced in her vision. "I don't . . . feel well . . ."

"Did you take your medicine this morning, my lady?"

Of course she had. Otherwise, he would've reminded her.

"Theron?" She pushed the button on her door to open it, but it wouldn't budge. She tried a few more times, growing more panicked by the second. "Open the door, please, I can't . . . I can't breathe . . ."

"Huh. It's jammed," he remarked, calm as ever.

"Theron!"

It worked. Her cry spurred him into action. He quickly opened his door and stepped out of the hovercar.

But he did not walk over to the passenger seat to open the door for her.

She pounded on the window. "Theron! Let me out!"

The old man slowly made his way to her side, peering through the window at her. His countenance remained the same: calm, collected. No hint of concern or remorse.

The darkness closed in. *This isn't real*, she thought. How many times did he submerge her into training simulations, each one more real than the last? She desperately fumbled for the lock on the hovercar door, and when it wouldn't release, she began to search for something, *anything*, beneath the seat.

It was just like when she'd been sinking into quicksand. She was running out of time.

"Theron," she croaked, collapsing on her side into the seat. "Let . . . let me out . . ."

~

WHAT DID YOU SEE?

Blanche's head throbbed. The voice was so loud it vibrated inside her skull.

"Nothing," she answered feebly. "Something was just wrong with the simulation."

The voice was not content with her answer. She realized this because before it asked her again, something raced through her body, bringing a searing pain before a terrifying numbness. When she cried out, it echoed all around her such that she didn't dare make a sound again.

What did you see Scarlette do? the voice demanded.

"She . . ." Blanche tried to recall when the simulation had gone weird. "She and Regulus Dara touched hands. He went off-script, asked her to dance. We couldn't see the other girl."

She braced herself for more pain.

This time, it did not come.

What do you think happened?

Whatever they'd done to her had already loosened her tongue. And her mind. Maybe it was whatever had been in the car. Maybe it was the effect of that current they'd pumped into her body. Thus, with no reservations, she answered, "She did something. I don't know what, but she did something. She would not let go of his hand. When she did, the simulation stopped."

She recalled Scarlette's face. "She was afraid."

What followed was a silence so thick she could hear the frantic beat of her heart in her ears. She tried to make out where she was, but a bright light was shining directly into her eyes, and she could barely move the rest of her body.

The voice returned. *You have seen too much. I'm sorry, child.*

Wait, she recognized that voice. "Theron?" It had to be. It sounded distorted, but that cadence, the accent, was familiar. "H-Help me, Theron . . . please . . ."

You have seen too much.

"No . . ." She didn't even understand what she'd seen. "No, please . . . I don't . . ."

Pain, unlike any other, blossomed in her chest.

And then, nothing.

~

THE WORLD SEEMED DIFFERENT. *She* seemed different. Blanche found herself re-energized in a way she hadn't experienced in years. There was a lightness to her that was unusual, a strength she did not recognize. Had it been the treatment? She *had* been on her way to the doctor, hadn't she?

The room she occupied even resembled that of the hospital over in the slums, old and close to falling apart. Beds with rickety frames filled the space, along with some outdated-looking machinery and trolleys of medical supplies. A woman in a shabby lab coat stood next to Blanche's bed, lips pursed together as she glanced from her clipboard to a screen mounted on top of some device that emitted a rhythmic beeping sound. Despite feeling well enough to go for another round in Theron's training simulation, Blanche found it hard to turn her head.

"Well, at least you won't have to worry about seeing a doctor again," a familiar voice drawled from the foot of her bed.

"Not *that* kind of doctor, anyway," the woman in the lab coat at her side agreed.

Blanche's gaze drifted to the source of the first voice, realizing that he looked familiar, too. "You're Regulus Dara," she said, equal parts certain and apprehensive. She'd seen enough of his movies with Scarlette to recognize him.

He didn't embody perfection like he did on screen, however. His nose was crooked and he suffered from a nasty pimple breakout on his forehead. She must've been glaring at him because he backed up a step and put his arms up in a gesture of surrender. "Regulus Dara is my Likeness," he corrected, bitterness lacing his tone.

"His Majesty sold his soul to the Corporation for a few hundred credits," the woman supplied, earning her a rude hand gesture that she returned with a laugh. "Now he doesn't even get royalties. Should've read the fine print, mate."

Blanche's expression softened a fraction. So Regulus Dara was only a woman's fantasy made real. She'd heard of Scanning; it was licensing your image to be used for whatever purpose, often for art and entertainment. Judging by his reaction and the teasing, it was clear that he had done it out of desperation. Scanning had been all the rage before Modding replaced it.

Still, she wasn't sure she liked him. She'd spent so much time being annoyed by Regulus Dara the actor that she had trouble detaching that impression from his actual person. "Then who are you, and what are you doing here?" she asked.

He raised a brow at her. "You crashed into my turf. I'll be asking the questions, thank you."

Well, that certainly didn't endear him to her. Maybe if he *acted* like Regulus Dara, he'd have more grace and charm. But he was all sarcasm and sharp edges, much like she was. Her temper rose. She straightened as she snapped, "*Your* turf? I was attacked!"

The woman's hands were gentle but firm as she guided Blanche to lie back down. "Slow down, girl. Your new heart's still getting used to your body. Don't push it too hard."

Blanche blinked. "My new what?"

Silence answered her. She scanned the faces of those around her, but the man who was not really Regulus Dara turned away, pretending to busy himself with checking out some tools and supplies.

The woman sighed softly, removing her surgical gloves and tossing them into the bin without taking her eyes off Blanche. "Your new heart," she repeated. "You died three days ago, Blanche."

~

BLANCHE HAD NOT EXPECTED death to be so unremarkable. Her life hadn't flashed before her eyes. She hadn't even seen a light she could walk toward. There had only been pain and darkness.

She couldn't even be certain *how* she'd died. Her deaths in the training simulation had bled together with the real one, giving her an ample supply of nightmares while she remained bedridden. She must have had some unprocessed fear of closed spaces, because her dreams constantly made up new scenarios when she'd had enough of the quicksand and the locked hovercar.

Being awake, however, proved to be just as annoying. Regulus Dara hovered like a hologram, always there whenever she woke, unusually interested in her progress but never directly speaking to her. Several times, she wondered if they had traded places; if this was not Dara's Likeness while they imprisoned the real one elsewhere, making him record hours and hours of cringey videos for the amusement of the masses.

It was odd how she was feeling more than she ever did when she had a human heart. When they'd explained that they couldn't repair her heart and had to replace it with one made of metal and wires, she'd feared she would become a shell of herself. But since the incident, she hadn't had a moment of peace. She feared the dark and what else it might bring now that she'd experienced death in its arms. She wondered about the people who kept her company and what their interests in her were. Why did they save her? They'd crafted the heart using parts that were clearly stolen from the

Corporation. Why would anyone go through all that trouble for her? There had to be a catch. People did nothing out of the goodness of their hearts—human or mechanical—anymore.

Most of all, she could not comprehend the fate that had befallen her. Why had Theron taken her life? Was he in league with the rebels? Did he seek to bring down the Corporation from the inside?

Was Scarlette in danger?

The thought of her sister spurred her recovery. She *had* to go back. If Theron genuinely posed a threat to her family, Scarlette would be vulnerable and easy to prey upon.

Blanche's funeral had taken place a week after her "death." It had been all over the news channels, which she watched with morbid fascination alongside Dara and the doctor, Sol. (Sol had to be a codename, she thought. A few others had come in and they'd been named Do, Re, and Mi.)

Scarlette looked ill throughout the ceremony and the press conference that followed, and Blanche didn't blame her . . . especially not with Theron standing behind Scarlette, gripping the handles of her wheelchair. He still looked as unfazed as ever.

Meanwhile, Adriana convincingly played the role of grieved mother. She even let a well-timed tear streak down her perfect face. Nevertheless, that was the extent of the emotion she displayed regarding her stepdaughter's passing. She spent the rest of the event making a target of the slums, painting them as brigands and terrorists who sought to destroy the City's peace.

Dara scoffed at that, which was most curious. Blanche was convinced he was on the Corporation's payroll.

"What?" he asked in a huff when he noticed her looking at him.

"She's my mother, you know," she pointed out, ignoring the pit that opened in her stomach as she said the words. Adriana had never cared for her. Blanche knew that, but she'd been so desperate for things to change that she was willing to hold on to the smallest shows of motherhood Adriana granted her.

"Stepmother," Dara reminded her. When Blanche recoiled, however, his countenance changed, leaving no trace of arrogance on his face. Instead, he shifted in his seat and faced her. "We need your help," he said, with no fanfare.

She frowned. "But I have nothing to offer you. That was my funeral you just saw—"

"Which is perfect," he interrupted, his infuriating grin returning. "You're dead to the world. But your biometric information will still be intact. They probably won't even bother to wipe it."

She glanced at Sol, who'd also turned away from the holoscreen to pay attention to their conversation. Blanche was beginning to see what they were getting at. "You want me to help you break into the Corporation," she concluded, her mechanical heartbeat picking up as the implication dawned on her.

She expected them to deny it, and was therefore disappointed when Dara only shrugged. "Don't you want to take it back? It's rightfully yours."

Blanche blinked. She'd never really thought about it that way. She didn't have a head for business; Adriana had been grooming Scarlette for the job, not her. Still, the reminder that the Corporation was hers, *rightfully*, through her father gave her pause.

Eventually, however, all she said was, "It was just a misunderstanding . . ."

Dara rolled his eyes so hard, for a moment she wondered if they would remain stuck at the back of his head. He shot Sol an exasperated glance but at least had the grace to try to temper it down when he turned to Blanche again. "I don't know, Blanche. They could've poisoned your food, had you run over. But they cut your heart out." His expression darkened. "Looks to me they don't want you back there. Not ever again."

Unconsciously, her hand came up to rest in front of her chest.

"Will you take my heart back if I refuse?" she asked them.

He raked his fingers through his hair and sighed. "No. We're not like them."

~

WE'RE NOT LIKE THEM.

Blanche turned the words over and over in her head that night. Who would have thought that *Regulus Dara*, of all people, was the leader of a resistance cell?

The more she pondered the incredulity of it, however, the more it made sense. Having a Likeness on the loose—and a popular one at that—might restrict his movements, but not his influence. *Everyone* loved Regulus Dara. His real self might not be as charismatic, but there were certain ways he could leverage his image to his advantage.

Why, though? Despite her efforts to get him to share his life story, Dara didn't disclose anything to her. It seemed a little overkill for him to have gone rogue only because the Corporation cheated him out of his share of royalties. There had to be something else, a reason far greater than revenge.

She promised to give her answer in the morning. It hadn't really been hard for her to decide. She wanted to get back at the Corporation just as much as he did. He might even help her get Scarlette to safety. Yet before anything else, she had to ascertain if she could trust him.

She had to make him talk.

Deciding she was past waiting, she carefully sat up and stared down at the wires connected to the thing now housed inside her chest. She wasn't squeamish; she simply found it a curious sight. There were no traces of blood or flesh or anything organic. Instead, there was a hollow space where her heart had been, its walls made of silicone. Encased was a device the size of her fist and the color and texture of a withering apple, its soft light pulsing rhythmically.

There was a good chance it was going to kill her, but she started detaching the wires from the device, anyway. When she'd pulled them all free and her body didn't spasm or suddenly shut down, she heaved a sigh of relief, then slid the cover closed. For a group of rebels with limited resources, they'd done a fantastic job. If not for the little arrow-shaped tattoo that hinted where the opening of the latch was, she wouldn't have been able to tell there was something else under all that skin.

She got up and searched the building for Dara, hoping she didn't trip any alarms or sensors along the way. All the other rooms were unoccupied, except for the one where they had hidden her away. The rebels at least had the sense not to be in the same place and risk being annihilated with one blow. She couldn't say the same for her family, despite Adriana's constant assurances that it would take an army to storm the Corporation and a nuclear explosive to take the building down.

The first rays of the morning sun broke through the horizon. Never having seen the city from this vantage point, Blanche took it in. She moved closer to the railing and watched the sky change colors. It wasn't anything like the sunrises she'd seen in the simulations—the clouds were too dark with smog to offer a good view—but it was *real*.

People said the City never slept, yet the rising sun clearly brought change. Buildings switched power sources, unfurling their solar panels. Even the roads suddenly got busier. More people visibly hurried about, crowds forming in the streets as they rushed to get to offices and factories. The aroma of food filled market stalls; the rebel infirmary was only a few floors high, and close enough to the slums that Blanche even caught whiffs of the delicious scents. Her stomach rumbled, reminding her she hadn't truly eaten in days.

Maybe Dara *could* wait. Her decision was further helped by the fact that one room along the corridor was some sort of locker room, and there she found a man's jacket hanging on a coat rack. She put it on, tugging the hood up over her head and stuffing her hands into the pockets. It stank of sweat and overuse, but it would have to do.

She kept her head down as she weaved through the crowd. The Corporation had drones patrolling the streets, but since the world believed she no longer existed, she was confident nobody would come looking for her. Dara and Sol might, though surely they'd be smart enough not to run into the market screaming her name. She had time.

It fascinated her to be wandering around unchecked. She'd never really had that freedom. Adriana had insisted that the slums were dangerous, and the few times the sisters were allowed outside, Theron marched them through along with a detachment of bodyguards. Scarlette couldn't touch anything without the item needing to be sanitized. Blanche couldn't wear anything that wasn't black, since her stepmother was worried about unglamorous pictures of her leaking onto the Net.

There was so much to take in. One stall sold bread and pastries in varieties she had only ever seen in pictures and holograms. The owner even offered samples to taste, and she tried out several types of cookies. Her favorite replicated the nutty flavor of an almond. She sighed in delight as the treat crumbled in her mouth.

More food stalls lined the street. One serving porridge was particularly busy, with the queue snaking down the block; she'd accidentally bumped into someone when she turned the corner with how crowded it had been, the impact nearly knocking her into the line. A man peddled some kind of sweet tofu dessert, wandering the streets balancing two metal buckets on a pole and stopping to mix a concoction right in front of a customer. Blanche didn't have any credits with her, so she only looked on forlornly as he passed her by.

"A treat, my dear?"

She turned toward the source of the voice and found an old woman behind a display of caramelized fruits. Her mouth watered at the sight. Despite the regulation of her intake due to her health, she had a fondness for sweets.

Thankfully, her lack of credits meant she couldn't give in to the temptation.

Blanche's regret must've been clear on her face because the old woman offered, "Oh, you poor thing. You can have whatever you like."

The people's kindness perplexed her. She had been taught to be wary of them. They'd killed her father, after all. Yet, it was a member of her own family who had made an attempt on her life, not the alleged scum of the streets.

She stepped closer to the stall and surveyed her options. In the mix were pears, apples, peaches, mangoes, and banana slices. How was it possible for her to only choose one?

In the end, she closed her eyes and extended her arm, reciting an old rhyme she learned from her father. Squinting an eye open, she found her hand hovering above the basket of apples. She was more than satisfied with the outcome. Perhaps she had even been wishing for it all along.

The old woman, bless her, gave Blanche the biggest one, spearing a stick through it and handing it to her. "Enjoy, dearie."

Blanche found it hard to believe her luck. The apple had a bright red color and was coated in a layer of sugar candy. She gave it a cursory lick, exclaiming in wonderment at how delicious that alone tasted. *Just a bite*, she promised as she helped herself to a supremely generous portion.

"There you are."

Dara materialized by her side, his fingers clamping around her forearm. He was alone. Unlike Blanche, he didn't bother concealing his face.

The old woman grinned at him, her two front teeth missing. "Morning, Rexie. I see you've made a new friend." Her tone was thick with implication.

He snorted. "She's not my friend."

It took a while for Blanche to say anything in response because she was still in the act of munching down her apple. Finally, she swallowed and backed Dara up, saying, "He's not my friend," while she wiped the frosting off the corners of her lips. "Thank you for the treat, ma'am."

Before she had the chance to finish, he pulled her away and back toward their hideout. She desperately clutched the stick of her candied apple as she glared daggers at him. "What's your problem?"

"You're not supposed to be out here."

"Why not? You're out here."

He stopped and turned to her, his face suddenly so close she could smell his cologne. Hah. Typical of Regulus Dara to still take the time and effort to primp himself, though she supposed he didn't need to do much apart from dealing with his acne since he already had such pretty green eyes and a nice jawline.

She blinked. Where did *that* come from?

And why wasn't he saying anything?

"What?" she huffed in annoyance—both from the

way he looked at her, and from how she couldn't wrench herself away from his hold.

He watched her for a moment longer, his face scrunched into an inscrutable expression. Then his gaze drifted to the apple she carried. "Leave it. We have work to do."

"I haven't even said yes!" she shouted after him as he walked away.

~

THEY SPED toward the Corporation on Dara's motorcycle, Blanche sitting behind him and gripping him around the waist. The man only proved more and more to be nothing like the characters his Likeness portrayed; for one, he had a clear disregard for traffic rules, driving through stop lights and speeding like there was no tomorrow. Corporation drones even chased them at some point, though he lost them easily, disappearing into a dark alley before blending with the rushing vehicles on the expressway. It was impressive and infuriating at the same time.

The sight of the Corporation's gleaming skyscraper no longer brought Blanche relief. She would not be safe within those walls—not after Theron had so casually betrayed her. She wished Dara would go faster. The longer they delayed, the greater the danger Scarlette faced.

"We have two minutes tops before they realize

someone used my ID!" she shouted to be heard over the noise of the wind and racing cars, forgetting that she shared a comm line with Dara and Sol back at headquarters.

"*Pipe it down, B. I can hear you and your frantic heartbeat just fine.*"

"*Stop messing with her, Rex.*"

"*Sol, you should see how tightly she's holding on to me.*"

Blanche's face grew hot. She *would* let go just to disprove his point, but they were flying at breakneck speed and she wasn't exactly keen on dying a second time. "Shut up and drive," she snapped.

"*As you wish, princess.*"

She directed him toward one of the employee side entrances. There were security cameras in place, but having helmets on would buy them some time. She had her fingerprints and retina scanned. The acknowledging beep and green light marked the beginning of their two minutes.

He didn't bother to park, leaving the motorcycle in front of the building entrance. Sol would deal with it for them. Anyway, if everything proceeded according to the plan, it wouldn't matter that they didn't have a getaway vehicle.

That was a very big *if*.

The first sign that something had gone awry came after they cleared the sliding doors and arrived at a deserted lobby. Employees worked in the Corporation in rotating shifts, so the building was never empty. Yet they found no signs of life—just the steady hum of machinery.

The second was how quiet Dara suddenly was. He was trailing behind her just moments ago, but she could no longer hear his footsteps. Neither was he making some ill-timed quip about their situation. She turned around to be sure he still followed her.

He was gone.

From the corner of her eye, she caught the door to the fire exit swinging shut. "What the hell are you doing? This wasn't the plan!" she hissed into her comm line, abandoning her path to the elevators to chase after him. Great, he probably thought he was being clever. Just because he was the boss of some gang didn't mean he knew this place better than her. She *lived* here—or had, at any rate.

The door creaked shut behind her and plunged the stairwell into darkness. A moment later, the emergency lights flickered to life, giving her an eerie red-carpet welcome. She cursed under her breath. Theron must've already discovered their presence.

She spun around and attempted to go back to the lobby, but the door was locked from the inside. The sound of static in her ears and the echo of rushing footsteps above her only further drove the point home: There was nowhere else for her to go but forward.

Blindly, she hurried up the stairs and into the doorway waiting on the landing. In hindsight, she should've questioned why there had been no door, only a gaping mouth that opened into a familiar bright field with rolling green hills in the distance. Overhead was a stunning blue sky. It took her breath away.

"Don't move."

Dara appeared in front of her, but he looked almost translucent against the vivid backdrop. Squinting, she saw pixelated squares instead of internal organs, a stark contrast to the lush blades of grass and the cotton-soft clouds drifting in the sky.

The only way out is in, a voice echoed from somewhere behind her, like a distant memory. She glanced down at her feet and saw that she stood on quicksand, though she didn't remember moving from her spot.

Her mouth became dry as it crashed back to her.

She was in Theron's training simulation.

"This isn't real," she whispered as she began to make her way out of the quicksand. But it wouldn't let her. She tried to reach for Dara, but she could not bring her arms out far enough before the quicksand grabbed and pulled her deeper into its embrace. "This isn't real!"

Despite her panic, he remained unfazed. "I know." He dropped to one knee and ran his palms over the grass, searching for something on the ground. What was he doing?

"We're in a simulation," Blanche explained, urgency in her tone. "Get me out—"

He huffed in exasperation, but he did not stop. "I *know*."

Deeper and deeper she sank. "Rex, please," she called out, and the use of his nickname surprised him enough that he stopped for a moment to glance at her. Their eyes met; his were as green as the grass. She realized she could get lost in them in the same way she could wander these endless fields forever.

He reached for her hand, his face lined with determination. "It's okay. I got you, B."

~

"You have *got* to stop dying."

The world came back into focus one color at a time. Cool blues. A splatter of red, slowly staining the walls like blood. The glowing yellow of a lightbulb. Shadows, dark and foreboding. Green, like the rolling fields of a world she would never truly see for herself.

Green, like Regulus Dara's eyes.

Blanche sat up with a start, sensing an unusual ache and exhaustion in her body. It took her a moment to place where she was. The building's interior appeared foreign, but through the broken windows, the rare scent of something other than death and decay wafted through. Very faint, but also there: salt.

They were very far from the Corporation, then; on the opposite side of the peninsula, near the sea.

Dara walked over and handed her a clean shirt before turning away to let her dress. Was she seeing things, or had it been concern on his features? "What happened?" she asked, pulling the garment over her head.

By the foot of the bed, Sol paced, squinting at the tablet in her hand before finally looking up to regard Blanche. "Do you remember what happened? Before you . . ." She trailed off, hesitating.

"You shouldn't have left."

"*Rex*," Sol said in a warning tone.

"She pulled off the wires! That could've killed her!"

Blanche blinked in astonishment. She remembered this Regulus Dara from the movies—full of righteous anger and protectiveness over whatever woman he loved. It seemed strange enough that he displayed any of that. What made it even more jarring was that *she* appeared to be the target of his outburst.

Perhaps she was just reading too much into it. She was their ticket into the Corporation, after all. Dara would be upset if anything happened to her.

"You know it's not that," Sol interjected matter-of-factly. She slipped the tablet into the pocket of her lab coat and moved to stand closer to Blanche on the opposite side of the bed. "You went to the market. Did you notice anyone suspicious?"

Dara snorted. "Everyone's suspicious."

Now Blanche was confused. "The market? We were in the Corporation." She scowled at him. "You went rogue and got us trapped in a simulation!"

The awkward silence and the exchange of glances

between Sol and Dara gave her the distinct impression they had *not* been in the Corporation.

From another pocket, Sol withdrew a corked vial and carefully handed it to Blanche. Inside lay a robotic creature the size of her fingernail, caked in blood and something else. It no longer moved, but Blanche remained careful not to disturb it in its prison.

"You were Bugged," Dara said, scowling.

Blanche's jaw dropped. Bugging had been a surveillance process that rose to popularity just before the Crash. People had shrunk cameras to the size of ants, rendering traditional security systems obsolete. If you wanted to spy on anyone, you just had to get the device into their bodies, and people did that by creating carriers designed after insects. Hence the name.

Bugging had become illegal after the Crash. For one, it had nasty side effects, which wasn't surprising considering it was a very intrusive form of technology. Bugs didn't just monitor a person's actions from the inside, either. The more advanced models could affect bodily systems, even linking with the nervous system to control the body or to extract information directly from the brain. Those Bugs caused hallucinations, and they were so real, they drove most of their victims mad.

"Rex pulled you out," Sol explained. "Don't let that pretty face fool you. He used to be a deBugger, and a damn good one at that."

"For the Corporation?" That presented a potential

motive. An entire department was laid off by the Corporation once Bugging was outlawed, but it appeared that its far greater sin was the continued use of it.

Dara made an exasperated noise. "Haven't you been listening? *You* were Bugged. Can we focus on that, please?"

He snatched the vial with the Bug away from her hand so suddenly that she flinched, for a moment alarmed that the glass case would break, and the Bug would force its way into her body again. That certainly grabbed her focus, albeit unintentionally. "If everyone thinks I'm dead, why would they have Bugged me? And how?"

The dread on Dara's face indicated that she had finally started asking the right questions.

It also confirmed that something had gone wrong.

"They know," she concluded.

She thought back to what she'd believed had happened: the trip to the market, their infiltration of the Corporation. Dara had confirmed that he had found her wandering the stalls with a candied apple in hand—which meant the rest of it had been a figment of her imagination.

"It was the Bug trying to extract information. Most people think they're just daydreaming, so they never realize they've already leaked sensitive information," he explained, launching into a lecture on how Bugs worked once they were inside the body and locked into their target's system. He also assured her that he had completely purged her of the Bug, though that wasn't the reason she was mortified.

If she'd daydreamed the motorcycle ride, then what was that banter with him all about? Worse, she'd *liked* it.

She shook her head to clear her thoughts of Regulus Dara, choosing to focus on the things she still lacked answers for. With how busy the market had been, she never would've noticed when she'd gotten the Bug. Had it been when that stranger had collided with her? In something she ate? Or on the ground, watching and waiting for her? A device smart enough to tamper with one's nervous system would be smart enough to track its prey. Or perhaps someone controlled it remotely.

"They know," she repeated, the awful truth finally sinking into her. The why or how wasn't important now. In fact, only one thing mattered: getting Scarlette away from the Corporation.

"You'll be safe here," Sol assured her, mistaking Blanche's reaction for concern for her own welfare. "This is as far away from—"

Blanche shook her head and pushed herself off the bed. "No, you don't understand. I need to go back for my sister." Theron and whoever else he was working with would be after Scarlette next, she was sure of it.

"They'll know we're coming," Dara said, but he didn't sound entirely opposed.

She fixed him a stare. "If you're such a hotshot deBugger," she challenged, "they won't."

WALKING through the front doors of the Corporation was out of the question now. So was sneaking in through the employee side entrance—the Bug had already trans-mitted that idea back to Theron for sure. But according to the evening weather report, a storm was coming, which was a rare window of opportunity—especially coupled with having access to the Corporation's security system via Blanche's biometric data. She'd dubbed it Reverse deBugging and gloated about it to Sol's amusement and Dara's annoyance.

The ease and efficiency by which Dara and his group executed their plan astounded her. She hadn't been able to interrogate them, but her gut told her they long had their pieces in place and had simply been biding their time. And unlike her Bug-induced daydream of breaking into the Corporation like the stars of an action movie, Dara did not stray from the plan this time. If anything, he trusted Sol to guide their path and their other comrades to clear the way for them, which must have been difficult considering the stakes.

"Are you sure your sister will be in her room?" he asked once he'd set up shop in the server room.

"Are you sure you can give me five minutes?" she retorted.

He grabbed her hand. His touch was gentle despite his calloused fingers. She fell quiet as she wondered what he was going to do, but in the end, he only switched the timer of her watch on. "Five minutes," he assured her without a hint of sarcasm or arrogance. He yanked down her night-vision goggles, his fingertips lingering on her cheek a little longer than necessary. Not that she minded. "Good luck, B."

She scrambled away before she made things weird, her heart pounding in her chest in a way she hadn't thought possible since they had replaced it. How peculiar was it that she had never truly experienced emotions until after her death? She loved her parents, and she loved Scarlette too, but other than that, her life had been one of routine and compliance. All this—rebellion, adventure, *attraction*—were new, and they scared her.

The lights died, as did the hum of everything electronic in the building. She crept out into the hallway, grateful for the self-defense training Theron had put her through. The simulation exercise was a later addition, aiming to further fortify her mind, but the more she reflected on her newfound knowledge of the Corporation, the more she suspected it was a test of some kind. Might Scarlette's condition, which showed no improvement despite the various treatments supposedly provided by Adriana, be because she was simply another test subject?

The voices at the end of the hall snapped Blanche out of her thoughts, and she slipped into the Security locker room. The guards were mobilizing, and from the sound of it, they'd found the source of their troubles easily enough:

the server room. She wanted to turn back and warn Dara, but it was impossible for her to leave her hiding place without being seen. They'd deactivated their comms when they got into the building as well; unlike Blanche's earlier daydream, Sol had thought it too risky for chatter of any form.

She told herself he'd be fine. Besides, why did she have to worry? They were just two people with a common enemy, and the enemy of her enemy was her friend.

The guards filed out. Without even needing to check her watch, she was aware that she was taking too much time, but she counted to ten anyway before finally moving. She slowly approached the elevators, confident that at least one was operating on emergency power, and used her credentials to gain control. Thankfully, Dara's assumption was correct: The Corporation hadn't yet deactivated her access. It would only be a matter of time before she'd be tracked, however, even if Dara had promised her she would have five minutes.

She glanced at her timer. Just about three minutes left now. *Damn it.*

The elevator shot up toward the sky; Blanche had never before felt it was moving too slow. Moreover, it was unsettling that she was going in blind. What if guards awaited her at her destination? What if they were given orders to shoot first and ask questions later? She wouldn't be able to overcome a group of armed guards with just one gun and sheer stubbornness.

However, the floor remained silent upon her arrival. She didn't like it. Theron was definitely not that dumb. There was surely a catch, but what? Was she moving through a rolling field of green again only to end up in quicksand? That seemed like Theron's signature tactic.

She intended to count another ten seconds before stepping off the elevator, time be damned, but at four the elevator wailed in warning, and she became more concerned about being locked in than facing whatever waited for her outside. She stepped onto the floor as lightly as she could manage, pulling her phase gun from its holster on her hip and hoping she wouldn't trigger any sensors that might be in place.

Silence. She wanted to be relieved, but the dread at the pit of her stomach only grew as she continued on.

This place was her domain, at least. Even in the dark —though the night vision goggles helped plenty—she made her way to Scarlette's room easily.

But where were the guards? Was this a trap? Had they already taken Scarlette?

Heart in her throat, Blanche hurried to her sister's room. The door was locked. She cursed under her breath, opening the panel to input the access code. For the first time, it asked for further identification. Relief coursed through her as that only proved Scarlette was still inside, but it was fleeting. With shaking fingers, she scanned her prints and then her retina.

The door slid open with a soft hiss. "Scar?" she called

out as she entered, no longer bothering to be discreet. She was left with, what—just over a minute?

Scarlette's room was much fancier than Blanche's, which only proved Adriana's favoritism. It faced the open sea, which, while gray and stinky most days, still offered a better view than the decaying city. The room even contained a reception hall, a spacious area with floor to ceiling windows on two sides, enhanced by synthetic potted plants and exotic flowers. As breezy as it appeared, to Scarlette it still felt stifling, despite Blanche's efforts to distract her sister by goofing around and inventing silly races as she wheeled her around.

A rustling sound made Blanche spin around so fast, her finger pressed into the trigger of her phase gun enough that it emitted a soft whining sound.

The end of her weapon was pointed right at her sister's face.

"Blanche," Scarlette said, a quiver in her voice. Her reaction cut like a knife through Blanche's heart. Her sister was afraid. Of *her*.

Blanche held up her hands in a gesture of surrender. "Hey, it's okay." Her voice also wavered, and she swallowed to clear the lump that formed in her throat. "It's okay, Scar. I'm not here to hurt you. I would *never*. But Theron, he—"

"Blanche," Scarlette repeated, her voice rising in pitch and urgency.

A flash of lightning from the incoming storm momentarily illuminated the room, exposing what had terrified Scarlette all along. Their mother, Adriana, stood behind her wheelchair with Theron by her side. He, too, carried a phase gun and had it pointed at Blanche.

It took a few seconds for it all to sink in. And even after Blanche reached the only conclusion, she found herself vehemently denying it. "I don't . . ." She took a step forward, only to be greeted by the warning whine of Theron's weapon. Any closer and he would fire it, she didn't doubt that. And yet: "I don't understand . . ."

"I'm not letting you take Scarlette," Adriana said, the sharp lines of her face made harsher by the random bursts of illumination from flashes of lightning.

Blanche turned to Theron, desperate for answers, but he only looked back at her with regret. *You have seen too much*, she recalled his voice saying, though she never figured out if any of that was real. But seen too much of what?

"I know what you are," Adriana pronounced, venom in her voice.

She possibly just imagined it, but Blanche felt her metal heart rattle in its cage. She also harbored anger toward her stepmother's hypocrisy. Adriana, renowned for pioneering aesthetic modifications, had the gall to paint her a monster for having a synthetic body part that she otherwise would've been dead without?

"He did this to me!" Blanche retorted, waving her hand with the gun at Theron's direction. When she realized that the attempt to change her stepmother's opinion of her was futile, she turned to Scarlette instead. "Scar, please. You know I would never hurt you. You're my sister!"

The lights flickered back on. Blanche didn't want to tear her gaze away from her sister, but she saw movement out of the corner of her eye and responded in kind. She rushed forward, grabbing the gun from Theron in a move the old man himself had taught her.

A shot rang out. Scarlette screamed, but the weapon was no longer aimed at anyone. Instead, it burned a hole through the window, ushering in a dose of angry wind.

Adriana attempted to retreat with her daughter in tow, but Scarlette, in a rare show of defiance, wheeled herself away from her mother's grasp. When Adriana used the device around her wrist to override the controls, Scarlette threw herself off the chair and onto the floor, crying out at the impact and at how she could no longer move.

Alerted to her sister's plight, Blanche turned away from her scuffle with Theron to come to her aid, only for him to grab her by the hair, dragging her back before hurling her toward the wall. The impact was strong enough to make spots dance in front of her eyes, but she pushed herself up and let her anger drive her onward. She ran for Theron with a roar, jumping onto the man's back before he could pick Scarlette up from the floor and deposit her back into her wheelchair. They wrestled;

Blanche no longer cared about fighting with honor in the way he had previously taught her.

Theron threw her off him, sending her crashing into a window. Scarlette screamed again, her voice squeezing the air right out of Blanche's lungs.

Then the whine of the pulse gun filled the room. Blanche opened her eyes just in time to watch Theron get blown back by the blast. Terror overcame her; never in her wildest dreams did she think Scarlette would ever need to fire a weapon.

But it had not been her sister.

Regulus Dara stood with his arm outstretched, looking every bit the hero in the movies his Likeness had appeared in. "That was for my mother," he declared.

A second shot left Theron lying on the floor with a gaping hole in his chest.

"That was for Blanche."

∽

BLANCHE STRUGGLED to stay still as Sol probed and examined her heart, even without experiencing any physical discomfort. She would have to get used to this now unless she wanted to just one day keel over from heart failure.

The rebels had stormed the Corporation, and with them came Sol and some medical personnel. Scarlette was being examined by one of the rebel doctors, though other than some bruising and her elation at being in the presence of Regulus Dara, she was unscathed.

"Poor Rex," Sol remarked. "He hates it when people fawn over him."

Blanche saw that he did, but she wasn't about to start being nice to him in front of other people—Sol most of all. "Doesn't look it from here," she scoffed. "If he so much as holds her hand, she's going to faint, I tell you."

That only caused Sol to give her a teasing smile. "Jealous, B?"

"What? No!" Blanche exclaimed, her face suddenly hot. "Why would I be?"

That was for Blanche, Dara's voice replayed in her head, and it certainly didn't help her case. Thankfully, Sol dropped the matter—perhaps because she had made her point.

"There's no sign of Adriana," Sol relayed instead, serious again. "None of our people saw her leave the premises, and we swept all the floors. Are there any secret passageways leading out to the City?"

"Not that I'm aware of," Blanche answered with a sigh. "We should ask Scar. I've been in the dark with what's going on with her since they came into the picture." A touch of bitterness laced her voice now; she was too exhausted to filter her feelings.

Scarlette had no knowledge of any secret tunnels either, so they had to be satisfied with preventing Adriana's access to the Corporation's systems and assigning a few rebels to guard the building in case she came back.

The sisters decided to get some sleep in the movie room. Scarlette didn't feel safe in her quarters, and Blanche's room was only big enough for one person. While Scarlette cleaned up, Blanche stripped her bed of its mattress, pillows, and blankets with Dara's help, carrying them over to the other room together.

It felt incredibly strange to have the actual Regulus Dara standing in the same room as where she had seen his Likeness countless times.

"Hey, B," he began when they finished laying out the blankets. He ran a hand through his hair, uncharacteristically nervous. "I . . . I could stay and keep watch. If you like. Just in case."

"Yeah. Sure. Just in case." It was a good idea, wasn't it?

He chuckled, and it seemed as though he was about to speak further, but she looked away. What was taking Scarlette so long? What the heck was she supposed to do now?

They fell into an awkward silence. For lack of anything better to do, she plopped herself down on the mattress she'd claimed as her bed. He followed without waiting for her invitation, though he kept himself perched on the edge and at a considerable distance.

"You okay?" he asked her. "I know it's been . . . a lot."

She sighed and leaned back, resting her palms on the mattress. After a moment, she shook her head. "I don't know." Idly, she scuffed the toe of her boot against the floor.

The floor rippled. Startled, she jerked and straightened, only to find the floor covered in water. "Rex—"

"I see it." He'd stilled, frowning at the water that should not have been there. "You said this was a hologram room?"

"Yeah, but . . ." She put her hand into the water and immediately trailed off. It was wet and cold. Holograms weren't supposed to feel like anything. Special effects had to be added in for the complete experience, but water was only ever used for a little drizzle since it would otherwise wreck the equipment.

They were in a simulation.

They had been Bugged.

But there were no rolling green hills and blue skies this time. Instead, they found themselves in the middle of a storm that only took seconds to form. The mattresses had disappeared, and she dangled over the side of a small rowboat. In panic, she hastily hauled the rest of her body inside, rocking the vessel even more.

"Get us out!" she screamed, straining to be heard above the roar of the waves. Despite being aware of their existence in a simulation, it was only a matter of time before her body fully accepted everything as truth. Drowning would be such a terrible way to go.

Lightning exploded overhead. Rain poured, drenching them with water so cold her teeth clattered.

"I can't!"

"What?"

"I'm in the sim *with* you! I can't get us out!"

The boat rocked so violently that Blanche was hurled overboard. Just before she hit the water, however, a strong pair of arms grabbed her, pulling her back into a tight embrace. "I'm sorry, B," Dara murmured, and while she shouldn't have been able to hear him through all the noise, the words slammed straight into her.

"What a terrible way to die," she tried to joke, fighting back tears.

"I know."

"You're not supposed to say that!" She pulled back far enough to punch him playfully in the chest. Maybe this was why people preferred dying alone. Dying made people stupid, and now she was making a fool of herself in front of Regulus Dara. "You're a hero, Rex. If you can't get us out here, then you can at least make dying worthwhile."

She had no idea what she was saying. He probably didn't get it, either.

Or maybe they did come to an understanding, because he leaned forward, and so did she, their lips meeting in a desperate last kiss. Blanche's resolve reignited; there *had* to be a way out of here. Sailors of old had weathered storms before. If they could just—

Then a furious gust of wind ripped through the sea and blew them apart.

Into the waves Blanche sank, toward a dark, dream-less sleep.

~

"So . . ." Scarlette bit her lip. "Are you and Rexie . . . ?"

Blanche looked over her sister's head and found Dara staring back at her with those infuriatingly green eyes. Were she and him *what*? She honestly had no idea. Friends? Sure. But that was likely not what Scarlette was asking. Scarlette had been in their mother's clutches for the past week, and she'd been hanging out with her sister's crush.

And what happened in the boat—or, rather, in the simulation—wasn't exactly the stuff of friends, was it?

"What? Of course not," Blanche said in answer, sounding more defensive than she intended.

He raised an eyebrow at her. She glared at him.

"Hmm." Scarlette didn't sound convinced either.

Blanche switched the topic, not wanting to subject herself to further scrutiny. She wasn't sure she could stand it; lying had never come naturally to her. "I still don't get it," she said, turning away from the window to gaze at their mother's still form on the bed.

Adriana lived, but she wouldn't be waking up anytime soon. The rebels hadn't seen her leave the Corporation because she'd hidden herself in the movie room, intending to ensnare Blanche in a simulation of her own design. She'd almost succeeded—if not for Scarlette, who had arrived just in time to intervene.

Sol's findings proved to be even more unsettling, however. Scarlette apparently possessed the ability to manipulate simulations. The girl didn't seem to realize it. Nor did she seem to be aware of the damage she'd inflicted on Adriana's psyche when she tampered with the program. Adriana had made the unfortunate decision to use a Bug, which allowed her to influence the elements of the sim directly. But Scarlette was no deBugger, and her method of stopping the simulation had been far from methodical.

Blanche thought back to that incident with *The Secret Prince*, as well as the message in Theron's voice, which made little sense until now: *You have seen too much, child.* Theron had to have known. Adriana, too. Was that why she had been so interested in Scarlette? All the monitoring, all the tests . . .

And there stood the other question. "Why did she have me killed? What did I ever do to her?" Even after everything, Blanche didn't really want her stepmother dead, though part of it was because she wanted answers, too.

"She had evidence you would surpass her one day," Scarlette replied as she wheeled herself over.

Blanche snorted. How preposterous. She had no interest in running the Corporation. In fact, she didn't know what they were going to do now that Adriana was out of commission. She hadn't really thought that far ahead.

"How?" The real question came from Dara, his brows furrowed in suspicion. He seemed to know something, but when Blanche tried to catch his attention, he pretended not to notice her.

Scarlette's expression was suddenly unreadable. She shrugged. "Algorithmic predictions."

Something about her sister's answer bothered her, yet Blanche couldn't put a finger on it. It also got pushed aside as Scarlette continued, "That, and legalities. Mother was still operating with the emergency powers the Board granted her when your father fell ill. It was only a matter of time before she would have had to step down and let you take over, as intended."

"Fancy that. Queen B in a suit," Dara teased.

"Shut up." The prospect of running the Corporation was becoming more real by the second, and Blanche didn't like it.

The wheels of Scarlette's chair creaked as she glided closer to her mother's bed. Adriana still looked beautiful, even while under a medical coma with her mind torn to shreds. How unfair.

"Will Mother be okay?" Scarlette asked, looking up at Dara.

His jaw tensed. Blanche could see he was planning to lie, so she was relieved when he opted instead for the truth, no matter how difficult it might be for them to hear. "Whatever happened back there . . . it's broken something in her. Sol and I will have to examine the Bug further. I've never heard of Bugs being used that way before. But her body will heal. It just might not be the same as it was before."

Blanche shot him a grateful look. It was kind of him not to blame it on Scarlette, even if it *had* been her doing.

"I managed living with this," Scarlette said with a small, enigmatic smile, patting the arm of her wheelchair. "She'll learn. We'll be here to help her through it." She stroked her mother's forehead, tucking a stray lock of hair behind her ear. "We're family, after all."

</FIN>

Some words, when strung together in the right manner, at the right time, were powerful enough to alter the future of humankind.

Others were meaningless.

It was a paradox I'd once delighted in. But I was tired of looking for the hidden meanirgs.

WILD SWAN *Chase*

Meghan Tomlinson

Lark

From the thinly-padded pilot's seat, I glared at the white blip that indicated my position on the nav screen. Unfamiliar constellations in glowing silver and teal blinked back in the silence. For the last thirty-odd days, the blip had mocked me as my underpowered flyer moved millimeter by millimeter through the nav display of the solar systems of Svaneunge, while I searched for a sign—any sign—of my brothers.

Not for the first time, I regretted taking *Dawnsinger*

instead of hiring a newer, faster ship out of Leda Station. But that would've drawn unwanted attention. And in the wake of my brothers' disappearances and the attempts on my own life, it was the last thing I should do.

If only Father had seen fit to give me a *Wild Swan*, I thought bitterly. The newly commissioned Cygnus-class ships were compact but loaded with enough firepower to take on an Eagle-class cruiser or escape an Albatross. And they were fast, making intergalactic travel a breeze. *Wild Swan I* through *IX* were prototypes for the new fleet being commissioned for our navy and would, if my brother Falconer's predictions were correct, end the war with the Aghavni decisively in our favor. All of my brothers had received one three months ago. Even the triplets had been given a ship to share, no matter that at 16 they needed to hire a pilot to fly them around.

My anger at being overlooked once again by my father gave way to guilt and fear. Somewhere out there, my brothers needed me. If I was very, very lucky, and if the Uni was generous, I'd find them healthy and whole. Maybe stranded on an uninhabited planet with a trashed warp engine. Or returning from a reckless trek into unclaimed space, one that they hadn't told anyone about.

Yeah, I had a hard time believing either of those scenarios, too. Especially in light of the abduction attempts made on me.

In the weeks leading up to the disappearances of my brothers, I'd noticed shadows following me on my way to work at Senator Iolana Drake's office, but I'd thought I was being paranoid. Then there was the altercation at a peace rally where I'd been attacked and nearly stunned by a couple of protestors. At the time, I'd thought it was simply a few uncouth political supporters of my father's attempting to scare me into submission. But after my brothers had gone missing, it was clear someone had been trying to make me disappear, too.

I might suspect my father's supporters of trying to abduct me (to them I was a traitor), but they loved my brothers and all their antics. Over the years, my brothers' exploits had branded them as the Wild Svanurs and darlings of the media. Although none actively campaigned for Father to maintain his seat as High Chancellor, they garnered him goodwill wherever they went by simply being his sons. So that ruled out my father's supporters (Senator Drake's fiercest political adversaries) as the culprits. And while Drake wanted to defeat my father in the upcoming election, this wasn't her style.

Who else could want the Wild Svanur brothers gone?

I'd already discarded the idea of opportunists and fortune hunters. If my brothers had been taken to beggar my family, there'd have been a ransom request by now.

That left one group. I shuddered despite my thermal leggings and thick turquoise tunic at the thought of my brothers being captured by the Aghavni Royal Forces. The recently late King Arnoldo's policies were downright draconian in comparison to my father's. My brothers, however, would make sensational hostages for the new Aghavni king—but so far, King Jonas had disavowed all involvement, both publicly and privately, to my Father's office. My fingers curled into a fist over Aghavni space on the nav display. They were probably only biding their time until they could marshal their forces for another attack on our weakening line of defense.

Frustrated with the lack of answers, I stood to stretch my short legs and my stomach growled. I'd bought *Dawnsinger* with an inheritance from my mother's estate, and I loved every nook and cranny on her. But the Sparrow-class flyer was meant more for planetside travel, not long hauls, and she barely consisted of a cockpit, a sleeping berth, and a head. She hadn't come outfitted with an insta-ov, so no hot meals for me. But I couldn't survive even short trips without hot caffeinated beverages, so I'd paid for the installation of a beverage station. I'd been living on hot chai lattes, meal replacement bars, and freeze-dried fruit.

As I rummaged in the depleted pantry compartment for a bar, the insistent beeps of an incoming message in code punctuated the small space and chased my dark thoughts away. While *Dawnsinger* was equipped to translate the archaic subspace signal of long and short dashes of light into an automated voice message, I didn't need it. The code was long burned into my brain by my grandmother, who'd been an enthusiast of old tech.

As I half-listened to the beeps, I slid back into the

pilot's seat with my meal bar to check my long-range probes for a report. Two had transmitted their findings on the two habitable planets in this system. One had a small colony, and the other was barren. But neither probe had found anything matching the unique mineral composite of the *Wild Swan* ships. *Wild Swan I* through *VIII* had gone missing along with my brothers. I chewed my lip. By now they could've been separated from their ships, especially if the Aghanvi Royal Forces were involved, but it was all I had to go on. I couldn't visually search every city on every planet. Besides, the local authorities would be doing just that. And by now, every citizen in Svaneunge was on the lookout for the missing Svanur brothers.

The beeps finished, and I mentally sorted the code while chewing the dry food without tasting it. Which was a shame because it was my last chocolate-raspberry bar.

[Greetings, Skylark. Any luck on your search today?]

Despite my ever-present hope that the message would be from my brothers, I wasn't disappointed to hear from Dove. He was the one silver lining in this mess. Twenty-one days ago, he'd answered a vaguely coded message I'd been sending out on repeat in hopes of making contact with my brothers without drawing attention.

Few used code anymore, as it was slow and cumbersome when audiocasts or vidcasts were available and transmitted via the much faster comm network of beacons and satellites. But Dove had replied to my message [Lost swans, sing and be found.] using the same subspace signaling code, [Do doves count?]. And we had been corresponding every day since.

[Greetings, Dove. No luck. How about you?]

From previous conversations, I'd gleaned he was sifting through space on a search for a ship his family had lost or that had been stolen. It gave me some comfort to know I wasn't out here searching alone.

[I seem to be all out of luck. I don't suppose you ever feel like giving up and running away? Maybe starting a pumpkin farm on a far-flung colony where no one knows you?]

The question hit me like a stun charge. I *had* run away.

Three years ago, when Father had returned home from his annual rejuvenation treatment with his new wife, Sarika Finch, in tow, I'd borne the abrupt change to our lives with grace, at first. But the bewitching Sarika was like a force of dark energy, filling my universe with negative pressure and ultimately driving me away from my father and brothers, who had hitherto been the stars and moon of my galaxy.

Suffice it to say we didn't get along, and I didn't like her influence on Father. But he was happy, so I held my tongue.

I held it when she redecorated my mother's rooms for her pet cybernetic birds; when she invited the dullest and shallowest of her former medical colleagues to sit next to me during state dinners; when she threw lavish parties for the elite of Svaneunge; and when she canceled our late mother's annual gala benefit for youth in need to fund some bio-medical company's research, probably to do with longer rejuv times.

After a year of holding back my opinions to keep the peace, however, I'd snapped and moved out. At twenty-five, it was time, even if all my brothers still lived at home, including the three older ones. Though it should be noted that Altair, the eldest, spent all his waking hours working in his lab, and Falconer, second eldest, had been deployed at the time. While Griffin . . . well, no one truly knew how Grif spent most of his days, but he generally turned up for supper twice a week.

But give up my search? *Never.* Of course, Dove didn't know who I was searching for. He might have the impression I was a bounty hunter. In our messages, I tried to be careful how much I revealed about my identity as the daughter of the High Chancellor of Svaneunge. Too many times I'd been befriended only to get closer to him. And while ship computers usually tuned out the archaic signals as white noise, Aghavni intelligence or my brothers' captors (who might be one and the same) could be listening in.

While I'd been considering my response, another message came through. [So that's a definite no on the gourds and running away?]

I chuckled under my breath. Was he being serious? It was so hard to tell over code.

[I tried running away once, and it only caused more problems.] And maybe, if I'd stayed at home, my brothers wouldn't be missing right now.

Or you would have been abducted along with them.

At least I'd be with them. The uncertainty was driving me out of my mind, so much so that arguing with myself had become the norm.

[More problems?] he prompted.

My fingers hovered over the console as I deliberated if I should confide in a stranger. If Dove figured out who I was and who I was searching for, that information was probably quite valuable. It wouldn't surprise me if the Aghavni king had taken a bounty out on my entire family. Under an alias, of course.

On the other hand, Svaneunge and Aghavni consisted of numerous solar systems. I could use an extra set of eyes.

[My search is very personal to me.] I finally tapped out. [Giving up is unthinkable, but maybe after I find who I'm looking for, I can meet you at your dream pumpkin farm.] Before he could reply that he'd only been kidding about meeting in person, I sent another message. [Are your family farmers?]

There was such a long pause, I feared he'd ghosted me. Then the code started rolling in.

[Thank you, Skylark, for the image of my mother toiling in the soil. I haven't had such a good laugh in a long time, and I was in desperate need of one. We are not farmers, but you could say we deal in agriculture. Once, I visited a gourd farming community in the autumn. It's one of my happiest childhood memories, but it doesn't fill my dreams.]

My brows rose as I finished my meal bar. [What does?]

[It's more an absence. Something I'm desperate to hear, and I keep searching for it.] In the pause, I leaned forward, curious what he would say. [What your voice sounds like.]

Warmth filled my chest. I'd also wondered from time to time about Dove, but it was neither here nor there. Despite what I'd suggested about meeting up, our galaxy was huge. We'd probably stop conversing at some point and then lose track of each other.

Another message came in a flash. [I can't believe I sent that. I must be oxygen deprived or the solitude is getting to me. Honestly, I wasn't dreaming of you in a creepy way. It must be because I haven't seen another human in months.]

I smiled to myself at his earnestness. Since Dove didn't know what I looked like, there was very little he could dream of. [All good.]

[Thank you. To be honest, I cannot run away either. My search is of great importance to my family. If I fail at this, everything my brother has been working toward will be lost. I'm afraid I'm already failing him.]

A burden I could relate to. We'd skirted around these edges before. I'd known his search was important. That he had been traveling through systems like me, meeting failure after failure. Strangely enough, it sounded like he was on a quest straight out of a fairy tale. And I supposed I was on one, too. I prayed to the Uni there was a happy ending for us both.

I made a decision. [I'm searching for my brother. I suspect foul play involved. He wouldn't just disappear like that.]

Not for this long. Not all of them at once. It hurt that Father hadn't informed me personally of their disappearances. Instead, I had learned along with everyone else when the story broke. It had been splashed across all media outlets, and it was still dominating the headlines and trending on various platforms.

I'd thought the story was a prank by my brothers until none of them responded to my messages in our secure sibling chat. At the time, it had been over a month since I'd participated in the chat. Work had been eating up all my free time as the campaign had ramped up for the final months. But I should've made time. Then I would've suspected something was amiss when I hadn't heard from my brothers.

Deep down I feared they had been abducted to silence me and my work to elect a new High Chancellor of Svane-unge Space in the upcoming election. But there'd been no contact. No demands. And the Aghavni were denying any involvement.

Finally, my resolve to cut all communication with my

father broke in desperation to understand what had happened. But either he was screening my calls, or he was in fact on a silent wellness retreat with his wife as his office maintained. I couldn't believe it. The galaxy was in turmoil as speculation ran high on why and how my brothers had disappeared, and the High Chancellor was on a spa week?

When it became clear Father had left his deputy chancellor in charge—a man perhaps rightfully more concerned with the warfront than 11 missing men who were known for wild jaunts about the galaxy—I'd walked out of my condo on Svaneunge III and taken on the search myself.

Dove's reply roused me from my brooding. [How can I help, Skylark?]

The selflessness of the question caught me off guard, and my teeth worried my bottom lip. As much as I wanted to, though, I knew I shouldn't divulge my identity. [Thank you, but there's not much you or anyone can do.] Not without telling more than I wanted to. [Maybe keep an eye out for shipwrecks?]

There was a pause. [Will do.]

I hesitated. [Dove, I can't give up, and I suspect you won't either. And I won't contemplate failure—for either of us. If you're still searching after I've found my brother, I'll help in any way I can.]

[That is a generous offer. And you are correct. I cannot walk away from my duty. But if you're still looking for your brother after I've located the item for my family, I'll join your search, Skylark.]

His promise set off unexpected warmth in my chest, and I realized it had been a long time since I'd had anyone other than my brothers to rely on.

After Dove signed off, I stared listlessly at an unfolding nebula until the ping of a returned probe had my fingers dancing over the console for the report. My mouth went dry and my heart skipped a beat at the read-out. A mass with the same composition of a *Wild Swan* ship had been found in the nearby Cygnet system.

Hold on, brothers. I'm coming.

~

WHITE ROCK, biting wind, and little else greeted me when I landed *Dawnsinger* in the northern hemisphere of Cygnet IV. It had taken 16 hours of pushing the flyer to its max to get here that quickly, but every minute had felt like an eternity. The uninhabited planet supported human life and was earmarked for future colonization by Svaneunge. It wasn't off-limits for exploration, so it was conceivable there were other people on-planet. *Dawnsinger* didn't have the capabilities to scan an entire planet for lifeforms without taking nearly 24 hours—time I couldn't waste.

So far, the war hadn't come to the Cygnet system. With the Aghavni border a mere stone's throw away, however, there was a chance I'd come upon a rogue

Aghavni patrol, scouting the area before advancing their fleet. With time not on my side, I had proceeded without the scan but with caution.

To the utility belt around my waist, I'd added a small energy pistol, and I'd chosen a landing zone a couple klicks from the site marked by the probe in case the abductors (if there were any) or rogue Aghavni soldiers were about. I'd also donned a lightweight jacket over a stretchy black suit that covered me from my neck downward. It doubled as both thermal regulation gear and protective wear. Basically, it would keep me warm or cool and stop most physical and energy blades, even stun rounds. The year before I left home, it had been a birthday gift from my elder brothers, Altair and the eldest twins Falconer and Griffin. (Yes, there were two sets of twins, plus the triplets, in our family, courtesy of the best artificial surrogate wombs money could buy and my mother's desire for a large family.)

I'd also stashed a few meal bars and hydration packets in the pouch on my belt, while in my hands I carried my padlet to track the unique metal composition my probe had detected. There was a slight possibility that this mass wasn't a *Wild Swan* ship, but just some other shipwreck. Best not to get my hopes up too high.

Underfoot, deep grooves scoured the smoothed rocks, evidence of Cygnet's past ice age. Here and there, violet-blue lichen speckled the unrelenting terrain like the paint dabs of some abstract-expressionist water-colorist. As I followed the path on screen, I noticed pale yellow flowers, smaller than my thumbnail, sprouting up through crevices in the rock. The flora looked too delicate to withstand such a harsh climate, yet their hardiness in the face of adversity buoyed my spirits.

After thirty minutes of swift walking, I crested a rise in the rock and used my padlet to zoom in on the area below. According to its readings, I should have been looking directly down on the mass of chromium and platinum. I scanned the area three times, and once more with my eyes.

There was nothing there but barren white rock covered in purple splotches.

Dammit. If this was a fluke deposit of raw minerals matching the near exact composition of my brothers' ships under these rocks, I was going to lose it. Desperately, I recalibrated the search parameters.

Same results. My padlet insisted the mass was in the valley—not below the ground, either. Was it a trap? I scanned the area in a one klick radius for life signs and got nothing, so I decided to get closer until I was standing almost on top of the area that should hold a ship.

The padlet must be malfunctioning. My heart plummeted. Had this been nothing more than a wild goose chase?

I blew out a long, hard breath while staring up at the cloudless indigo sky beginning to darken at the edges. Tears pricked at the corners of my eyes, and my stomach felt like I'd swallowed a fistful of rocks. Dusk was falling. It was time to head back to *Dawnsinger* while the light was still decent.

I half-turned to head back when the hair on the back of my neck stood up. The air around me seemed to shimmer and crackle with an electrical charge. I took a step back as silver lines appeared out of nowhere, joining up with each other to form the outline of a ship.

A ship I recognized immediately. The outline solidified into a white, sleek craft that resembled the body of a bird, with a rounded bow and tapered stern, sitting as if it had tucked its wings together to settle in for the night.

"Great wings of glory," I murmured in awe. "Altair finally did it."

The ramp was open. It seemed too good to be true that I'd find my eldest brother inside. As I made my way into the quiet ship, an uneasy feeling had me biting down the urge to call out my brother's name. I suddenly wished I'd sent Dove a message to let him—or anyone—know where I was. *Dawnsinger* was programmed to send a distress beacon out if I didn't input a code within 48 hours, but I still cursed my lack of forethought. As always, I'd rushed into things without thinking about the consequences. Like the day I'd run out on my brothers.

As I ascended into the belly of the ship, I held my pistol in hand. It was compact, like me, but packed a wallop and was versatile. A stun shot at maximum setting would knock an average human out cold for three to six hours, but it could also be set up to be lethal. It would deliver five shots at maximum or two at the lethal level before needing recharging. I was a decent shot, but I hadn't spent much time in target practice since moving out and starting my new job.

I'd only been on *Wild Swan I* once, but all nine ships had the same layout. A track of blue emergency lighting along the floor directed me toward the command center, but on my way I noticed the hatch to the engine room was open. A faint muttering, along with the clicks of switches or tools, drifted up from the access shaft. The voice was too indistinct to tell if it was one of my brothers yet.

Swallowing the growing lump in my throat, I peered over the edge. Not much of the engine room was visible, but someone was definitely down there. So far they hadn't noticed me. The smart move would probably be to seal them down there until I could ascertain their identity. But apparently my legs didn't receive the message. I was halfway down the ladder with my pistol stowed on my utility belt before I realized the reckless nature of my decision. If it was an intruder, I was a sitting duck. But I had to know, right now, who it was.

Once my boots were on the floor, I drew my pistol, scanning for targets in the dark while I crouched behind the crescent-shaped engineering console that ringed the deactivated warp coil in the middle of the room. With only the emergency lights on, most of the room was cast in shadows. Had the ship suffered damage that forced one of my brothers to land here?

On the other side of the console, the person—man, I suspected by the broad shoulders that were spread generously under a tight grey undershirt—stood hunched near the warp coil, with his back to me and his hands deep in the ship's circuitry. Unlike my brothers, he had a golden swath of short, curly hair. The sleeves of a blue and gold flight suit were tied around his waist as if he'd been down here working for a while. I didn't recognize the colors. They weren't the forest green and silver of the Svaneunge military or the black and gold of the Aghavni Royal Forces.

"Come on, *lille fugl*," he crooned to the unit while tapping out some instructions on the console. Light flooded the cabin, making me blink, accompanied by a cry of triumph from the interloper.

I rose, my pistol trained on him. "Who the hell are you? And what are you doing on my brother's ship?"

The muscles in the stranger's back tightened before he slowly turned around, hands in the air in the universal sign for "don't shoot." He didn't need to worry about that. I wouldn't be shooting him until after I found out what he'd done to my brothers.

My lips parted as I finally got a good look at his face. It didn't have the look of a labourer as the rest of him did— more like a ruggedly handsome vidstar. *What would a vidstar be doing mucking about your brother's ship?* Yet something about his chiseled features was familiar.

At the sight of me, his lake-blue eyes widened. Maybe it was the pistol. Or maybe it was my slight stature. People had been underestimating me for years on account of my height.

"There was no one here when I found it." His tone was calm and measured, as if he didn't want to spook me. Smart. Then his gaze narrowed. "This is your brother's ship?"

Scavenger. That's what he was. At best an opportunist; at worst, a smuggler. He was either stealing parts or trying to get the thing to fly. The owners or kin of a ship owner had thirty days to retrieve shipwrecks, or they were free for the taking under salvage law. Technically, he was here first, and it was over thirty days. He could take me to court and win, but it would be over his dead body.

I ignored his question and stepped out from the ladder to get a better angle on him. "Mighty convenient there was no one here when you arrived." Some underhanded scavengers skated the line of piracy and had been known to make survivors disappear. "Looking for survivors in the engine room, were you?"

"I'm not a scavenger." But he looked as if I'd caught him with his hand in the proverbial cookie jar. His face had paled, and crease lines furrowed his brow, but none wrinkled around his eyes. I guessed him to be younger than my 28 years. "I scanned the surrounding area before I landed. *Svalaug* detected no human life forms."

Sympathy tugged at his full, soft lips. "If your brother survived, he has vacated the vicinity."

He looked *genuinely* concerned.

Damn, he was good.

I frowned, that feeling of familiarity coming back. "What's your name?"

There was a slight hesitation before his shoulders drooped. "I go by Dove."

It couldn't be. The Uni was playing a huge prank on me. One I didn't deserve.

"My Dove?" As soon as the words slipped past my lips, my cheeks heated with embarrassment. He wasn't mine, even if he was the same Dove that I'd spoken with only hours ago. I'd asked him to keep a lookout for my brother's ship, and here he was looting the place less than a day later.

A harsh laugh erupted before I could swallow it. "You work fast, Dove."

"Apologies, but have we met before, ma'am?" There was a slight accent to his voice, and it grew stronger with his confusion. But I wasn't buying it.

Shame on me for trusting someone to not stab me in the back again, I supposed. Somehow, he must have known who I was from the beginning. Tired from the confrontation and holding a pistol for so long (I was out of practice), I lowered it and gestured him out from the warp coil toward the bulkhead. He complied as if his life depended on it. If he kept calling me *ma'am*, it would.

Bitterness and hurt twisted my lips. "And I thought you simply wanted to hear my voice, Dove."

If possible, his eyes widened further—the pupils as round as satellites—and his brows disappeared into his wealth of curls. "Skylark, is it you?" He swallowed hard. "This is *your* brother's ship?"

"I thought we'd established that already," I said testily as I brought up the ship's log on the console. It was encrypted, but luckily it was *Wild Swan I*, and Altair always entrusted his password key to me. He'd also invited me to make use of his ship whenever I wished.

"That means . . ." He swallowed hard, then muttered something under his breath.

"It means you need to get off this ship. Find another one, Dove." I glared up at him. "One not belonging to my family."

He met my glare with the solemnity of having accidentally run over my dog. In any other situation, I'd have gobbled up his earnestness, which was in short supply among those who worked alongside politicians. It was sweetly adorable on him—and that irritated me even more. I'd rather he give me a reason to shoot him.

"Please, Skylark. You must believe me. I had no idea you were . . . that your brother . . . brothers," he corrected. A red flush flooded his face and he clamped his mouth shut. It was clear he'd checked the ship's registration. And he knew I was the daughter of the High Chancellor of

Svaneunge. Maybe he'd been hoping to sell the ship back to Bors Svanur for a finder's fee.

"I'll believe you, Dove. When your actions speak louder than words. Now you're welcome to leave and continue your search. You will, of course, be handsomely rewarded for finding *Wild Swan I*."

Instead of jumping at the payout as I expected, Dove knelt down on one knee and placed his palms flat on the ground. "Please allow me to assist you with your search, Lady Svanur. Let me show you by my actions the truth of my soul."

It was my turn to be speechless. It didn't happen often in my line of work. I'd already told him to get lost, but I hesitated at repeating my words. The air between us seemed fraught with tension and somberness of something sacred. The growing silence unnerved me. Maybe it would be better to know where he was and what he was up to.

"Fine. But since I don't feel like being double-crossed today, I'll take your weapon." To my chagrin, I hadn't noticed it until now. But not once had he gone for it to try to turn the tables on me.

In a fluid movement, he rose and handed me the deactivated pistol from his thigh holster. It was larger than mine, an expensive model I didn't recognize, keyed to his print so I wouldn't be able to use it against him. It looked military-issue and had probably been obtained on the black market. *Huh*. Dove was full of surprises.

"Please understand the *svalaug* prevents me from harming you."

"What?"

"The oath I swore." He sighed at my unimpressed look, running a hand through his curls. "Actions, not words. I remember."

That's right. I dealt with pretty words all day long. And while my boss didn't make a habit of going back on her word, too many politicos like my father did.

The engineering console responded to my demands for the ship's log and a status report. The good news was the ship had warp capability. No repairs were logged, so Altair must have landed on Cygnet on purpose. But why?

The bad news was his personal log was less enlightening. The last entry was nearly two months ago, the date startling close to my twenty-eighth birthday, which I realized I'd completely worked through in the hectic lead up to the senator's appearance at the peace rally.

The log stated that Altair and the three youngest— Tern, Rook, and Starling—had travelled to Leda Station. But that couldn't be right. I'd searched Leda Station's records for any trace of my brothers via a few untraceable bribes. I pursed my lips. Someone must have paid a hefty sum to the station master or an underling to wipe the docking records for *Wild Swan I*.

After refueling, Altair had flown here, to the Cygnet system—but why? There was nothing on this rock. A growl of frustration escaped before I could help it.

"No leads?" Dove leaned against the far bulkhead, giving me a great view of his deltoids and biceps as he crossed his arms.

I purposely turned away from him. "*Wild Swan I*, this is Lark Svanur. Do you know where your captain and crew are? Or why you landed on Cygnet IV?"

"Greetings, Lark Svanur. I detect two life forms aboard, but neither conform to Captain Altair's biometrics or those of your younger brothers."

"Were you forced to land here?" My gaze slid to Dove. The outside of the ship looked pristine, but that didn't mean they hadn't been coerced by a larger ship.

"Negative. Captain Altair directed my landing of his own free will. Before he and your brothers departed, he put me in sleep mode and activated my stealth drive, which should be noted is no longer turned on."

I glanced at Dove, who remained silent, his capable-looking arms now tucked behind his back and his expression unreadable. How much did he know about the stealth drive? Well, he'd deactivated it with his tinkering, so he either knew what it was or had been trying to figure it out.

I sighed, unable to stop my shoulders from slumping. "Did Altair say where he was departing to, *Wild Swan*?"

"Your birthday party, Lark Svanur. Did you not attend?"

What the hell? I scrolled through the logged footage

to find my brothers leaving the ship of their own free will on the day of my twenty-eighth birthday.

Dove edged closer to the console and me. "If your brothers left on foot, I have an idea where they were headed. May I?" At my nod, he called up a terrain map of the planet, then entered the coordinates he wanted. It zoomed in on a trio of buildings. "On my flightpath here, I flew over this installation. It's about five klicks southwest of here. I can take you."

I snorted, glancing up at him. "So your colleagues can take me hostage and make off with my brother's ship?" And the stealth drive, the first of its kind? "I don't think so."

I'd been thinking Dove was a scavenger, but this installation made me doubt that. He could be a merc working for whoever owned the building—it wasn't registered under Svaneunge law, so it obviously wasn't legit. Or he could be Aghavni Special Forces. If they'd established a base on-planet, their fleet wouldn't be far behind.

Either way, I couldn't trust him.

Dove's jaw clenched before his expression smoothed out. "I've sworn on my honor to assist you. I am here alone."

"Words."

And I'd heard so many words before. Ironic that I used words both as weapons to tear apart inequitable legislation and as tools to disseminate forward-thinking policy changes. Some words, when strung together in the right manner at the right time, were powerful enough to alter the future of humankind. Others were meaningless. Not worth the air it took to breathe them into life. It was a paradox I'd once delighted in. But I was tired of looking for the hidden meanings behind what people said.

His nostrils flared at my cool perusal of him, but I gave him points for keeping his composure. Even experienced politicians had difficulty when confronted with my glare. "I am trying to show you with actions, Lady Svanur."

At his repeat of my title, I pursed my lips in displeasure. Then, I sighed. Remaining this acrimonious was exhausting, and there was no point in letting him stay if I wasn't going to give him a chance. "Just call me Skylark."

"Skylark."

My codename on his tongue was soft as a whisper. The earnestness was laced with a promise of more. A declaration of intent. And that alone set my toes curling. "So what actions do you propose, Dove?"

~

IN THE END, Dove proposed we wait. Night had fallen, and while the darkness would cloak our movements, it would also make the trip on foot that much more difficult, as I didn't have a night-visor. If Dove did, he wasn't volunteering it. And a trip on foot it would have to be in order to keep a low profile. So we agreed to leave at first light to scout around the buildings.

Rather than reveal *Dawnsinger's* location to Dove, I remained on *Wild Swan I* and tried to re-activate the stealth drive with little success. While I didn't demand that Dove stay, I was glad he chose to. I told myself his presence made me happy because I could keep an eye on him.

It was only half a lie.

Dove's presence, however, meant I had to figure out how to get some rest without worrying if he would steal the ship or the stealth drive in my sleep.

In the end, he solved the problem for me. After a quick supper of rehydrated vegan chili in the insta-ov, there was nothing left to do but find a spot to sleep. Thankfully, there were several crew cabins, plus the captain's suite. Dove ducked into a cabin with four bunks. The light had dimmed to simulate night inside the ship, and soft shadows wrapped around him like a blanket as he curled his long form into a bottom bunk.

"You can direct the ship to lock my door and key it to your voice command." His voice was low and soft.

I nodded, lingering in the doorway while I imagined we had met under different circumstances. But we hadn't.

"Then goodnight, Skylark. Don't for-gourd about me in the morning."

A groan escaped against my will at the terrible joke. Had he winked at me? It was too dark to tell, but I thought

I saw a flash of a grin when I rolled my eyes. "Goodnight, Dove."

<hr />

IT PROVED impossible to forget that Dove was across the hall from me, or forget the fate of my brothers, and I spent a restless night tossing and turning on the too firm bunk.

The sun rose early on Cygnet IV, and so did I. Though part of me was tempted to leave Dove locked in his room so I wouldn't have examine my feelings for him, I decided I wanted to know if his actions would back up his words. Plus, the way he had asked me specifically not to forget him last night made me think he was used to being disregarded.

And I didn't like that.

At my voice command, his door unlocked and slid open. I walked in on Dove doing crunches on the limited floor space, in nothing but his grey undershirt and under-shorts. He froze halfway up as he saw me standing there. Sweat lined his brow and dampened his shirt in a dark V. He'd been up and at it for a while. If my mouth was hanging open, I couldn't be blamed.

He scrambled up, allowing me an even better view of his well-toned body, and grabbed his flight suit from the bed to hold in front of him like a shield. "I didn't think you'd be up this early."

"Early bird gets the worm. That's what my mother

used to say." Since sleep had eluded me, I'd already showered and dressed.

The poor man's cheeks pinkened, so I kept my gaze trained on his eyes—it wasn't a hardship. "If you want to shower, I'll make breakfast. Eggs okay?"

At his nod, I headed back to the galley, but I couldn't resist calling back. "And Dove? I have 11 brothers. There's nothing you have I haven't seen before."

But the fact that I wanted to see more did surprise me. While Dove took my suggestion, I proceeded to Altair's well-stocked galley. My eldest brother liked to experiment with food as well as play with an object's index of refraction. On his insta-ov, I whipped up a hot breakfast of eggs with freeze-dried cheese and chives for us. The fresh produce in the cooler had gone bad, but there were many staples. I added some chopped up plant-based protein and hot sauce, plating it just as Dove returned refreshed from his shower.

With a hearty appetite, we both dug in: Dove, I suspect, because he'd already squeezed a workout into his morning, and me because I hadn't eaten anything as delicious for the last month.

"What's it like having 11 brothers?" he asked, pouring tea for the both of us. "I only have one, and sometimes that's more than enough."

The question caught me by surprise, with a huge forkful in my mouth. When I was younger, I was often asked this question by journalists. "Busy? There are 12 of us. After our mother died, I sort of became the designated person to attend all their competitions, science fairs, and recitals. Father was too occupied with running Svane-unge. He'd just been elected for his first term." I shrugged. "My older brothers look out for me"—I grimaced and Dove chuckled—"but I do the same for the younger ones. Truthfully, life in a big family is unpredictable. You never know what will happen at any moment. But it's heartening, too. There's usually someone around to lend a hand or a shoulder to cry on."

Except I hadn't been around that last few years for them. I'd flown the coop and left them to fend for themselves. A heavy silence stretched between us as we finished our cold eggs. I'd taken life with my brothers for granted, and now it might be lost forever.

After Dove placed our dishes into the recycler, we were on our way. I couldn't turn the ship's stealth drive back on, so the best I could do was lock it. How Dove had found and infiltrated the ship would be a conversation for later.

The tundra, awash in soft oranges and pinks of sunrise, was peaceful. Dove led the way and I trailed him, with both pistols on my utility belt. While I couldn't use his, I wasn't foolish enough to think he might not be helpful if the situation with my brothers' abductors escalated—assuming my brothers were in these buildings and being held against their will. That was also assuming Dove wasn't working with their abductors, which my gut told me was true. But that was a lot of assumptions.

After about an hour of walking, I broke the silence. "Were you ever planning on contacting me after you found my brother's ship?"

Dove stumbled but quickly recovered. "Would my words mean anything if I gave them to you right now, Skylark?"

I winced. "I guess I deserve that." I stopped to rehydrate, trying to hide how his response had hurt, and Dove backtracked toward me, contrition writ upon his face. Why was I now feeling like I'd kicked a puppy?

"You deserve the truth."

Why did I hear a big "but" coming?

"But I do not think you will like it any better."

"That's saying a lot, since I don't like *this* very much at all."

He sighed and retrieved a pair of micro-binoculars from a flap on his flight suit. Travel-sized. Wasn't that handy?

After sighting through the lenses, he pointed to a craggy rise in the distance, then passed them to me. "We're almost there."

Sure enough, I could just make out the flat roof of a building. "Shall we go see who's home?"

～

EITHER THE CLUSTER of buildings had no active security system for trespassers (I'm not sure why one would be needed for an uninhabited planet) or we had triggered silent alarms, because we walked right up to the compound without issue. We did pass by anti-aircraft silos, however, nestled in the white rock, which led me to believe they expected trouble to come from above.

There were three buildings, just as Dove had shown me. One was four stories high and had a rectangular design that gave it an industrial prefab look. The siding, however, was a white stucco, used—I presumed—more to blend in with the surrounding rock than for any aesthetic purposes. Beyond it lay a larger, domed building, which we agreed was a hangar, and to the west lay a smaller cube-like structure, also in white stucco. Gravel roads connected all three. So far, we hadn't spied a single soul.

Five meters ahead of me, Dove lay prone in a shallow ravine, where the escarpment created a natural shield from the buildings. In his cobalt blue flight suit, he didn't exactly blend well. I hoped his suit had built-in protective measures like mine, because if he got hurt, it would be my fault for dragging him into this.

No—he had offered to help me. He was an adult who'd made his own decisions. One of which had been to raid my brother's ship. But I'd still feel terrible and responsible if he was harmed helping me find them.

"I don't see anyone outside or visible cameras," Dove

commented after peeking over the edge with his binoculars. "They might be using satellite imaging. The buildings are shielded from scanning."

So we had no idea how many people were inside. Head down, I scooted over to him and rested a shoulder against the exposed rock face. "I think we should try the small building first. It might control all the security for the compound." And it had comm dishes on the roof for communicating off-planet. I could admit when the situation was becoming larger than I could handle. It might not be a bad thing to have a Svaneunge battleship en route. If the deputy chancellor would authorize one.

Before Dove could respond, the sound of a metal door opening silenced us. Gravel crunched as someone walked along the path from the direction of the larger building. I crouched lower, my hand sliding my pistol out while watching for Dove's reaction. Would he betray me?

Then, his hand latched onto my wrist, and I jammed my pistol in his side before I realized his hold was light. And he was tapping on my pulse point using the same short and long sequences as our code. He had to do it twice before I fully caught on.

[I'll lure them out. You stun.]

I lowered my weapon, nodding, and he let go of my wrist. My heart was thumping—half from the fear of discovery, half from the lingering effects of his warm touch—but he seemed unperturbed by it all.

He threw a pebble at an exposed rock face a few meters to our right. The footsteps above stopped.

"Is someone there?" a high voice called out. The footsteps came closer, and I set my pistol to maximum stun.

Dove, meanwhile, was making his way backward away from the ridge. Soon, our target would see him. I held my breath as he lay down on the ground, playing possum, and threw another pebble.

The white toe of a shoe peeked over the edge of the rock. "Deryn, if you're playing a trick—oh! Are you alright?"

I jumped to snake my hand around her ankle, and then my body weight and gravity pulled her down. As we slid down into the ravine, she screamed before the stun pistol in my other hand connected with her thigh. Quickly, I let go of her as she convulsed. A few seconds later, she was out cold.

"Are you okay?" Dove asked as he crouched over the coppery-haired, light-skinned woman, checking her pulse. She appeared to be some sort of medical personnel, dressed in a desert rose lab coat with light beige scrubs underneath. On her chest was an ID tag and photo. *Perfect.*

"Fine." I unzipped my jacket and dropped it on the ground before taking her shoe off. "Can you help me get her clothes off?"

The woman was ten centimeters taller than me and curvier, but I'd make do. After a slight hesitation, Dove helped me carefully strip the woman's outer clothes in a thoroughly professional manner. I left my black suit underneath the scrubs for protection. I also kept my boots, as her rubber-soled shoes were too large. My cropped brown hair wouldn't match the woman's photo, either, but hopefully no one would be looking too closely.

I tucked my pistol into the back of my pants under the lab coat. I couldn't wear my utility belt with the extra weapon without standing out. I made a decision and handed the belt and weapon to Dove. He hadn't betrayed me since I found him in my brother's ship. And I was beginning to wonder if that hadn't been something of a coincidence after all.

"You might need your pistol. And I can't carry this."

He nodded and slipped the belt around his narrow waist but holstered the weapon on his thigh.

I felt bad about leaving the unconscious woman out in the elements, even if she was complicit in the disappearance of my brothers. There weren't any large predatory animals in this sector according to the Svaneunge database, but it still seemed wrong to leave her practically naked. So I laid my jacket over her top torso for some protection from the sun. Dove pulled a small foil packet from yet another cargo pocket. Really, the man was a walking wilderness survival kit. With the emergency blanket covering the rest of the woman, I felt better. She should be unconscious for hours. Plenty of time, I hoped, to find my brothers and get them out.

In whispers, we hashed out our next steps. Since we didn't know if the woman had access to the smaller building, I would try to gain access to the larger building, which in view of her apparel appeared to be some sort of medical treatment facility. Dove offered to go first, but only one of us looked like we belonged.

The creases in his forehead returned. "I doubt her ID tag alone will get you access. They'll have fingerprint security at minimum."

It was my turn to produce something useful. From my utility belt, now around Dove's waist, and I pulled out what looked like an oval stone. It was the size of my thumb, black and smooth. I'd picked up the printscan on the black-market side of Leda Station while refueling there. It would lift a fingerprint and reproduce it for scanners—every security chief's nightmare.

Our plan set, I approached the double doors with my shoulders back and head up, as if I had every right to be here. Whether it was facing down political adversaries out for blood or breaking into a high-security building, confidence was key.

"If it turns out my brothers are here getting rejuv or augments," I muttered to myself as I pressed the fingerprint gadget to the scanner, "they will sorely regret the day they were born."

The door clicked open, and I slipped inside. It was a brightly lit foyer with terracotta tile, but it lacked all the accouterments of an office building. Without plants, wall art, or a front desk, it seemed institutional. In the far left corner of the room was a surveillance cam. That would need to be taken care of. After all, a tall stranger like Dove couldn't go unnoticed for long.

Under the camera, the foyer opened up into two hallways and an elevator. Every few minutes, someone in a lab coat like mine wandered between rooms in the hallway, but no one paid me any attention. As if checking my work messages, I pulled out my padlet from the coat's pocket and brought up an app that had cost me more credits than I cared to think about, but had paid for itself time and time again. I'd had this one for years, as it had allowed me to escape my father's security detail while I was living at home. Something my dates had often appreciated. Being the daughter of the High Chancellor had more drawbacks than advantages, in my opinion.

As I approached the camera, I raised the padlet as if peering at the screen. In short order, the app hacked into the cam and jammed it. Or that's what it should have done. Whoever was watching the surveillance screens should have seen static in this area now. However, the cam's signal would only stay jammed while my padlet was in close proximity, so I leaned it against the wall before backtracking to let Dove inside. Someone might be sent down to inspect the malfunctioning unit, but we'd be gone by then, the cam's signal restored with no one the wiser.

With me leading and Dove half crouching behind me,

we started down the hallway to the right. The first door had a small window inset and appeared to be a break room, with several people in lab coats sitting around a long table on their devices with mugs of hot beverages. Past the door was a laundry hover cart. Dove rifled through the discarded clothes and plucked out a larger lab coat with what I hoped was a coffee stain. Though it was still tight through the shoulders over his flight suit, it was better than nothing.

The next door on the left was labeled SECURITY and had no window. After taking up position on the left of the door, Dove gestured at me. I pressed the printscan and my ID tag to the door, hoping it would work. It blinked red, but then the door unlatched from the inside.

"—looks like the camera's working now," someone was saying. In a blink, Dove opened the door and pushed the surprised guard back inside.

"What—" came a muffled voice as I followed behind, closing the door behind me.

When I turned around, one guard in a green uniform of an armored vest and cargo pants lay on the ground, while another was face-down at his console below a wall of screens covering the inside of the compound. I started as Dove holstered his pistol. Were they . . . ?

"They'll be out for the next three hours. We should plan to be gone by then." Without further discussion, he pulled each guard to the back wall of the cramped room.

Plastic ties were produced out of another pocket to secure the guards' hands.

"Do you always come so well prepared?" I blurted, impressed despite myself. He was rather adept at subduing and securing hostages, and a tendril of unease slid through me. Was anything he'd told me about himself true? Granted, he'd told me very little, despite all our coded conversations.

"Three years' mandatory service before university entrance," Dove replied, without pausing from his task. "I chose search and rescue. We trained for many different situations." He shrugged as if that was nothing out of the ordinary and moved onto securing the other guard. "And I like being prepared."

"I'm sensing that." My gaze flicked from his hands to his holstered pistol. Bounty hunters also liked being prepared.

"I told you, I'm not a scavenger. Or a bounty hunter." He stood and looked me straight in the eye as if he could read my mind. "But I admit I was trying to relieve *Wild Swan* of her stealth drive. I'm not proud of it. But when you found me, I decided I didn't want it at the expense of your brothers' lives."

I considered his words. For some reason, I believed him. "How did you know Altair had developed one?"

A muscle twitched in his cheek. "A good guess. It's long been rumored your father's scientists have been close to a breakthrough." Industrial espionage or Aghavni

408

intelligence? "When your brothers were reported missing, I decided there was a fair chance at finding one of their ships and a working device."

Once he finished with the guards, he joined me at the screens, where I'd been scanning over the live images. The upper floors only had cameras in the hallways, but those floors looked like a dormitory for the staff. A blonde-haired woman in a lab coat and heels strolled through the hallway on the top level and disappeared into a room. Something about her was familiar, but the angle of the camera didn't allow a good look at her face.

Most of the rooms on the ground floor held medical equipment, including a diagnostics lab with technicians studying vials of blood and one that looked like a cyber-netic shop. Another room appeared to be an aviary with bird cages and lush greenery. Were they illegally experi-menting on birds? Because whatever was happening here, in the middle of nowhere, likely wasn't on the books.

But what did it all have to do with my brothers?

Then, my gaze snagged on a room full of patients lying in medbeds with some kind of medical apparatus over their heads, and my mouth went dry. "Can you pan around that room?"

With the tap of a few keys, the camera swept over the room as I counted. Eleven occupied beds, arranged in a hexagonal pattern, with two walls for more medical equipment.

Rejuv? Altair was only 32, and the triplets were the

youngest at 16. Most people didn't start rejuv—if they could afford it—until 40. No, something more sinister than erasing wrinkles was happening here.

Curse words I didn't recognize startled me out of my thoughts.

I looked back to find Dove halfway into one of the guards' uniforms. The dark green cargo pants were zipped up, but I caught a glimpse of his muscled back and a tattooed crest of two doves across his shoulder blades before he shrugged into the arms of the long-sleeve shirt and vest.

"Are those your brothers?" he asked, handing back my utility belt.

"I think so." It was difficult to make out clear features because of the medical equipment. But who the hell else could they be?

"Can you carry this? I don't want to leave it behind to be found." In his hand, he held out his flight suit, impeccably folded into a blue square.

I secured the belt under my lab coat and stuffed the compressed suit into one of the pouches, while he finished putting on his new guard gear. A lump was growing in my throat, panic rising with every breath. I was a PR manager. What the hell did I think I was doing here?

A gentle hand squeezed my shoulder. "We've found them. Now we'll get them out. Together."

THE MEDICAL STAFF barely batted an eye at me or Dove as we strode down the hallways with the laundry cart, confident now in where we were heading. I'd called up digital blueprints of the building in the security room, and my brothers' room was labeled as TRANSFER. Increasingly more disturbing ideas of what was happening to them popped into my head, such as illegal body augmentation or organ harvesting, until my chest threatened to explode and a wave of light-headedness assailed me. Dove's steady hand under my elbow kept me upright and moving forward.

"You got this, Skylark."

I could do this. I had to do this. For my brothers.

In the quiet hallway of the Transfer room stood a lone guard in green. He was on the shorter side, stocky, and sported a neat brown beard. When he saw Dove, he broke his stance. "About time, man."

Dove quickened his pace, pulling ahead of me and the cart. The guard frowned as Dove came within arm's reach. "You're not Krowe—"

Lunging forward, Dove jabbed him in the neck with a small shock baton that must have been part of the guard's kit. "I'm not."

Krowe was currently out cold in the security room.

Dove caught the twitching, unconscious man as he crumpled; then he made use of his fingerprint and ID

411

badge to gain us entry. With the guard slung over his shoulder and his pistol at the ready, Dove pushed through the unlocked door.

Right on his heels, I maneuvered the laundry cart inside, leaving it to block the door. It wouldn't stop the determined, but it would slow them down. My padlet was already configured to jam the surveillance cameras in the room—just in case anyone else had access to the feeds.

An eerie pall blanketed the sterile, bland room. Soft beeping sounds and filtered oxygen set my nerves on edge and dredged up unpleasant memories of visiting my mother's bedside. No one shot at us, thankfully. In fact, the room appeared empty except for the patients.

While Dove moved along the walls, scanning for threats, I made a beeline for the closest medbed. The heads of each patient lay beneath a transparent screen, above which a neuro scan of their brain was displayed. A closer look revealed they weren't, in fact, rejuv chambers. At least, not any I'd ever seen before.

Gathering my courage, I peeked over the screen at the face of the patient. My blood froze. "Crane?" His freckles were more pronounced on his pale face, his eyes closed as if running mathematical equations in his sleep. He didn't wake.

I ran to the next bed, my heart in my throat. *Lonan.* He was barely 19. Unlike Crane and me, he took after our father in looks with thick black hair that curled at the ends and a dark olive complexion. The next bed held

Griffin's muscular form, mouth in a smirk even in repose. Then the younger fraternal twins, Phoenix and Hawke, side by side with dark red and black hair, respectively. They always were inseparable. After them was Wren, the poet in the family. I found Falconer, laying stiff as if at attention and sporting an unfamiliar beard. After him came the identical triplets—Tern, Rook, and Starling—looking unbearably young with rounded cheeks and their black-brown locks sticking out every which way.

Finally, I stopped at the last bedside and gazed down at my eldest brother's peaceful face. Out of all my brothers, Altair resembled our father the most with a thick head of black hair, a widow's peak, and a strong nose over chiseled lips.

"Altair, wake up," I said, my voice trembling. "This isn't funny." He didn't move, but from the corner of my eye, I saw Dove approaching a second door in the corner. When he saw me looking, he raised a finger to his mouth.

He must have hearing augments. With my pistol gripped in my hand, I followed on silent tiptoes.

"We can't wait," said a familiar-sounding voice from the other side of the door. "One of us needs to get to the ship."

"Then what, bird-brain? Who will help us looking like this?"

Was that Griffin? And Phoenix? But how? My hand closed around the door handle of its own volition, opening it. As I flung myself through, motion on the periphery of my vision told me Dove lunged after me.

Against the bright light from the glass ceiling, I squinted at the scene before me: a regal swan, a fierce eagle with paws, and a majestic crimson bird with a long tail conversed by a green pond. All three turned to stare at me.

"Brothers?"

Looking back, I'd recall the vacant look that filled their eyes after I spoke. But the next instant, a flurry of wings, beaks, and claws was heading towards us. "Dove," I yelled behind me, "duck!"

I felt the air warm before a solid wall of muscle slammed into me, taking me to the ground. Hot flame singed the air above us, followed by a cacophony of squawking. The impact, along with Dove's weight, forced the air out of me, and I gasped. We'd fallen on our sides, but Dove had most of his body wrapped around me. It took a few dazed seconds for me to realize the birds were attacking him, drawing blood in areas not covered by his light-armor vest. More flames singed the air, and I prayed his guard uniform was fire retardant.

He raised his pistol in the air. Dammit, he couldn't shoot them. Feebly, I tried to swat at his chest to get his attention, but my arms were pinned under me.

"Dove, don't—"

An electromagnetic pulse filled the air and the birds dropped, thudding as they hit the ground. Usually a pulse such as that would momentarily stun or slow a crowd of people. But the birds didn't seem to be stirring.

Not birds. Your brothers. If he had hurt them . . .

I grabbed Dove by the back of the neck, pulling his head down toward me so we were nose to nose. He had three bloody slices across his cheek from talons or claws. Those soft lips of his parted, as if he, too, felt the pull to close the miniscule distance.

"Stunned," he said, interrupting my fantasies of how his lips might feel against mine.

"Get the hell off her!"

Grif. I'd recognize that voice anywhere. Tears spontaneously streamed from my eyes. I wasn't a crier, but stressful situations triggered it. The fact that Griffin's voice came from the eagle-lion creature brought me back to the present situation.

"Will you attack us again?" Dove demanded, not moving a centimeter.

The eagle-lion was the first to have recovered, and it staggered over to settle at my head. "What? I'd never hurt Lark." With his eagle eyes, Grif peered down at me. "I knew you'd come for us. But I don't know what came over us. Altair?"

This can't be happening.

Dove seemed to realize that the birds weren't going to harm me and rolled off me, but he remained alert and kept his pistol at the ready. Slowly, I sat up, taking in the tropical oasis around us. Empty bird cages hung from cables among trees and shrubs with broad leaves. The swan had slipped into the lily-pad covered pond of deep green water, situated amongst artfully placed rocks and the stone path. The others had dispersed to the trees or stands of birdseed.

"Skylark, do you remember where we are? Do you feel dizzy or nauseous?"

Bright light flashed in my eyes as Dove's hand touched my cheek. In his other hand, he used his padlet to scan my head.

"Don't speak, Lark," Altair ordered. At least, it was his voice, coming from the swan. "I hypothesize that we've been programmed to attack at the sound of your voice. A safety mechanism, perhaps, should you come to rescue us. Or another nefarious scheme of Sarika's. She must have assumed you'd come looking for us."

Our stepmother, Sarika Finch?

"Auditory recognition would have a higher success rate than visual recognition," Crane added. I blinked at the slender white bird standing in the tall water grasses.

The swan dipped its head toward Dove. "Quick thinking on emitting an electromagnetic pulse wave. I believe it reset the trigger response, but I'd rather not risk another episode, Lark."

I frowned. This last bit was directed at me. No talking. Yet, I had a million questions for my brothers.

"Is no one worried about who the hell he is?" Griffin groused. His grouchiness toward the men in my life was so familiar that a laugh bubbled out of me, earning a sharp glance from Altair and Dove. Maybe I was losing all touch with reality. Maybe I wasn't on Cygnet IV but at work, having a mental health crisis.

"I don't recognize you as one of Sarika's guards, so who are you?" the vibrant red bird with curling orange crest feathers asked Dove. *Phoenix*. At fifteen, he'd hijacked a speeder and flown it in across the planet before being caught.

Again Dove glanced at me, his own pupils dilated, like maybe he'd hit his head when we'd fallen to the ground. "We subdued a couple on our way in. Borrowed the uniform." To me, he said, "I take it these are your brothers —somehow?"

More birds had come out of the foliage to chirp my name in excitement. In addition to Altair, Griffin, Phoenix, and Crane, I counted a falcon, a hawk, a blackbird, a wren, a rook, a tern, and a starling. Someone had gotten cute with my brothers' names.

No, not someone. Father's new wife.

I growled in frustration at not being able to speak. A gentle touch on my back reminded me that I wasn't facing this situation alone, for which I was intensely grateful. Especially since it gave me an idea. I couldn't speak, but that didn't mean I couldn't communicate.

I grabbed Dove's hand and tapped out a message to him in code. [We can talk like this. I'll need you to relay my messages.]

He nodded, not breaking eye contact with me. "As to who I am, I'll let Skylark introduce us."

[Tell them you're my friend. Ask them what happened to them.]

Dove relayed the message, including his name.

Altair ruffled his wings, sending droplets of water flying. "We can explain, Lark. But time is of the essence. We've overheard the staff talking. A new procedure is scheduled for this afternoon. Dr. Finch will be here to oversee it. You need to get out of here before she sees you."

That was the second time Altair had mentioned our stepmother.

"Your sister has been searching for you since you disappeared, I doubt she's going to leave you now." Dove looked at me for confirmation, and I nodded, glaring at Altair.

"Fine," said my swan-brother in defeat. "You saw our bodies in the transfer room? Well, Sarika Finch has developed a way to extract human consciousness and download it. While we may look like true avian specimens, we are in fact housed in robotic bodies. Under our wings there are cybernetic ports for the transfer."

Clearly Altair thought he was stating the obvious. Dove looked as dazed as I felt.

Air whooshed by us, and a falcon landed on a platform nearby. "You know, I never thought Sarika had a sense of humour." He shrugged his wings, as if making a point. *Falconer.*

Black feathers flapped in my face as a blackbird landed on my shoulder. "Her sense of humor sucks," Lonan grumbled. "You'll get us out of these bird drones, won't you, Lark?"

I nodded, my heart breaking for the travesty carried out against my brothers, and his head rubbed against the side of my cheek.

"I assume you came on a ship? And you have weapons?" Falconer asked, ever the soldier.

"Two energy pistols and a mini shock baton," Dove replied. "Which one of you is Altair? We found your ship."

That initiated a round of introductions on Dove's behalf. The highlights were that Sarika Finch had lured my brothers to Cygnet IV on the pretense of a surprise birthday party for me. Once inside, they'd been tranquilized and prepped for the transfer.

"Then we woke up with beaks and wings," Grif said grimly.

[How could Sarika do this?]

I didn't care for the woman my father had married, but it seemed unbelievable to imagine her as the villain behind this horror. She was a rejuv doctor turned socialite.

Grif snorted, his tail flicking against my leg. "She's a resourceful platinum digger with a doctorate in biotechnology who gathered up a team of brilliant wackjobs with a desire to extend human life beyond the limits of cell regeneration. Don't underestimate her like we did."

"I suspect she has backers and external sources for materials here though," Altair mused, as if commenting on a scientific puzzle. "Perhaps the Aghavni are bankrolling her."

"She could be a spy, sent to destroy the house of Svanur from the inside," Hawke added from the trees.

The hand in mine stiffened at that, but Dove dutifully relayed my next question. [Is Father involved?]

"That we don't know," Falconer cut in before Altair could launch into his many hypotheses on the subject. "But that's neither here nor there. Any minute, she'll be here. From what Tern and Rook overheard, this will be the next step in her experiment."

There was an uneasy silence at this. *Next step*. What was the next step?

[Then we need to leave. Now.] I tapped out on Dove's wrist.

"We can't leave without our bodies!" Phoenix cried, landing down beside us in an display of shimmering crimson, dramatic as usual. "It's why we haven't escaped yet."

"That's where you come in, Lark." Altair waddled out of the water to join us. "We need you to transfer us back before Sarika can carry out her next transfer."

It was already 13:15 hours. How long would a transfer —11 transfers—take?

"Can we wait until after this next human-bird is created?" Dove asked, anticipating my question.

Once again, Crane startled me. "Oh, Sarika's not transferring another human mind into a robotic bird. She's transferring another human mind into one of our bodies."

~

AFTER HASHING out a quick plan of action together, we barely had time to get into position in the Transfer room before my stepmother came marching through the lab door. With my eyes closed under the medical blanket in my brother Wren's spot, I couldn't see her, but those heels clicked imperiously as they had in the marble hallways back home.

"Alert Commander Culver to the missing guard," Sarika ordered in her usual high-handed way. "I'll not put up with such laxity."

Someone left to do her bidding, and Dr. Finch directed the staff who remained. Two, by their voices. Dove was also positioned in a medbed—in Altair's spot. Though they looked nothing alike, they were both quite tall. We'd taken the chance on replacing them since Tern and Rook had reported the staff mentioning Subject Blackbird in regard to the experiment. Now Altair and Wren's bodies waited in the laundry cart in the bird room with the rest of my avian brothers.

The hiss of a medbed entering the lab interrupted the hushed medical chatter. The new subject.

I risked a peek through slitted eyes. Without moving my head, I could see the two assistants. The one at the main medical console against the wall near the door had a black braid down her back, medium brown skin, and several eyebrow piercings. The other—a lanky, pale-skinned man with thinning blond hair—crouched in front of Lonan's medbed, while Sarika checked readings on the neuroscanner above the new subject's bed in the middle of the room.

My stepmother was so close I could see the ashy lowlights in her perfectly coiffed hair and smell her lilac perfume. But I couldn't see the subject over the rails of the medbed. Who in the Uni would sign up for this? Or had she abducted someone else?

My toe twitched. Did anyone notice?

I forced myself to relax every muscle when all I wanted to do was loosen the tight chest binding under my borrowed medical gown, sit up, and bean Sarika Finch over the head with something heavy. *Soon*, I told myself. *You can shoot her after your brothers are safe.*

"Is Subject Blackbird ready to accept the transfer?" Sarika asked sharply.

That was close enough.

As I rose from the medbed, my pistol coming up from under the covers, one of the techs replied, "Yes, Dr. Finch." Across the room, I saw Dove mirroring my actions.

422

"Hands in the air, Sarika!" I shouted.

The shock on my stepmother's usually composed face was priceless. It didn't last long.

"I told Bors you'd find your way home sooner or later." For someone staring down a pistol, my statuesque stepmother seemed calm, and it irked me. What did she know that we didn't?

"Step away from Lonan." I slid out of the medbed, the gown bunching around my hips and revealing my black suit underneath. Sarika complied, taking a step toward the new subject, but an arrogant smile spread on her permanently rose-tinted lips. Behind her, Dove, also in a medical gown, had corralled the two lab techs with their noses against the wall and their hands on their heads.

"Surveillance?" I asked him.

From where he stood, he shot the camera above the main door. There was another one over the entrance to the bird room, and he eliminated that one, too.

Security might have already seen us, but we'd decided against using my padlet again. Disabling earlier might have tipped Sarika off, and we needed her as our hostage for my plan to work.

"Can you unplug the transfer cables next?" I asked, unwilling to take my eyes off my stepmother.

A strange smile lit Sarika's lightly tanned face. "Are you certain you wish to do that? After all, you have many brothers, but only one father."

Father?

I would have been less floored by a meteorite crashing through the ceiling. My lungs burned for air while fire shot through my solar plexus and tears pricked at my eyes. It definitely felt like the time Piper Jackdaw sucker-punched me for eliminating her in the last round of the prestigious Halcyon House debate tournament.

When I could focus again, I saw that Dove had secured my stepmother's hands behind her back with another plastic tie—I seriously needed some of those—and sat her on Wren's empty bed.

"You're lying," I accused.

"See for yourself, Lark."

I edged closer to the patient who had been about to be transferred into Lonan's body, praying it was anyone other than Bors Svanur. Under the thin, mint-green blanket lay a sleeping, shriveled old man. Not my pugnacious father. The man had run a marathon only last year. Now his widow's peak was as white as swan feathers, as if his age had suddenly tackled him. Rejuv treatments were like that sometimes. After a while they no longer worked their magic, the body's cells having become acclimatized to the regeneration process. But by my calculations, Father should still have twenty-five years left before this could happen.

My shock gave way to the harsh bite of betrayal. "Why?"

"He's dying, Lark," Sarika said quietly.

A trembling rocked through me. Firm but gentle

hands turned me so I was staring into Dove's kind blue eyes. So clear and vibrant. So alive.

"I know you're hurting right now, Skylark. But if you want to proceed with your plan, we need to do so. I'll initiate the lab lockdown procedure, but the longer we're here, the sooner we'll be discovered."

Every lab had a containment protocol, and we'd discussed with Altair how to activate the one here. I ordered the techs to turn around, my voice steady again. Their cooperation would be essential, as I couldn't trust Sarika near a console.

"You'll be transferring my brothers back into their rightful bodies. Starting with Falconer."

My brothers had decided amongst themselves who would go first. If the transfer failed—and if the consciousness was lost—then they would need someone with the ability to reverse engineer Sarika's experiment. That ruled out Altair and Crane as first contenders. Falconer, the second-eldest and a retired major from the Svaneunge Armed Forces, had volunteered without argument.

Sarika scoffed. "Revna and Arno aren't capable of such a delicate—"

I swung the pistol over to the techs. "Then I guess we don't need them. And if you think I'm bluffing, just remember no one knows we're here, and if my brothers have to remain birds the rest of their lives, I have no qualms about burning this place and anyone complicit to the ground—including you."

I guess I was just as ruthless as my father.

The threat gained the swift cooperation of both techs. Neither, it seemed, were willing to die for their research. Under my watchful gaze and Sarika's glare, the duo began prepping Falconer for the transfer. Alarms rang in the background, sounding the evacuation for the whole building. Now the lab and bird room were in lockdown, and the security guards, who I assumed were swarming the hallways, wouldn't be able to override access to either.

"We need Subject Falcon's avian unit," Revna said from the main console. If she was afraid, she didn't show it.

I left Sarika under Dove's careful scrutiny to fetch my brother. With Falconer-the-bird in earshot, I wouldn't be able to speak again. But I really didn't know what to say. That Father had been working with Sarika to use his son's body? There was no time to process the tornado of emotions whirling inside me. So for now, I kept quiet.

Soaring through the open door into the lab, Falconer stretched his wings for one last time. He settled above his tall, thin human body on top of the neuroscanner in front of where Arno stood. The tech audibly gulped as the brown-and-white-flecked bird of prey pinned him with his beady stare. A silent promise of retribution if the tech should fail.

Altair and the others had also joined us to watch— and to wait their turn. Grif landed within arm's reach of

Sarika, and while I was delighted Sarika finally looked less than sanguine, I was worried my vengeful brother wouldn't be able to keep his claws off her until the transfers were complete. As a child, Grif had used his fists more often than not if he thought someone was picking on one of us. But if her techs couldn't reverse the transfer, we'd need her.

I had absolutely no guilt about using Arno or Revna, since they'd willingly gone along with Sarika's experiments. No doubt they had their reasons, but whatever they were, it didn't excuse their involvement.

"Once the avian unit is connected to the neural transfer equipment, I'll need to put it into stasis mode to receive the transfer." Arno licked his thin lips. "We've never reversed the process, though theoretically it should work fine. But there is a chance we could lose"—he swallowed hard—"the download."

From the empty medbed, Sarika scoffed, but it was unclear whether it was at her employee's lack of confidence in her work or the entire situation.

"Do it." Falconer lifted his wing, and Arno opened the port to plug in a grey cable. Then he tapped in commands to the neuroscanner and Falconer's eyes shut. His entire avian body stilled, looking like an imperious statue with his brown-flecked chest puffed out.

"He's in stasis now," Arno reported, eyes trained on the screen before him. "Initializing re-transfer."

My chest hitched as I held Falconer's cool hand.

Would my brother wake up in his body, or would I lose him forever? Would the rest of my brothers be condemned to life as robotic birds?

The equipment beeped, and pathways throughout Falconer's brain began to light up on the neuroscanner, but his body remained still.

"Cardiac arrest," Revna reported. "Arno, get the defibrillator."

Arno deftly extracted a red box from the neuroscanner and placed it on Falconer's bare chest. "Clear for shock."

A split-second later, his body arched. Then a steady beeping returned. But still his eyes remained closed.

"If it didn't work, I'll be happy to eat her for supper," Grif growled, though how he managed that through a beak, I didn't know. His tail flicked at Sarika, who wisely stayed silent.

I gazed down at the familiar contours of Falconer's sharp nose and auburn beard, longer than the usual close clip he kept. But his hazel eyes stayed closed. *Come on, Falconer.*

"It should've worked," Arno stammered. Sweat glistened on his forehead as Revna rechecked the data on the main console.

"The avian unit is wiped," she reported with a "don't shoot the messenger" expression. "Normal rhythm and neural activity has returned to the body. He should be waking up."

"Coma is a possible side effect of a failed transfer,"

Sarika offered with a curl of her lip. "So is a psychotic break."

Grif lunged—I thought he was aiming for her throat —but he sailed past our stepmother to land on Falconer's barely-rising chest. "Up and at 'em, soldier!"

At the order, Falconer's hazel eyes flew open, and my knees sagged. For a long moment, he didn't say anything. Didn't move. Just stared at the impossibility that was his twin. Then Grif leapt off him, and Falconer cursed the air blue.

A smile spread across my face as I caught his hand and gave it a squeeze. With my hand in his, Falconer sat up slowly, taking in his brothers' bodies and their bird forms on each bed. He swallowed. "I was hoping it was all a nightmare, but I was a goddamn bird, wasn't I?"

"The nightmare isn't over for some of us," Hawke grumbled.

Falconer turned to me in wonder. "Thank you, Lark, for not giving up on us. For being there for us, even if we weren't there for you. Maybe if we had taken your qualms about Sarika seriously, we wouldn't be here now."

Tears pricked at my eyes at the deep well of affection in Falconer's low voice. As he pulled me into a tight hug, the rest of the birds hooted and twittered in a strange cacophony of celebration. From across the room, Dove smiled at me, and I smiled back.

"One down, ten to go," he said with a worried glance

at the door, his thoughts plain: Where was Sarika's security team?

∽

FORTY MINUTES LATER, there were only Altair and Starling left to transfer.

"You're sentencing your father to death," Sarika hissed. "He'll die without a new body."

Only Sarika seemed not to comprehend that she was sentencing either Altair or Starling to death instead—or a robotic avian existence—by saving her husband.

"Can someone shut her up?" Phoenix was recovering more slowly. He still sat on his medbed, red head between his knees, trying to orient himself to his human body.

It didn't seem like we needed her conscious, so I raised my pistol. Sarika straightened, looking me dead in the eye. Rejuv had kept her looking in her early thirties, though I recalled the birthdate on the marriage certificate. Maybe four more treatments until her age started to catch up with her.

"At least hear what your father has to say before he dies," Sarika hissed at me. "He talked about you every day you were gone, you know. Mostly railing about whatever latest speech you'd written for those pacifists. But for all he hated your politics, he admired your statecraft."

Her knife slid home, and I lowered my pistol, nodding to Revna to wake him up.

Because I did want to hear what he had to say. Or I'd always wonder what his role had been in all of this.

His frail hand, covered in dark spots, twitched first. Then his creped eyelids opened. "Sarika?" he whispered, voice thin and reedy. "Is it over?"

"There were complications, dumpling." A saccharine sweetness colored her voice. She approached the medbed from the other side, her hands still bound behind her. My fingers clenched around the pistol. If she tried anything, I could still shoot her.

I opened my mouth to tell Father I was here, too, but I remembered I couldn't speak without triggering an attack from Altair's and Starling's bird forms, who perched with their bodies waiting for their transfers. My gaze narrowed at Sarika. Had that been her plan? To cause a distraction?

Dove was half-helping, half-carrying Phoenix to the bird room where we'd evacuate from, so I couldn't use him as my interpreter.

I tapped on my father's wrist, and his head rolled slowly over to my side of the bed.

"Lark?" He drew out the syllables of my name as if he couldn't quite control all the parts of his mouth, but his voice was filled with warmth. A surge of conflicted affection rose inside me. "You left me without a word. Lark? Why won't you speak to me?"

I looked daggers at Sarika, and she blanched. Clearly, she hadn't informed Father of all her plans.

Before I could get my padlet out, there was a fluttering

of iridescent black wings on my left side before Starling landed on my shoulder. "She did tell you, Father, by her actions. But you weren't listening. Sarika made Lark's life miserable at home."

Tears pricked at my eyes at being seen. I had thought no one had noticed Sarika's ill-treatment, especially not one of my youngest brothers.

Starling tilted his head, as if something had just occurred to him. "She was—is—afraid of Lark's influence over you, Father. Now, she's silenced our sister. If Lark speaks, she'll set off an attack program in these robotic birds of hers, and Altair and I will be forced to hurt her."

"Altair?" Father rasped.

"Your sister and that senator," Sarika snarled, "will single-handedly undo nearly a century of sacrifices by our colonists to protect our planets from Aghavni plunder and set back decades of research into mind uploading. She'll forget those who died to protect us, and she'll kill thousands more, starting with your father."

I'd had no idea the woman harbored such fear and hatred. Vaguely, I recollected the late Aghavni king outlawing mind uploading experimentation years ago and a whisper of Sarika's brothers and parents being killed in a Aghavni attack on their colony during the last war.

Confusion clouded my father's eyes, but I saw the truth in my stepmother's. She hated me and everything I stood for. And she was jealous of the love my father held for me, no matter how thin and brittle that love might be.

"All of us are here, Father." Altair flapped his large wings to cross the short distance from his human body to Father's blanketed feet. I couldn't tell if Father was surprised his eldest was a swan or not. "And Starling speaks rightly. Lark found us and stopped Sarika from sentencing us to a life trapped in these mechanical birds. You won't be receiving one of our bodies anymore. Though I shudder to think why you needed all 11 of us. Two lifetimes weren't enough for you?"

"My boy?" Father's rheumy eyes narrowed on the looming swan. "No . . . that can't be you. You're dead. All of my boys . . . killed by the Aghavni—the monsters! General Ptak retrieved your bodies—I saw them. Lifeless. This must be a trick." His voice trembled and broke. "Saree, tell me this is a trick." When she didn't say anything, he mewled, "What did you do?"

So he had thought his boys dead—and agreed to Sarika's mad idea to transfer his consciousness into one of them to extend his life. It wasn't as bad as I had thought, but it was still horrifying. Suddenly, her plan—and my father's—made a twisted sort of sense: my father would take on Lonan's much younger body, and with Sarika's assistance, rise to the chancellory after Bors' apparent death.

Rage and revulsion curled in my gut, along with all the words I couldn't speak.

"Bors, you're dying. It was the only way to continue your vision for Svaneunge's future." Sarika turned to me when he didn't respond, except to close his eyes. "You can still save him. If not one of your brothers' bodies, choose someone here. Anyone. Please." She bit her lip, and I almost felt sorry for her. "Please, Lark. Don't let him die on me, too."

Out of the corner of my eye, I caught Arno bowing his head, and I suddenly knew Sarika had promised my brothers' bodies to her people. For compliance or wealth or both, it didn't matter.

Angrily, I jerked my head in Arno and Revna's direction to get them moving on the final transfers. On my padlet, I typed out *I will not sacrifice anyone for my father* and then pressed the text-to-speech function.

Disgusted by both of the pair of them, Altair had turned his graceful swan's back on his progenitor and flown back to his medbed.

Like me, Starling didn't say anything else. He had climbed on top of my head, nestling himself in my short brown hair. Carefully, I scooped him up and set him over on his neuroscanner for his transfer, pressing a kiss to his soft, feathered back. Then I returned to my father's bedside. On the other side, Sarika hovered over him, eyes splotchy and red, her hands still tied behind her back, and my father's face turned away from her.

Had she committed such crimes out of love for him or hate for the Aghavni? Or both?

I didn't care. Taking my father's hand, I squeezed it to get his attention. Leaning down, as if to give him a kiss on the cheek, I whispered in his ear for him alone to hear. "There's something I forgot to say when I left." He looked at me expectantly, as if he couldn't believe I'd have anything but a daughter's love for him. "Goodbye, Bors."

Then all hell broke loose.

~

FLAMES LICKED around the heavily reinforced steel-composite door, like someone was sawing it down with pure fire. It took me a few seconds to realize it wasn't a natural flame, but an enhanced laser weapon, one long outlawed in both Svaneunge and Aghavni space.

From the bird room, Dove, now wearing his blue flight suit again, ran toward me, pistol in hand. "Take cover!" With his free hand, he grabbed mine and brought me to the floor before taking position behind one of the empty medbeds.

"The transfer isn't complete!" Arno shrieked, cowering behind Altair's neuroscanner.

Dammit. We still had Starling to transfer as well. Dove and I exchanged a weighty look before he trained his pistol on the door.

"Keep the transfer going," Dove called back to Arno. To me, he said, "*Svalaug* is hovering in position above the compound. Your other brothers are all aboard. They are waiting on Altair, Starling, and us. We'll get them out, Skylark. You cover Altair and Arno. I'll bring up the rear with Starling. We can figure out how to transfer him later."

I also had my pistol trained on the door, but I nodded, rising to make my way to Altair.

"Stay low," he cautioned, squeezing my hand. "We have maybe ten seconds before they're through."

As I passed by my father's medbed, I met Sarika's gleaming eyes from where she knelt on the floor. Confidence once again radiated from her too-perfect smile. "Leave us Starling's body and I'll call off my security team. You have the others. What's one brother out of 11, Lark?"

Never. I raised my pistol to stun her silent, but Starling was suddenly flying in front of me. He'd broken the connection with his port transfer.

"Lark will never agree to that," he said, still fluttering before Sarika until he landed on the foot of Father's bed. "But I'll do it, if you promise to let us go peacefully and not come after us."

I wanted to shake my feathered brother. He had his whole life ahead of him.

"You have a deal, Starling." Sarika eyed me warily. "Make sure your sister keeps her end of it."

I got on eye level with Starling, trying to convey how not okay this was with hand gestures.

"I'm sorry, Lark. But it's safer this way. Sarika would never let us leave without getting what she wants."

"We have incoming!" Dove yelled as the flaming door fell down.

I shooed Starling away, gesturing for him to join the others on the ship, and he flew after Revna, who was already running to safety in the bird room. Then I dashed across to Altair as energy shots laced the room and Sarika began screaming for a ceasefire. I assumed she didn't want Bors' or Starling's bodies damaged.

As I reached Altair, Arno wailed from behind the console, his limp blond hair slicked with sweat. "I don't want to die. That was the whole point of this."

"Once the transfer is complete, you're free to stay here with Dr. Finch or come with us. I can't guarantee your safety either way, but I will do what I must to keep my brothers safe." Like blow this lab up so Sarika couldn't perform any more transfers. Or just her. Really, that seemed the best solution. But would the guards keep fighting if Sarika was dead, or would they desert?

I eyed Arno. "What are you getting out of this?"

He couldn't look me in the eye. "A new body. I'm terminally ill. So is Commander Culver. Others were promised money or favors."

I couldn't spare any sympathy; my attention was now focused on the phalanx of guards moving into the room behind riot shielding. They converged around Sarika and my father. And where was Dove? He was falling back between the medbeds while exchanging energy shots.

Altair's neuroscanner beeped. "Transfer complete."

Out of the corner of my eye, I saw Altair's legs twitch under the blanket. *Good.* I glanced up to check Dove's progress. He stood in the open, lifting the neuroscanner off the top of Starling's medbed. What the hell was he doing?

One of the guards saw an opportunity and fired.

"Dove!" I screamed

The blast grazed the side of Dove's head, and he fell. I didn't see any movement, but the guards would be on him in seconds. And I had gotten him into this mess.

From behind the console, I sighted my pistol on the guard nearest to Dove and shot. She collapsed in a twitching heap.

"Sarika!" I yelled.

She was hiding behind the phalanx. I'd lost my chance at her. But I could still save Dove. I willed the cursed words past my lips. "You get Starling's body, we get to leave peacefully. That was the deal, Sarika."

For now, I told myself. I wasn't giving up on saving my last brother.

The guards had nearly reached Dove, but they waited for Sarika's orders. That meant Dove must be out cold and no threat to them. I didn't dare consider what else it could mean.

There was grumbling among the guards. "What about the bodies promised to us?"

A liver-spotted hand rose from my father's bed, now protected by two guards. "Let her go, Saree." Bors' weak voice erupted into coughing. "Please."

"More bodies can be procured," Sarika murmured to her restless guards. Louder, she said, "I am true to my word, Lark Svanur. Leave Starling and take your brothers and your man before I change my mind."

The guards formed a protective line around Starling's body. I turned to Arno. "Are you staying or coming?"

"Staying," he mumbled, head down.

I stunned him. I didn't need any other surprises. Then I hoisted a semi-conscious Altair over my back so his arms were slung over my shoulders and his feet dragged behind. He had about 25 centimeters on me. This way I could still keep my pistol in one hand. But I had no idea how I would get Dove out, too. "Altair, can you walk?"

But all I got was a mumbled response. By the time I reached Dove, he was stirring. Blood smeared one side of his face and the top of his right ear was mangled. Black burn marks covered his blue flight suit. He must have taken a few shots.

"Are you okay, Skylark?" His eyes looked glassy, but he focused on me when I spoke.

"You're the one who got shot, Dove."

"Yeah. I don't think I can shoot anymore."

"Never mind. Can you walk? We need to get to *Svalaug*."

He rolled onto his stomach, and I thought he wasn't going to get up. But then he managed to get to his knees. I started off with Altair. I could come back for Dove, assuming Sarika kept her word. Behind us, I could see her prepping for another transfer.

My stomach clenched. It felt so wrong to be leaving without Starling's body, but I couldn't do anything else right now. It wasn't far to the bird room. Through the broken glass-dome ceiling, a cable dangled from a beast of a ship, lowering a large rescue net. As soon as I could, I laid the semi-conscious Altair down in it, then tugged on the cable to signal it was ready.

I was overjoyed to find Dove was halfway to me. His curls were darkened with blood and he was crawling, not walking. Exhaustion rolled over me as I stumbled toward him, keeping an eye on the activity in the room behind him.

"Skylark," he gasped as I gave him a hand up. "You should've gone up with Altair."

The truth was I couldn't leave him. *Show me with actions*, I'd said to him. And he had. He'd done all he could to help my brothers. Playing possum. Subduing guards. Offering his ship. Even trying to get Starling back. Done it all without complaint. Done it all for no reason except to help me. At great risk to himself.

"Dove, if we don't—I don't want to die without—I mean if we don't die, I'd like to find out—"

"Find out what, Skylark?"

Every time he said my name it sent a shiver down my back. He said it with such intensity, such gravity, as if he were swearing an oath. It gave me the courage to utter the rest. "If we could be more than enemies?"

Warmth bloomed on the side of my face as he cupped my cheek, and I pressed myself into his solid hand. "Me too, Skylark."

The rescue net hurtled down from above as the air crackled with an energy shot. Dove's body jolted into me, nearly taking me to the ground. I clutched him as his knees gave out to the convulsions and his eyes rolled back into his head.

Over Dove's shoulder, a thin-looking guard with his visor up and pistol raised was coming through the doorway of the bird room. "Screw that chick. I was promised a new body. And I want this one."

But I'd already raised mine from behind Dove. I didn't remember choosing a setting or pulling the trigger. But the shot hit the man in his unprotected face.

"Sorry, he's mine."

∼

ONCE AGAIN I was surrounded by the whir and beeping of medical equipment. The white noise both soothed and unsettled me as I sat by Dove's medbed; it was both a steady reassurance that I hadn't lost him and a grim reminder of Starling's absence.

Nearly 24 hours had passed since we'd left Cygnet IV, and Dove hadn't woken yet. His vitals, however, were strong. So far I hadn't worked up the courage to ask his ship where his family was located in the event he took a turn for the worse.

My hand brushed over his golden curls as I drank in his peaceful expression. "Who are you, Dove?"

Only Dove's heart monitor beeped in reply to my question.

You know he's not a scavenger.

Everything on *Svalaug* was tasteful and expensive-looking. The plush, tan walls of medbay rose into a domed ceiling of artificial light that mimicked a blue sky with fluffy clouds. Though I'd never personally met scavengers before, I didn't think they had ships as luxurious or as large as this one.

Under the thermal regulating blanket, I watched his broad chest rise and fall. I'd washed away the blood from his hair, face, and chest, and cut his damaged flight suit off. Despite my bravado to him on *Wild Swan I*, I'd left him modestly clothed in his grey undershirt and shorts. The medbot had delivered an antiseptic spray, and his main injuries were above his shoulders. But he needed proper medical attention, more than a bot could provide.

"Captain Lark," chimed *Svalaug* over the comms,

"there's an unidentified ship that will intercept us in the next ten minutes if we maintain our present course and speed. They're not broadcasting their registration."

At some point, Dove thought to assign me full rights and privileges of captain in case our escape didn't go as planned. He'd been prepared for the worst case scenario —and it was a good thing, too, because after we evacuated without Starling's body, Sarika reneged on our deal. She must have realized that if any of us survived, we'd contest her version of the events and "Starling's" rise to the chancellory.

That, or her security team had truly gone rogue. Maybe they hadn't liked that I'd killed their commander.

As *Svalaug* pulled away from the buildings, the anti-aircraft silos had engaged, along with a dozen missile drones. While Grif helped me carry the unconscious Dove to the medbay, Falconer had taken over piloting, with Crane on navigation and Phoenix and Hawke on weapons, and they'd had their mettle tested before Altair had been able to remotely pilot *Wild Swan I* to offer assistance.

I'd been preoccupied at the time getting Dove hooked up to the emergency medbot. The second shot he'd sustained had been a stun round, fortunately. However, with it coming so soon after the blast that grazed his head, his nervous system was in what the medbot labelled "traumatic shock." There'd been some bleeding and abnormal arrythmia, along with swelling in the brain. The medbot had corrected most of the minor issues within a few hours, but there wasn't much else it could do about the swelling without nano treatment.

But once we were free from Cygnet IV, my brothers and I had decided on a course of action: While they took *Wild Swan I* and hunted down Sarika and Father, who we assumed was now uploaded into Starling's body, I would fly the unconscious Dove to Leda Station—the closest medical facility in Svaneunge space. *Svalaug* had assured me his autopilot would do the hard stuff since I'd personally never flown anything larger than my flyer.

"Captain Lark, shall I engage warp engines, or do you wish to parlay?"

The reason we hadn't yet warped was Dove's medical condition. The high Gs could exacerbate his injuries.

"Are they pirates?" *Svaluag* had a dizzying weapons array. We could probably fight off pirates with ease.

"Sensors report the ship matches the schematics of an Aghavni Royal Forces destroyer."

Alarm bells clanged in my head. What were the Aghavni doing in Svaneunge space?

"Shall I hail them with our diplomatic registration, captain?"

Wait, what? Did *Svalaug* know who exactly I was? I glanced at Dove, but no answers were forthcoming. "Will that work? And diplomatic for who?"

It might have been my imagination, but *Svalaug*

sounded indignant at my ignorance. "Why, for Prince Svale of Aghavni, of course."

⁓

IN THE END, our diplomatic registration didn't stop the Aghavni boarding party. Not that I tried.

My hand tightened over Dove's as the medbay's door whooshed open and six soldiers in tactical black, along with an officer in Aghanvi black and gold, marched inside. The soldiers circled us, weapons pointed at the ground, as the officer strode forward. *Svalaug* had done all the talking with the destroyer's comm officer on my behalf, including detailing Dove's medical condition. Once I learned that the ship's captain had been searching for the missing Prince Svale on orders of his brother, King Jonas, for almost as long as my brothers had been missing, I'd realized no one would take better care of Dove than his people.

The middle-aged officer took a step forward. His blond mustache radiated displeasure, as if I might further injure his prince by breathing next to him. "Step away from the prince, miss. You are free to go with *Svalaug*"— he grimaced, none too happy, I took it, that Dove had signed the ship over to me along with captain privileges —"wherever you wish. We will accompany the prince home."

I could relinquish my responsibility for Dove to this

officer and join my brothers' hunt for Sarika and Starling's body. That's where I should wish to be. But eight of them were adults, with three not far off, and all were more than capable. I'd done all I could for them. My brothers didn't need me anymore. Neither, perhaps, did Dove.

But now that his people were here for him, I found myself unable to let him go. There was something between us, and it couldn't be settled until he awoke.

"Step away from the prince," the captain ordered again, his voice like a steel door slamming closed on my heart.

I straightened my spine to refuse, the perfect excuse rolling off my tongue. And I didn't care that it made me a liar.

~

FROM MY BALCONY, I looked down on the cherry trees in full bloom outside the palace walls. While words—the powerful and the persuasive kind—danced in my head, pale pink blossoms floated along a lazy river that wound around the palatial grounds. Or so I'd been told. I hadn't been given the freedom to investigate that claim. In the weeds along the bank stood a crane, patiently fishing for his breakfast, while a handful of doves pecked at the breadcrumbs in my palm and scattered on the balustrade to tempt them.

Although my movements had been curtailed, I had not been idle. My thoughts drifted to where my brothers might be and whether they'd been successful in their pursuits.

It had been nearly 30 days since I'd seen them. Thirty days since the Aghavni Royal Forces had escorted Dove and me back to Aghanvi III. Thirty days since I was locked in this tower, afforded the luxuries of a lady, but with no freedom. Thirty days since I last held Dove's hand. Thirty-one days since I'd last seen his lake-blue eyes or heard his calm, measured tones that made me want to kiss him until he lost his composure.

A rustle of satin followed by the click of a key announced the Dowager Queen's daily visit. I turned to face her, still wearing my black flight suit. I'd eschewed all her gifts of dresses and suits fancier than I'd ever owned on principle.

Like me, Dove's mother was petite, and her voluminous lavender skirts smothered her. Her auburn hair was streaked with grey—a bold statement in these times, but I didn't put her chronological age past fifty. The likeness between her and her youngest son tugged at my heart.

"Lady Lark, I trust you slept well."

It was a trick question, or so it seemed. Despite the quality of the mattress and bed, I'd slept terribly except when exhaustion had overcome my worries for Dove and my brothers, and then my nightmares featured Sarika turning us all into swans, like a sorceress in a fairy tale.

When I didn't respond, soft lips, much like Dove's, pursed. "Your silences grow tedious, my dear, and do not support your claim."

My claim was a lie, but when Officer Reiher had refused my request—well, demand—to accompany Dove back to Aghavni, I'd claimed we were married. It seemed to work in the vids. I was hoping he'd forgive the lie when he woke up.

But he hadn't woken yet.

I suspected the only reason I wasn't in a dungeon or interrogation room was because of the possibility my claim was true. Dove had, after all, given me the majority ownership in his ship, which was probably worth fifteen times my salary.

"Mamma." The gentle reprimand came from behind the queen. King Jonas was shorter than his younger brother, with straw-blond hair that fell as straight as a poker to his shoulders. He must have taken after their late father in his features, but they shared similarly kind eyes. Today he was dressed in an ornately-cut double-breasted suit of cobalt blue silk with gold buttons and tassels. "We don't have any evidence that she is responsible for Dove's injuries. Certainly, it would be odd for her to have stuck around if she was."

So if I was an assassin, I was a stupid one.

Queen Paloma sniffed, conveying in one sound that she thought me at worst to be responsible for her son's predicament (which wasn't entirely wrong), and at best out to marry rich and profit from her youngest's demise.

"How is Dove? Has he awakened?" I demanded.

Jonas cut me a measuring glance. "Svale fares the same, I'm afraid. Internally, his wounds are healed, and the swelling in his brain has subsided. My personal physician is optimistic he could wake tomorrow. But then, it could also be a year from now. Or never."

My hopes soared briefly, only to take a nosedive and explode in a fiery ball. My determination hardened. "I don't believe in never. He'll wake up."

Queen Paloma's lips turned cruel. "Then you will have no qualms about enjoying our hospitality until then."

I held her gaze and inclined my head. I was in no hurry to leave, though I suspected the tentative armistice between our two nations teetered on a dangerous precipice. We could be back to all-out war by now for all the news I had.

After the dowager queen flounced out the room, I made for the balcony again. I needed fresh air and my coterie of birds to bolster my flagging spirits.

The speeches for peace . . . I should work on those. There must be an uproar back home at the continued absence of my father and all his children. A vacuum of power Sarika must mean to fill with the "discovery" of Starling. It must be her and my father's plan to have "Starling" (a.k.a. my father—that still made me want to vomit) run for the High Chancellery as soon as he came of age.

Or maybe they'd planned to vanish into the stars to live out the rest of their days together. But I didn't think so.

It wasn't long before a presence loomed behind me.

"It would help your claim if you could explain why Svale took off and entered Svaneunge space, breaking the armistice. Was it for you?" Jonas chuckled darkly. "Of course it was. Svale is unable to resist playing the rescuer."

"Actually, it was for you." A few things clicked into place. "He was trying to rescue you and your whole empire, wasn't he? He had it in his head that if he could find the lost ships of the Svanur brothers, he'd get his hands on our prototype stealth drive. Which he could then bring back for your scientists to reproduce."

Jona looked like I'd sucked all the wind out of his sails. "What? Why would he risk himself like that?"

"Because he thought it was the only way he could help you and the Aghavni in the war. And he'd felt he failed you somehow." I scrutinized Jonas, but his expression had gone blank. "I bet the transition from your father's way of doing things hasn't been easy."

A stiff nod acknowledged my statement as true. "Perhaps. And did Svale succeed?"

"Not in the way you think. But he did come to my aid. He put his life on the line for my brothers. For me."

A long sigh escaped Jonas, and he looked a decade older as he leaned against the balustrade and stared out at the cherry trees. "That is Svale's way—to help those in need. Tell me, does his help have anything to do with your stepmother Sarika Finch and your brother Starling Svanur crossing into Aghavni space a few weeks ago?"

I jerked in surprise. What was Sarika up to now? Could I trust Jonas with the whole story? Had my brothers followed them in their stealth drive?

"Of course, our military escorted your stepmother's ship to Aghavni III. She has proved as tight-lipped as you on why she's absconded with her stepson across our border." He paused, but I kept my thoughts that Sarika must have an influential investor here to myself. Eventually, Jonas got to the point.

"My mother thinks the timing of both you and your stepmother and brother too much of a coincidence to be anything other than a Svanur plot to undermine the Aghavni monarchy. Of course, with your other brothers and father missing, and you, your brother, and Sarika Finch as our special guests, there isn't anyone left to sit in the High Chancellor's chair except that deputy fellow. It makes Svaneunge quite vulnerable. And if what you told me about a stealth device is true, then we should act to reclaim our lost colonies before your fleet has a widespread advantage."

My teeth ground together. "For what it's worth, Dove

swore an oath—a *svalaug*—to help me. And I owe him my life."

One impeccably groomed brow rose. "So you married him?"

I looked out at the river, seeing nothing but lake-blue eyes. "Nothing I say will matter unless he can corroborate it, will it?"

I felt Jonas' too-keen gaze sweep over me. "Your actions have already said much to those who are paying attention. Whether my brother owes you his life—or his death—in return remains to be seen. But please understand that if Svale dies, my mother is a vengeful woman."

Dove

N ight without stars. I drifted . . .

∽

WHEN THE OPPRESSIVE fog of darkness lifted, I awoke with a pounding head and the feeling of having been tossed down a mountain. Where was I? Someone groaned. Me. The dim lights were too bright by half, and I closed my eyes against the onslaught.

Images, sounds, and sensations flooded back to me: A small but fierce woman with pixie-short brown hair pointing a pistol at me. Skylark. Calling my name. *Dove. Dove. Dove.*

A bird shooting fire. A talking swan. A room full of medbeds and comatose men. Sarika Finch's lab of horrors. Bright flashes of energy shots. Burning flesh. Mine.

I'd been hit at least twice during the rescue, the last shot rendering me unconscious in Skylark's arms. Not my finest hour. Yet despite the fact that I probably weighed twice as much as her, she had delivered me to safety.

Of all the snatches of memory, it was her voice calling my name as she frowned over me in *Svalaug's* medbay that pierced my soul. Where was she?

But this wasn't the medbay on *Svalaug.* As my eyes

adjusted to the light, the chamber, became achingly familiar. It was spacious, with many windows opening onto a terrace by the river, and only one medbed with an empty armchair beside it. King Arnoldo, my father, had taken his last breath here. Maybe in this exact bed. I wasn't certain because I'd been involved in an off-planet SAR at the time. The guilt of not being home when my family needed me the most cut deep.

I sat up, and nearly fell over. Alerted by some silent alarm, a nurse in gold scrubs entered to check my vitals, asking me about how this or that felt. *Fine.* I knew if I said anything else, he'd call the doctor. As he held a cup of water to my lips, he detailed my condition and procedures for the past thirty days (including ear reconstruction) while I drank the bland liquid, if only to wet my throat so I could ask the only question that mattered: "Where is she?"

Skylark had brought me home. Which meant she now knew who I was. Did my family know who she was?

The answer had me pulling out my IVs and barking orders at the royal guards on duty outside the room. In a few minutes, I had an assortment of clothing—leather breeches and a loose white shirt—and a pair of boots that a guard graciously gave up for me so I didn't have to run barefoot through the palace. I made a mental note to repay everyone for their kindness.

The guards fell in line behind me as I ran—okay, jogged—as fast as my pounding head could handle down the arched hallways of my childhood home. I didn't wait for the befuddled porter to open the tall doors, flinging them open myself to barge into the hallowed courtyard, a space once reserved for beheadings and now used for trials and celebrations. We believed in seeking justice under the celestial sky, as well as rejoicing under it. A charge of espionage held a life sentence or death, depending on how the king was feeling. During my father's reign, he had rarely felt lenient toward the spies of his enemies.

Today the courtyard was set up for a trial. My jaw clenched as I tried to order my thoughts and rampant emotions at the tableau before me. When my gaze lighted on Skylark as she stood with her back to me in her singed flight suit on a block of wood known as the questioning box, all those thoughts and emotions dwindled down to one: *mine.*

It was a startling state of being for someone known all his life for his even temperament and generous nature.

A smattering of doves and pigeons flew out of my way as I stalked across the cobblestones, the silence ringing with the slap of leather against the stones. "What in the sky's heavens is going on here, brother?" I demanded.

Skylark froze at the sight of me, eyes wide. "Dove?"

My name on her lips nearly bowled me over, and I stumbled in my course. Maybe she wouldn't appreciate my interruption. She'd probably already argued a winning defense. But then, she jumped down from the box and ran toward me, hope and joy lighting up her face.

"Skylark." And I suddenly felt like I could (and would) take on the universe. For her.

As our bodies crashed together, I lifted Skylark off the ground in a tight embrace, despite my legs wobbling from the exertion. With her head on my chest over my heart, the tension there, which I'd attributed to my injuries, eased. The universe—me—everything—finally felt complete.

"You scared me half to death." She bit her lip, lifting her head to hit me with the full force of her gaze. "I'm so sorry—"

"None of that now." I'd endure it all again if I could be by her side.

"We aren't finished." It wasn't a question.

I set her down, not releasing my hold on her. "Not in the slightest. Are you alright? Your brothers?"

"I've not been allowed to communicate with them."

"Svale?" The tortured cry of relief came from Mamma, but I didn't particularly care about her feelings right now. Selfish, maybe. But she'd orchestrated this entire farce and kept Skylark from her family.

"Is it true then, Svale?" Jonas rose from his elaborately-carved chair in one of his tailored suits and with a circlet upon his head. "Do you support her claim of being your wife?"

The way Jonas phrased the absurd question made me

hesitate, like he was priming me for a certain answer. The ancient laws. Then there was a tapping on the palm of my hand.

[I may have said we were married so the boarding party would allow me to accompany you back to Aghanvi.]

Boarding party? There was a lot I needed to catch up on. "First, I want to know what is happening here, brother." I included Mamma in my glare, and she looked horrified at my lack of courtesy. But then, she wasn't used to me raising my voice.

As if we were discussing the chance of rain tomorrow, Jonas shrugged. "Oh, Mamma was concerned that this Svaneunge woman had tried to kill you in some elaborate plot with Lady Finch, who broke the armistice by crossing into Aghavni space—some say on an assassination mission. Though she's wanted back in Svaneunge for questioning about the disappearance of the High Chancellor and his sons. Of course, I know you broke the armistice first." Jonas pointedly glanced at my hand wrapped around Skylark's and a grin twitched along his thin lips.

My eyes narrowed on my brother. "So you saw fit to arrest Lady Svanur as well? Without any evidence?"

"We didn't arrest her," my mother protested, picking at her silk ruffled skirts. "We kept her safe, here in the palace. We were simply questioning her. You must admit,

Svale, that it seems extraordinarily convenient timing for her to claim you married her."

"So if she's not an assassin, she must be a crown hunter?" I demanded, side-stepping the question for now.

Jonas stepped down from his dais, eyes twinkling. I'm not sure why, as I was likely to lay him flat as soon as he got within reach. "I told you they were married, Mother. Svale wouldn't be so upset if they weren't."

If glares were laser beams, my brother would be ashes —from both Mamma and myself.

"He hasn't confirmed their status!" she trilled, clearly hoping my brother was wrong.

Quickly, I tapped out a message on Skylark's wrist as she seemed to be waiting for me to explain to them it was all a lie. And while it was an outrageous idea to marry someone I'd only known for a few months, I didn't want to let Skylark go.

The universe had brought us together.

[If you say yes, I'll call you my wife. If you likewise claim me as your husband, by old Aghavni law, we'll be legally bound to one another. If that's not something you wish, I will take care of this travesty of a trial and continue to help you and your brothers.] I raised her hand to kiss it, desperately hoping she'd say yes, though I knew it to be a wild shot in the dark.

For a breath, she stared up at me as I waited on tenter-hooks. "Yes."

That one word opened a floodgate of possibilities, and

all my plan Bs, Cs, and Ds crumbled into dust. "I confirm this woman as my wife."

Mamma pretended to faint, and Jonas's grin widened.

[Do you trust your brother?] Skylark asked me.

[Present circumstances aside, I do. I trust him with my life.]

[Follow my lead?]

[Anywhere.]

Skylark approached the judicial pulpits, but Jonas was already halfway across the cobblestones. He moved to greet her as one of the family, but I intercepted him and we ended up in our first hug in years.

"Svale?" It was a question and a statement of brotherly love.

"At some point soon, I will forgive you for putting her on trial," I murmured, "but if you greet my wife with a kiss before I do, I might have to ruin that perfect nose of yours."

He laughed and released me. My body naturally found its way back to Skylark, where I belonged. *Dritt*, but what about her brother Starling?

"Your majesties," Skylark began, "I believe we have more important matters to discuss, such as the threat of Sarika Finch's body-snatching experiments and the continuing peace treaty between our nations . . ."

I could only stand back as Skylark disclosed her stepmother and father's actions against her brothers and with brutal honesty began weaving a spell over my brother on the advantages of a formal peace treaty with her nation.

My mother, however, was a tougher sell.

"Young lady—"

"Princess Lark, Mamma," I reminded her, but Skylark didn't miss a beat.

"As cordial as it was, Your Highness, I am willing to overlook your imprisonment of my person, which no doubt breaks the armistice, as well as your incursion into Svaneunge space after Prince Svale, and Prince Svale's own incursion and attempt to steal the property of my brother Altair. But only on the following conditions. One, you surrender Sarika Finch and Starling Svanur's body into my custody so that my brother's mind can be properly restored; two, you open your finest medical facilities and physicians to my brothers for this transfer to take place; three, you invite my brothers to Aghavni III for this transfer and our wedding; and four, you agree to a hundred-year peace treaty—"

Mamma made a squawking noise. "The Aghavni empire won't be sweet-talked into a one-sided deal—"

"A hundred and *fifty-year* peace treaty," Skylark argued, unyielding in the face of the dowager's glare. "In exchange, my brother Lord Altair will cede you a stealth drive for your scientists to reproduce and improve upon at your leisure. The rest of the details concerning our borders can be negotiated between our diplomats."

"And why would Lord Altair do that? Why would you?" Jonas asked cautiously.

Instead of answering him, however, Skylark turned to me, her eyes gleaming like a supernova remnant basking in all its brightly ejected stellar material. So many colors: greens, oranges, yellows, and hint of blue. But more than that, I saw her determination, her loyalty, and her sense of justice shine from within, just as brightly as any living star.

Wings of glory, she was stunning. But like Jonas, I was waiting for her words—for it was her words that first made me fall in love with her.

"Altair owes me and Dove, big time. As for why I would . . ." She shrugged, her smile growing mischievous as her palm slid up my pounding chest. I leaned down so her hand could capture my chin. "Consider the stealth drive a wedding gift to my husband."

Those last two words unleashed me. I'd been waiting for this kiss for what seemed like a life cycle of a star. My lips brushed against hers as I gathered her in my arms. One desperate kiss turned into two, and then a third more passionate one. The galaxy could have imploded around us while we explored each other for the first time.

When we finally broke apart for air—to the repeated clearing of my brother's throat and the scandalized noises my mother was making—I blurted, "I can't believe you said yes."

One brow arched, and she grinned cheekily. "I did promise to join you after my search was over, Dove."

I'd made a promise, too.

"And we make a fabulous team. But we will need to discuss living arrangements. Though after my father's actions come to light"—her eyes became steely—"I doubt Senator Drake will need much more of my help to win the election."

"True, but I think Jonas will need all the help he can get. I hear he's about to negotiate with the galaxy's best," I whispered.

Capturing her lips in mid laugh, I took my time making each kiss a new promise to fulfill to my bride. If she had her way, I'd have at least a hundred and fifty years of peace to do so.

Much later, after more action and fewer words, Skylark tapped a message on my chest that gave me the second best laugh of my life.

[You were joking about pumpkin farm, right?]

THE END

ABOUT THE AUTHORS

By day, Amy Johnson is a wrangler of middle schooler children who, more often than not, are taller than she is, and by night, she's a craftsman of worlds. She has written several science fiction novels, including the Idyllic Series, and has several other projects in the works. In her spare time, she loves spending time with her son Elliott, reading and playing cozy video games together.

Follow her on Instagram: @amyjohnsonwrites

Dawn Christine Jonckowski is a writer / editor / dancer / musician / shoe connoisseur, author of the Stars and Suns trilogy, and lover of the Oxford comma. She is married to her very own rebel leader and they live with two adorable yet spoiled dogs in North Carolina under a single sun.

Follow her on Twitter and Instagram: @dawncjonckowski

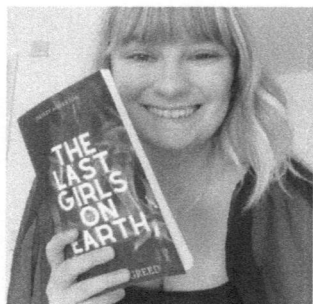

Hayley Anderton is an author and ghostwriter who loves to bake. She is now diving into the world of self-publishing to share her stories, and she runs indie sale events in her spare time. Follow her on Instagram, @hayley_a_writes

Destiny Eve has been writing since childhood, dabbling in several styles including fiction, nonfiction, short stories, flash fiction, and poetry. As a novelist, she primarily writes love stories with a dark edge. She currently resides in Northwest Minnesota with her husband and three children. Learn more about Destiny Eve by visiting www.destinyeve.com.

Meri Benson has always been in love with the written word. She loves spinning retellings, be they mythology or fairytale, and that includes her co-authored series *The Prophecies of Ragnarok* series which spins Norse mythology. You can find her online at www.meriscorner.com or on

Instagram, TikTok and Twitter @meriscorner.

Marie Sinadjan is a Filipino fantasy author, singer-song-writer, and musical theater actress. She is the co-author of *The Prophecies of Ragnarok* series, and her short stories have been published in anthologies, magazines, and literary journals. You can find her online at @marienettist or at www.mariesinadjan.com.

Meghan Tomlinson fell in love with stories so much so, she studied them for many years, earning her Master of Arts in English Literature. She now writes fantasy and science fiction (with romance!) and makes her home with her husband, kids, and dog along

the shores of Great Lake Superior (on the Canadian side, eh?). Follow her on Instagram @meghantomlinsonwrites for updates on her writing and TBR pile.

Milton Keynes UK
Ingram Content Group UK Ltd.
UKHW021858130324
439338UK00004B/36

9 798224 487998